D0519403

A2 612 134 5

TILL THE END OF TIME

JUDITH GOULD

TILL THE END OF TIME

LITTLE, BROWN AND COMPANY

A *Little, Brown* Book

First published in the United States of America by Dutton 1998
First published in Great Britain in 1999
by Little, Brown and Company

A CIP catalogue record for this book
is available from the British Library.

ISBN 0 316 84799 2

Typeset in Minion by
Palimpsest Book Production Limited,
Polmont, Stirlingshire
Printed and bound in Great Britain by
Clays Ltd, St Ives plc.

Little, Brown and Company (UK)
Brettenham House
Lancaster Place
London WC2E 7EN

To Susan Jervis
the Derbyshire lass
who provides the best medicine:
laughter

PART ONE

SPRING

For once, Leonie Marie Corinth, who normally paid at least a semblance of attention to the posted speed limits and warning signs, was decidedly not in her usual attentive, organized – even, some would say, pragmatic – state of mind. But she had Alberta Hunter in the cassette player, and listening to her rendition of 'Always,' Leonie shook her head and scowled. According to the song, love was for always. Maybe, she thought. Maybe for Alberta Hunter and whoever wrote the music, but not for Leonie Corinth. Ha! What a joke the whole notion of love was. She had loved and lost and never wanted to love again.

She was also distracted by the vibrant spring weather here in the Hudson River Valley. The sky was cerulean perfection, with huge puffy cotton balls of the whitest clouds scudding across it. Had the sky in Manhattan ever looked this beautiful? she wondered. Had the air ever smelled so fresh? So clean? Had the light – that famous light that artists loved so much – ever been this beautiful in New York's canyons? She didn't think so. Manhattan had its own charms, to be sure, but this! Well, it was a whole new world of earthly delights, full of heavenly colors, smells, and sights. As she blithely swung off the Taconic State Parkway at the Chatham exit, she must have been doing at least fifty, glorying in the beautiful spring day; Alberta Hunter's flawless inflection, phrasing, and poignantly eccentric voice; and her own extraordinary luck. When the Range Rover loomed up directly in front of her, its dark-green rear end like an impenetrable wall filling her windshield, she was caught completely unawares.

Jesus!

With an audible gasp and maneuvers worthy of Richard Petty, she slammed on the brakes with a screech and swung the wheel sharply to the right shoulder of the road, agonizingly gritting her teeth as the rear end of her car fishtailed to the left. She gripped the steering wheel with all her might, as if by sheer willpower alone she could make her ancient Volvo station wagon grind to a stop before making contact.

To no avail.

There was a dull thump as Volvo met Range Rover, and she watched in horror as the Range Rover jumped forward, then jerked to a halt. After a long moment of paralysis, Leonie finally loosened her grip on the steering wheel and expelled a lengthy lungful of air.

Oh, God, no, she thought. What now? I'm going to be late. Late!

The Range Rover's driver's side door quickly swung open, and Leonie's eyes widened in alarm as she watched a man leap out and take quick, purposeful strides to the rear of his car, a not-at-all-pleasant scowl etched into his features.

He stopped between the two cars, hands on hips, intently examining the damage in what was undeniably a posture of fury.

Well, at least he doesn't look like a gun-toting Neanderthal that'll blow my brains out, Leonie thought. Nevertheless, she took a deep

4

breath, squared her shaky shoulders, and opened her car door with a feeling of trepidation. Here goes, she thought. A lamb to the slaughter. She unbuckled her seat belt and slid out of the car to stand on the pavement, tossing her head to the side to flip her rich chestnut hair out of her eyes.

Now the man was squatted down with his back to her, running a finger along the mud-coated bumper of his Range Rover. He didn't look up. In fact, he didn't indicate in any way that he was aware of her presence. Finally, Leonie cleared her throat and stepped forward, impatient with nervous energy.

'I . . . I'm awfully sorry,' she blurted. 'I hope you're all right?'

She was met with stony silence.

She almost danced on her feet, barely able to contain her anxiousness. 'Is there much damage?'

Nerve-racking silence.

Jesus! What was it with this guy?

'I'm in a terrible hurry,' she said. 'To a very important meeting. I . . . I didn't even see you.'

The stranger shifted around on his feet and studied the front end of her car. He still ignored her, deigning neither to look up nor to speak – something as alien to the beguilingly intense and commanding Leonie Corinth as a pox.

At five feet, ten inches in her stockinged feet, with a trim, well-toned body and a head of rich chestnut hair highlighted with streaks of darkest ruby and magenta, Leonie Corinth was not used to being ignored. Far from it.

She was considered strikingly, if not conventionally, beautiful by one and all – even other women, who had to concede that Mother Nature had gone out of her way to endow Leonie with a physicality so rare that it could not be ignored.

And few were the men who could look into the depthless pools of her button-black eyes, set like obsidian gemstones in skin as porcelain pure, unblemished, unlined, and fresh as a newborn's, and not be mesmerized. Her full lips seemed to have a life of their own, but they always held promise; and her straight, aquiline nose spelled well-bred refinement. Her exquisitely fine bone structure seemed the work of a Michaelangelo, rendering her face with high, prominent cheekbones, her limbs and torso with elongated elegance.

Hers was not a voluptuous beauty, not a voluptuous body, but its elegant proportions invited and intrigued.

Above all, Leonie exuded presence. There was an air of intensity, of undeniably being there, that customarily attracted attention whether she asked for it or not.

That this was not the case now was baffling to her.

Well, this is no time to play the shrinking violet, Leonie thought. I've got to get the hell out of here.

With that, she sprang forward, leaning over the stranger to inspect the damage for herself. God! Both cars were so dented, so battered, so coated with filth from the springtime roads, that she couldn't really tell whether or not the accident had caused any damage. What's more, she didn't really give a damn, right now. Certainly not about her old heap of a Volvo. And as for his Range Rover! Well, it looked like it had been driven through the Kalahari and back more than a few times.

'Look,' she asked with a tinge of exasperation in her voice and a fretful tap of her foot, 'couldn't we just exchange names and addresses or whatever we need to do for the insurance companies?' She looked at the gold Cartier Tank watch on her wrist. Damn! 'I've really got to get—'

The man suddenly looked up and locked his eyes on her, seeming to take her in, in one brief but all-encompassing, all-knowing sweep of her body. Then his features relaxed, the lines of concern – or was it anger? – disappeared, and she glimpsed a flash of white teeth as a smile crossed his face. He seemed, in his short scrutiny of her physical attributes, to have come to some sort of decision, as if he were a judge at a beauty contest – or a dog show, she thought.

Slowly he eased himself up to his full height – what a tall drink of water he was! – still eyeing her with what now appeared to be obvious relish, tucking his hands, palms out, in his back pockets. After what seemed like an eternity to Leonie, he shrugged. 'No harm done,' he said with a hint of amusement in his voice. 'I don't think either one of these cars is any the worse for wear.'

Leonie felt a wave of relief flood through her. Thank God, she thought. He's not going to be a shit. 'Oh, that's great,' she said, her voice brimming with gratitude. 'I don't need this headache right now. You know what I mean.'

'Forget it,' he said. 'I don't think our insurance companies even need to know about this.'

Leonie cupped a hand over her eyes to shield them from the sun and returned his look for the first time. And she was stunned. Yes, she, Leonie Corinth, blasé woman of the world and nobody's fool, was stunned – by the wickedly penetrating green-blue? – of his eyes. She felt the power of that relentless gaze, and looked away, strangely discomfited.

Normally never at a loss for words on any given occasion, Leonie was suddenly speechless and felt herself flush with embarrassment. But finally, the urgency of her errand propelled her tongue back into action. 'I really appreciate it,' she said. 'Thanks again. I . . . I'd better be going now.'

He smiled again. 'We can both get a move on.' But he stood there, making no moves toward his car, his eyes boring into her.

After a moment's hesitation, Leonie forced herself to turn on her heels and head for the Volvo's open door. She waggled her fingertips at him over her shoulder, the flippancy of her act a transparent cover for her disconcertedness.

She slid onto the driver's seat, closed the door, fastened her seat belt, then fired up the engine. When Alberta Hunter's voice boomed out of the tape deck, she quickly turned the volume down. He must think I'm a complete fool. Then she shifted the Volvo into reverse and backed up a few feet, put the car in drive, and started to pull away.

Through her windshield, Leonie could see the stranger, arms folded across his chest, feet planted firmly on the pavement, watching her with a grin – or was it a smirk? – on his face. Then he turned and lazily sauntered back to his Range Rover.

Easing her car by him, she paused at the Yield sign, then hooked a right, on her way west.

God, she thought. I hope this isn't some sort of an omen.

But considering the accident, Leonie very practically decided that if indeed it was an omen, it was a good omen. After all, the man had said forget it, hadn't he? And he could have been a real bastard, right? Right. No doubt about it. So. So, she had lucked out.

Yes, she had lucked out, had a reprieve. And even if she felt a bit unnerved by the accident and the mystery man, she was not going to let anything, certainly not a trifle like this, interfere with this glorious spring day. No. She would put the whole unpleasant business out of her mind. The man, too. Especially the man. And his predator's eyes.

I will not let this take the shine off of my day! she told herself.

She reached over and turned the volume on the tape player back up, and began singing happily along, her voice a discordant warble even she herself had to admit was anything but easy listening. Speeding on, she was a bit more cautious now.

The countryside quickly absorbed her attention as she glanced around, observing this pristine land coming to life now after winter's long, deep sleep. On both sides of the road, the stately conifers rose in darkly beautiful contrast to the muted pastels of the new growth of the deciduous trees – maples and birch, beech and oak, ash and cherry, aspen and poplar – all unfurling their springtime foliage in every conceivable shade of green, grateful for the ravishing sunlight of the Hudson River Valley.

It was a light of such beauty and rarity, such golden-pinkish luminosity, Leonie thought, that it was no wonder it had influenced a whole school of painting with its own inimitable style.

It was this special light that bathed the gardens of the well-tended farms dotting the landscape she gazed at. She reveled in the colorful tulips and daffodils and hyacinths, was thrilled by the virginal wedding veil lushness of spirea – and the lilacs! She couldn't wait to fill vases to overflowing with these heavy purple wonders. She would mix them with her favorite, palest pink peonies. Yes, lilacs and peonies, her favorites, bar none. And even in her trusty old Volvo, Leonie thought she could imagine the air redolent with a perfume so sweetly ethereal, yet so sensuous, so – yes, voluptuous! – it almost made her woozy.

She rolled the window down all the way, and took a deep, intoxicating breath of the cool spring air. Ah, bliss, she thought. Pure, unadulterated bliss!

She drove on at a steady pace, thinking about this magical valley she had found almost by chance and had fallen so in love with. She'd heard about the Berkshires to the east and the Catskills across the river to the west, but she had known almost nothing of the valley itself. It was, she had discovered, a land that seemed truly lost in time. And she had come to think of it as God's country.

She loved its gently undulating hills, and she loved the old houses which populated them – throwbacks to a more gracious, less hectic era. There were simple vernacular farmhouses, grand Georgians and Federals, Eyebrow Colonials and Greek Revivals, Queen Annes and Victorians, Gothic Revivals and Arts-and-Crafts – you name it, the length and breadth of American architectural history was represented here. And it was, in part at least, the architecture which had brought her here.

It was strange, Leonie thought. Strange that because of her passion for old buildings and their architecture she had ended up moving to a place she had barely known.

She'd had an architectural salvage shop in New York City's Soho. Architectural Elements, as she had named it, had flourished in her capable hands. To keep it stocked, she had regularly scoured the countryside around New York City, usually New England and New York State, for merchandise that appealed to her, and as her business had proven, her choices had appealed to a large and wealthy clientele. Business had been phenomenal. Which is how she'd first come to the Hudson River Valley – so close in physical proximity to the city, yet light-years away in every other respect. She'd found it a rich depository of architectural artifacts, and she'd been successfully mining it for several years.

During those years of shopping, she had never imagined that she would live here. That she would, in fact, ever leave New York City. But she hadn't known the extraordinary changes the failure of a marriage could bring about.

She and Henry Wilson Reynolds, her husband of fifteen years, had divorced after a marriage she'd thought had been made in heaven had turned into – what? Hell? No, not that. At least not precisely that, unless hell was a kind of nothingness. Because that was what had happened: Their marriage had simply turned into nothing. They had drifted so far apart while living together that they were virtual strangers, and hard as she tried, Leonie couldn't bridge the gap. Hank Reynolds hadn't wanted her to.

If their drifting apart had made her unhappy, Hank's increasing coldness and ruthlessness had put the lid on the coffin. She had slowly begun to feel like a victim of one of his corporate takeovers, and ultimately like nothing more than an ornament for his arm on those occasions when he felt it was important and appropriate for her to be there.

It had not been an amicable divorce, and Leonie did not miss Hank Reynolds. Hell, no! But she sometimes worried that she would miss the city and her shop. She was that rarity: a native born-and-bred New Yorker, and she had always felt at home there. The city was in her very bones, and all that concrete and pavement had been like a security blanket – at least that's what she had thought. But after the divorce battle, she felt she needed a change, and new challenges.

Sometimes, she was not altogether sure what she wanted and even had doubts about her instincts, those same instincts that she had once trusted implicitly. But who wouldn't, she thought, after finding out you'd married some kind of a monster?

There were, however, a few things Leonie Corinth had absolutely no doubts about. She relished her newfound independence, and even though she knew there would be lonely nights – and hadn't there been lonely nights with him? – she also knew that she wasn't about to sacrifice her independence just for someone's company. She wanted to stand on her own two feet for the first time in years and not be beholden to anybody. Certainly not to a man.

She felt burned – used, duped, and humiliated – by Hank Reynolds in particular, and men in general, and she didn't know if she could ever trust another man.

But another thing she did know was that she was not going to be a victim. No, ma'am, thank you, ma'am. She was going on with her life – a new life, in a new place. She was going to carve out a home for herself and, come what may, she would not dwell on the past. The past may be a part of her, there was no denying that, but it was not her. No. She had made up her mind to live very much in the present, in the here and now, with an eye on the past and the future.

She gave a snort of derision as she slowed down for a Stop sign on the road ahead. Ex-wives clubs were not for Leonie Corinth! No way, she thought. No fucking way! Let other women continue to identify themselves through the men they had once wed and bed, but she wasn't about to. It was a trap all too easy to fall into in New

York City, or anywhere else, she imagined. She'd seen it happen to too many of her friends.

She had quickly grown sick of being the extra woman for dinner parties – as if there weren't enough more-than-presentable divorcées swimming around in New York's social scene like so many starved piranhas. She wasn't about to join their hungry, oftentimes unhappy, vindictive, and bitchy hordes! And she truly detested being referred to as the ex-Mrs. Henry Reynolds. Had hated it so much, in fact, that she'd gone to court to take back her maiden name. Corinth. That's me, she thought. Plain old Leonie Corinth.

She laughed aloud and gave the steering wheel a slap with her hand. What have I done? she asked herself for the thousandth time. Soon hitting the big four–oh, my biological clock ticking away like a time bomb, with no husband, no children, and some would say, no prospects. I've moved to this truly beautiful, but utterly foreign, valley, plain old Leonie Corinth, the proud owner of a derelict house that no one else wanted – at least no one in his right mind – and only one single friend to my name in the entire county. One.

Have I lost my mind? Definitely not. Am I a little scared? Damn right I am!

And it was a truly frightening prospect, this new adventure, especially on the heels of a divorce she was still reeling from. The fears of loneliness, of being financially strapped, of being a stranger in town, of actually living in a place she had only visited – these fears reared their ugly heads with alarming regularity. But she constantly reminded herself that she wanted this new life, a new beginning in a new place. She wanted to shed her past like so much old, familiar snakeskin and venture forth into the unknown, as frightening as that may be.

New York City, although familiar, had begun to reek of failure, and the reminders of a former married happiness were too often like smacks in the face. Her wounds were still fresh, too livid to take the constant beating that the city so freely offered.

Now, she took some comfort from the ravishing pinks, oranges, purples, and golds painting the late afternoon sky as she slowed down, nearing the picturesque village of Kinderhook. Somehow the play of the light and color reassured her.

Yes, she had made the right decision. A good decision. A sensible decision. Above all, a practical decision. And practical she had to be at this stage of her life.

She may have survived the divorce in spirit, but she had barely gotten out alive financially. With Hank's power and money and his influential friends in very high places – plus a very serious threat to ruin Leonie's best friend, Bobby Chandler – he had managed to take virtually everything they had built up together over those fifteen years of their marriage.

The duplex on Park Avenue and its art and antiques – his. The huge shingle-style mansion in Southampton with its lavish contents – his. Their brilliantly performing portfolio of stocks and bonds – his. The Bentley Turbo and the Jaguar convertible – you got it! – his.

It was not a common scenario, though becoming more so. She knew divorcées like herself who had wound up with settlements in the tens of millions of dollars or more. But Hank Reynolds had succeeded where lesser – or more noble – men had failed.

Leonie had wound up with her shop in Soho, Architectural Elements, which she had put on the market. It was now sold, for a handsome sum, except for some final paperwork that she and Hank had to sign once it was drawn up. The shop's healthy bank account had also been hers to take, as well as the old Volvo station wagon she was now driving. Luckily she'd had an assortment of furniture and assorted decorative items in storage – all of it possessions that she and Hank had gradually replaced with finer and pricier objects over the years. She'd planned on sending everything to Christie's to auction, but now she was grateful that she had all this booty because some of it was sure to come in handy decorating her new house in the country.

Leonie took a deep breath to steady herself. Now that she'd bought the house with the shop's bank account, she could probably slide by financially for another year, two, at most, if she was extremely careful. But that was about it. The proceeds from the sale of the shop would pay for the house's renovation and leave some living expenses.

Knowing that she would soon be low on cash, she'd developed a plan. Her Recovery Plan. Part of her recovery effort was to buy this property, renovate it, decorate it, and sell it for a handsome profit to reinvest in another property. And repeat the process, until? Well, she didn't know right now. She only knew that with her innate taste, her abilities for decorating and landscaping, and her knowledge of what the property should look like, she couldn't go wrong. She would do what others feared to do – and make them pay the price.

She had the wealthy client list from her former shop, and she felt confident that many of them would spring at the chance to purchase a property that she had renovated and decorated, so taken with her style were they.

She was also debating the idea of opening another shop here in the valley – at home, perhaps, or in Hudson. A small town on the river, Hudson was home to over sixty antique shops, and was swarming with curiosity seekers and buyers from all over the Northeast on the weekends. That, plus her invaluable list of former clients, just might make a shop not only feasible, but quite profitable, at that.

In any case, she was going to take it a step at a time, a day at a time, and test the waters of possibility.

She stepped on the gas now, anxious to get to her new home sweet home, ruin that it may be, and her friend of long standing, Fiona Moss. Mossy, dear Mossy. Mossy of the caustic wit, the devastating irony, and the unerring eye for the meat of any matter – along with a heart and soul of purest platinum. It was Mossy, a local

14

real estate agent, who had sold her the property – the Dump on the Lump, they had affectionately dubbed it – and it was Mossy, she knew, who was waiting at the house with a local architect who specialized in renovating historic buildings.

Leonie felt confident about a lot of the work that needed to be done. Certainly the interior decoration. God knows, she thought, I've had enough experience. But when she was restoring an old house in Southampton, she'd discovered that she really needed an architect's help to get some things exactly right.

It had irked her to realize that she needed help, but it had been a good experience, allowing her to discover her strengths and her weaknesses. She had also learned that the architect had probably saved her both time and money in the long run, because she wasn't making mistakes that required costly redoing.

Now, nearing her latest challenge, she was determined to rely on as little outside help as possible. Finally emerging from beneath the very powerful and suffocating thumb of Hank Reynolds and his whole stuffy, Wall Street–Park Avenue–Social Register set had only served to fuel her drive for independence, to reinforce her instincts to keep her own counsel.

Now, she wanted nothing more than to prove herself capable of going it alone.

Home alone, she thought. Not most ex-wives' idea of a good time, to be sure. But in my case, just what the doctor ordered.

Little did she know that fate had an entirely different future in store for her.

Leonie's excitement mounted with the anticipation of seeing her new home, and she had to force herself not to give the old Volvo more gas as she approached a curve in the highway, knowing that the octagon house lay just around the bend.

She reached over and turned off the cassette player, then in the sudden silence looked up. And there it was, on the western side of the highway, rising in all its faded glory atop a hillock with a view of the Hudson River and the Catskill Mountains beyond.

She slowed to a snail's pace now, appraising the house and its setting, letting the magic it had imparted the first time she had seen it envelop her once again. A smile slowly crept across her face. It resembled nothing so much, she mused, as a once-beautiful debutante, now an aging dowager gone to seed. But what magnificent seed it was!

The house was built of wood, clapboard – as were the outbuildings – once painted white, now all peeling paint, with heavy, classically inspired moldings. Its windows were long and narrow, many with broken or missing panes, and the first floor had French doors leading outside to overgrown bluestone terraces. Its shutters, many loose and hanging askew, had once been green. It was an octagonal-shaped wonder, two stories high, with a third-floor attic leading to the lantern cupola, also an octagon, centered on the roof.

The cupola, she thought, somehow managed to be formal and stately but whimsical at the same time. Its beautifully wavy old glass was cracked in places and a few panes were missing. About a hundred feet to the south she could see the old clapboard barn with its twin cupolas. They were identical but smaller versions of the one atop the main house. Even the carriage house was crowned with a duplicate though smaller version, this one topped with a weather vane. It was a verdigris-covered copper horse at full-stretch gallop.

The buildings and grounds had been meticulously laid out in the 1840s. The whole property, in fact, was designed along formal, classical lines, but had about it an air of fantasy, of not being quite earthbound, not quite practical. It was a house saturated in romance. A gracious home, she thought, built on a gentle land. Someone had once lavished love on it, of that she was certain. As I will, she told herself.

Turning off the highway, she slowly wound her way up the rutted pea gravel drive which trailed through about a hundred yards of unkempt but luxuriant green lawn. She knew that a lot of the color came from the crabgrass and other invasive grasses which had taken over, but that didn't dispel her proprietary feelings about every single blade of it. Majestic but long-neglected trees and shrubbery dotted the lawn, flourishing in the rich soil along the river.

Circling around the north side of the house, she pulled into the forlorn courtyard between the main house itself and the carriage house, which was now used as a garage. Mossy's elderly but spiffy white Acura was parked there, and before Leonie could even put her car in park, Mossy herself came out the back door of the house, ever-present cigarette in hand, her confident stride belying her diminutive stature.

'Bloody hell, Leonie,' she called in her crisp, aristocratic-sounding British accent as she walked to the car, 'took our time, didn't we?'

Leonie quickly unbuckled her seat belt, grabbed her enormous leather Fendi shoulder bag, and slid out of the car with a wide smile on her strikingly beautiful face. 'Mossy!' she all but shrieked, flinging her arms around her friend. 'You are a sight for sore eyes.'

They kissed cheeks, neither being careful about the other's makeup or hair.

Mossy stepped back and eyed Leonie from head to toe. 'Aren't we looking chic today,' she said throatily. 'I guess you've already heard the architect's an absolute dreamboat.'

Leonie caught the mischievous gleam in Mossy's eyes and quickly retorted: 'As for the architect, I don't know a thing except what you've told me, Mossy.' She pointed an accusatory finger at her friend. 'And as for the clothes, well . . .' She slung her bag over her shoulder and twirled around in place, then stopped, facing Mossy. 'You likee?'

'I likee very much indeed,' Mossy replied, fingering the nubby beige and chocolate wool. 'Who, may I ask, did it?'

'Yohji Yamamoto. Isn't it fab?' Leonie beamed.

'Divine,' Mossy replied. 'I love the big jacket and the braid trim. Ooooh, and those super wide-legged trousers.' She exhaled a voluminous plume of smoke. 'But it does look like old Yohji's having a good laugh at Coco Chanel's expense.'

'Paying homage, Mossy. 'Paying homage,' Leonie said in Yamamoto's defense.

'Whatever,' Mossy said dubiously with an arch of an eyebrow. She flicked a long ash onto the ground. 'Anyway, it looks great with your hair color.'

Leonie ran a hand through her rich chestnut A-line-cut hair with its hints of ruby red and magenta. 'Thank you, Clairol!' she crowed with a sparkle in her button-black eyes.

Mossy laughed, then cocked her head to the side, eyeing Leonie's feet critically. 'Best watch your boots, dear,' she said. 'We don't want a couple of thousand bucks getting mucked up in this nasty country mud, do we?'

Leonie looked down at her chocolate leather booties. 'A couple of grand!' she snorted. 'They may be Christian Louboutins, but they were nowhere near that,' she said defensively.

'Teasing, dear,' Mossy said. 'Let's go in, shall we? I have a little something for you.'

'Oh, Mossy,' Leonie asked, as the two walked arm in arm to the back door, 'what?'

Mossy ignored her question, held the door open, and gestured Leonie in. 'Age before beauty, dear.'

Leonie laughed and stepped into the hallway.

'Now into the parlor with you,' Mossy directed her. 'Get comfy. I'll be there in a flash.'

'Good God, Mossy,' Leonie said with exasperation. 'Why so mysterious?'

But Mossy was already off to the kitchen.

Leonie's boot heels clicked loudly on the bare parquet floors as she headed to the parlor's wide, graceful entry with its beautiful classical molding. She lingered in the doorway, standing with arms akimbo, her eagle eye scrutinizing every minute detail of this large, high-ceilinged room. She was asking herself for the millionth time if she had been in her right mind when she decided to buy this wreck and renovate it.

'Home sweet home, not!' she murmured to herself.

Wallpaper hung in sheets from the cracked plaster, and the painted woodwork was chipped and peeling. The fireplace mantel was a once-white stained and cracked marble. And the floors! Leonie cringed. The once beautiful parquet was in such a state of disrepair she wondered if it was even salvageable.

Worst of all, she was having trouble seeing any magic in the grime that covered every surface. She saw only expensive and time-consuming drudgery. At least, for the moment.

I can't believe I'm going to be living here while all the work is going on, she thought. But she wanted to be close to the project to keep her eye on the work, and there were financial considerations, of course. She didn't want to spend her precious dollars to rent something for the next few months, when she was certain that she could somehow manage here, even with the work going on.

Well, I won't think about all that right now, she decided. No. I'll be Scarlett O'Hara today.

She glanced at the huge Napoleonic-style daybed, now covered with several sheets of protective plastic. It was one of the few pieces of furniture she'd taken out of storage in New York City and had sent up here. It would serve her quite nicely as a bed, while doubling as a couch.

She ambled over to it, let her shoulder bag slide to the floor, and forced herself to sit on the inhospitable plastic. She grimaced at the awful crinkling sound it made under her weight and its sticky-feeling surface. Then she took off her booties and spread out her legs. At nearly six feet in her heels, she'd had the daybed custom made to accommodate her full length and allow the possibility of somebody else sitting at the end. Perhaps with her feet in his lap? A nice thought – at the time.

She wiggled her toes and massaged her calves. There. Much better. But she'd hardly stretched out when she heard Mossy coming down the hallway.

'Here we are,' Mossy announced, coming into the parlor. She was carrying a silver tray on which perched two crystal flutes and a bottle of champagne in a sweating silver bucket.

21

'Oh, Mossy,' Leonie cried, jerking back up. 'You shouldn't have.' Then she grinned. 'But I'm so glad you did.'

She jumped up to help, but Mossy had already set the tray down on an overturned box and was pouring champagne into the two flutes. Then she lifted them, handing one to Leonie, who took it gratefully.

'Here,' Mossy said, lifting her flute in a toast. 'Let's dispense with the usual bread and salt ritual, shall we? A bit of shampoo is what's called for. To celebrate your arrival on these hallowed grounds.'

'Mossy, you really are too much,' Leonie replied, lifting her flute and chiming it against Mossy's. A gas-blue refraction of light flashed in her eyes. Then, a feeling of warmth, of gratitude, of thanksgiving for this, the very best of friends imaginable, flowed fervently through her, and she suddenly and unexpectedly had to fight back the tears that threatened to spill at any moment.

Leonie took a tiny sip. The champagne tasted smooth and dry, and she loved the way it felt bubbly on her tongue. She cleared her throat and found a croaky voice to say, 'Yummy, yummy. Mossy, this is heaven. It's such a surprise.'

'Only an inexpensive Perrier Jouet,' she said. 'Not at all what you're used to, I'm sure.'

'Oh, come off it, Moss. You know me better than that. If I ever was a wine snob, I certainly can't afford to be one now.' She gave Mossy a significant look. 'Not in my present strained circumstances,' she added with a sigh.

Leonie plopped down onto the daybed, and Mossy kicked off her low-heeled pumps, sat down, and drew her feet up under her.

'Well, not to worry,' Mossy said, 'I'm sure all that's going to change for the better in the not-so-distant future.'

'I know it will. It's . . . it's just that sometimes it seems so damned hard to adjust to all the changes,' Leonie said fretfully.

'You know what the Twelve Steppers and all those feel-good groups say nowadays: "This is but a moment in time."'

Leonie groaned. 'Yes, Mossy. And I know that other old chestnut, "This too shall pass."'

'Bloody assholes,' Mossy said through gritted teeth. She paused and sipped her champagne, then abruptly smiled. 'But you know what, Leonie? They're right.'

Leonie was staring down into her glass. She dipped a finger into her champagne, then licking it off, looked up. 'I suppose so,' she said.

'I know they are,' Mossy said, 'even though it's not much comfort now, is it?'

Leonie shook her head.

Mossy eyed her thoughtfully. 'You know what else, Leonie?' she continued. 'I think taking on this place' – she swept an arm out and around dramatically, as if to encompass the entire house – 'was one of the best things you could have done for yourself. You're going to be soooo busy you won't have time to be blue.'

Leonie arched an eyebrow and scanned the room herself. 'You can say that again.' Then she laughed and took a gulp of champagne.

'Just remember what I always say.' Mossy paused to take another quick sip of champagne. 'If one has too much on one's plate, one simply eats faster – and chews harder.'

Leonie laughed again. 'I'll be sure and keep that in mind when I'm knee deep in construction debris around here.'

'Yes, well, it is going to be a challenge, dear,' Mossy said. 'But I'm sure you'll rise to it.'

'Yes, I'll manage,' Leonie said with a certainty in her voice. 'I'll move from room to room as the work progresses. All I'll need is a single room to live in. Hopefully, we can work it out so that I can camp out here in the parlor for a while, then move to a bedroom upstairs, or vice-versa. I'll just move, depending on where the work is going on.'

'It's not going to be easy,' Mossy said.

23

'No.' Leonie shook her head. 'But I don't care, Mossy, I've got a hot plate—'

'Hot plate!' Mossy cried.

'Yes,' Leonie said. 'Don't look so scandalized. There'll be days I can't use the kitchen while it's being worked on. So, I've got a hot plate and all sorts of things I can hole up with in a room out of the way.'

'I must say, you've got a pioneer spirit,' Mossy said.

'Whatever it takes,' Leonie said. 'If I have to take sponge baths for a while, so be it! If I have to eat takeout pizza or sandwiches, that's okay! If you don't see me in anything but old blue jeans, that's tough!'

'That is the spirit,' Mossy said.

'Damn right,' Leonie said, slamming her fist on the daybed.

'Oh, shit.' Mossy was feeling around in her jacket pockets. 'Left my cigarettes and lighter in the kitchen. Got to have a pee, too. Back in a jif.' She hopped up and strode out of the room in her stockinged feet.

Leonie watched her go, a smile of contentment softening her features. There is nobody else like Mossy, she thought. Nobody.

She thought back to their first meeting. God, was it serendipitous! Mossy had come into Architectural Elements to look at a small stained-glass window on display. She had balked at the price, in fact had balked at the price tags on everything, letting Leonie know in no uncertain terms that she could easily find similar merchandise in her area of the country for a fraction of the price. She said that she saw this sort of merchandise all the time in her rambles through the countryside, showing property in the real estate business. 'You know, crumbling houses, tumble-down barns, ruined gardens. In some cases, people are glad to be rid of the stuff. Sometimes they don't have a clue as to what they've got. And what's more, they don't care. They'll happily take your cash.'

They'd ended up having dinner together that night, and Mossy had become one of Leonie's 'pickers' – getting a finder's fee for objects she unearthed and Leonie bought for the shop. It had been a very successful business and personal relationship from the start.

Over the last few years, Leonie had made countless trips up to see Mossy and her 'finds,' more often than not immediately snatching them up. She discovered that Mossy had a very good eye indeed.

And chutzpah. In her friendly but aggressive manner, she often simply approached strangers about the possibility of buying this, that, or the other column, gate, window, garden urn, or what have you. And oftentimes, she had to call upon all her reserves of charm and use a subtle form of persuasion to part these people from their treasures. And it had paid off for both of them.

What had begun as a high regard for each other's business savvy quickly grew to an appreciation of each other's wit and intelligence, and finally matured to an easy intimacy, an unjudgmental acceptance of each other's foibles.

Despite the fact that they were living in utterly different worlds – on the surface at least – they seemed cut from the same cloth.

Leonie was married to an enormously rich and successful Wall Streeter and moved in the rarified social circles of Manhattan's Upper East Side and Southampton. Hers was a life of immense privilege.

In contrast, Mossy was long divorced and living comfortably, though by necessity frugally, and enjoyed a much less glamorous and hectic social life in the country. It was a life of constraint.

Yet they felt like sisters under the skin.

Mossy's youthful exuberance, her droll, ironic sense of humor, her kindness and generosity, her undyingly optimistic, yet down-to-earth and commonsense approach to life, topped off with a fierce and unflagging loyalty, had won Leonie over. Not surprisingly, they were all qualities Leonie herself possessed.

This kinship with Mossy, in part at least, had led Leonie to decide to settle here.

She looked up now as she heard her friend pad back into the room on her childlike feet. Watched as she set her champagne on the mantelpiece, placed an ashtray alongside it, and then lit a cigarette. She took a deep drag and blew a plume of smoke ceilingward, eyeing the room critically.

All their years of friendship had seen little change in Mossy, Leonie thought. She didn't remotely look the fifty-odd years she now admitted to.

She was still petite, no more than five feet tall, fine boned, and had tiny hands and feet. She was in excellent physical condition, due to her thrice weekly aerobics classes and careful eating habits, and had boundless energy and enthusiasm. This despite her insatiable appetite for cigarettes.

Her hair drew your attention immediately. It was dyed a wildly flaming orange which made no pretense at being her own color, or anywhere near it. As Leonie always affectionately told her, it was a color that did not even occur in nature. And as if it were frosting on a particularly festive cake, it was always styled to look as if Mossy had stuck a perfectly manicured fingernail in an electrical outlet.

But this most unnatural, even outrageous of looks seemed perfectly natural on Mossy. Somehow, Leonie thought, it suited her personality perfectly, and she carried it off where no one else she knew could have.

If her hair attracted attention, it was her eyes that held it. They captivated, held you in their thrall. Topaz, almost an amber, and shot through with glittering shards of gold, they were appraising, critical eyes, which seldom missed a trick. They were knowing eyes, Leonie thought, eyes which seemed always to be able to read your innermost thoughts, your innermost secrets.

She was never groomed less than immaculately, with minimal but expertly applied makeup. And despite the fact that she could spend very little on clothes, she was always dressed simply, elegantly, and in the very best of taste. As she was now, in well-tailored gray slacks and matching blouse, with a stylish shocking-pink jacket.

Mossy took the last sip of her champagne and made a beeline for the bottle. 'Ready for more bubbly?' she asked, holding it up.

'You bet.' Leonie extended her flute for a refill. Then she reconsidered for a moment. 'But only if you promise you won't let me get snockered before the architect gets here.'

Mossy looked at her watch. 'I wonder what's taking him so long. He's already thirty minutes late.'

'Well, I can see now that I needn't have rushed,' Leonie said. 'I was in such a hurry that I rear-ended some guy coming off the Taconic.'

'You what?' Mossy pronounced with suddenly widened eyes.

'I rear-ended this man at the Yield sign,' Leonie replied. 'You know. The one where you get off the Taconic at Chatham.'

'Bloody hell, Leonie!' Mossy said agitatedly. 'Why didn't you tell me? Are you okay? You weren't injured, were you?'

Leonie rolled her eyes. 'Mossy, do I look injured? I barely bumped the guy. It didn't even hurt the cars.'

'My God!' Mossy said, 'You could have been killed!'

'Mossy!' Leonie protested. 'It was nothing! The guy said to forget it.'

Mossy paced the floor in circles, smoking furiously, wound up to her most dramatic mode. She was a coloratura now, Maria Callas perhaps, in full throttle. Abruptly she stopped and turned to Leonie. 'Who was it? Who was this man? My God. You could have hit some local yahoo. In a pickup. With a rifle!' She punctured the air with her cigarette. 'You could have been shot!'

'Oh, Mossy, do stop with the histrionics. It was nothing like that,' Leonie assured her. 'The guy was in one of those ridiculously expensive Range Rovers. He was harmless.'

'Harmless? How do you know? What did he look like?' Mossy drilled her in rapid-fire fashion, not even stopping to take a breath. 'Who was he?'

'How should I know?'

'Didn't you get his name?' Mossy stabbed out her cigarette. 'Was he a local?'

'I have no idea, Mossy!' Leonie cried with exasperation. 'He looked at the cars and went on his merry way. We didn't even exchange names.' She paused and took another sip of champagne. 'And I have no idea what he looked like, either. I was so flustered, I don't even remember. All I saw were eyes and teeth.'

'What do you mean, eyes and teeth?' Mossy persisted, as she lit another cigarette.

'Exactly what I said. I saw lots of big white teeth, and his eyes were ... they were ...' Leonie struggled for the right words. 'Oh, I don't know what they were. Blue. No, green. Maybe. I really don't know.'

Mossy took a deep drag off her cigarette and exhaled a blue-gray plume of smoke. 'Well,' she finally said in an imperious tone of voice, as she continued pacing, 'you must be very careful driving up here in the country. What with the drunks, the wild turkeys, the deer—'

'Oh, for God's sake, Mossy,' Leonie interjected. 'You're the one that hits all the deer.' She pointed an accusing finger at Mossy. 'You should have a license to kill for your car. Or register it as a lethal weapon. If there are any deer left for me to hit hereabouts, I'd be surprised.'

Mossy burst into peals of laughter, spewing out cigarette smoke. 'You're too right, of course. Absolutely. I think the bloody deer smell my car coming and lie in wait.'

'No doubt,' Leonie said. 'Maybe that's what's happened to our architect. Maybe he hit a deer on the way over.'

Mossy stubbed out her cigarette in the ashtray. 'Not this fellow,' she said, walking over to the daybed, easing herself down, and getting comfortable. 'From what I hear, he gets everything right. And I do mean everything.'

'What's that supposed to mean?' Leonie asked.

'Oh, like I said before. He's an absolute dreamboat. You know. He looks right. Went to the right schools. Married into the right family, the right architectural firm. Runs in the right social circles.' She suddenly made a face of utter disdain. 'The horsey set, with their hunts and all that folderol. Sod it! Lives in the right house, drives the right cars.' She paused thoughtfully, taking a sip of champagne. 'And probably is a bloody good screw, too.'

Leonie laughed and slapped her lightly on the hand. 'Mossy, you are so bad!'

Mossy smiled drolly, then continued: 'But he comes highly recommended, I must say. His work is respected by one and all. On that score, at least, I've never heard a discouraging word.'

'I just hope I'll be able to communicate with him,' Leonie said. 'You know. Make him understand what it is I want here. I don't want somebody to tell me what I should do.'

'Ha! He's a man isn't he?' Mossy retorted scornfully. 'So you might as well prepare yourself for a bit of patronization at the very least.'

'Oh, I hope not,' Leonie said with genuine worry in her voice.

'I don't mean to scare you off, Leonie,' Mossy added hastily. 'I would never have recommended him unless I thought he was right for the job. I've seen his work and it's brilliant. First rate, I must say. No, I think he is certainly the best man for the job from what I know.'

She jumped up, strode to the mantel, and lit another cigarette. 'They say he's trustworthy,' she continued. 'You won't get ripped off. And that is the exception, my dear, not the rule, with a lot of these local yokels around here doing renovation work.'

She gave Leonie a significant look and exhaled a streamer of smoke.

'Well, that seems to be the way it is just about everywhere,' Leonie said. 'It certainly was in Southampton and New York.'

'I think you'll find that it's just as bad or worse here. But Sam Nicholson is supposed to be different, and he has a good bunch of workmen at his disposal. Very loyal to him, too, I hear.'

Mossy knocked a long ash off her cigarette into the astray. 'Just like that wife of his.'

Leonie looked up. 'What do you mean, Mossy? She's very loyal to him, despite—?' Leonie stopped mid-sentence as they heard a car in the rear courtyard.

'Finally!' Mossy said. 'That must be our man now.'

'Good,' Leonie replied, and quickly reached down for her suede booties and began pulling them on.

Mossy put out her cigarette and padded over to the daybed where she slipped into her heels. 'You needn't get up, Leonie. I'll see to the door.'

'I'll take this stuff out to the kitchen,' Leonie said, gesturing at the champagne bottle and the glasses.

Mossy went on ahead to the door, while Leonie gathered up their glasses and the bottle. She grabbed Mossy's ashtray to empty, put it on the silver tray, and started for the kitchen, loaded tray in hand.

She could hear the scraping of boots, the screen door moaning on its hinges, and Mossy's amiable chatter. Then she saw Mossy straight ahead, more diminutive looking than usual, her short-ness emphasized by the very tall man standing just inside the back door.

'Leonie,' Mossy called to her, 'your long-lost architect is here at last,' she said with laughter in her voice.

'Sorry about that,' a deep rich male baritone apologized. 'I had a little altercation with—'

He abruptly stopped speaking when he saw Leonie standing before him, tray in hand, staring up at him open-mouthed, as if she'd seen a ghost.

'Leonie Corinth, this is Sam Nicholson, the architect, of course,'

Mossy said. 'Sam Nicholson, meet Leonie Corinth, my dearest friend and the proud new owner of Octagon House.'

There was a brief moment of silence, and Mossy looked with curiosity from Sam to Leonie, and back again to Sam. She had never seen the unflappable Sam Nicholson at a loss for words, but she didn't know him that well. As for Leonie, well, she'd never seen her in this light either, and she thought she knew her quite well.

It was Sam Nicholson who finally broke the uneasy silence. 'I think we've already had the pleasure.'

A wide smile spread across his face, revealing gleaming white teeth. Perfect teeth. The teeth Leonie remembered. And his eyes – the eyes she could not quite describe – danced mischievously, even wickedly, she thought. She saw now that they were an aqueous green with shards of blue, giving them a hint of turquoise.

Leonie suddenly felt weak with – what? Embarrassment? Oh, yes. And acute at that. Disbelief? Yes, even though the man she had rear-ended was unquestionably standing here right in front of her. Surprise? Definitely. She had never expected to see him again.

And she felt something more, something much more powerful. Something – dare she even think it? – something that could only be described as chemical.

She finally found her voice and said, 'Yes, we have had the pleasure.' She laughed easily. 'If it could be called that, under the circumstances. Anyhow, I'm glad to meet you now. Let me just put this down in the kitchen. Why don't you two go get comfortable?'

'What the devil—?' Mossy began.

'Mrs. Corinth and I had a little altercation coming off the Taconic,' Sam said.

'It was you,' Mossy squealed. 'I don't believe it. This is too funny.'

'That's why I'm late,' Sam said. 'Then I had to stop by the office afterward and pick up some stuff.'

31

'Well, come on in to the parlor,' Mossy said. 'I'm sure Leonie will want to give you the grand tour.'

Leonie listened from the kitchen, taking deep breaths, trying to gather her wits about her. Her mind was racing, but not in any one direction. No, her thoughts and feelings were in a muddle of confusion, of uncertainty, flying around in every direction at once.

How silly, she thought, laughing at herself. How perfectly silly! What's happening to me? And why didn't Mossy tell me he had this effect on people? That he had such devastatingly handsome looks?

Now what? she wondered.

L eonie stood transfixed.

She was unobserved as she lingered in the shadows of the parlor's arched entryway. She watched Mossy and Sam Nicholson, Mossy smoking and chattering away as the two of them talked, looking out a window on to the lawn.

But it was as if Mossy were a smoke-wreathed ghost in his presence. She did not quite exist, not standing next to him as she was.

For almost against her will, Leonie focused intensely on Sam Nicholson and knew that, despite herself, despite all the determination she could muster to the contrary, she was gone.

Gone.

There were men who exuded power because of their relative money and position, and there were men who exuded power because of their sheer physicality. For Leonie, Sam Nicholson was both. More than both. In his case, she mused, two plus two equaled a great deal more than four.

He had about him an aura of such power – such maleness –
that it transcended his obvious physical attributes, overwhelming
though they were. It placed him on a plane with all the gods on
Olympus, she thought.

And like those gods, she suspected that he must be very complicated, perhaps flawed, and certainly not easy. Not easy to know.
Maybe not easy to like. But he attracted her nonetheless, drew her
to him as no one ever had before.

So this is what they mean by animal magnetism, she thought.

Sam Nicholson was surely the most attractive and virile-looking
man she had ever laid eyes on. At least six feet three inches tall,
and somewhere around forty, she guessed, he was lean but very well
built, with a strong neck set on wide, powerful-looking shoulders.
She could imagine the massive chest beneath his dark brown leather
bomber jacket, and the long torso descending to narrow waist and
hips. His boyishly thick hair was worn slightly longer than the
average cut, and had the slightest curl. It was light brown, streaked
with blond and silver.

Kissed by Apollo himself, she thought.

She could see a scar running across the bridge of his prominent
nose, sun-burned though it was. Had it been broken? she wondered.
Was it an accident? A fight? Beneath it, demanding lips were set
above a strong, square jaw.

In their blue jeans, his long legs looked surprisingly solid for one
so tall, and they seemed planted firmly on the ground in their worn
construction boots.

His was a maleness which Leonie was unaccustomed to seeing, even in those ultimate male corridors of the power elite
on Manhattan's Wall Street. It was a massive maleness which
was slightly intimidating to her, until he turned and she saw
the wounded, somewhat haunted look in those dazzling blue-
green eyes.

What, or who, could have possibly injured this supreme Adonis?

she wondered. What has life dealt him – this man to whom nature has been so generous – that has caused this dim flickering of sorrow which is intimated in his gaze?

Leonie felt a shiver pulsate through her chest. She didn't want to think about what was happening to her, why she even cared, but suddenly she felt she had to know everything about this man, that she must find a way to make him reveal himself to her, scary as the proposition might be.

The easy smile which crossed his face as he turned and saw her did not quite conceal that look of sadness in his eyes.

'There you are,' he said in his deep rich voice, a voice full of possibilities, of danger. A voice which sent jolting currents of electricity through her very being.

Oh, God, she thought. He's so damned comfortable in his own skin. So relaxed, yet so alert. What's wrong with me?

'Oh, Leonie,' Mossy chimed in, 'Sam knows quite a lot about the history of this place. You have to get him to tell you.'

'Really?' Leonie replied in as casual and cheerful a voice as she could manage. She quickly crossed the room toward them. 'I can't wait. I know hardly anything about it myself.'

'Well, I know a little bit about this place in particular,' Sam said offhandedly, looking at her. 'I do know a lot more about the history of the octagon houses around here.'

Leonie wanted to get down to business, and fast, because she felt she must focus on something, anything, other than Sam Nicholson. 'Why don't we do a tour now, and you can give me a history lesson later?' she asked. 'Is that okay?'

'You got it,' Sam said, looking at his watch. 'We better get started because I've got to get a move on before too long.'

'Where would you like to begin?' Leonie asked. 'Up or down?' She gestured her hands. 'In or out?'

'Why don't we start in the basement, work our way up, then outside?' He was all business now.

35

'Makes sense to me,' Leonie said. 'The basement stairs are back in the kitchen. Just follow me. I'll lead the way.' She turned to Mossy. 'Aren't you coming, Moss?'

'If you don't mind,' Mossy replied, 'I'll stay up here. I've shown this place so many times, I know the mice by name.'

Sam and Leonie both laughed as they headed through the hallway and back to the kitchen.

Leonie found the light switch at the top of the stairs and carefully led the way down the steep steps. 'It's awfully grim,' she apologized. 'Straight out of a horror movie.'

She reached the bottom of the stairs and flipped another light switch. 'But on the bright side, it seems to stay dry. Mossy's seen it in all kinds of weather, and has never seen a single leak.'

'All your mechanicals down here?' Sam asked.

'Yes. At least I think so,' she said, brushing a cobweb away from her face. 'Oil-fired furnace. Water heater. Water holding tank. Washer and dryer hookups. All that really glamorous stuff.'

He laughed, and began looking around in the eerie, uneven light cast by naked overhead bulbs. 'Have you got a copy of the engineer's report?' He turned to her and stared.

'No.' Leonie shrugged. 'I didn't get one because I figured that in a worst-case scenario everything would have to be replaced anyway.'

'So why pay somebody a small fortune just to tell you that, huh?' She saw the flash of those perfect pearly whites again.

'Exactly,' she said, tossing a chestnut strand of hair out of her eyes. 'So now, it's play it as it lays, I guess.'

'Fair enough,' he said, and began wandering around.

He stopped at the huge, old furnace and squatted down, looking closely at it, then stood and examined some duct work. Soon his attention turned to the water heater, the holding tank, and the antiquated electrical fuse boxes. Finally, he began to examine the foundation's stone work and then the huge beams that supported the house.

Leonie watched as he moved slowly around the basement, looking, touching, almost caressing the heavy, hand-hewn old wooden beams.

'They sure don't do work like this anymore,' he said.

'Is that work good or bad?' Leonie half-joked.

'It's very, very good,' he said with seriousness.

'They really are quite beautiful, aren't they?' she said, lightly rubbing her hand against one of the beams, then patting it.

He looked at her. 'Yes, I think so, too,' he said. 'It's one of the reasons I like doing old barn conversions. Sometimes the beam work is really special, and they can make beautiful rooms.'

Leonie was pleased to hear this appreciation in his voice, to hear that he saw the beauty, the strength, and the possibilities in something as simple as these old beams. Maybe, she thought, he is that rarity: a man with imagination. Not to mention a cute ass.

He continued looking around the basement, nodding to himself occasionally, sometimes asking her questions, completely absorbed in what he was doing. Finally, he turned to her. 'Ready to head upstairs?' he asked. 'I think I've seen everything down here I need to.'

Leonie couldn't read his expression. Was he pleased by what he'd seen? Disappointed? Appalled? It was impossible to tell what he was thinking.

'Sure,' she answered, and started toward the stairs.

'I'll get the light down here,' he said, 'and you can start up.' He gallantly waited for her to get a head start, then followed her up the stairs, trying unsuccessfully to keep his eyes off the shapely body he visualized beneath her expensive clothes.

What a great-looking package, he thought.

He admired her lithe, quick way of climbing the steep steps, even in her high-heeled boots. Her eager, energetic gait that must be matched by her spirit. He could certainly appreciate her apparent willingness and fearlessness to take on this project and what it might involve. She must be one very gutsy lady. And, he considered, despite her refined, well-heeled look, she didn't seem like the type who would be afraid to get her hands dirty.

He liked that. He liked that a lot.

At the top of the stairs, Leonie stepped into the kitchen and turned to him. 'Kitchen next? Okay with you?'

'Great,' he said, flipping off the light switch and closing the basement door behind him.

'You know,' Leonie said, using her hands to lift herself onto a countertop, where she sat frowning at someone's bad attempt at modernization years before, 'we really haven't talked about the overall approach I want to take toward renovating, and I think this is an ideal place to begin.'

'That's a very good idea,' he replied, staring at her. 'Doing it now, before we look at the rest of the property. Because at this point, I don't know how far you want to go.' He looked at her levelly. 'Renovation can mean a lot of different things to different people. Everything from tearing down a place to nothing but a fresh coat of paint.'

Leonie laughed. 'Well, this isn't Southampton or Beverly Hills, so I don't consider this place a tear-down, that's for sure.'

'I'm glad to hear it,' he said. 'You would be doing architectural history a great disservice.'

'On the other hand,' Leonie said, 'it's going to take a lot more than a fresh coat of paint. Like in here.' She hopped down from the counter. 'This floor. This horrible, disgusting, filthy linoleum!'

'My guess is that underneath this crap' – he lifted a torn piece of linoleum with the toe of his boot – 'you are going to find wide-board pine floors.'

'I was hoping you'd say that,' Leonie smiled.

'And I would also guess they'll clean up and look like a million dollars.' Just like you, he thought. After a moment, he added, 'If that's the approach you want to take.'

'That's exactly what I had in mind,' Leonie said. 'I want to give this a country kitchen look, but with all the modern conveniences. New appliances, of course. But. And this is a big but.' She looked directly into his eyes. 'Wherever possible, I want to use original materials. Like those old cabinets. I love their shape and the old hardware on them and the old glass-paned doors that some of them have. Do you think they're worth trying to salvage?' She looked at him questioningly.

'It wouldn't be cheap,' he said, 'but you bet they can be. And I would go for it. They can be stripped, then stained or painted, whichever you prefer. And if there are parts or pieces that need replacing, we can match them up. No problem.' He paused again, eyeing her critically. 'Now I think I have a pretty good idea of where you're coming from.'

Leonie smiled self-consciously. 'I hope so. I'm not always so great at translating my ideas about these things into words that people understand. Sometimes ... sometimes I feel like I'm on an alien wavelength.'

'I think you're doing just fine,' he said.

'Thanks.' Leonie felt herself blushing and turned away, suddenly feeling foolish. 'Anyhow, moving right along. See this horrible lowered ceiling?' She gestured up with a hand. 'I want to take it down. I don't have any idea what we'll find, but this has got to go.'

'There're probably great old beams up there, hidden when somebody decided to modernize the place. If you want to use them.'

'Exactly!' Leonie enthused.

They continued going over ideas for the kitchen, then moved on to the dining room and library, Leonie and Sam both excitedly exchanging thoughts on what should be done. Their ideas seemed almost identical. Or, Leonie thought with a touch of atypical cynicism, he's a real smoothie who certainly knows how to say and do the right thing.

But somehow she didn't think that was the case. He had a

spontaneous, natural enthusiasm for the house and everything they discussed, and contributed his own opinions without hesitation. She didn't think he could fake his reactions that well. And why would he want to, anyway? she asked herself.

'Well,' Leonie finally said. 'I think that about covers everything down here, except the parlor. How about we do it, then head upstairs?'

'Okay,' he said, and followed her into the parlor, where they found Mossy, spread out lengthwise on the daybed, thumbing through an Italian *Vogue*, wreathed in the ubiquitous haze of cigarette smoke she created wherever she happened to be.

'Don't mind me,' Mossy intoned. 'I helped myself to one of your magazines, and I'm having a look-see at all these gorgeous things I'll never be able to afford.' She looked at them over the tops of her Ben Franklins. 'But then, from the looks of them, neither can the models,' she drawled. 'They look as if they spend all their hard-earned dollars on heroin.'

Leonie and Sam laughed.

'Don't let us interfere, Mossy,' Leonie said. 'You just pleasure yourself. We won't be a lot longer.'

'Take all the time in the world,' she said. 'I've only just begun planning a complete makeover for myself.'

Leonie and Sam exchanged amused glances. Then Leonie got down to business.

'In here, like the rest of the downstairs, I'm really worried about the parquet.' She indicated the scarred and broken flooring, which, like a giant jigsaw puzzle, was missing many of its once beautiful and intricately fitted pieces. 'Should I just forget it, or do you think it can be saved?'

'Absolutely, it can be saved,' he said in an assured tone. 'And I hope you do.' He squatted down and picked up a piece of the chipped parquet, then examined it closely.

'There are several places nowadays where we can get the wood to match what's missing,' he said, getting back up and holding the pieces of parquet out for her to look at. 'And I've got some very talented craftsmen who can do the work. It's really not a big problem. Just a little tedious and time-consuming.'

'I love it,' Leonie said. 'And I'm willing to go out on a limb to save it.' Then she reached out and ran a hand down a crack in the plaster-work. 'What do you think? Is this going to be a big problem?'

'If you've got the money, I've got the men,' he said with a grin.

'I bet you do,' she countered.

They examined the fireplaces, mantels, windows, and molding as they had in the other downstairs rooms, then took a peek into the tiny powder room off the hallway.

All the while, they discussed the myriad alternative approaches to rescuing the crumbling old mansion. Afterward, they headed up the elegant but time-worn and rickety staircase to the bed-rooms above.

Leonie turned to Sam and said, 'As you can see, any hint of grandeur that's left is all downstairs. The upstairs has been completely let go. Over the years, they've closed up the fireplaces, and you can see in places where they've patched up the plasterwork – badly. Even some of the moldings have been ripped out.'

Sam walked from room to room, surveying all of them quickly, knocking on a wall here, stomping on a floor there.

Finally, he turned to her. 'You know,' he said, 'this looks a lot worse than it is. It'll be a snap to get the fireplaces opened up and working again and to redo the plasterwork, if that's what you want.'

'That's exactly what I want. The way they were, once upon a time. Including all the right moldings, which I know means a lot of work,' she said.

'That's not a problem, either,' Sam said, 'because it looks like they're all stock moldings.'

Leonie paused, pacing from room to room again, absorbed in her own thoughts, with Sam trailing along just behind her.

Suddenly she stopped. 'I think the only thing that I want to do up here that might be a challenge is adding bathrooms, without intruding on the architectural purity of the place.'

She turned to him, looking into his eyes. 'That's where I really need help,' she said. 'I'll have to rely on your architectural expertise and ideas.'

'Not an easy problem to solve,' he considered, 'but I'm sure we can figure out something that'll work.'

'If I've got the money, you've got the know-how, huh?' she said with a grin.

'Touché.' He shrugged and smiled at her.

It was a smile, Leonie thought, that almost but not quite spread to those sadly beautiful blue-green eyes of his.

She suddenly felt acutely uncomfortable again, even though she was more at ease with him now. The irony was not lost on her, but she felt unnerved nevertheless.

Keep busy, she told herself. Idle hands, she remembered her mother used to say, are the devil's workshop. She quickly got back down to business again.

'Should we look at the attic and the cupola while we're up here?' she asked.

'Definitely,' he replied. 'I should get a good look at this side of the roof. See what kind of shape it's in.'

Leonie led the way to the tiny enclosed staircase that led up to the attic, and Sam followed closely behind her, once again finding it impossible to keep his eyes off the shapely body springing up the steep stairs ahead of him.

He suddenly realized that he should get the hell out of here, but he also realized that a much more powerful urge was exerting itself. I don't want to leave, he thought.

Leonie opened the door at the top of the stairs and stepped into the attic. She quickly flipped on a light switch as Sam drew up beside her.

'Whew!' He let out a low whistle, muscled arms akimbo, as he looked about him at the imposing space in which they stood.

'Are you as impressed as I was when I first saw it?' Leonie asked with a hint of a tease, having known almost certainly that he would be.

'My God,' he replied, with awe in his voice. 'This is a dream come true up here. The possibilities . . . !'

He surveyed the huge, open octagonal space with its eight bull's-eye windows all around, one to each section of the octagon. In the exact center of the room was a small open staircase that led up to the lantern cupola. The roof was supported by huge hand-hewn beams like those in the basement.

'Now watch,' Leonie said. She flipped the light switch off again, and looked at Sam to try to judge his reaction.

Early evening light spilled into the attic from every direction – the opening to the cupola and through the bull's-eye windows. Its effect was diffuse and dusky but hauntingly beautiful, bathing the room in an almost unearthly luminescence.

'Don't turn the lights back on yet,' Sam said, and he began carefully making his way from window to window, taking in the 360-degree views they afforded. After making a complete circle, he climbed up to the cupola, then back down again, and came over to Leonie's side, where he stopped.

She looked at him questioningly.

'What do you plan to do up here?' he asked.

'I have a couple of ideas, but I'm not absolutely sure yet,' Leonie answered. 'I guess most people would turn it into servants' quarters, or children's rooms. You know, to get them out of the way.'

'You're right about that,' he said with a laugh.

'But I thought that it would make a great master bedroom suite. Exposed beams. Slanting ceilings. Really gigantic, with a huge his and her bathroom and a little wet-bar, so you wouldn't have to traipse all the way downstairs to the kitchen for midnight snacks.'

She looked thoughtful for a moment, then continued. 'It would be like a haven, a sanctuary, away from the rest of the house, the rest of the world for that matter. It's a great place to be meditative, to be alone. Or with someone special.'

She looked up into his eyes. 'What do you think?'

'That's a fantastic idea,' he said. 'It's almost like a separate world up here. A totally different world. And it would change with the light all day long and during the night. Even though you'd be at the top of the house, in a way you'd be close to nature – the sun, the moon, the stars and clouds. Sunrise and sunset and everything in between. Then you'd have a spectacular view of the river and the mountains, if you wanted to take advantage of it.' He glanced at her. 'And you're right, it would be a great sanctuary, a retreat where you could be alone, or – who knows?' He smiled at her.

She returned his smile.

'The cupola's going to take a lot of work,' he said. 'There's a lot of cracked glass and missing panes, and there's been some water leakage. That's probably where a lot of the damage in the bedrooms downstairs comes from. Leaking down from here.'

'I thought so,' Leonie replied, 'but I definitely want it to stay. I realize it would be easier to just tear it out and roof over the hole, but I don't want to. And I just hate to replace that wavy old glass with new, but I guess that's what I'll have to do.'

'We'll see,' Sam said. 'Maybe . . . maybe we can come up with something that'll work right.'

'I hope so,' Leonie said.

'It's like the steeple on a church,' Sam said. 'You just don't want to tear it down, even if it is a pain in the butt. It's like the heart and soul of the house in a way.'

Leonie was aglow. She felt truly gratified with his reaction. It gave her ideas a validity that made her feel more self-confident. But more than that, his enthusiasm was infectious. It excited her all the more about the project, made it seem that much more

44

meaningful somehow, knowing that she would not be working in a vacuum, that there was somebody to share the little defeats and little joys with.

Suddenly she jerked herself out of her reverie. She had to slam a mental door shut on this train of thought immediately, she told herself.

Jesus! What am I thinking? Am I crazy? This guy hasn't even said he would work on it yet. Besides that, he may price himself right out of my league!

What's more, although they seemed to agree on a lot of her ideas, how did she know what working with him would be like? I don't! she reminded herself. It might be pure, unmitigated hell for all I know.

In fact, she didn't know much of anything about Sam Nicholson, even though she felt increasingly as if she had somehow always known him, that meeting him now was somehow meant to be.

Sam looked at his wristwatch. 'It's getting late,' he said matter-of-factly, 'and I've got to go soon. How about we have a quick gander outside before I take off?'

'Okay,' Leonie said hurriedly, 'but if you need to get on your way, we can leave it for another time.'

'Nah,' he said. 'It's okay. I'd like to get the big picture before I go.'

'If you're sure, then let's go,' Leonie said, turning and starting down the stairs.

He watched her go, wishing that they could stay up here awhile. Just the two of them. But for what? he wondered. Then he sighed and reluctantly followed her down the stairs.

'I think I'd like to see this staircase opened up,' Leonie said.

'That's easy,' Sam replied. 'Not a problem.'

In the entry hall, they spied Mossy, still stretched out on the daybed, engrossed in the Italian *Vogue* and a cigarette, seemingly oblivious to them.

Leonie led the way outside. 'I'll try to give you a quick-sketch artist's idea of what I'm thinking,' she told Sam.

She hurriedly guided him through the old carriage house. 'Two-car garage, caretaker's apartment or guest quarters upstairs,' Leonie said.

Then on to the barn they went. 'Maybe an artist's studio with some offices. Maybe.'

Finally, they did a hasty survey of the grounds. 'They were beautifully laid out once upon a time. They have good bones, just like the house. Now all they need's a major cleaning up, a lot of trimming, some replanting. All the old stone walls need work.' She looked up at him. 'You name it. The works,' she said with a laugh. 'But then that's not really your province.'

'Not unless you want to include repairing the pergola and the gazebo in my estimate,' he replied.

Leonie looked thoughtful for a moment, then nodded. 'Yes,' she said, 'do that. But separately, if you could, so I'll know exactly what the cost will be.'

'Sure,' he said. He looked around him. 'I've passed by here a million times,' he said, 'but I didn't realize these gardens existed. You can't see them from the road.' He strode over to the Doric-columned pergola, now almost smothered in wisteria vines which were not blooming, with Leonie trailing closely behind.

'This could be really beautiful,' he said.

'Yes,' Leonie said. 'I'm going to have to trim back this wisteria mercilessly, and I bet it blooms next year.'

'Think so?' he asked.

'Probably,' she said. 'There was an old one like this at a friend's house in Southampton. He nearly killed me for giving it a major haircut a couple of years ago, but he's thanking me now, because it's absolutely covered in flowers.'

She pointed to the formal parterre, a quadrant broken up by overgrown bluestone paths. In the center of it stood a crumbling birdbath, its bowl broken off completely. 'The parterres are planted with roses, mostly,' she said. 'I'll have to wait for them to bloom to see what kind exactly, but I suspect they're very hardy old-fashioned varieties. What else could survive these winters?'

He nodded. 'I guess you're right,' he said. 'We have some at home, but they take a lot of tending.'

'Anyway,' Leonie continued, 'they're going to require a major trim job, too. So are those on the gazebo.'

They walked over to the lattice-work gazebo, a fanciful, once-white structure that overlooked the river on one side. Like the pergola, it was smothered in vines, in this case climbing roses which had yet to bloom.

'These are going to take a lot of cutting back,' Leonie said, 'Just to paint the gazebo. But it'll do the roses good, too.' She turned to Sam. 'I was thinking of placing a swimming pool between the gazebo and the pergola,' she said. 'What do you think?'

'It's the most perfect spot imaginable,' he said.

'I thought that I would try to make the swimming pool look something more like a reflecting pool,' Leonie said. 'About eighteen feet wide by thirty-six feet long. Not huge. With no diving board, and no ladders. Just steps down into it at the shallow end. Then I'd put in a black liner.'

'Black?' Sam said in surprise.

'Yes,' Leonie replied. 'I know it sounds spooky, like creature from the black lagoon territory. But it's not. I've seen it done, and it looks fabulous. You can see to the bottom – it's not creepy – and it looks like a classical reflecting pool. But it has the distinct advantage that you can swim in it.'

'I'll trust you on this,' Sam said with a grin.

'Good,' Leonie said. 'Because, believe me, it works.' She looked around her, then turned to Sam. 'All this overgrowth is awfully romantic,' she said, 'but I think it needs a little careful attention before the vegetation takes over completely.'

Sam smiled. 'Yeah, it's very picturesque, but getting close to jungle.'

'I wonder about the people who used to live here,' Leonie said wistfully. 'What sort of people they were, to let it go like this. I only dealt with lawyers since it was an estate sale. They said there were no heirs.'

'You know it belonged to the Wiley sisters, Grace and Eleanor Wiley,' Sam said. 'They've both been dead for quite a while. Neither one of them ever married.'

'I wonder why,' Leonie said.

'I don't really know,' Sam replied. 'They were both supposed to have been great beauties in their day, back in the roaring twenties. One of them painted, landscapes mostly, and a few portraits. She was pretty good, too. The other one gardened quite a lot.'

'I guess that accounts for the layout here,' Leonie said.

'Probably,' Sam said. 'Their father was a politician. I think he was actually in the Cabinet at one time. Secretary of the Interior or something like that. He had been a very powerful man. But that was decades ago.'

'Did he build the house?' Leonie asked.

'No,' Sam said. 'His father – Grace and Eleanor's grandfather – built it in the eighteen-forties. He was a doctor and a gentleman farmer. He also owned some of the banks around here. He was a very rich man, but after he died, his son gradually sold off acreage over the years, farming a little as a hobby.'

'What about the daughters?' Leonie asked. 'What do you know about them?'

'Grace and Eleanor were true eccentrics, to say the least,' Sam answered. 'I don't know anybody who ever really knew them. Hell, I don't know anybody who ever even saw them off of this property. Not for years.'

'You're kidding,' Leonie said.

'No, I'm not,' Sam replied.

'I wonder how they lived? Two elderly women. All alone out here.'

'They had this ancient little man, Pete Blanchard was his name,' Sam said. 'He had worked for the family all his life, and lived here on the place. I guess he was about the sisters' age. Anyway, Pete did all the shopping, all the maintenance, everything that had to be done. When anybody tried to ask Pete about the sisters, he clammed up totally. Wouldn't say a word.'

'How odd,' Leonie said.

'It was odd,' Sam agreed. 'They lived here as recluses, really complete recluses. I remember passing by here once, years ago,' Sam said. 'It was in the spring, toward dusk, and there was a light rain. I saw – I think it must have been Eleanor, I think she was the only one alive then. Anyway, I passed by and saw her making her way through all these weeds – it was a lot more overgrown then – in the rain, around the side of the house. It looked like she was headed somewhere around here, where we are now, the gazebo.'

Leonie felt a shiver run through her. It was all so odd.

'She was wearing a long nightgown,' Sam continued. 'It looked white and lacy, or like it once had been, and it billowed out behind her in the wind. She had snow-white hair piled up on her head. I could tell it was really long, because it was coming undone and blowing around her.'

'What a weird scene that must have been,' Leonie said.

'It was,' Sam said. 'Mostly because it's the only time I ever saw her. The only time. I guess that's why I've never forgotten it. I almost stopped to see if she needed help, but I'd always heard stories about how they would slam the door in people's faces, so I decided to leave well enough alone.'

'I wonder what she was doing,' Leonie said. 'I wonder why she was outside in a nightgown. Why she was outside in the rain.'

'I don't know,' Sam said, 'but there was something mysterious about it to me.' He shrugged. 'I guess I'll never know the answer.'

49

'What about their workman?' Leonie asked.

'Pete Blanchard?' Sam said. 'After Eleanor died, Pete disappeared.'

'Disappeared?' Leonie said.

'Yes,' Sam said. 'Disappeared. He was never seen or heard from again.' He turned to Leonie. 'They used to say that Pete was a little slow, mentally and all, but I don't really know. Anyway, he vanished from the face of the earth.'

'Good Lord,' Leonie said. 'It gets stranger and stranger.'

Sam nodded. 'Finally, when Eleanor died, she left this place and all the money – and there was a lot of it – to the Humane Society. And that's all I know about them,' Sam said.

Leonie laughed. 'I think that's plenty,' she said. 'They do sound a bit eccentric. I only hope that if there're ghosts, they're friendly.'

Sam smiled. 'I'm sure they will be. For you.'

Leonie felt herself blush slightly. 'Oh, I wouldn't be so sure,' she retorted. 'Maybe they would feel like I'm a usurper on their territory.'

'I think they'd be pleased,' Sam said, 'to see someone as young and vibrant as yourself restoring their home to its former glory. Even if they didn't bother, for whatever reasons, I feel like they'd appreciate your efforts.'

'Maybe so,' Leonie said. His proximity, combined with his flattering comments, was making her feel distinctly uncomfortable again. She looked to the west, across the river, and saw that the sun was an enormous fireball descending over the Catskills. It was spectacularly beautiful, but served as a reminder that Sam Nicholson should be on his way.

'It's getting late,' she said, 'and I know you were in a hurry. I've kept you long enough.'

He looked at her. 'You're right. I'd better go say good-bye to Mossy and get on my way.'

They returned to the parlor, where they joined Mossy.

50

'Well, what do you think?' Mossy looked up at Sam critically. 'Do you see any merit in saving this tumble-down disaster? Do you think it will be a challenge? Do you think you're interested in doing it?'

Sam smiled at her rapid-fire questions. 'There's no question but that it should be saved,' Sam said seriously. 'And, yes. It will definitely be a challenge, but it will be more than worth it.'

He paused and turned to Leonie. 'I don't know whether I'll be working on this project or not, but it's definitely interesting.'

'I'm glad you think so,' Leonie said somewhat formally. 'When you think it over, there are a couple of things to keep in mind.'

Sam stared at her.

'What I want to do here is make a very big ripple with a very small stone. Do you see what I mean?'

'I think I do,' he replied.

'I'm big on effect,' Leonie said, 'and a little short on money.'

He laughed. 'That I understand perfectly.' Then he gazed at her thoughtfully. 'I think you can take one of three approaches to a job like this.'

Leonie listened carefully.

'One,' Sam said, 'is perfection. That is usually expensive, and it would be very, very expensive here.'

'I guess I can live without perfection,' Leonie said half-jokingly.

'Two,' he continued, 'is acceptable. A whole lot less expensive and looks good.' He eyed her significantly. 'Three is unacceptable. And I personally won't even think about doing a job that way, and I don't think you should, either.'

'I don't have any intention of handling this place like that,' Leonie said defensively. 'I may be doing this place up to put on the market, but I want to do it as if I myself were going to be living here. So, I want to do it as lovingly as possible. I want to return the place to its former glory, give it some dignity, and show it some respect. It deserves it.'

'I didn't mean to offend you,' he assured her. 'It's just that there are a lot of architects and contractors out there who will go for something super cheap. And it's usually super wrong,' he said. 'Sometimes it may look okay, but that usually only lasts awhile before everything starts falling apart.'

'I don't want to use shoddy materials,' Leonie said. 'But I do think that I'll probably be forced to compromise and go for acceptable as opposed to perfect in most cases.' She looked at him. 'Do you think you could live with that?'

'Yes,' he said, 'I could.'

'Bloody hell,' Mossy suddenly interjected. 'It's almost completely dark out!'

'Oh, I'm sorry,' Leonie said to Sam. 'I'm keeping you. Again! Why don't you get going. When you've had a chance to think this over, give me a call. Okay?'

'You got it,' Sam said.

'You have the number, don't you?' Leonie asked.

'Mossy gave it to me,' Sam answered

'Well,' Leonie said, 'I'll show you out.'

'Mossy,' Sam said, holding out his hand for Mossy to shake, 'it was good to see you, as always. And thanks a lot for recommending me for the job.'

'Pleasure to see you too, Sam,' Mossy replied, shaking his hand. 'Stay out of trouble.'

'I'll try.' He grinned.

He turned and started to the hallway, with Leonie following along behind him. When he reached the back door, he turned to her. 'It's been a pleasure to meet you, Leonie,' he said. 'Maybe something will work out here.'

Leonie nodded. 'I hope so.'

He offered his hand for a shake and she took it. His grasp was firm and warm and lingering, as if he were reluctant to let go.

When she looked up at him, she saw that his eyes were searching out hers, the blue-green glint of intensity in them almost overwhelming. They made her feel naked and helpless. Vulnerable and lost. She felt a quiver burn hotly through her and suddenly felt weak.

She struggled to control herself. This is ridiculous, she thought. Just plain silly. He's probably playing with me.

But the mischievousness that she had seen in those eyes earlier was gone, replaced by something much less playful, something much more serious. Once again, she knew beyond a shadow of a doubt that she was gone. She felt it in her very bones, in the depths of her very being.

Finally Sam broke the silence.

'Good night,' he said, his resonant baritone voice barely audible. Then he turned and quickly left without another word or backward glance.

Leonie closed the door behind him, turned around, and leaned back against it. She took a few deep, slow breaths as she listened to him start his Range Rover, steadied herself when she heard the crunch of gravel as he pulled out. When she could no longer hear his car, she waited a moment, ran long fingers through her hair, then walked back into the parlor.

Mossy was perched upright on the daybed, an omnipotent and all-knowing look on her face. After a moment, she flicked the ash off her cigarette into an ashtray, all the while studying Leonie intently, then spoke: 'At last!' she said theatrically. 'Why don't you come have a sit down by poor, dull, old Mossy.' She patted the daybed beside her. 'You must be exhausted.'

Leonie looked over at her as she slowly walked to the daybed and sat down. 'Exhausted?' she answered in a suspicious tone. 'No. Not at all. Why would you say that, Mossy?'

'Bloody hell, Leonie. You can't fool an old warhorse like me. The air in this house has been so fraught with sexual tension since Sam

Bloody Nicholson walked in the door that I'm a complete wreck from the bloody vibrations between you two!'

'That is complete nonsense, Mossy,' Leonie retorted, with more conviction than she felt and more hostility than she intended.

Mossy was slightly taken aback by Leonie's defensive posture. She looked at her, arching an expressive brow. 'Ooooh,' she said. 'We've hit a nerve, have we? Sorry, dear. No offense meant.'

'None taken,' Leonie said. She sat quietly with an uncharacteristically closed expression on her face, challenging Mossy to breach her inaccessible defenses.

Mossy gazed at her friend with an expression that was both quizzical and tender. After a moment she reached over and put a hand atop one of Leonie's. 'Listen, dear,' she said softly, stroking her. 'I really didn't mean to upset you, you know. I suppose I get carried away sometimes, drama queen that I am.'

Leonie couldn't help but laugh. 'Drama queen!' She put an arm around Mossy's shoulder and squeezed her. 'That you are, Moss. That you are.'

Mossy drew away and leaned over to get a cigarette out of the pack which had fallen to the floor beside her. 'But he is a divinely sexy specimen, you must admit,' she said airily, relentlessly steering the conversation back to Sam Nicholson.

'Yes,' Leonie conceded, 'he is. And besides that, he seems like a very nice man.'

'Ummm,' Mossy murmured as she lit a cigarette. She blew a streamer of smoke, directing it away from Leonie's face. 'Nice. Oh, yes. That too.'

'And you know what?' Leonie said. 'He seemed to understand everything I said. Everything I wanted to do here.'

'Really,' Mossy drawled throatily.

'Not only that,' Leonie continued, 'but we seemed to be on the exact same wavelength.'

'Indeed.'

'And—' Leonie suddenly stopped, hearing the sardonic tone in Mossy's voice. She looked over at her, and saw that the smile on Mossy's face was both perceptive and sly.

'You ... you scallywag ... you ... you rogue ... you ... you witch ... you—' Leonie sputtered.

'Bitch, dear. B-i-t-c-h,' Mossy spelled. 'That will suffice. I know I am, and you can call me that anytime. You will most definitely not be the first.' Mossy paused and took a drag off her cigarette, then continued. 'But what I think you would like to say to me, is that Mr. Sam Nicholson is right for the job – and a whole lot more. I think what we have here is a serious case of the hot pants?'

'Oh, you are awful!' Leonie laughed despite herself.

'Yes. And I'm right!' Mossy trilled. 'Two cases, actually. You and Mr. Nicholson. Serious cases. He could hardly get out of here, the condition he was in.'

'Do you really think so?' Leonie asked through her laughter. 'I don't think he paid any particular notice to me.'

'Bloody hell! Don't be so naive, dear,' Mossy said. 'The poor bastard could hardly keep it in his pants.'

'Ohhhhh!' Leonie wailed, slapping Mossy's wrist. 'Stop! Right now!'

'It's the truth,' Mossy insisted. 'He was like a buck in rut. And, if my curious eyes didn't deceive me, you were slightly atwitter yourself. Not that you weren't the perfect lady, of course.'

Atwitter! Leonie thought. What a silly-seeming word. If Mossy only knew! Atwitter hardly began to describe what she was actually feeling. But then, she wasn't certain she could describe it herself. Quite simply, she didn't think she had ever felt this way before.

'Well,' Leonie said at last, 'I just hope at this point he'll want to do the job, and give me a good estimate. He really does seem to be perfect for it.'

'I'm sure he is,' Mossy said. 'Perfect man.' She paused thought-fully. 'And now the poor bastard is headed home,' she continued, 'stuck with the common scold.'

'Common cold,' Leonie corrected.

'No, dear,' Mossy said. 'Common scold.'

'What do you mean?' Leonie asked.

'Don't ask,' Mossy replied darkly. 'You don't want to know.'

4

'What the—!' Sam Nicholson slammed his hand against the steering wheel of his Range Rover and then slowly eased over onto the shoulder, off the road. He rolled to a crawl, braked, and put the car in park. He had just barely avoided plowing head-on into a deer leaping across the highway.

A beautiful white-tailed doe, he thought. And I could have killed her.

He didn't know why, but it was almost always a female, never a male, that made a target of itself on these roads. In all his years here, he'd only seen three or four stags on the roads, but countless does. He knew well that this was not an uncommon occurrence in this neck of the woods, but his near-miss was wholly uncharacteristic of him. He prided himself on being one of the few people he knew around here who had never actually hit a deer, or any other animal for that matter.

In fact, he'd always felt a ripple of repulsion run through him when he'd seen the signs on the road advertising cutting and wrapping deer. Although he'd hunted with his father when he was a boy and still ate meat occasionally, he somehow found the idea revolting, illogical as it may be on his part. As for killing animals, he couldn't bring himself to do it, certainly not for sport. Perhaps, life – any life – had come to seem too precious and fragile a thing to consider extinguishing it, whether intentional or not.

Now he had to cool off, relax, let his adrenaline return to normal. Get back in control.

What the hell's wrong with me anyway? he wondered. But he knew the answer to that question beyond any shadow of a doubt. Knew exactly and specifically what was wrong. I'm just not paying attention, that's all, he rationalized. It was as simple as that. Or was it?

Why, then? he asked himself. Why am I being so damned inattentive? Why am I losing control? Because . . . because . . .

He exhaled an audible sigh of annoyance. He did not want to pursue this line of questioning any further. Not under any circumstances. No way.

He reached over and switched off the radio. He liked Sinatra, but had decided the man either must have owned or had a lot of stock in WABY radio, because sometimes it seemed as if they played no one else. Right now, he was not in the mood for Old Blue Eyes and his crooning. No. Absolutely not. Love ballads were the last thing he wanted to hear, and he didn't need the distraction of the music – any music. That much was obvious.

Besides, he wanted to be alone with his thoughts. Those same thoughts, ironically enough, that he didn't think he should be having in the first place.

Ah, hell, he decided. Sitting here is getting me nowhere.

He slammed the Range Rover in drive, checked for traffic, and swung the big car back out onto the highway. Across the river to the west, the sun had already performed its final, brilliant, pyrotechnical display of the day and had been swallowed up by the Catskill Mountains. Continuing north in the quickly diminishing light, Sam once again became absorbed in thoughts of the old octagon house and the idea of saving it.

What an exciting prospect it was, he thought. And what an extraordinary old property. Its historical importance alone made it a gem. Any architect worth his salt would jump at the chance to work on the project, and would deem himself the luckiest of men to even be considered for the job.

And by God, he thought, I sure would like to have a hand in it. It was right up his alley, precisely the sort of project he could sink his teeth into.

But, he told himself, I'm never going to be able to work with that woman. Leonie Corinth.

Not that he didn't think she would be great to work with. No, it wasn't that at all. In fact, it was the very opposite. He wanted desperately to work with her. Every instinct he had told him that they would be ideal partners, that working with her would be a highly rewarding experience, a tremendous creative challenge – and, possibly, a whole lot more.

And therein lay the problem.

The stirring he'd felt when he first saw her reasserted itself now. Leonie Corinth. That tall, slender, desirable body. That rich, dark hair and pale, creamy skin. And those eyes! Black as pitch, shiny as obsidian, and, he thought with a smile, capable of being mischievous as all hell. Had he not seen the soulful wariness and hurt that lay beneath their glittering, good-humored surface, he would have thought that she was, well, some kind of superwoman, too together, too perfect. But those eyes rendered her vulnerable, approachable . . . human.

Sam didn't know when he'd felt this bewitched by a woman, if ever. The attraction had actually been chemical, he thought. A feeling of affinity deep within his gut that touched his very being.

Something elemental: a force of nature both primitive and grand, ruthless and overpowering – and inescapable.

'Jesus,' he swore aloud. He was approaching Kinderhook. He flipped on the turn signal and slowed down to make a left onto the road leading to his house.

Inescapable, a very powerful word, that. But, for some unfathomable reason, he felt certain that their meeting had been predestined, that it was a meeting he could never have planned or predicted, not in his wildest imaginings. And it made him very uneasy to think that it was a coming together – a convergence of forces – over which he had no control whatsoever.

But, he told himself, it had happened, and now . . . well, now it was something to which he felt he must submit, come what may. It was almost as if he had no choice in the matter because he was dealing with a power that seemed infinitely greater than himself.

On his right, huge iron gates loomed, black and elegant and forbidding. The entrance to Van Vechten Manor.

He sighed, a vague sense of dread needling at his consciousness, then he turned in, braked, and buzzed down the car window. He punched in the security code on a steel panel set into one of the massive brick piers on either side of the drive and watched the video cameras watch him.

This place is a paranoid's paradise, he thought. He could understand Minette's desire for security on this vast estate, but he thought she'd gotten carried away with all the technological devices she'd had her cousin Dirck install to turn it into a stronghold.

The gates slowly swung open and he drove the big car through, watching them close behind him in the rearview mirror.

He gazed out at the magnificent old conifers – hemlock, spruce, and pine – lining either side of the drive. Tonight, they were eerie, monolithic sentries guarding the approach to the manor, their usual majestic lushness transformed into a menacing austerity. He slowed down, not anxious to reach the house, still absorbed in his thoughts.

Perhaps, he thought, the most shocking revelation today had been that he had felt anything at all. Leonie Corinth was undeniably an incredibly alluring creature, but over the years he had met many beautiful and exciting women – and he had never felt this way before.

He had met women, he was certain, who were as well heeled, and as exoticly beautiful, as vibrant, and as smart as she seemed to be. Some of them had thrown themselves at him, others had hinted at possibilities, flirting behind their husbands' backs. But none of them had had this indefinable impact upon him. No. In fact, it had been so many years since he had experienced a feeling remotely this powerful that he was truly amazed that he still had the capacity to feel at all.

He looked up at the light spilling out of the perfectly proportioned Palladian windows of Van Vechten Manor. Its classical Georgian symmetry rendered in old pinkish brick, which usually gave his architect's mind such a rush of aesthetic pleasure, failed to have any effect this evening. If anything, its grand and stately formality made it seem like a beautiful prison, a formidable fortress which, in all its vastness, had no room for his soul.

This place is anything but a home, he thought.

He crawled to a stop in the circular drive at the foot of the brick steps leading up to the front door, put on the brakes, and killed the engine. Then he reluctantly climbed out of the car, punched the alarm-lock button on his key chain, and started up the steps to the elaborately pedimented front door. Before he reached it, it swung open.

'Mr. Nicholson.' It was Erminda, the only live-in servant. She held the door open for him, her voluptuous figure with its ample bust barely concealed beneath the dowdy gray uniform Minette Nicholson made her wear.

'Hey, Erminda,' he said, forcing a smile as he stepped into the entrance hall. It was a suitably grand entry, with its black-and-white checkerboard marble floors, sparkling antique Waterford chandelier dripping crystal, and hand-painted eighteenth-century wallpaper, which depicted hunt scenes, over carved wainscotting. 'How are you tonight?'

'I'm fine, Mr. Nicholson.' Her dark eyes glittered provocatively. 'I hope you are, too.'

'Sure thing, Erminda,' he replied. Sam tossed his car keys into a large famille rose porcelain bowl which rested atop an elaborately carved gilt and mahogany console.

'Mrs. Nicholson is in the conservatory. She says to see her the minute you get here.' Erminda stared up at him, patting the lustrous jet-black hair that she wore pulled back into a severe bun at the base of her neck, the hairdo being another rule of Minette's.

'Do me a favor, Erminda, would you?' Sam said, trying to keep the smile cemented on his face. 'Tell her I'll see her in a little while. I have some things to do.'

Erminda smiled brightly. 'Yes. I'll go right now.'

Sam noticed Erminda's obvious relish in delivering a message to his wife that she knew would not make Minette happy.

No love lost between those two, he thought mirthfully. Strange that in the last few years she was the only live-in servant Minette had been able to keep around for more than a few weeks. Erminda had been with them for two years now, and though she remained something of an enigma to Sam, she had silently and obediently catered to Minette's every whim during that time, setting something of a record for longevity in the household.

Sam dodged the big round center table with its enormous arrangement of fresh flowers, and quickly climbed the antique Talish runner on the stairs, which elegantly curved like a perfect nautilus. In the hallway, he paused a moment, then hurried down it and through their bedroom to his bath and dressing room. He shut the door behind him and locked it.

He pulled off his leather jacket, boots, and socks, then took off his blue jeans and shirt, and his underwear, leaving everything in a pile on the highly polished wide-board pine floor. He padded over to the huge pedestal sink on bare feet, where he twirled an old-fashioned brass tap for cold water and then splashed his face several times. He toweled off vigorously and stood looking at himself in the mirror. Really looking, for the first time in as long as he could remember.

Not bad for a man my age, he thought, examining his handsome features from various angles. No. Not bad at all.

But, he thought, it's all going to waste. I'm going to waste. Been going to waste for years.

He walked into his dressing room, and spread out on the Stickley oak daybed, its brown leather squeaking under his weight. He ignored the Roycroft lamps, the Stickley leather-and-oak chess table he used for a desk, the Voysey arts-and-crafts rug on the floor, the Grueby and Rookwood earthenware, his favorite old, foxed architectural drawings and maps, and all the other precious objects which normally nourished his sense of well-being.

This was his little domain, furnished with things he cherished, not done up with the extremely formal and very finest of American antiques that Minette preferred. She, in fact, loathed this room, and didn't come near it.

On the daybed now, he brooded.

Why am I wasting myself? he wondered. Throwing myself away? For what? But he knew the answer: a loveless union. A union born of his own sense of guilt and shame. A union born of sacrifice. Sacrificing himself to a marriage that had become so suffocating he thought he had become totally numb to the world around him, smothering his own dreams and ambitions, his own chances for any emotional life whatsoever.

He realized now that he had been marking time, content to let the days run their course, sleepwalking through them, not living really, allowing himself to be consumed – eaten alive – by this guilt and shame. He knew now, more than ever, that this loveless union had robbed him of any possible joy in this life.

And he realized something else, too. Something perhaps more frightening in its own way: that his capacity for joy had been reawakened, that he did not have to spend the rest of his life in this somnambulant state, denying himself an emotional life. And this, he knew, was because of Leonie Corinth.

Meeting her had forced him to face up to a reality he had been denying for a very long time – this loveless and sacrificial union. And meeting her had roused his slumbering capacity for feeling.

Leonie Corinth, he thought. Maybe, just maybe, it might be possible for me—

Sam jerked up, his thoughts abruptly interrupted by the disembodied voice of his wife summoning him over the intercom.

'Sam, darling,' Minette Nicholson was calling out, her voice eerily distorted by the speaker.

He sat there listening.

'Sam, what are you doing?' There was a pause. Then: 'Sam? Sam! Where are you? Answer me, dammit!'

With a sigh of disgust, he jumped up from the daybed and dutifully went over to the intercom on his desk, where he punched the answer button.

'I'm in my dressing room, Minette,' he said. 'Be down in just a second.'

'Whatever are you doing,' she whined. 'I've been waiting for you forever.'

'I'll be right there.' He turned from the desk and went over to a Harvey Ellis dresser where he took out fresh underwear and socks, then got a shirt and clean jeans out of the walk-in closet. He quickly dressed, then slipped on ancient topsiders, and headed out through the bathroom, where he viciously kicked at the pile of clothing and boots on the floor, and went on downstairs.

He wound his way from the hallway through the darkly gleaming mahogany-paneled library to the French doors which led to the conservatory, one of his favorite rooms in the house. He paused in the doorway, peering in.

It was a large Georgian-style structure he had designed himself to harmonize with the rest of the house. Its floors were of antique French limestone with black cabochon inserts, and its glass walls soared to over twenty feet. Two identical crystal chandeliers, large neoclassical Russian antiques, were suspended from the ceiling. During the day, they fractured the light into all the colors of the rainbow, casting them about the room kaleidoscopically, and at night, they flickered romantically in the candlelight.

The room was filled to overflowing with greenery of every description, from towering palms and ficus trees to smaller lemon and orange trees to roses and orchid plants. Ivy ran rampant on the wall of the house to which the conservatory had been attached, and it was overlaid with wisteria, which draped theatrically throughout the room, the scent from its huge grapelike clusters of lavender blossoms almost overpowering. Here and there classical busts and statues of weathered marble peeped through the verdure, frozen observers of the dramas played out before them.

From the doorway, he could see an unearthly blue-gray light flashing off the chandeliers and glass walls. No candlelight tonight. Minette was watching television.

She was unaware of him as he stepped in and gazed at her, sitting with the remote control in one hand and a drink – Jack Daniel's and water, he assumed – in the other. Her shoulder-length, pale blond hair glowed lustrously in the light from the television set, and her large ice-blue eyes were focused intently on whatever was on the large screen.

She turned and looked out toward the pool, and Sam saw

her face more clearly. As always, her makeup was expertly but minimally applied to her once-perfect creamy complexion. Lips the palest shell-pink, with the merest hint of blusher, eye liner, and mascara. And she was meticulously dressed – this evening in one of her favorite fawn Zoran cashmere sweaters with matching cashmere pants. Her feet were shod in custom-made, bottle-green, quilted velvet flats with the Van Vechten family crest embroidered on them. Pearls shimmered palely at her ears and around her neck. Gold bangles inset with diamonds, rubies, emeralds, and blue sapphires encircled both wrists, flashing brilliantly when she made the least movement with her hands or arms.

God, she is a beauty, he thought. One of the most beautiful women I've ever seen. Except—

'There you are!' Minette eyes grew wide when she caught sight of him.

Sam walked over and bent down to give her a kiss. It was perfunctory, no more, but that's the way they both seemed to want it these days. Simply going through the motions, he thought.

Minette took a sip of her drink as if to wash the taste of him away, then gazed up at him with a questioning look on her face. 'Where've you been, handsome?' Her voice was husky and dry from the alcohol. She set the drink down on the table next to her and pressed the mute button on the remote.

'I was out looking at a job downriver,' he told her. 'The old octagon house.' Sam sat down on the chaise longue on the other side of the table, and looked at her. 'I might put in a bid on renovating it.'

'Oh, that,' she said disparagingly.

'What do you mean, "Oh, that"?' he asked.

'What I mean, darling,' Minette said, 'is that I think it would be a waste of your time. You don't have to work at all if you don't want to. So why bother with that place? It's not a particularly distinguished house, is it?'

Acting as if his reply didn't matter, Minette continued without pausing for him to answer her. 'Nobody really important has ever lived there. A couple of crazy ladies.' She took a generous sip of her drink and smiled at him sweetly. 'It's a tear-down, if you ask me.'

'I don't believe you're saying this, Minette,' Sam replied, exasperation in his voice, for he was truly perplexed by her reaction. 'I would think that you of all people would be interested in saving the place. As much time as you spend working with the historical society, you know better. You know it's an important house architecturally.'

'Relax, darling,' she said. 'I just think there are a lot of other houses around that are more worthy of attention. Certainly of your attention, I should think.'

'You know as well as I do that the octagon houses in this county are disappearing,' he retorted. 'And fast.'

'Maybe this one should.' She took another sip of her drink, then said: 'Besides, I heard through the grapevine that some New Yorker bought it. The sort of nouveau riche divorcée who'll probably ruin it.' She gave him a significant look. 'Want you to ruin it for her.'

Sam stared at her. 'That's bullshit, Minette,' he said, 'and you know it. You've been talking to Andrea Walker.'

'You needn't resort to coarse language, darling,' she replied. 'And what if I have talked to Andrea? She had that old eyesore listed with her real estate agency for ages. So she knows all the dirt on this deal.'

'Uh-huh,' Sam said, realization dawning. 'So that's it. Now I know what all this is really about. Andrea Walker's gotten you to help blacklist the new owner before she even has a chance around here.' He emitted a sigh. 'Just because she bought the house through somebody else. Andrea lost a commission.'

Minette ignored him, gazing into the bottom of her glass as she swirled the drink in it. Then she looked up. '"Blacklist" is an awfully nasty word, Sam. Especially for somebody who wouldn't have a chance of becoming part of our set anyway. I've heard all about her, and believe me, I know.'

She gave an ugly, derisive laugh, and tossed her head. 'She's some New York nobody divorcée who's already buddy-buddy with that British tart, Fiona Moss, if you see what I mean.'

'Yeah, Minette.' Sam sighed with annoyance. 'I think I do. I think I see exactly what you mean.'

He got up and strode over to the drinks table. Typical of Van Vechten Manor's formal, priceless, and he thought, stuffy furnishings, it was a classic nineteenth-century mahogany and gilt New York pier table with a white marble top. He poured a generous portion of Scotch into a crystal Baccarat old-fashioned glass, added a few ice cubes, then a little water. He took a sip and walked back over to the chaise longue and eased himself down again.

Minette sat there quietly, following him with her eyes, a smug look of satisfaction on her face.

Finally, Sam broke the silence. 'Well, whatever you and Andrea and your little clique of local rich snobs think, I'm excited about the prospect of doing this job. I hope it works out.'

Minette appeared not to have heard him. She depressed a button on the intercom which sat on the table next to her. 'Erminda,' she said, in a clipped manner. 'We'll be dining in a few minutes. Get things ready.'

'Right away, ma'am,' came the voice over the intercom.

How like her, Sam thought. Not to say 'please' or 'thank you,' words which were virtually alien to her vocabulary. Especially where the help was concerned.

He looked at Minette with a glum expression on his face. Why, he wondered, does it have to be this way? Why is it always like this? Always niggling little battles?

Minette turned to him and smiled brightly. 'We're having one of your favorites tonight, darling,' she said. 'I had Katie make one of her fruits de mer before she left. This one's lobster.'

68

'That's great,' he replied unenthusiastically.

Minette looked at him with superior disaffection. 'Well, you needn't pout, darling,' she said.

When he didn't respond she added, in her best and most irritating baby-talk, 'You wook wike somebody wicked all the candy off your apple, wittle boy.'

Still Sam didn't rise to the bait.

Minette suddenly grew irritated with her little game, and drew herself up with self-righteous indignation. 'I was just giving you my opinion, Sam. I'm not the big bad wolf, you know. Perhaps it's time you finally gave up this little . . . hobby of yours and stayed at home with me.'

'Absolutely not,' he shot back. 'I've made money at it – I'm making money at it – and I enjoy it.' There was fire in his eyes and deadly determination in his voice.

'Okay, okay,' she said, backing off. She realized that this was not the time to pursue this line of discussion. 'Whatever makes you happy. But I still think you're wasting your time and your talent. Certainly on that house.'

He looked her in the eye. 'Let's drop it, Minette, okay?' he said softly. 'I'm not in the mood for this conversation right now.'

She brightened again. 'Yes,' she said. 'Let's do that. Let's drop it.' She threw back the last of her drink and set her glass down on the table, then looked at him questioningly. 'Shall we go in to dinner? Erminda should have things ready for us now.'

'Yes,' Sam replied, taking a quick sip of his Scotch.

'Take me in?' Minette asked.

'Sure.'

Sam got up and dutifully walked around to the rear of her wheelchair, reached down and released the brakes, then began rolling her forward, toward the dining room.

And another lonely dinner, he thought, with a little quiet blood-shed.

5

Leonie tossed the scrub brush in the plastic pail of dirty gray suds, and sat back on her haunches.

'Lawdy mercy, Miz Scarlett!' She scowled. 'I ain't made for scrubbin' no floors!'

Getting to her feet, she pulled the Bluettes off her hands with an elastic snap! and flipped them into the kitchen sink, then wiped the back of her hand across her brow. She pulled off the scarf she had tied around her hair and shook her hair free.

'There,' she said aloud, 'that's better.' Then she inspected the cleaning that had been done, slowly walking from room to room, deciding that, if not perfect, it was certainly a lot better.

Her inspection finished, she went to the kitchen and poured herself a glass of white wine. Then she grabbed the bottle and her glass and went to the parlor, where she sat down on the daybed.

Ah, she thought, alone at last. Now, I can kick off my shoes and relax a bit. The little army of helpers that Mossy had found for her had come, done a great job of cleaning, and left.

The house now sparkled, as much as that was possible, from top to bottom. The better to dirty it up with workmen, she thought with a smile. She'd decided, quite simply, that renovation or not, she could not tolerate the idea of somebody else's dirt. So first she had cleaned. Now she would start making her own mess to clean up again, beginning in her own idiosyncratic way to put her personal mark on the house.

After housecleaning, the unpacking had begun. First in the kitchen, which she planned to use as much as possible during the renovation so as to save money. Then the few bibelots she didn't think she could live without. Finally, she had made her daybed and the twin beds upstairs, and readied the bathroom downstairs and one upstairs for use.

She planned to live as much as possible in the parlor, kitchen, and bath downstairs, then move to an upstairs room when necessary. She knew she would probably be moving all over the house – from room to room – as the renovation progressed. It was not going to be easy, but she would manage somehow.

She hadn't imagined there'd be so much to do since she'd left most of her belongings in storage, knowing that they would only be in the way and might possibly be damaged. But, as it turned out, there had been more than she'd bargained for.

Well, she told herself, if I'm going to be camping out, I might as well camp out in style.

Plus, now she could have a friend or two for weekends, although she couldn't think of anybody among her New York friends who would relish the idea of roughing it with her in a construction site.

No, indeed. Most of her New York friends' idea of country weekends was swimming parties, perhaps horseback riding, walks through beautiful, lovingly tended gardens, scrumptious gourmet meals, a bit of antiquing and sightseeing, and showing off the newly acquired designer clothes they'd purchased just for the country weekend. Lots of big straw hats and flowery dresses.

Hah! she thought. Here they would be confronted with minimal luxury, to say the least. No pool, at least not yet. No horses. Make-do food. A garden gone utterly to seed. A tumble-down house.

Perhaps they would be content with a few black flies? No? Then, deer flies? Some mosquitoes? Maybe a snake or two among the luxuriant weeds? Construction debris? And possibilities!

No, she decided. Not most of the people she knew.

Oh, hell, so what? If Pammy, her sister, and James, her brother-in-law, made the annual summer pilgrimage from Italy, they wouldn't mind . . . would they?

She surveyed her realm from the daybed and considered that with the help Mossy had found for her, she had accomplished a minor miracle. She felt gratified. Proud of herself. And rightly so.

But she also felt agitated. Highly agitated. There was this niggling worry in the back of her mind which simply refused to let go.

So she rose from the daybed and crossed her arms in front of her and paced.

And paced.

If this parquet wasn't worn through before, she thought, it certainly is going to be now.

Finally, she sat back down and sipped her wine, but the wee leprechaun of irritation in her head still wouldn't leave her alone. She sighed.

Sam Nicholson, she thought. Sam Nicholson is the problem. I can't get him off my mind, and I've got to do something to quit obsessing on him.

But nothing she could do seemed to work. All through the cleaning, the unpacking, the preparing of little snacks, making a zillion phone calls – handling all the quotidian details of settling in – one single thing, and one single thing only, burned in the back of her mind.

Scratch that, she told herself. Not at the back of my mind, but at the front.

And that, of course, was Sam.

Sam Nicholson.

She had to admit that the intrusion was a welcome one, that it offered inviting respite from all the drudgery facing her. There was something so appealing about him. His looks, of course, were undeniably stunning, but it was much more than that. Yes, much more. She felt that perhaps, despite his visible and distinct masculinity, there was definitely something of the lost puppy about him. He seemed very much here – his was a commanding presence – yet he seemed adrift in the world. Like a boat come loose from its anchor, she thought, with no direction in mind, but aimlessly bobbing atop the waters of life, a little lost.

Something – what could it be? she wondered – was, if not very wrong in his life, then at least not quite right. Then she remembered his eyes, those mesmerizing, depthless, blue-green eyes. There had been an air of sadness about them. His was a haunted look.

It was a look Leonie understood all too well. Because it was one she had seen in the mirror not so long ago, one that she still saw from time to time.

Leonie sighed and poured herself another glass of the dry white wine to sip.

She had no way of knowing whether or not Sam Nicholson had been injured by a woman – he is married, she reminded herself – but she knew from her own experience that it was a man, her ex-husband, who had caused that same lost and haunted look on her face.

Perhaps he had never set out to do it, but Hank Reynolds had nearly destroyed her, as surely as if he'd put a gun to her head and pulled the trigger.

In the beginning, when they'd both been younger and poorer, struggling to get Hank through Wharton and the M.B.A. he dreamed of, they had both worked like slaves. But they had worked together, rejoicing in their labors, celebrating their little triumphs, consoling one another when life dealt them a defeat. Those had been difficult years, but they had been full of fun and joy and a caring she didn't think would ever end.

After graduate school, he had been recruited by Endicott, Weismuller, the venerable New York brokers and investment bankers. It was the start of the heady 1980s, and Hank had made money hand over fist from the very beginning. After the struggle of graduate school, they were suddenly awash in money, and their climb to the pinnacle of monied society had begun.

Leonie had to admit that she enjoyed the perks and privileges of their position and all those greenbacks. She had given vent to her artistic impulses on their increasingly commodious and lavish apartments and houses, throwing herself into their decoration with a vengeance. Not content to rely on the expertise of others, she had schooled herself in the fine and decorative arts, becoming something of an expert on period furniture. These things had always held a great deal of interest for her, but now they became obsessions as she refined her already discerning eye.

She had become a habitué of the auction houses and the best antique stores and art galleries in New York, London, and Paris, and she had become a fixture on the charity ball circuit, serving on committees and chairing glittering society events. But she had gradually become disenchanted with that lifestyle. She was tired of living for the next party, the next dress, the next piece of very important French furniture or the next Impressionist painting to go on the auction block.

That was when she had decided to open Architectural Elements, the shop she had come to devote herself to. It had given her great pleasure, a feeling of independence, and a feeling of accomplishment, and had been a great success financially.

Hank, in the meantime, had become head of Endicott, Weismuller's leveraged buyout sector, then branched out on his own, putting together takeover deals that rapidly filled their coffers with more money than she had ever imagined. He had joined all the 'right' clubs and allied himself with the willing old rich and the most acceptable of the nouveau riche, dropping anybody on the way up whom he no longer found useful or who didn't measure up to his exacting standards. She knew that he had trampled on more than a few custom-shod feet on his way up.

But as he became richer and richer, more and more powerful, there had developed a chasm in their relationship which Leonie was at a loss to explain. Hank had ceased to show any interest in her sexually and still insisted that they wait to have children, even though she desperately wanted a family. His long hours at work, his obsession with social climbing, his fastidious attention to building, building, building – these things she understood. What she didn't understand was his growing lack of interest in her.

Gradually, as Hank became more and more ambitious and greedy, he had become ruthless and selfish. They hadn't just grown apart, Leonie was convinced. Hank had begun to push her away, slowly, but surely, apparently deciding that she no longer was useful, like some of his former business associates.

He hadn't been content to shove her aside, but had tried to destroy her. It was as if he wanted no reminders of the struggles, the sweat, and the toil it had taken to get where he was. Leonie thought that perhaps he had to believe that his life had always been as monied, privileged, and luxurious as it was now. That he had always been the powerful Wall Street figure he had become.

But she knew different, and Hank seemed to resent that. She had always known that his was a fragile ego, that he needed constant reassurance as to his worth and accomplishments, but she had never realized just how delicate his ego really was.

He was apparently getting the necessary ego boosts from his business victories – often at the expense of a lot of pain and suffering to others. After all, she asked herself, what had happened to the thousands of people whose jobs were eliminated as part of some of his leveraged buyouts? She had begun to fear that their lavish lifestyle was built on a trail of tears. She had questioned him, but to no avail.

Then Hank had dumped her. Like so much stinking garbage.

But she had survived. And quite well, too, she thought. I've worked at keeping myself together, and I've been fortunate—

The loud jangle of the telephone interrupted her reverie, and Leonie reached over and picked up the receiver. 'Hello?'

'Leonie, dear, it's Mossy.'

'Hi, Moss,' Leonie said. 'How are you?'

'So-so,' Mossy said. 'I called on the spur of the moment to ask you to dinner.'

'Oh, Moss!' Leonie cried. 'I've been cleaning all day, and I look like something the cat dragged in.'

'You are incapable of looking like any such thing!' Mossy said. 'Now throw on something captivating, and I'll pick you up in thirty minutes or so.'

'Thirty minutes!' Leonie protested. 'But I—'

'No buts, dear,' Mossy interjected. 'See you in thirty.' And she hung up.

Leonie looked at the receiver for a moment, then replaced it in its cradle. 'Lawdy mercy,' she said. 'What will I wear?'

An hour later they were on their way to the Old Chatham Sheepherding Company Inn for dinner. Leonie knew that it was expensive and a treat that Mossy could ill afford, but Mossy wouldn't take no for an answer. There, in the beautifully restored and decorated inn, over a superbly cooked meal of grilled quail, spring lamb with couscous, and a rich apple tart, Leonie, at Mossy's relentless prodding, had poured out her heart to her friend, who had offered the most sustaining and constructive succor.

'You've got to create a new life for yourself,' Mossy said. 'That's what I did. Had to do. You needn't forget the past, Leonie, but don't dwell there.'

'That's exactly what I'm trying to do, Mossy,' Leonie replied. 'Make a new life, I mean. I know this area and love it – and its affordable in my present circumstances.'

'Have you thought about what you'll do with the octagon house? Keep it or what?' Mossy asked.

'Yes,' Leonie said. 'You already know that I'm going to renovate it. Then I plan to decorate it and put it up for sale. Hopefully make a small bundle, then repeat the process, saving a bit from each move up to build myself a tidy nest egg. Maybe eventually have a shop like the one in New York. With the weekenders, plus the clients I've gotten to know in the city, I think I could make a go of it. A lot of my best clients wouldn't hesitate to travel up here to shop.'

'We have long winters,' Mossy said, playing the devil's advocate. 'And the nights can be lonely. Especially when you're a single gal. I know, dear. I've been there.'

'I know,' Leonie said, 'but that's true in the city, too.' She held up her wineglass and nodded toward Mossy. 'Besides, I've got you.'

Mossy beamed. 'Indeed you do,' she replied. 'For what it's worth. But what about men? It's most definitely not the hunting ground New York City is, and I'm afraid a lot of the locals would think you're from Mars.'

Leonie laughed. 'For the time being, I've had it with men,' she said. 'Up to here.' She drew a line across her throat.

'Good girl,' Mossy said enthusiastically. 'I say use and abuse them. Turn the tables on the whole sodding lot.'

Leonie laughed again.

'It's true,' Mossy said. 'I think Lysistrata had the right idea. But why don't we continue this conversation at home? It's getting late, and we can have a nightcap there.'

'That's fine with me,' Leonie said.

After Mossy paid the bill with her credit card, they left the idyllic country inn with a complete sense of satisfaction.

When they arrived at Mossy's small, ultra-modern house in Chatham, she immediately drew open the immense draperies in the double-height living room, with its enormous wall of glass. In the distance, they could see lights twinkling in the houses perched in the foothills of the Berkshires, and above the hills, the heavens sparkled with millions of stars.

Mossy retrieved a crystal decanter of brandy and two snifters from a small serving table in the dining area. She placed them on the coffee table, poured two hefty portions, and handed Leonie one.

'To your health and happiness,' Mossy said.

'And yours,' Leonie said.

They both sipped at their brandies and settled down for a talk, Mossy spread out on a loveseat and Leonie in a large, comfortable chair.

Mossy lit a cigarette, blew out a streamer of smoke, and looked across at Leonie. 'To get back to our conversation at the inn. I think you're coping beautifully, considering what you've been through.'

'Thanks, Mossy,' Leonie said. 'I don't know how I would have done it without you. I've hardly discussed the divorce with anybody. It's been so difficult to open up about it, and I don't think most of the people I know in New York even want to hear about it. You know, they're mostly the kind of people who want to hear nothing but party talk. Or all about your latest success.'

'Well, I am the voice of experience,' Mossy replied, 'if not always reason.' She took another drag from her cigarette, then continued. 'After Larry traded me in for a newer model, I decided that I would never let another man talk me into love and marriage. I've yet to meet a single man that I think is capable of being honest and faithful for more than the time it takes to get you to bed.'

'My, my. We are cynical, aren't we,' Leonie said with amusement.

'Damn right,' Mossy retorted. 'And with good reason.' She stabbed her cigarette out in an ashtray. 'Men,' she spat. 'They're all alike, the whole sodding lot.'

'Are you going with anybody now?' Leonie asked.

'Going with! Hah! I have a good old-fashioned roll in the hay now and again, but I don't go with anybody.' Mossy sipped her brandy, then set it down with a bang and lit another cigarette.

'But don't you date?' Leonie asked. 'I mean go to a movie, or out to dinner, or any of that good old stuff?'

'We've just had a lovely dinner, haven't we?' Mossy answered.

'I can't deny that,' Leonie said.

'Oh, sure. I sometimes go to a movie or dinner with a guy,' Mossy said. 'But more often with a lady friend. Sometimes with Thomas, an elderly widower I'm fond of. But as for the boys – love 'em and leave 'em is my policy.'

Leonie laughed.

'Right now, it's a local nurseryman I met. He's young and tall and blond and built like a horse. He's also a liar, a cheat, and a bit of a drinker. But he's sexy as all hell, and very energetic in the sack.'

Leonie laughed again, then took a sip of brandy. 'I wish I could be like you,' she said, setting her snifter down on the coffee table.

'It's not easy being me,' Mossy replied, 'even if I have a reputation for being an easy woman. Some of these boys actually expect something from me, besides sex, that is. And they are not going to get it.'

'You really are a confirmed bachelorette, then?'

'You bet I am,' Mossy said. She looked at Leonie. 'But enough about me. This conversation is supposed to be about you. You don't regret moving up here, do you?'

'Maybe a little,' Leonie confessed. 'It's still all so new.'

Mossy reached for the brandy decanter. 'In that case, you must be ready for a refill. We might as well finish this off.'

'If you say so.' Leonie handed Mossy her snifter, and Mossy splashed brandy into it, then refilled her own.

'There,' Mossy said, setting the decanter back down. 'So you are having second thoughts?'

'Not really,' Leonie said. 'I do get a little nervous when I think about all the changes.' She paused, brushing at imaginary lint on her silk blouse. 'And I know it's not going to be a picnic living in a house while renovation is going on, but I don't have a choice.' She sighed. 'I just don't have the money for anything else.'

'Are things really that tight?' Mossy asked.

Leonie looked at her and nodded. 'Yes, Mossy,' she said. 'I can buy a house and renovate it, maybe live for a year or two on what's left over. If I'm careful. Very careful. But that's about it.'

'The son of a bitch really did screw you, didn't he?' Mossy said.

Leonie nodded again. 'Yes. Royally.'

'I knew you'd taken a beating, but I didn't know it was that bad,' Mossy said.

'Well, now you do,' Leonie replied. 'So you can see the wisdom of my staying in the house while the work's being done.'

Mossy took a long draw on her cigarette. 'Yes. But you're always welcome here if things get to be a bit much, dear,' she said, smiling.

Leonie looked into Mossy's eyes. 'Thanks, Mossy. You're the best. But you have your life to lead and so do I. All little birdies need their nests. And we're no different.'

'Still, you're welcome. Just remember,' Mossy replied, 'the door is always open.'

Leonie smiled. 'You always make me feel better, Mossy. I really do wish I were more like you.'

'You must have taken leave of your senses!' Mossy exclaimed.

'Hardly,' Leonie replied. 'You're so independent. You have a lovely home. A career. You have a busy social life. You aren't beholden to anyone, really. And you've done it all on your own, without a man.'

Mossy blew out a stream of smoke, then looked at Leonie. 'And you can do the same,' she said emphatically. 'Remember, Leonie. No matter what that ex-husband of yours did to you, you are still young and beautiful and resourceful. You have brains, wit, and charm. He can't take any of those things away from you, regardless of what you might have lost. Nobody's powerful enough to rob you of those things. You must keep looking within. It is there that you will find your worth as a human being. Not from what some man – or anybody else, for that matter – tells you. Certainly not from a man who has apparently been as ruthlessly cruel and vindictive as Hank Reynolds.'

Tears threatened to come to Leonie's eyes as she listened to these words of comfort, and when Mossy finished speaking she couldn't reply at first. Finally, in a hoarse voice, she said, 'Thank you, Mossy. I needed that vote of confidence.'

'Whatever are friends for?' Mossy said.

Leonie took a sip of her brandy. 'Hank really was cruel, you know. I still don't quite understand it.'

'Was there another woman?' Mossy asked.

'No,' Leonie said. 'At least not that I know of. If there is, she hasn't surfaced so far.'

'Then how in the name of God did he end up with nearly everything?' Mossy asked. 'Or am I being too nosey?'

'No, not at all,' Leonie said. 'In fact, I'm glad you asked. I've hardly discussed this with anyone, either. Partly because I feel like such a fool and partly because ... well, I didn't want talk going around New York about some of the details.'

She took a deep breath, then began. 'To make a long story short, Hank grew more and more distant. Then he got to be downright nasty, when he was around. We finally got around to discussing divorce, and he suggested I get a lawyer. I discovered that I hardly knew my own husband. You know how I'd been busy decorating the apartment in New York and the house in Southampton. And running my shop. So Hank and his lawyers had always handled our business affairs, except for the shop. It turns out that the apartment in New York was in Hank's name only—'

'You must be joking!' Mossy interjected.

'I wish I were,' Leonie said. 'But wait, it gets worse. Not only was the apartment in his name only, but so was the house in Southampton. And of course the stock portfolio.'

Mossy sat there, stunned to momentary silence. She took a deep drag off her cigarette, staring at Leonie, shaking her head. 'I can hardly believe my ears,' she finally said.

'I know,' Leonie said. 'I was such a fool I blithely sailed through life, trusting Hank to take care of everything.' She paused a moment. 'And he did. Making certain in the process that he could, like we said, screw me royally, if and when he decided to.'

'My God,' Mossy said. 'I would have thought you would get millions of dollars. Everybody knows that Hank is worth hundreds of millions. He's always in the newspapers and business magazines.'

'Yes,' Leonie said, 'and he intends to keep it all to himself. I get the proceeds from the sale of my shop, and what was in my checking account. Plus some furniture and personal things. Of course, the lawyers ate up a lot of that.'

'There is no justice in this world,' Mossy said. 'Wasn't there anything your lawyers could do? My God, you'd been married for years, and you helped him get where he is.'

'If I had decided to fight it,' Leonie said, 'it would have cost a fortune I didn't have. And I was having trouble getting a really good divorce lawyer in New York to go up against Hank's team. They were all afraid of his power. Plus – and this is what clinched the deal for him – Hank had some 'evidence' against me that he threatened to use if I fought him.'

Mossy looked at her with a curious expression. 'Don't tell me,' she exclaimed. 'You had a little hanky-panky on the side!'

Leonie laughed. 'No. But that's what it might have looked like,' she said. 'You know how close I was to Bobby Chandler.'

'Oh, yes,' Mossy said. 'That blue blood investment banker. A nine-goal polo player. Always in the society pages with some heiress on his arm. Always being photographed with Prince Charles or some other rich toff at some polo match or other.'

'That's Bobby,' Leonie said. 'Robert Winston Chandler the Fourth. Well, Bobby and I got to be very close friends. We were always running into each other at parties in the city and out in the Hamptons. When he was decorating his house in Southampton, I helped him. Actually, I practically did it all.'

'Aha!' Mossy crowed. 'I knew it! You and Mr. Chandler had a thing!'

'No!' Leonie laughed. 'And this is where the secret comes in. Bobby . . . Bobby's gay.'

'You've got to be joking!' Mossy was genuinely surprised. 'But he . . . he seems like such a jock! And he has such a reputation as a heartbreaker.'

'Yes,' Leonie said. 'You're right on both counts. He is a jock. Plus he has the old heartbreaker reputation. And he wants to keep it that way. He is very discreet. The investment bank he works for would find some way to drop him, and I mean in a New York minute, if he came out of the closet. Plus his family would cut him off. And believe me, Bobby certainly doesn't want to lose one cent of all those Chandler millions.'

'My God,' Mossy said. 'I would have never guessed. Not in a million years.'

'Hardly anybody knows,' Leonie said. 'He cultivates his man-about-town reputation. Anyway, Bobby and I got to be very close. He's like the brother I never had – that close. He stayed out at our house in Southampton a lot while his was being renovated. Then while I was decorating it, he was at our place practically all the time. One weekend when Hank was off in Tokyo on business, Bobby was staying over. We went to a dinner party together, then went back to the house and went swimming. Skinny dipping, in fact. We were both a little drunk, and I thought, what the hell, Bobby is gay. Afterward, we sat up in bed talking half the night and clowning around. Bobby with his arms around me, kissing me, just monkeying around. All totally innocent.'

'Oh, my God,' Mossy said. 'I think I see what's coming.'

'Yes,' Leonie said. 'Our little bedtime party was videotaped. Interestingly enough, without sound. So that a lot of our fooling around looked incriminating. If you could have heard our conversation, that would have changed everything. Because of course, we were being totally silly. In fact, we spent most of the night talking about some of Bobby's sexual exploits. And I don't mean with women.'

'So Hank actually was looking for something like this,' Mossy said. 'He must have planned it very carefully.'

'Obviously,' Leonie said. 'He'd probably paid one of the servants to run the video camera at just the right time. At least that's my guess. Because Raimondo – he was the butler – up and left right after that. No excuses, nothing, just left. So anyway, when I told Hank I was going to put up a fight over a divorce settlement, he threatened to use the videotape of me and Bobby. Said he would ruin me in court.'

'But for God's sake, Leonie,' Mossy exclaimed, 'if Bobby Chandler is gay, Hank wouldn't have a case!'

'That's just it, Mossy,' Leonie said. 'Don't you see? I couldn't expose Bobby. It would ruin his career, his whole life, if I had claimed he was gay. I just couldn't do it, no matter what.'

'Did Hank know that Bobby's gay?' Mossy asked.

'Oh, yes. Absolutely! But he also knew that I probably wouldn't want to expose Bobby, and that if I even tried, it would be hard to prove. The whole thing got to be so . . . so sordid, that I just gave up. I took what I could get without a fight just to get away. I guess I was exhausted from the filthiness of it.'

'And that's why you're strapped for funds now,' Mossy said.

'Yes,' Leonie said. 'But I'll change that. I've made it before, and I can do it again.'

'I should think that you would have lost any faith and trust in the human race that you might have ever had. Certainly in men.' Mossy sighed. 'The things we do to one another. Just remember dear, I'm here for you. Always.'

Later that night, after she had dressed for bed, Leonie paced the parquet in her parlor. She was lost in thought, thinking about Mossy's generous and kindly advice. Deserted by many of her fair-weather friends in New York City, she appreciated Mossy's reaching out to her, offering any help she could give. She had been a great listener and had helped Leonie bolster up her badly abused self-esteem, to keep her sense of worth intact.

She sat down on the daybed and took a sip of her wine and sighed.

I must be crazy, she thought. To even think about a man like Sam Nicholson. He seemed to be much too complicated a man, and despite his confident masculinity and easy charm, he was one of the walking wounded, of that she was certain.

He's also too good looking, she thought. He must have half the women in the valley chasing after him all the time. Yes, she decided, he must have a very involved life. A history she knew nothing about.

And besides, Sam Nicholson is very much a married man.

She put her wineglass down and pursed her lips. That settles it, she thought. I will definitely not allow Sam Nicholson to insinuate himself into my thoughts. For the most obvious and practical reason of them all: He's a very married man.

Two weeks later, Sam Nicholson heard the answering machine on his private line click, but he didn't bother to listen immediately. He had just come in from his early morning horseback ride, and was changing clothes in his dressing room. One heel in the bootjack, he pulled, then eased the dusty custom-made riding boot off. He repeated the process with the other boot, then stripped off his tan jodhpurs and tossed them on the daybed. He pulled his sweaty socks off, then his black polo shirt, and finally his jockey shorts. Leaving everything in a pile on the floor, he padded naked over to the answering machine, turned up the sound, and hit the playback button.

When he heard the voice, a thrilling sensation went through him, and he found himself breathing a little faster than usual. Just the sound of that unmistakable, smoky contralto awakened in him a sensual pleasure he had all but forgotten was possible.

'. . . Mossy took me by the Cranstons' place yesterday,' Leonie was saying, 'and I really loved what you did with it. The plans were brilliant, and the workmanship was beautiful. I'm convinced you're the right person for this job, if the price is right. So get in touch with me as soon as you can. The number here is—'

Sam hit the rewind button. He didn't need Leonie Corinth's number. It was engraved in his memory forever. Like the woman herself, he thought, it was unforgettable.

It seemed that no matter how hard he tried, he couldn't get her off his mind. She had an allure that was unique. Her ravishing looks, coupled with her vibrant and independent spirit, made for a combination that he was finding impossible to resist. He remembered her bouncy walk up the stairs. Those legs, that . . . Jesus, he had to stop thinking about her!

Leonie Corinth, he sensed, was far too independent a woman to be interested in him. She seemed to have a very active life entirely of her own making, and he was sure that she was strong-willed and had a mind very much her own that would exclude a relationship with a man right now. Certainly with the likes of me, he thought.

He knew who she was, of course. Who didn't? After all, her ex-husband was constantly in the press, and their social coups and lavish lifestyle had been chronicled in gossip columns and the business press for several years. And now, even if she was divorced, Sam realized that Leonie had come from another world. A world that was light-years away from his own. Sure, Minette had money and connections, and they lived in a world of privilege and luxury relative to most of the villagers here in the country. But the ex-Mrs. Henry Reynolds had been exposed to the stratospheric heights of international business and society. Not tens of millions of dollars but hundreds of millions, even billions. It was one thing to be well-to-do and prominent in a rural area of farms and small hamlets and towns, like himself and Minette, but quite another to have been part of the global elite such as Leonie. She might hire Sam Nicholson to do a job, but she wouldn't give a man like him the time of day otherwise.

After having been married to a man of such great wealth and power, she must look upon men like Sam as nothing more than one of the servants, there to cater to a very rich mistress's needs. I'm not rich like she is, Sam thought. Never have been rich in my own right, and practically everything I have is Minette's.

Why then, did he feel such an affinity with her? A powerful physical, even chemical, affinity, he reminded himself. Certainly, part of it was that hint of wariness about her. She had been through a lot, he guessed. Probably the divorce. If Henry Reynolds was the shark at home that he was on Wall Street, then there was no telling what Leonie might have endured at his hands.

He paced the dressing room floor, wondering what to do, how to respond to her message in light of his feelings – and Minette's. But he quickly came to the conclusion that Minette's obvious distaste – even hostility – regarding the project shouldn't color his decision. She had raised objections to his working in the past, and he wasn't about to consider giving in to her selfish demands now.

What the hell, he decided. Keep it simple. Leonie Corinth wants me to do the job, and I want to do it. So I'll give her a call.

He picked up the telephone and punched in her number. After two rings she picked up.

'Leonie,' he said, 'it's Sam Nicholson returning your call.'

'Hi,' she said. 'I don't want to rush you, but Mossy took me by the Cranston place last week, and I had to call. It's really beautiful, Sam. Just the sort of work I had in mind.'

'Thanks a lot,' he said. 'That was a tough one, but it worked out pretty well, I think. I tell you what, Leonie. What if I put together some preliminary figures and rough out some ideas I have about the project, then we could get together to go over them later this week.'

'That would be great,' she said. 'I want to try to finish before winter sets in. If that's possible.'

'I don't think that would be a problem,' Sam said. 'If we decide to work together, I think we could finish everything before Christmas. There might be some detail work to polish off, but nothing major.'

'Okay,' Leonie said. 'How about coming by Thursday or Friday, then. Would that be all right?'

'Let's make it Friday,' Sam said. 'That would give me plenty of time to get some figures and plans together. How about Friday morning, say about ten o'clock. Is that okay?'

'Perfect,' Leonie said. 'I'll see you then.'

'Okay,' he said. 'See you later.' He hung up the phone, scratched the day and time in on a memo pad, then headed for the bathroom. Time to shower and dress for breakfast.

And time to tell Minette what he was doing.

Jesus, he thought, what have I gotten myself into?

'How was your ride?' Minette asked, as she sipped strong black Colombian Supremo from a delicate antique Minton cup. Sunlight streamed into the glass conservatory where they were breakfasting and made her hair gleam more golden than usual.

'Great,' Sam said, smiling. 'Jicky, that two-year-old gelding we got from the Whitneys, is one fine horse.'

'It has a great lineage,' Minette said. 'Blood always tells, doesn't it?'

'I guess so,' Sam said in a distracted manner. He wanted to tell her he was going to be working on plans for the octagon house and get it over with. He knew her reaction was not going to be positive.

'Did you see Dirck this morning?' Minette asked.

'Yes,' Sam replied, 'as a matter of fact, I did. Just for a minute though. He was rushing off someplace. I meant to ask you about it. He said he talked to you late last night and you told him you were going to see the doctor in New York again. I thought you'd just had a checkup last week when Dirck took you in.'

'I did,' Minette said. 'But Dr. Nathanson's office called yesterday

90

while you were gone. They said he wants to run some sort of tests, so they scheduled me for another appointment in a month.'

Sam looked over at her with surprise. 'What kind of tests?'

'I'm not sure, Sam,' she said in a miffed tone of voice. 'The receptionist didn't say, and I didn't ask. I just scheduled the appointment.'

'That's pretty odd, isn't it?' Sam said. 'Not telling you what kind of tests?'

'No,' Minette replied. 'She said I haven't had a complete physical in some time and the doctor wants to do one.'

'Do you want me to take you into the city?' Sam asked. 'Or do you want Dirck to take you?'

'You,' she said hastily. 'I want you to take me in this time. So mark it on your calendar. I wrote it all down. Next month.' She handed the piece of paper over to him, and he took it.

'One o'clock,' Sam said. 'We'll leave about seven to give us plenty of time.' Strange, he thought. She nearly always had Dirck take her in so they could talk, mostly about family matters, he supposed. He wondered why she wanted him to take her this time, but decided not to ask.

As if she could read his mind, Minette said: 'I would have Dirck take me, but I'm furious with him.'

'What's he done now?' Sam asked.

'Oh, he's been seeing this dreadful little tramp.'

'Margy Newsome,' he said.

'The very one,' Minette said, with distaste. 'She is t-r-o-u-b-l-e,' she spelled. 'With a capital T.'

'Well, if she makes Dirck happy . . .' Sam began, setting down his coffee cup.

'Ha!' Minette spat. 'She's probably made every farmhand in the valley happy.'

Sam grinned. 'I guess you're right,' he said. 'She does have a certain reputation for keeping the boys satisfied.'

'Well, if I have anything to do with it,' Minette snarled, 'Little Miss Margy's going to be peddling her wares elsewhere.'

'He's your cousin,' Sam said. 'I'd stay out of it.' He took a sip of coffee and looked across the table at Minette. Might as well get it over with, he thought. 'Minette,' he said, 'I'm going to be working on plans for the octagon house this week.'

She stared at him for a moment in silence. Then she sipped her coffee and cocked an eyebrow. 'Well,' she said, 'have it your own way, Sam. But I do hate to see you waste your time on that place. And for that trashy divorcée, whatever her name is.'

'Ah, come on, Minette,' he said, trying to humor her. 'The house is well worth saving, and you know it. As for Leonie Corinth, she's hardly trash. She seems like a very fine lady to me.'

Minette's eyes flashed with barely suppressed fury. 'Fine she may seem to be, but I doubt if she could afford to pay you enough to keep you in riding boots!'

Sam put his cup down and looked at his wife. 'That was unnecessary, Minette.' He could see that no amount of humoring her would work this morning. 'You get angry every time I take on a new commission, unless it's for some friend of yours.'

'At least they're worth your time,' Minette said angrily. 'You don't have to work at all. I have tons of money, and you could devote yourself to the estate and the horses.'

'Minette, we've had this conversation before, and I don't want to have it again,' Sam said quietly. 'This work is important to me, and you know it.'

'Your work,' she spat out, 'is nothing more than a hobby!'

Sam calmly folded his napkin and placed it beside his plate. 'I'm sorry you feel that way, Minette, but I won't change my mind.' He rose to his feet. 'I'm going down to my office now and get busy. I'll see you later.' He left the room, ignoring the look of fury and rage on his wife's beautiful face.

*   *   *

He hurried to the office off the kitchen, where he grabbed his briefcase, then stopped in the kitchen when he saw Erminda, shaking with her own barely suppressed fury. Her face was red and distorted with a scowl, and her eyes bulged with rage. As he watched, she carefully put down the knife she had been using to chop scallions and stood staring at it.

'What's wrong, Erminda?' Sam asked quietly.

She looked up at him. 'I . . . I couldn't help but overhear your conversation, Mr. Sam,' she said. And your wife is an evil witch, she thought, who's heartless and cruel, and deserves to be punished for the way she treats people.

'Don't worry about it, Erminda,' he said. 'Minette just doesn't feel well today.'

Erminda nodded. 'Okay, Mr. Sam,' she replied. Doesn't feel well today! she thought. She never feels well. She makes me work like a dog and treats me like a common puta.

Erminda picked up the knife again and began chopping the scallions.

'I'll see you later, Erminda,' Sam said.

Erminda nodded again. 'You have a nice day, Mr. Sam,' she said. Chop, Chop.

'You, too,' he said, leaving the kitchen.

Erminda watched him go. She sees how he's nice to me, she thought. That's one reason she's so mean to him – and to me. And she continued chop, chop, chopping.

In the entrance hall, Sam snatched his keys from the porcelain famille rose bowl, then dashed out the door to his Range Rover. He started the engine and pulled out, anxious to get away from this insufferable prison, yet ravaged with the inescapable guilt that he was displeasing the woman he had crippled for life.

93

7

The mist burned off, and it turned into a true blue dream of a morning, the sky a cerulean canvas without a wisp of cloud in sight. A few chirping birds at earliest light gradually swelled to become a battle of conductorless symphonies, so that Leonie felt she was inside a giant aviary. Then, as the birds seriously sought out breakfast, they quieted down, so intent were they on hunting and pecking. She watched the robins for a moment, their heads bobbing up and down as they fed on the lawn, and listened to the noisy chatter of the chipmunks and squirrels as they scampered about in the giant old white pines. Somewhere near the carriage house, doves cooed, and in one of the old flower beds, she saw two white butterflies performing a pas de deux.

Leonie was making good use of an old garden table which had been left behind at the house. She'd dragged it onto one of the stone terraces at the back of the house, and draped it with a sunny yellow cotton cloth with a tiny pattern of red flowers. She had bought it in Provençe longer ago than she cared to remember. Centered on it was a creamware jug she'd overstuffed with fragrant purple lilacs which grew on enormous old bushes on the property. She had set out two creamy old ironstone plates with matching bowls, cups, and saucers, a platter with cranberry bread she'd just taken out of the oven, bowls of strawberries and peaches, a pitcher of cream, fresh-squeezed orange juice, and a pot of rich hot coffee. Her early-nineteenth-century Russian silver flatware sparkled in the sun.

She had risen early and quickly applied a modicum of makeup, then taken special care dressing very simply in a cool white cotton peasant dress. Very Carmen, with ruffles and a scooped, off-the-shoulder neckline. She wore simple white sandals with it.

As she surveyed her brunch table, she thought that it was picturesquely beautiful and that it would impress any man. Any man with any degree of sensitivity, that is. And despite convincing herself that she would make this effort for any guest, she knew deep down inside that she had tried to make an extra good impression because it was Sam Nicholson who was coming.

Last week, she and Sam had met and gone over the property again, this time with a fine-tooth comb. After discussing it with her, he had also brought over a couple of engineering experts for advice about her septic system, furnace, well, water purification system – all the basic mechanicals. Not very glamorous, but essential. In the end, she and Sam had been left alone to look over his preliminary plans, specifications, and rough financial figures.

Leonie had been extremely impressed with his professionalism, the sheer volume of work he'd produced in a very short period of time, his vision, and his choices. She had been left to choose between perfect, acceptable, and the merely do-able – but never unacceptable – so that the budget was hers to approve. More than ever, she was struck by the feeling that they were on the same keen wavelength as to exactly what the house needed to breathe new life into it. They had been in complete agreement after hours of going from room to room, studying his plans, and listening to each other's suggestions. They had finally reached the decision that he would do the work, if she approved his final plans and figures.

This morning he was coming with those and a contract, should she decide to sign. Leonie thought the possibility of there being some hitch which would prevent her giving the go-ahead was next to nil. But practical woman that she was, she knew that anything could happen. The renovation work on her own home in Southampton had taught her that. There, endless revisions, contracts to renegotiate, firing, hiring, substitutions, and so on and so forth, had been the order of the day. A certain amount of barely controlled chaos had ruled.

But it had been her first project, and enormously successful in the end. A triumph in fact. *Architectural Digest* had featured the house on its cover, making her the envy of many a Hamptonite.

She heard the unmistakable sound of Sam's Range Rover on the gravel drive, and a flutter went through her. She had anticipated his arrival this morning with nothing less than bated breath. The almost overwhelming physical attraction was still there, perhaps more powerful than ever, even after a few more hours of time spent together.

She quickly dashed into the powder room and checked her hair and makeup. Looking in the mirror, she ran a hand through her chestnut hair with its magenta and ruby highlights to muss it a wee bit. '*Voilà,*' she said to her image, and dashed back out to the table, where she perched on an iron garden chair, trying not to look like an overexcited schoolgirl waiting on her first date.

Sam parked and got out of the Range Rover. He stood staring at the sight before him, briefcase in hand and rolled-up plans protruding from a large leather carryall. A smile spread across his face, revealing those perfect white teeth. As he strode toward her on those long, well-muscled legs, she was stunned as always by those depthless turquoise eyes, his sun-burnished skin, and that boyish hair, all on a body ... well, stop there, she told herself.

'What's this feast?' Sam asked good-naturedly. 'Looks great.'

'I thought that if I put on a little spread, I might be able to bargain you down a bit on your price,' Leonie said with a hint of amusement in her voice.

Sam laughed. 'Not a bad idea, actually.' He drew up a chair and sat facing her. 'But to be honest, I don't think it would work.'

'Ah, Sam,' Leonie joked, 'you're a disappointment to a New York gal who learned to bargain with the best of them.'

'Seriously,' he said, 'I think you'll be pleased with the figures. I've done my damndest to keep costs down without compromising quality too much.'

'I'm sure you have,' she said. 'Do you want me to have a look at the contracts and figures now, or after we've had a bite to eat?'

Sam grinned disarmingly. 'Better afterward,' he said. 'I want to be sure to be able to enjoy some of this beautiful food.'

Leonie smiled at him and then poured coffee and juice and served the cranberry bread, strawberries, peaches, and cream.

He dug right in, eating heartily. 'This is delicious,' he said.

'Thanks, Sam,' Leonie replied. 'Glad you like it. It's simple, really, but sometimes simple is the best.'

'I couldn't agree with you more,' he said. He looked at her surreptitiously over his coffee cup, and felt the same sensual thrill running through him that he always did. God, he thought, she is so beautiful, so smart, and so damn nice. How could any man have left her? he wondered. He wanted to get up and sit beside her, put his arm around her while they ate, feel her radiant skin against his own.

Leonie saw him gazing at her and a fiery blush rose up into her face. She quickly looked away, irrationally afraid that he would be able to read her thoughts. His masculine presence, his sexuality, still had the power to unnerve her, and she simply could not control the fantasies which had been going through her head ever since the first time she had seen him. She wanted to touch him, to hold him, to feel his strong body against her own, and sometimes she felt a nagging emptiness because she could not. But no, she told herself, I cannot have him. I must not.

Sam sensed her uneasiness and set his coffee cup down. He cleared his throat, then began discussing the house. 'The engineers' reports were even more positive than I'd hoped for,' he said.

Leonie hastily agreed. 'I was prepared for the worst,' she said. 'So I've been pleasantly surprised. They really don't build them like they used to, do they?'

'No,' Sam said, 'they don't. Luckily, this place looks to be in much worse shape than it actually is.'

Leonie smiled. 'I think I really lucked out, don't you?'

'Yes, Leonie,' he said. 'I think you did. And the whole area lucked out by having you take an interest in it. It's been sitting here, unused, like an eyesore for a long time.' He looked into her eyes. 'So we've all benefited by your coming along.'

Leonie took a sip of coffee and returned his gaze. 'Thanks, Sam,' she said. 'That's . . . that's especially nice coming from you.'

They finished brunch at a leisurely pace, talking about the valley, its natural beauty, its history, and the diversity of architecture dotted across the landscape.

It was Leonie who finally, reluctantly, got down to business. 'Okay,' she said. 'I've put off the inevitable long enough.' She looked over at him. 'How much is this going to cost me? Let me see your figures.'

Sam set his battered old tan calfskin briefcase up on the table, unlocked it, and pulled out a sheaf of papers clipped together. He handed the paperwork across the table to Leonie, who took it from him and began studying the first page.

'I've broken all the costs down,' Sam said. 'Labor, supplies, architect's fee, and so on. I've also separated out the costs for each structure – house, barn, carriage house, and pool. Even the gazebo and pergola. It'll be easy for you to know exactly what each structure is going to entail cost-wise, so if you want to cut back or make other changes you can.'

'Good,' Leonie said, intently examining his figures.

'You can see where every penny is going,' Sam said, watching her, searching for clues as to what she was thinking.

Leonie finally finished flipping through the pages of costs and slapped them down on the table.

Sam looked at her questioningly. 'Well,' he said, 'what do you think?'

Leonie looked over at him and nodded. 'I like what I see,' she said in a businesslike tone of voice.

Sam looked relieved.

'I'm ready to sign on the dotted line,' she added, 'if your contract suits me.'

'I don't think you'll object to anything in it,' he replied. He took a copy of the contract out of his briefcase and passed it over to her. 'If you need me to explain anything, just say the word.'

'Okay,' Leonie said, and began reading through it.

Sam watched her while she read, admiring her no-nonsense, practical approach to things. She seemed to be that way about everything, he thought. She was nothing like the fluttery, helpless female that a lot of people might have expected a rich divorcée to be. He hoped and prayed that she would sign because at this moment there was nothing in the world he wanted more than to work with this exquisite creature for the next few months, as closely as possible.

Leonie finished reading the contract and laid it down. 'Well,' she said, looking up at him, 'I don't have any problems with this. Have you got a pen?' She smiled.

'You bet,' Sam said, returning her smile. He pulled a Cartier Pasha fountain pen – a very expensive present which Minette had once given him – out of his briefcase and handed it to her. 'Here you go,' he said. 'And here's another copy of the contract.'

Leonie took the pen and the second copy of the contract. She signed both copies, then handed the pen and one contract back to Sam. 'I keep one, right?' she said.

'Yes,' he replied. He placed the contract and pen in his briefcase and snapped it shut, then stood up and extended his hand. 'Looks like we have ourselves a deal, huh?'

'Yes,' Leonie said, shaking his hand, 'I'd say we do. When do we start?'

'Tomorrow morning,' Sam said.

'Tomorrow morning?' Leonie asked, surprised.

'About seven o'clock,' Sam replied.

'Seven a.m.?' Leonie echoed.

He smiled. 'That's right,' he said. 'You want this done in a hurry, right?'

'Right,' Leonie said. 'Well, I guess my peace in the valley has come to an end.' She looked up at him. 'I'll be here, ready and waiting.'

And she thought: I've never looked forward to so much work in all my life.

June's early morning light flooded her bed with its brilliance, and the usual bird chorus was as raucous a symphony as ever. But Leonie slept soundly. It was still cool this early in the morning, but later in the day the sun would warm up the temperature to a perfect seventy degrees. The sky was cloudless and azure. It was summer at its most ideal in the Hudson River Valley.

The alarm clock shrilled loudly in her ear and Leonie rolled over and searched for it with one hand, her eyes still closed against the early morning light.

Damn, where is it? she wondered, her hand scrabbling over the table next to the daybed, delving among the books, magazines, water glass, tissues, lotions and creams, and . . . success at last! There it is! She slammed the Off button firmly with her hand, and the piercing sound of the offending alarm clock quieted.

'Ooooohhh,' she moaned aloud. 'Thank God.' She yawned and slowly opened her eyes, rubbing them with her hands, and then gradually eased herself up into a half-sitting position, her back against the pillows.

'Ooooohhh,' she moaned again. She stretched her arms and legs, her shoulders and her spine, then her arms and legs again.

She was sore from the top of her head to the very tips of her toes, every fiber of every muscle in her slender body rebelling against a workout such as they'd never before experienced.

I ache all over, she thought. All over. Even my fingernails ache. My hair aches!

Gardening, she thought with a pang. Gardening. It will be the end of me. The end!

Still, if nothing else, she had made noticeable progress in the last few weeks, and she had never slept better in her memory. Last night, for example, after a long soak in a hot bath and a hearty dinner of a cholesterol-rich cheddar cheese and salsa omelette with buttered toast, she had curled up in bed and managed to read about two pages of the diverting little mystery novel that she had begun last week before she'd fallen asleep, book in hand, bedside lamp still burning. At this rate, she would be reading it all summer long. But she felt that her physical exhaustion and deep, untroubled sleep was restorative, even if she was sore all over.

She stretched again and turned her head to gaze at the clock. Five thirty-five! Busy, she thought with alarm. I've got to get busy! She threw off the sheet and leapt out of bed, then slipped into rubber thongs – so practical around the house, just rinse them off if they got dirty – and made a mad beeline for the bathroom.

She quickly splashed cold water on her face once, twice, three times, then patted it dry with a towel. She brushed her teeth vigorously and combed her hair. Eyeing herself in the mirror, she snatched up her makeup bag and started to apply a little blusher and lipstick, but suddenly put the little bag aside.

Why? she mentally asked the image in the mirror. What for? I'm just going to go outside and get filthy.

Then her mind flashed on the perpetually tanned and handsome Sam Nicholson, and she snatched up her makeup bag again. But before she had opened it, she decided that the flawless Mr. Nicholson would have to learn to like her the way she was. Naked, so to speak. Her usual meticulous grooming was, she decided, a waste of her precious time and energy under the present circumstances.

She flung the makeup bag back down on the vanity and dashed back to the parlor where she quickly shed her nightie and slipped into bra, panties, a long-sleeved tee shirt, and old, paint-stained khaki pants – all of which had been carefully folded and placed atop a fully packed suitcase at the foot of her daybed. She closed the suitcase – the better to keep unnecessary debris from coating her clothes – then pulled the covers up over the pillows on the daybed, not really making it, but neatening it a bit. That done, she grabbed a huge sheet of heavy plastic, unfolded it, and carefully spread it over the entire daybed. There! That would keep the worst of the sawdust and plaster dust and all the other various and sundry debris from dirtying her little oasis in the midst of this project.

Thongs back on, she rushed to the kitchen and ground coffee beans and filled the coffee maker. Waiting for it to brew, she got two mugs out of a cabinet, found the Sweet 'N Low, and retrieved skim milk from the refrigerator. She flipped on the radio–WABY in Albany.

'Oh, no!' she said aloud. 'Not again! Frankie baby, it's too early in the morning, far too early in the morning, for your soulful love songs. I love you, but not before noon.'

She flipped the dial from Old Blue Eyes to 89.1 FM, a classical station. Mozart. Good, she thought, some relatively quiet, soothing piano music. The perfect thing for early morning.

She got two slices of whole-wheat bread and plopped them into the toaster, then grabbed margarine out of the refrigerator, and searched through the jams. Ginger preserves. No. Gooseberry. No.

105

Black currant. Again, no. Aha! Thick-cut Seville orange marmalade. Just the ticket this morning.

The coffee brewed, she poured herself a mug, stirred in Sweet 'N Low and skim milk, then smeared the toast with margarine and marmalade. She put the mug and toast on a plate and headed to the back door. There, she grabbed a sweatshirt and her old straw hat off a wall peg and exchanged her thongs for gardening clogs, then headed out to the gazebo.

She'd put a small metal garden table and chairs in the gazebo, and she settled there now to enjoy her coffee and toast to the accompaniment of the early morning bird chorus, a cacophony that had awakened her at first light for the first few nights she had slept here, but which now couldn't penetrate her heavy slumber.

Shivering in the chill morning air, she slipped into the sweatshirt. She knew it would be coming off again when she got physically active in the garden and the mist slowly burned off with the heat of the sun.

Munching on the toast and sipping her hot coffee, Leonie's gaze shifted from the house to the garden, over to the Berkshire foothills to the east, then down to the river, and west to the Catskills beyond. It was moments like this in the early morning beauty and tranquility of the landscape that she felt she had made a wise decision in acquiring this place. There certainly were moments during the hectic, busy days and worn-out evenings when she had doubted the wisdom of her choice, but invariably this magical spot would remind her that her goal was a worthy one and that her decision had indeed been wise and practical – perhaps, she thought, even inspired.

She quickly finished her toast and coffee and rose to her feet and donned her big straw hat, positioning it just so, in order to protect her face from the sun. She headed out to the barn where she kept her gardening cart, always loaded down with tools and supplies. It was a big wheelbarrow-type affair with large wire-spoked wheels.

She donned her gardening gloves, which had been perched atop a bucket filled with small tools. They were long kidskin ones, to protect her from thorns, and although they were new, they were in a state of near ruin from the work she'd already done.

Ah well, she sighed, another trip to the local nursery was on her agenda anyway. The garden was eating up supplies as fast as she could buy them.

She grabbed hold of the cart with both hands, pulling it behind her as she made her way to the parterre, studying her handiwork on the rose-enshrouded gazebo and the wisteria-laden pergola as she went.

The gazebo had been relatively easy, involving cutting out a mountain of dead rose canes and trimming back a lot of the junglelike growth. It didn't look particularly pretty now, but Mother Nature would take care of the rest with the summer's growth. She was satisfied with her work and looked forward to the growth and the flowering she knew was to come. Plus, with her trimming, the gazebo would be easy to repair and paint now, without interfering with the roses.

The pergola had been another kettle of fish entirely. She'd had to use a saw and giant loppers as well as pruners to trim back the thick, rampant growth of the old wisteria vine. She knew it wouldn't reward her with blooms this year, but she felt certain that it would next spring, if not for her, then for the new owners, whoever they might be.

She pulled her cart to a stop at the parterre and surveyed the task at hand. Trimming, trimming, and more trimming. Fertilizing and mulching. Spraying. Would it never end? she asked herself.

She had begun by hoeing and weeding in these formal beds, because the whole parterre was so overgrown that the rose bushes were hardly discernible from the rest. Likewise the paths between the quadrants. It had taken her two days simply to weed and prune back the growth between and around the bluestone walks.

However, she thought, the roses here will reward me like those climbers on the gazebo, and my work here will increase the attractiveness and value of the property for future buyers.

Taking her snippers in hand, she began trimming in one of the four quadrants of the parterre, careful to avoid thorns as much as possible, although she inevitably would finish with scratches here and there. She only had a few bushes left to do in this quadrant, and it would be finished. Making quick work of it, she split open a bag of Moo Doo with a shovel and began to work it in around the bushes, smiling at the irony that such disgusting-smelling stuff worked to produce such exquisitely aromatic flowers.

She had barely begun when she heard Sam's Range Rover on the gravel drive. He was always the first to arrive in the morning – and usually the last to leave in the evening – and oftentimes had a cup of coffee with her while they discussed the progress on the project.

Leaning on her shovel, she looked out toward the drive and watched him get out of his car and walk over to the carriage house. He had set up a sort of makeshift headquarters there, with big tables of plywood resting on sawhorses where plans were spread out. As materials came in, most of them were unloaded there or in the barn and he carefully inventoried everything.

'Sam,' she called out to him.

He stopped short of the carriage house, looking for her. When he spotted her in the parterre, Leonie could see the smile which spread across his face.

'Hey,' he called back to her, then started hurrying toward the parterre.

'If you want some coffee,' she said, 'it's on the kitchen counter.'

'Great,' he said. 'Do you want some, too?'

'Please,' Leonie said, pushing the straw hat back on her head. 'We can have it in the gazebo. Okay?'

'Be right back,' Sam said.

Leonie propped the shovel against her gardening cart, then

removed her gardening gloves and slapped them off against her khakied thighs. 'Whew!' she said aloud. She walked to the gazebo where she took off her hat and shrugged out of her sweatshirt, then she shook her hair. It wasn't quite seven o'clock, and she'd already worked up a sweat that sheathed her body in a sheen. She wished she could work in shorts, but that was impossible in the thorny roses, unless she wanted her legs to look like bloody roadmaps.

She sat down just as Sam ambled in with two mugs of hot coffee. 'Oh, thanks, Sam,' she said, taking one of them from him.

'You're welcome,' he said. He looked at her with a curious expression. 'You look like you've already been at it for a while,' he said. Then added: 'As usual.'

'Yes,' Leonie replied. 'I want to get as much done as possible before the sun gets too hot and the bugs are out in full force. At least some of the hard stuff.'

'I've got to hand it to you,' he said. 'You sure have worked miracles in the last few weeks.'

'You look surprised.' Leonie laughed.

'I guess I am,' Sam said. 'I guess I didn't expect you to take quite so much of a hands-on approach.'

Leonie set her coffee mug down and looked at him with interest. 'Why's that?' she asked.

Sam looked thoughtful for a moment. 'Well, to be honest, I guess I didn't expect a city slicker with your kind of money and looks to be out here in a garden spreading Moo Doo and all that stuff around herself. I'd have thought you'd hire somebody to do it for you.'

Leonie smiled. 'Believe me, I've thought about it,' she said. 'Hiring somebody, I mean. But I enjoy it.' She paused, taking a sip of her coffee. 'Besides, this way I save myself a few bucks and get it done the way I want it. And my kind of money, as you put it, is the kind that dwindles down to nothing very quickly if I'm not careful.'

Sam looked chastened. 'I didn't mean to be presumptuous,' he said. 'I just assumed—'

Leonie held up a hand. 'It's okay, Sam,' she said. 'Forget about it. Suffice it to say, I'm not the rich divorcée most people think I am. Anyway, why don't we have a look around. Okay?' She still felt somewhat uncomfortable discussing her circumstances with anyone – except Mossy – and wanted to change the subject. As much as she liked – a very tame and undescriptive word for the way she really felt – Sam Nicholson, she didn't yet feel comfortable enough to confide in him.

'That's a good idea,' Sam said, putting his coffee mug down. 'Especially since there wasn't time to yesterday. We'd better get a move on before this place is crawling with workmen.' He realized with a sense of disappointment that for whatever reason Leonie Corinth didn't seem to want him to get any closer to her, to know more about her.

They walked around the south side of the house where mounds of earth and rock ran the length and breadth of the new septic tank and line that had been installed last week.

'I wish they didn't have to wait to spread the rest of that dirt out,' Leonie said. 'I could go ahead and seed it with grass now and take advantage of the summer growing season.'

'The problem,' Sam said, 'is that the ground's going to sink where they've dug it up. If you wait at least until the end of summer, after the ground has settled some, then let them spread it, you'll end up with much more even ground to sow your grass on. If you do it now, it'll have to be done again, later on.'

'Well, I guess I'll just have to live with it for a while,' Leonie said with resignation. 'But it sure is an eyesore.' She turned and looked at Sam. 'But then, the whole place is an eyesore now, isn't it?' She laughed.

'Yes, but not for long,' he replied. 'For a while it's going to look like Armageddon, then . . . bingo! One day it will suddenly all start coming together.'

Leonie's gaze swept over the house itself now. Rotten siding, where it existed, had already been removed and replaced with new wood on all the buildings. On the house, the shutters had been taken down, either for repair or to be junked and replaced with identical new ones. The roof shingles had been partially removed. All of them would be replaced, and the remainder would come off today. She had selected the darkest green – almost black – shingles to replace the old ones, and they would match the paint she had selected for the shutters. It was an Essex green, very dark, with blue and black in it. Most of the French doors and windows were reparable, but a few had to be replaced, so that there was a mixture of the old and the new, along with a few empty gaps to fill.

'The house looks like a crazy quilt,' she said.

'It does, doesn't it,' Sam agreed. 'Patchwork.'

Leonie pointed to the huge Dumpster on the lawn. 'That thing is filling up fast, Sam,' she said. 'It's amazing the amount of debris tearing out makes.'

'Yes,' he said, 'but I think after it's emptied this time, one more load will do it. Most of the deconstruction is done.'

They came to another mound of earth and rock where the new electrical, telephone, and television cable lines had been laid underground. Like the septic line, it couldn't be spread and grassed until later in the summer. The new electrical meter with upgraded service equipped to handle all the modern conveniences was set in place on the side of the house.

'Another eyesore,' Sam said, grinning.

'But not for long,' Leonie answered, returning his grin.

Workmen were arriving now, their truck tires crunching on the pea gravel drive. They called out their 'Hellos' or honked their horns and waved. They were, Leonie reflected, a very friendly and easygoing group of men, and they all seemed to respect Sam, if not openly idolize him.

She had been somewhat surprised by their camaraderie at first, but began to see that it was largely because Sam worked along with

111

the men. He neither lorded it over them, nor patronized them, but actually made himself a part of their various teams. And she had seen something else that both surprised and pleased her very much: When any of the workmen needed help, when someone might be out for the day, or when a crisis of any kind occurred, Sam Nicholson didn't hesitate to jump right in and help, whether it was problem solving or helping fill a vital gap in the labor pool.

She had seen him get his hands dirty several times in the last couple of weeks. He was not some sort of elitist architect who stayed locked up in his office, issuing directives and visiting the job site merely to direct or criticize work. He did all those things when necessary, but he took a very hands-on, down-to-earth approach, mixing and mingling with the men, hauling, heaving, digging, sawing, hammering, doing whatever the moment and the job required.

What had she expected? she asked herself. Probably someone more along the lines of the very well-known, very expensive, and very snobbish architect she had worked with in Southampton. After all, Sam, she knew, was married to a local heiress, lived in a grand manor house on a large estate with horses, and had been educated at Yale. She had imagined quite reasonably, therefore, that he would be far removed – perhaps aloof – from the actual nitty-gritty of the day-to-day work. She was delighted to discover that he wasn't afraid to pitch in, that he was anything but a snob, and that, indeed, he wasn't afraid of getting his Ivy League hands dirty.

'Want a quick look around inside?' Sam asked her.

'Yes, if we won't be in the way,' Leonie said.

'Not yet,' he replied.

They stepped up onto one of the bluestone terraces, where stonework was being regrouted as needed and some of it was being replaced. In the kitchen Sam paused, looking around. 'You told me you'd be going to Southampton?' he said.

'Yes,' Leonie replied. 'Why?'

'Because that would be the ideal time to get as much done in the kitchen as possible. That way you could use it, or most of it, up until you leave.' He looked at her. 'When are you going to leave?'

'About three weeks, I think,' she said. 'Maybe four. I'm not really sure yet.'

'Well, we'll try to work around you, so keep me posted, okay?' He looked at her questioningly.

'Sure, if you can work it that way,' Leonie said, 'it would be great.'

'We'll have to tear out this cabinetry and the ceiling and pull up this lineoleum,' Sam said, 'but you'd still have the stove and refrigerator. I'll take out the sink last. How's that sound?'

'Perfect.' Leonie nodded.

The house was beginning to come alive with workmen and the various sounds of progress: saws, drills, hammers. It was music to Leonie's ears.

'Have you been up to the top floor since yesterday afternoon?' Sam asked.

'No,' Leonie said. 'I'm ashamed to say I haven't. But there was so much going on, I steered clear of up there. Then last night, I was too tired to climb the stairs.'

Sam smiled. 'Let's go have a look,' he suggested.

He followed her up the curving stairs to the second floor, then to the staircase leading to the third. It was no longer enclosed, but was now open and gave the hall a more expansive sense of airy spaciousness and light. They climbed up to the third-floor attic.

Leonie stepped in and looked around in amazement. The walls and ceiling were now completely insulated, and she could see that the heat ducts, wiring, and plumbing were already in place. The bathroom was framed in, and they were starting to put up the drywall. It was actually taking shape as the master suite she had envisioned.

'What do you think?' Sam asked, a smile on his face.

'What do I think?' Leonie repeated. She turned and looked up into those turquoise eyes of his. 'Why, Sam, it's fabulous. You know it is! It's going to be even better than I'd imagined.'

'It is going to be fabulous, isn't it,' he said, a hint of pride in his voice. Then he suddenly frowned. 'There's only one problem that still bothers me.'

'What's that?' Leonie asked.

'The cupola,' he said. 'I've got to do something about that glass before I can do anything about the rotten framework. And I'll be damned if I want to put new glass in.'

Leonie sighed. 'That's one of those concessions we may have to make,' she said. 'But I hate to do it, too. I really love that old wavy glass, and it's a shame we can't match it.'

'I'll think of something,' Sam said. 'Anyway, I'm going to try to get this whole room finished out before everything else. That way, you'll have a private hideaway, away from all the mess. We can just move you up here.' He turned to her and smiled. 'You can even sleep late if you want to.'

Leonie laughed. 'I doubt you're going to see any of that until this project is finito, but I appreciate your thoughtfulness,' she said. 'Besides, I've got that garden to finish taking care of. And as soon as the pool is in, I'm going to landscape around it.'

'All by your lonesome?' he asked.

'All by my lonesome,' she said.

'You really are amazing,' he said. 'You just dig right in, don't you? You get down on your hands and knees, up on ladders. You don't seem to be afraid of anything.'

Leonie looked thoughtful for a moment and felt her face flush slightly at his compliment. 'I wish that were true,' she said earnestly, 'but . . . but there are things that I'm afraid of, to be honest.'

Sam looked at her with a curious expression. 'Would it be too nosy of me if I asked what?'

Leonie hesitated a moment, then said: 'The unknown, I guess. Of being . . . of being out on my own again.'

He looked surprised, then his expression changed to one of compassion. 'I think I know what you mean,' he said.

'Anyway,' Leonie said brightly, to change the subject, 'I think this is looking great, Sam. Now, I'd better get back out to the garden. The snakes might be missing me.'

He laughed easily. 'And I'd better get out to that carriage house and get busy.'

Leonie led the way downstairs, and they parted company out in the courtyard. 'See you later,' she said.

'Yeah,' Sam said, 'see you later.'

He watched her walk off toward the parterre for a moment, then went on to the carriage house, his mind whirling with thoughts of this woman who seemed day by day to become more formidable in his mind. He had assumed that she was very wealthy. Everybody did. After all, she had been married to Henry Reynolds. Sam had initially thought that she wanted to economize on the renovation simply because she was doing it to put the house up for sale. It was not the perfect job she would no doubt do for herself, he thought. He'd also suspected that she was just another New York City rich lady who knew how to get blood out of a turnip – or would die trying. He had met several of those in the past. Always bargaining, bargaining, bargaining. So it had been surprising to discover that she seemed genuinely concerned about money.

He walked into the carriage house and flipped on the lights, then took his jacket off and hung it on a wallhook, unable to get her out of his mind. He had also thought that Leonie Corinth was absolutely indomitable, but he had to confess that he was gratified to discover that she was vulnerable. She had very real fears and had said so. Perhaps, he thought, she's a bit more human than I'd surmised. Maybe a bit more approachable, too. Somehow, this vulnerability, these fears she admitted to, made her all the more desirable to him.

She was still reeling from a divorce, he knew, and that could account for her reluctance to open up, to be more forthcoming with him. Perhaps she would gradually overcome that.

He wondered now more than ever: Who is this woman to whom I've become so desperately attracted? Now more than ever?

Leonie shoveled and shoveled and shoveled. She dug and dug and dug. Snipped and snipped and snipped. But no matter how hard she tried to concentrate, her mind was filled with thoughts of Sam Nicholson. Not unusual these days certainly, but now the cauldron of emotions she had been experiencing was stirred up anew, after talking to him this morning. She had been physically attracted to him from the moment she had set eyes on him. Who wouldn't be? she asked herself.

And while the initial physical reaction had only grown to be more potent than ever, there was another dimension to her attraction now. She liked him. In fact, she liked him a lot. Like the men who worked for him, she respected him. But it was much more than that. She could see that despite whatever wealth and status – and the inevitable privileges which derived from them – might be part of Sam's station in life, he was still a down-to-earth man without a haughty bone in his body. He was approachable, of this she was certain, and she felt he was ultimately so very human.

She was beginning to see that he was much, much more than the extraordinarily well-put-together specimen, with all the 'right' attributes, be they physical, social, educational, or otherwise, that Mossy had described to her. Mossy had been right, for he was all of those things. But she now knew that he had much more to offer than those immensely appealing surface characteristics.

Yes, she thought. He's just the sort of man that a woman could fall for. Just the sort of man I could fall for.

Quit beating around the bush, Leonie, she told herself. He is the man you have fallen for, more so now than ever.

*   *   *

The workmen had left for the day, but Leonie noticed that Sam's Range Rover was still parked out on the driveway. She took off her straw hat and grabbed an old bandana out of her back pocket. She wiped the sweat off her face and neck.

'Whee-ewww!' she said aloud. 'I think it's just about quitting time for me, too.' Then she remembered the birdbath. 'Well, almost quitting time.' She pocketed her bandana, put her hat back on, and walked over to the old Volvo. She opened its back and eyed the heavy cement birdbath.

'Mercy, child,' she said. 'What you do get yourself into!'

She reached in and pulled up on the bowl, leaning it out of the back. Then she managed to lift it out, letting it fall to the ground with a thud. Now for the even heavier pedestal. She rolled its heavy cement closer to her, lifted one end out over the lip of the back, and finally managed to roll it out, too. It joined the bowl on the ground with a louder thud.

She heard boots crunching on gravel and looked up. It was Sam.

He smiled. 'What the devil are you doing now?' he asked.

'I'm going to get this birdbath in place if it kills me,' Leonie said.

'Here, let me help,' Sam offered.

'No,' Leonie replied. 'You don't have to do that. It's getting late, Sam.'

He looked at her levelly. 'I don't bite, Leonie,' he said.

'I . . . I know that,' she stuttered. 'But I can do this myself.' She leaned down and started picking it up.

'I insist,' he said. He quickly leaned down to pick it up, brushing her hand in the process.

Leonie hesitated, then moved her hand away. She felt a thrill at his touch and a heated, electrical rush. Sam looked at her and she felt herself flush.

'Sorry,' he said, smiling sheepishly, perhaps a little shyly. He

117

picked up the heavy base effortlessly and walked to the center of the parterre with it, Leonie walking along beside him.

'Here?' he asked, setting it down.

'Yes,' Leonie said. 'Perfect.' She'd already moved the crumbling old one out of the way. Sam adjusted the pedestal so it sat straight, then walked back to the car and got the bowl, which he brought back and placed atop the pedestal.

Leonie stood back, eyeing it critically from various angles, as did Sam. 'It looks straight, doesn't it?' Leonie asked.

'Yes,' Sam said. 'Luckily, it fits right in the spot where the old one was.'

'Now, if it just didn't look so damn new!' Leonie complained. 'Oh, well, that'll change soon enough, and I'll help it along. Keep it wet, so moss will grow on it. Maybe start some ivy growing up it.' She looked at Sam. 'What do you think?'

'Sounds good to me,' he said.

'Well, thanks for your help,' Leonie said, bending down to pick up some clippings she'd left on the ground.

'Watch it!' Sam exclaimed. 'There's a snake right at your foot.'

Leonie jerked up, then she looked down. 'Oh, well, it's just a harmless little thing. They've got to eat, too, don't they?'

Sam laughed, as the snake slithered off to cover. 'I thought you'd be hysterical for sure.'

'Me?' Leonie said. 'No. I've gotten to rather like the little devils. But then I haven't run across anything too big, either. Snakes, in fact, are part of my new first rule of gardening.'

'Your new first rule of gardening?' Sam said. 'And what is that, exactly?'

'Don't look,' Leonie answered. 'Or not too closely. Whether you're trimming, or hoeing, or digging, or whatever. Just don't look. Because, if you do, you're bound to see something that will scare you off.'

Sam smiled. 'I guess that's a pretty good rule,' he said.

118

'On the other hand,' Leonie said, 'it is the direct opposite of my old first rule of gardening. Always look carefully to see what you may be raking out from underneath a bush or whatever. You don't want to rake a snake up onto your feet, do you?'

'I guess you're right on both counts,' Sam said. 'So what do you do?'

'I wish I knew,' Leonie said. 'I guess it's like life, isn't it? You think you have everything figured out, and then, boom! the sky falls on you.' She laughed. 'I guess all rules are made to be broken.'

'Yes, I guess you're right,' Sam said.

She looked at him and suddenly felt a little shy and embarrassed. 'I better get busy putting my tools away,' she said. 'I know you've got to get home.'

'No,' Sam said, 'I'm not in any hurry. Let me help you.'

Leonie started to protest, but didn't say anything. What the hell, she thought. I'm bone-weary, and if he wants to help, then I'll let him.

They both began picking up her tools and piling them onto her gardening cart, Sam carefully wiping loose soil off with his work gloves.

'Oh, wait,' Leonie said. 'Let me have those pruners just a minute.'

Sam handed them over.

'I see a couple of roses I missed over there,' she said, 'and I might as well get them now.' She walked over to the offending bushes and began pruning.

Sam picked up another pair of pruners and joined her, pruning on the rose bush she hadn't started on.

'Sam!' Leonie cried. 'You don't have to do that. Please! I know you have to get home.'

'No,' Sam answered, 'like I said, I'm in no hurry.'

Thirty minutes later, they had finished the pruning and had admired their handiwork. He helped Leonie put away her tools, taking the big gardening cart from her and rolling it into the barn where she kept it overnight.

'Would you like a glass of wine?' she asked when they were done.

'Sure,' Sam said. 'That'd be great.'

Leonie got the wine and two glasses, and they sat out in the gazebo, sipping their wine and enjoying the view across the river to the Catskills beyond.

'You seem to be settling right in,' Sam said. 'You think you're going to like it up here?'

'Yes,' Leonie said. 'I really love it.' She paused thoughtfully. 'I don't know what the future will bring, but I certainly do love it for now. Besides, the city's not going anyplace. It'll be there if I decide I just have to have it.'

'Do you miss it?' Sam asked. 'Get lonely for it?'

'Not so far,' Leonie said. 'Oh, sometimes, I guess I get a little lonely for friends and everything, but I'm always busy.'

'I know what you mean,' Sam said.

She looked at him and saw the haunted look in his eyes. 'But you've got a life here, don't you? I mean, you've got your work and your family and so on.'

'Yes, I've got my work,' Sam said, 'but that's about it. We don't have any children, and my wife . . . well, let's just say she has other interests.'

'I see,' Leonie said. God, she thought, he looks so lonely. So lost and unhappy. She decided that Mossy must be right about his unhappy marriage. She wanted nothing more than to reach out to him, to offer him comfort, to . . . Stop thinking this way! she told herself. It will get you nothing but trouble!

Sam suddenly put a smile on his face. 'Well,' he said, 'if there's nothing else I can help you do, I guess I'd better get on my way now.'

'No, Sam,' she said, 'and thanks a million for your help.'

'It's okay,' he said, 'and when you need something like that done, just ask me or Skip, the foreman, if I'm not here. Somebody will be able to help you.' But he knew that she wouldn't, that she was too independent, too self-reliant. And he liked that a lot.

'I will,' Leonie said, genuinely appreciating the offer, knowing that she would never take him up on it.

She walked him to his car and waved good-bye as it rolled out of the driveway.

She wished that he didn't have to leave now, that they could talk some more. She had really enjoyed his helping her, his gentle and unhurried manner. He doesn't have to act the macho male, she thought. Doesn't have anything to prove along those lines. And, she thought, he lets me be myself.

She couldn't think when she'd ever met a man who hadn't tried to impose his own will on her. Well, I have now. She thought that she appreciated this more than anything else. Then she remembered their hands touching, and she felt a frisson of excitement rush through her once more at the mere memory. I think I like that, too. Oh, yes. I definitely liked his touch.

PART TWO

SUMMER

The sun was beginning to die in the west, the fiery ball descending over the Catskills. It was getting late, and Sam bounded out of the Range Rover and up the brick front steps of Van Vechten Manor. He was whistling, tunelessly, but no matter. He was feeling exceptionally happy tonight. Work on the octagon house had continued to progress very well over the last month now.

The weather had been cooperating, and the work crews had made their best efforts. He honestly believed that part of it was because they saw Leonie, day after day, week after week, toiling out in the garden as if she were a field hand, working if not precisely with them, then alongside them. She also took the time to compliment them on their various endeavors, and if she had a complaint, it was always voiced in a positive, upbeat way that was encouraging rather than remonstrative. He felt certain now that they would finish the project on schedule, if not ahead of time, and that he would be able to keep it within budget.

His buoyant spirits, however, were more a result of his getting to know Leonie better. She was gradually beginning to be more at ease around him, and opening up to him. Tonight they'd had a glass of wine together after all the workmen had left, and she'd let him help her haul garden debris down behind the barn to a compost heap she'd started.

Strange, he thought, what joy doing these little things with her had given him – and he was certain that she had derived pleasure from them, too. It reminded him of the evening he'd helped her with the birdbath. It had been such a simple task, but had given so much joy. He had hated to see her leaving, but then she would only be gone a couple of days, she'd said. He would enjoy the work regardless, but he knew that without her, it would not be the same. Not by a long shot.

We make a great team, he thought.

As if she were psychic, Erminda opened the front door before he could insert his key. How does she do it? he wondered.

'Hey, Erminda,' he greeted her, the smile on his face tonight wide and genuine.

'Good evening, Mr. Sam,' she said. Her voice was a near-whisper, and she looked up at him with a solemn expression.

Sam knew immediately that something was amiss, for she always seemed delighted to see him. 'What's up, Erminda?' he asked.

'Mrs. Nicholson is waiting for you in the conservatory,' she said. She looked at him meaningfully. 'And she is in a very bad mood tonight.'

The smile quickly faded from Sam's face. 'Thanks, Erminda,' he said. 'I'll go see her right away.'

He tossed his keys into the famille rose bowl, dropped his briefcase onto an American Empire chair, and quickly threaded his way across the vast expanse of black-and-white checkerboard marble of the entrance hall toward the library, through its rich mahogany book-lined quiet, and out to the conservatory.

The moment he entered the verdant excess of the glass room, his wife turned to face him. He saw written on her features a look of studied quiet and calm, a deceptive tranquility that he knew could only mean one thing: Minette was seething with barely contained rage, a white-hot fury that she was about to let loose on him.

There were times when she would try to get him to coax the anger, and the reasons for it, out of her, a nasty, time-consuming game she seemed to enjoy more and more frequently. But tonight, he could sense that he wouldn't have to play this tedious little game. No. From all appearances, Minette was not in the mood for coaxing. Rather, she was going to vent her rage freely and copiously. Yes, she looked in just the frame of mind for a take-no-prisoners approach.

What now? he wondered, his earlier euphoria already evaporating at the mere sight of her face.

'Minette—' he began.

'How dare you!' she spat. 'How dare you!'

Her beautiful face had twisted into a mask of fury, and she slammed a bejeweled wrist down on the padded arm of her wheel-chair with such violence that she splashed a drink onto her silk-sheathed legs.

'What's wrong, Minette?' Sam asked in as calm a voice as he could manage. He was truly bewildered by her anger and swiftly crossed the limestone floor to her side.

He reached out a hand to touch her shoulder, but she quickly jerked back, glaring at him malevolently.

'Don't touch me,' she said. 'Don't even think about it!'

'What is it, Minette?' Sam said. He sat down across from her, arms on knees, looking at her. 'What in the world is the matter?'

'"What is it, Minette?"' she mimicked. '"What in the world is the matter?"' A vicious smile crossed her lips, but her large, widened eyes were still filled with hatred.

Sam sat staring, wondering what he could have done to produce

127

such vitriol, because there was no doubt in his mind that it had to be something he had done.

When I least expect it, he thought. For the last few weeks she had been surprisingly quiet about his working on the octagon house. She had expressed no interest in the project or curiosity about Leonie Corinth, but neither had she complained about his preoccupation with his work or his long hours away from the house. Now this. What the hell?

Sam finally broke the silence. 'Could you please tell me what it is that's upset you?' he asked quietly, pleadingly.

'Where were you this morning?' she asked evenly.

'What do you mean, where was I?' he said in a puzzled voice. 'You know very well where I was. I went to work as usual.'

Minette shifted impatiently in her chair. 'Work,' she said sarcastically. 'As usual. Ha! Well, if you'd taken the time to look at your calendar, you might have noticed that you were supposed to take me to New York City today. To the doctor.'

'Oh, God, no,' Sam moaned. He lowered his head into his hands, his fingers covering his face. 'Oh, God, Minette. I'm so sorry,' he said. 'I didn't—'

'You didn't what?' she said nastily. 'You didn't give a damn, that's what! That little shit, Dirck, had to take me.' She took a sip of her drink and eyed him over the crystal of the glass. Then she set it back down.

'Why didn't you call me on the cell phone, Minette?' he asked. 'Or call the octagon house? You have the number.'

'If you can't remember your responsibilities, Sam, I'm not here to remind you. You've made your priorities clear. You know I ask for very little from you, especially considering what I've given you over the years,' she continued. 'I almost never ask you for a favor. I almost never ask you to take me into the city. And what happens the first time in ages that I do? You ignore me, that's what happens. You simply disregard me. I'm just the pitiful old cripple you married and keep hidden away here at home while you gallivant around the countryside – at my expense.'

The muscles in Sam's jaws were locked in a grimace, and he hardly trusted himself to speak. He could certainly understand her anger, and he felt guilt, like an evil mantle, spread itself over him, cloaking him in a sad and despairing darkness. How the hell could I have forgotten? he asked himself.

At the same time, he knew that Minette was overreacting – she didn't have to humiliate him, did she? – and that she was probably making up for the last few weeks of her quiet and uncomplaining tolerance of his absences while he was working. She had been seething with anger all the while, he told himself, just waiting for the right time to attack. Well, he thought, I've given her the perfect opportunity to extract her revenge – in spades.

Still, he wondered whether or not something else could be going on, if there was something she was perhaps not telling him. She had always resented his working, but she had never been quite this vindictive, quite this full of rage. Was it merely an escalation in her continuing efforts to get him to stay at home? He simply didn't know.

He lifted his head and looked across at her. She sat staring at him with a look of triumph on her face, apparently satisfied with knowing that she had made him feel small and miserable.

'I can't say how sorry I am, Minette,' he said quietly. 'And I don't really have any excuses. I've always tried to be there for you, and I'm really sorry I wasn't today. I guess I forgot to mark it on the calendar.'

'Well, it's little wonder,' she said. 'It wouldn't have happened if you didn't insist on this stupid work. You've been so wrapped up in that old house, you've hardly been here at all.' She took another sip of her drink and set it back down on the table next to her. 'Take tonight, Sam,' she continued relentlessly. 'It's after eight o'clock.

I ask you! What the devil are you doing down there until eight o'clock?'

'I stayed late, Minette,' Sam said. 'Going over plans for the work coming up.' He may feel guilty, but he wasn't about to tell his wife that he'd been helping Leonie Corinth in the garden. Especially considering that he'd failed to be there for Minette today. 'I guess the time just got away from me,' he added.

'I guess it did,' she said.

'What did the doctor say?' Sam asked.

'What difference does it make?' Minette answered.

'Oh, come on, Minette,' he replied. 'You know I care. What did he say?'

'Nothing,' she finally said. 'Nothing. It was just a series of tests.'

'What kind of tests?' he asked.

'I don't know,' she said peevishly. 'Just tests. Blood tests and stuff. The usual.'

'But why?' Sam persisted.

'Who knows?' she said. 'It's all just part of a physical. Anyway, let's forget it. I'm sick of the subject.'

Great, Sam thought. Now that she's made me feel like a complete asshole, we can forget the whole thing. Right. 'Okay,' he said equably. 'But I hope you'll forgive me, Minette, because I'm really sorry.'

She waved a hand. 'Let's forget it,' she said. Her rage had obviously dissipated, leaving her a little weary, he thought.

She pushed the button on the intercom. 'Erminda,' she said. 'We'll have dinner now.'

'Yes, Mrs. Nicholson,' the voice came back.

Minette looked over at Sam. 'I see you're not wearing your watch,' she said.

He looked at her with curiosity. 'No,' he replied. 'I don't want to get it dirty at work.'

'Perhaps you should,' she said. 'It cost me twenty thousand dollars, and it might get you home in time for a drink before dinner.' She smiled. 'Now!' she said in a saccharine voice. 'Shall you take me into the dining room, darling?'

Sam felt his face redden and his jaw muscles clench again, but he swallowed his anger and got to his feet. 'Of course, Minette,' he said. My God, he thought, it can't get any worse than this, can it?

10

The sky was a monochromatic blue without a hint of a cloud in sight, and the sunshine was almost blindingly bright as Leonie took exit 70 off the Long Island Expressway and headed toward Sunrise Highway. She'd already forgotten how the light here in the East End of Long Island seemed to envelop you in its luminosity and intensity when at its brightest, as it was today.

Perfect, Leonie thought, and smiled wryly. And appropriate for this most perfect of seaside resorts. Everything here was so perfect, so exceedingly proper. On the surface, at least. But she knew that, like Palm Beach and Monte Carlo, this pristine enclave's residents could turn dangerously dark and stormy, just like the weather.

Then suddenly, as if by magic, all of her cynical thoughts were swept away by the air. Ummm, she thought, traveling along Sunrise Highway at a speedy clip, I'd almost forgotten what it was like. The first intoxicating smells of the ocean. The salty air filled her well-shaped nostrils with its tang and flooded her with memories – some sad, as well as quite a few happy ones – but finally left a distinctly acidic taste on her palate and an almost overwhelming feeling of dread somewhere deep in the pit of her stomach.

Dread for the unpleasant task at hand. A task she would gladly walk over hot coals – well, almost! – to be able to turn over to somebody else. But that was impossible, and she knew it.

She put on her right turn signal and slowly eased off the highway onto a sandy lane leading out into the woods and eventually the shore, or so she supposed. She pulled over and put the car in park, then reached over and got her compact out of her shoulder bag.

She checked her makeup, eyeing herself critically. Maybe, she thought, just a touch more blusher. Yes, just the merest dab. She got busy with the brush, delicately dusting her cheekbones with a terracotta-tinted powder.

Not having been out to the beach this summer, she would look a trifle pale in Southampton, and she certainly wanted to look her best today.

Is it pride? she wondered. Vanity? Who knows? She wasn't sure, and didn't think she much cared. But she knew that she wanted to look confident, secure – anything but wan and crushed. No, sirree, she was not going to look like a victim. She was not going to look like the woman whom Hank Reynolds had tried to smash like some lowly housefly.

She was Leonie Corinth now, she reminded herself, and damn proud of it!

I'm also scared shitless, she thought. Then amended that thought immediately with: Not so much scared as very, very nervous. She told herself repeatedly that there was absolutely nothing to be scared of, nothing to be nervous about, pumping herself up with positive, assertive thoughts, drumming into her head all the 'good' things that today represented. However, all of her assertions, with their mantralike repetition, seemed to be to little or no avail. She was still very anxious. And, she thought, with good reason.

She had gotten a telephone call from Bobby Chandler the day

before yesterday, telling her that he had decided to put his house in Southampton on the market. He also told her in the nicest – and firmest – way possible that he would appreciate it if she would kindly pick up the boxes of personal property that she had stored at his house – and 'tout de suite, cherie.' Then, it was 'ciaocito' before she'd had the opportunity to ask him what was going on.

Oddly enough, only a couple of hours later, Jeremy Sampson, the attorney who had handled her divorce and the sale of her Soho shop, telephoned to tell her that he had some paperwork that had to be signed and witnessed in one of his two offices – New York or Southampton – by both her and Hank Reynolds. Paperwork regarding the sale of her Soho shop. She could name the place, the paperwork would be waiting.

At last! she had thought, looking forward to the sizeable chunk of cash that the sale would bring her. Almost as important, she thought, was the sense of closure that she felt certain the sale of the shop would give her. It would also sever the very last link between her and Hank Reynolds, because even though the shop had been hers and the proceeds of the sale were going to be hers to keep – glory hallelujah! – he had to sign the paperwork, disposing of any interest he might have had in the shop and benefits from its sale.

So, to simplify matters Leonie had decided to drive to Southampton and sign the necessary documents. Being the middle of the week, there was no chance Hank would be in Southampton. He would be wheeling and dealing in New York City, so she wasn't worried about running into him. And she most definitely did not want to see him. No way! Why open old wounds?

Afterward, she would retrieve the few boxes she had stored at Bobby's place, killing two birds with one stone. Make a day of it, even if it was not altogether her idea of a perfectly enjoyable one.

For she did not relish the idea. No, not one single little bit. Jeremy Sampson, she felt, had let her down big time, and just seeing him stirred up feelings of defeat and hostility that she would just as soon

135

forget about. Then there was seeing Bobby's place – just down the road from the magnificent old house she had restored as a getaway for Hank and herself.

She had helped Bobby redecorate his house, and he had had a hand in decorating hers. Simply seeing the place, she feared, would stir up a hornet's nest of feelings. Feelings she did not want to feel right now. Feelings she didn't think she was ready to handle.

Oh, hell, she thought, just being in Southampton might trigger a grab bag of highly unpleasant emotions she could well do without. After all, Southampton was, she felt, the locus of her great failure: the breakdown of her marriage. For Leonie, it was like visiting the scene of a crime, a particularly bloody and vicious one. Murder perhaps.

Who needs it? she asked herself. Just when work on the house upstate was going so smoothly and she was beginning to actually forget the recent and highly unpleasant past. She had thrown herself into her new life, and now the past had reared its less than attractive head, insinuating itself into the steady, rewarding, and peaceful building of this new life like an enraged and evil Medusa.

However, she wanted to get these errands out of the way, and her practical side won out. Perhaps it wouldn't be so bad, she told herself. She could hardly wait to see Bobby, who was taking a few weeks off, spending them in Southampton. It had been months now.

Maybe she would spend the night at his house, have a good gabfest and catch up on all the latest gossip. Although come to think of it, he had been decidedly unresponsive – could it be, even chilly? – when she had mentioned the possibility.

Now that she thought about it, she wondered what was up with Bobby anyway. He hadn't been calling, keeping her posted on the society and celebrity shenanigans in the Hamptons this summer. Bobby, in fact, hadn't been calling at all, and it wasn't like him. He had always taken great pleasure in confiding his latest escapades and giving her the latest skinny on the triumphs and defeats of the power elite. She had to admit that she'd always enjoyed these confidences and the society gossip. Now, she missed them and wondered why Bobby wasn't calling.

Paranoid, she thought. I'm just being paranoid. Bobby's merely been caught up in the *de rigueur* summertime frolics in the rich and decadent precincts of this beachside Sodom and Gomorrah. He would be the last person on earth to let her down.

Giving her face a final inspection, she snapped her compact shut, tossed it into her shoulder bag, checked for any unlikely traffic, then made a U-turn back to Sunrise Highway and headed on toward Southampton.

First stop, the law offices of Sampson, Williamson, and Everett to sign the papers. She parked on Main Street in Southampton Village and dashed into the offices. I'll get this business over with in a flash, she told herself. Just like Elvis. Sign the papers and dash back out.

But reality, that great gorgon, once again asserted itself. While Leonie was sitting in Jeremy Sampson's inner sanctum, sipping a San Pelligrino while waiting for Helen, his assistant, to bring in the paperwork, it had happened.

Helen opened the door, a sheaf of papers in hand – and Henry Wilson Reynolds at her side.

Leonie was so stunned that she couldn't speak. She couldn't believe her eyes for a moment. She had been certain that Hank would be in New York City or elsewhere working. Even had he not been, she simply couldn't conceive of the fact that Jeremy Sampson had scheduled them both on the same day – at the same time yet.

She looked up at him, the man she had once loved so whole-heartedly, the man who had dumped her so unceremoniously, standing there resplendent in his tennis whites, blond hair tousled, tanned skin glowing, and felt her pulse begin to beat rapidly, then a burning flush rose from her chest and up her neck to suffuse her face with the red-hot heat of – what? Embarrassment? Anger? Humiliation? Probably all of the above, she thought. And a whole lot more besides.

Hank stood there for a moment, looking down at her from his six-foot-one advantage, with his best and smuggest King of Wall Street expression, the superior look of a needy ego that she had grown only too familiar with. He acknowledged her with a barely perceptible nod.

Leonie nodded back, struggling to keep her composure.

'Huh,' Hank uttered, 'didn't know you'd be here.' Sounding like she was the cleaning lady who should have already left for the day.

'I . . . I thought you'd be in the city,' Leonie responded, the mere effort to find her voice not an easy one.

'Decided to take a few days off, play some tennis, golf. Maybe do a little sailing,' Hank said offhandedly.

Jeremy Sampson cleared his throat, then spoke. 'Have a seat, Hank,' he said. 'This will only take a minute, then you can get back to your tennis.' He gave Hank Reynolds a smile that made Leonie feel the bile rise in her throat and threaten to make her be sick all over Jeremy Sampson's precious antique Majal carpet. In fact, she thought, I wish I would be sick all over his damn rug!

Whose lawyer is he anyway? she asked herself.

Hank made his lanky frame comfortable in the George II library chair next to Leonie's, crossing his long legs in a relaxed manner.

Leonie couldn't help but notice that he was very tanned, unlike the Hank she had known, who had always been too busy working, working, working to get out into the sun. She could see, too, that he was damp with perspiration, under his arms and down his chest; he'd obviously come straight here from the tennis court.

He looked, she had to admit, more handsome and healthier than ever. Hair blonder, teeth whiter, eyes a brighter shade of blue, body leaner and tighter. She hated to think that Hank Reynolds seemed to have a happier, more relaxed and contented air about him, now that she was no longer a part of his life. He seemed . . . content, she decided. That was it.

She wondered what could account for this. If he might be seeing somebody. Some beautiful, rich young socialite. If that was the reason for the somewhat more youthful and more laid-back Hank Reynolds who had shown up.

Well, she told herself, she would find out soon enough because Bobby Chandler was sure to have all the poop on her ex-husband.

Hank's voice jerked her out of her reverie. 'How you liking it up in cow country?' he asked, with more than a hint of derision in his tone.

Leonie felt his gaze and answered without looking at him. She was steaming now, but tried to control her voice. 'I like "cow country", as you call it, a lot,' she said. 'You know I always have.' Why does he make it so easy to hate him?

'Isn't it just a little bit too . . . provincial for your tastes?' he continued. 'No boutiques? No fancy clubs? No blue bloods?'

Why does he want to taunt me? Leonie wondered. If he wanted to irritate her, he was succeeding royally, but she could not, would not, let him know it.

She looked him in the eye now. 'I really don't miss all that, Hank,' she said mildly. 'It's a different life . . . not as glamorous, maybe, but it does have its rewards.'

'Really,' he replied, arching an imperious eyebrow.

'Yes, really,' she said. 'I've met a lot of interesting women and men,' she said pointedly.

Hank smiled at her. 'I didn't think farmers would be your style, Leonie.'

Before Leonie could respond, Jeremy Sampson called Helen and another assistant, Leslie, in to witness, then began passing the paperwork across the desk to each of them to sign on the Xed lines. The whole process only took a few minutes, but Leonie felt like a lifetime had passed before all the i's were dotted and the t's crossed.

When they finished, Jeremy Sampson rose from behind his desk and shook hands with Leonie. 'I'm sure everything is to your satisfaction, Leonie,' he said confidently. 'And, oh yes. Here's the check.' He handed the check across the desk.

Leonie took it wordlessly, folded it in half without giving it a glance, then dropped it into her shoulder bag on the floor.

'I'll overnight copies of everything to you in a few days,' Jeremy said, 'and that, as they say, will be that.' He smiled his shark's smile, bloodless but predatory nevertheless.

'Thanks,' Leonie said, and stood up and grabbed her big leather shoulder bag from the floor next to her chair. 'That's it, then?'

'That's it,' Jeremy said.

'See you,' Leonie said, and turned and started for the door.

'Leonie?' Hank called to her back.

Leonie froze. Oh, Lord, she thought, help me get out of here, away from this cesspool. She turned and looked at her ex-husband, eyebrows raised.

Hank smiled condescendingly. 'Have a good trip back upstate,' he said.

'Right,' Leonie muttered, then turned and left.

She rushed through the outer office in a daze of confusion, then out to the car, where she was tempted to sit and gather her wits about her. But she knew that Hank would be coming out here soon – his big midnight-blue Bentley Turbo was parked right next to her – so she fired up the engine, jerked out of her parking spot, and raced off, too fast and too erratically.

The creep! she thought. He knew I was here and just acted surprised to see me. He must have known I was here because he parked next to me.

After a few minutes, she pulled over on a side street and put the car in park. She didn't trust herself to drive, not now. She was shaking, literally shaking, with rage and humiliation.

Why, oh, why, she asked herself, did I allow this to happen? I should have made absolutely certain with Jeremy Sampson that Hank would not be anywhere near his office when I came in.

Too late now, she thought. Besides, she surmised that it was reasonable of her to expect that Jeremy Sampson would have had the decency to see to that himself. But then, she was now more convinced than ever that Jeremy Sampson – the filthy, lowdown, good-for-nothing – was in cahoots with Hank Reynolds. Jeremy, like most people, had been seduced by Hank's power and wealth. It was Hank, after all, who would be making and spending big buckaroos in New York and Southampton, not Leonie.

Hank Reynolds.

Just seeing him made her feel somehow defiled, ashamed, and inadequate. It also made her feel an anger such as she had never known, and a confusion she didn't know how to sort out. She had spent years of her life with that man, working for and with him, thinking that she knew him, that she loved him. But the man she had seen in Jeremy Sampson's office was a stranger, a man she didn't think she knew at all.

How, she asked herself for the millionth time, could I have been married to him? How could I have known him so little? How could I have been so fooled by him? How could I have been so wrong, goddammit?

She took a few deep breaths to steady herself, and thought: I've got to get on my way, put this out of my mind, and get on with my life. She took yet a few more deep breaths, then squared her shoulders.

She affixed a bright smile to her face – act as if, she told herself. Act as if all is well. She decided to put her feelings on cruise control, closing down, so to speak. Try to forget this nasty business, she told herself. Don't give Jeremy Sampson, that slick, remote, power-hungry shark who I am certain sold me down the river, any more of my precious time and thoughts. Ditto Hank Reynolds.

God, I feel like I need a bath! Just being around the two of them!

With that, she put the car in gear, pulled back out into the street, and headed for Bobby Chandler's, slowly but steadily.

At least with Bobby, I know where I stand, she thought. He's like an old shoe – so comfortable, so easy to be with. Bobby had very big shoulders to cry on, big arms to envelop her in a hug, and what's more, Bobby was a great listener, a highly attentive listener, who knew when to speak, when to shut up, when to give a stroke, when to leave well enough alone. He was like that treasured family member who, no matter what, would welcome her with open arms, with unconditional love.

Besides, she reasoned, nothing could be worse than this.

11

Over a month had passed since he'd begun working on the octagon house, and there had been moments when Sam wished he had never taken on this project. Minette, with her objections to his working, of course, was part of the reason, but there was something – no, someone, he amended – who was more at the root of his problem.

Leonie Corinth.

Leonie Corinth was driving him out of his mind.

Only not in the way most clients did, with changes, indecision, firings, hirings, and disputes of every kind. No. Leonie Corinth was proving to be as perfect a client as he had ever had, even if they had debated a few issues.

And therein lay the problem: their equally keen and discerning eyes, their agreeable, even happy, working relationship, their mutual—

Sam didn't want to think about it.

From the frying pan, into the fire, he thought.

Perhaps all those tired old adages were true. It certainly seemed to be the case with him. After all those tortured years with Minette, why was he allowing himself to start feeling something for another woman? Especially when there was no possibility of anything coming of those feelings?

Jesus! he thought. Am I nuts, or what? To let this woman insinuate herself into my consciousness the way she has. He was asking for trouble, as always, and he knew it.

As he ambled south down the highway toward the octagon house, he looked over toward the Catskills to the west. The sky was a uniform gray this morning, with the threat of a summer storm throughout the day, according to the radio. The humidity was suffocatingly unpleasant.

Perfect, he thought. Just like my frame of mind.

He reached over and started flipping the dial on the radio, not in the mood to listen to the crooners once again coming out of Albany. He hit a rock and roll station, playing the Rolling Stones – 'Let's Spend the Night Together.' Not his idea of early morning music.

But not a bad idea. No, not a bad idea at all, he thought. Just what the doctor ordered, in fact. Jeez, would I ever like to spend the night . . .

He quickly began spinning the dial again, then decided he didn't want to listen to anything at all. Not this morning, not now. He had too much on his mind, too many really serious problems to solve, and no solutions in sight. He quickly shut the radio off.

What am I going to do? he wondered for the umpteenth time that morning. What the hell am I going to do?

He drove on in silence, then slowed down when he saw the road to Leonie's up ahead. His pulse quickened, as it did every morning when he approached the site. And he knew, of course, that it wasn't just the job that excited him. Hell, no. He took a right off the highway, and drove up the lane to the octagon house, the anticipation of seeing Leonie making him want to pick up his pace, forcing him to control it.

He swung around back to the carriage house, but didn't see her old Volvo there, amid all the pickup trucks parked helter-skelter that belonged to the crew. He saw that Skip, the construction foreman, and the crew were swarming all over the property like so many worker bees.

In the last few weeks – very productive weeks, he thought – there had been a lot of progress, especially with the extra work crews he had put on. Right now, the property looked a mess. Little hillocks of dirt and rock, those eyesores Leonie hated so much, filled-in trenches, like so many ugly scars on the grounds, and steel scaffolding surrounding all the buildings now, were indeed a blight on the landscape.

But Sam knew that looks in this case were deceiving. A lot of the work that had been done was invisible – the basic upgrading of the mechanicals. He smiled when he remembered Leonie joking that it would be nice if wells and septic systems and all that plumbing and electrical work could be enclosed in Plexiglas, so that you could see where your money went.

Soon though, in just a few more weeks, all the labor, love, and money being lavished on the historic old house would begin to show, since the basics were nearly complete, and the time-consuming but more visually gratifying cosmetics would begin.

'Hey, Skip,' he called, jumping out of the Range Rover.

Skip Curtiss, the construction foreman, ambled over, taking off his hard hat and scratching his sweat-soaked head. 'Hey, Sam. How you doing this morning?'

'Okay,' Sam answered. 'You?'

'Can't complain.'

'Listen. I just wanted to remind you. When the pool people get here, I want you to accommodate them like you do everybody else. Try to keep the guys out of their way and let them do their thing.'

'No problem, Sam,' Skip Curtiss said.

'And be sure that either me or Ms. Corinth is here before they get started. We've changed the positioning a couple of feet,' Sam continued. 'I told them about it, but I want to make sure nobody forgot. You know how it goes.'

'Yeah,' Skip laughed. 'Don't worry about it. I'll take care of it.'

'Thanks, Skip,' Sam said. 'Everything going okay this morning?'

'Right on schedule,' Skip said.

'Good,' Sam said. 'I'll see you later.' He didn't see Leonie working out in the garden, so he turned and walked to the back door of the house, which was open. He knocked on the door frame, but there was no answer. Knowing that Leonie was expecting him, he went on in.

'Leonie?' he called out from the hallway. When there was no answer, he walked on into the kitchen.

No Leonie.

He went on into the dining room and parlor, then the library. Finally, he checked to see that the bathroom was empty. She was nowhere down here.

Bet I know where she is, he thought, suddenly smiling.

He bounded up the stairs, calling her name.

Still no answer.

On the second floor, he continued on up to the third-floor attic, which was quickly being converted into a master suite where she could hole up, as he had promised.

They had already finished the duct work, electrical, and plumbing up here, and had framed out the bathroom, finished the insulating and drywall, being careful to leave the giant old beams exposed to their best advantage. The cupola still worried him though, and he made another mental note to do something about it soon.

He stepped into the giant room and looked around.

It was empty, except for a couple of busy carpenters, who nodded to him then went on about their business.

Where the hell could she be? he wondered. Then he recalled that her car wasn't downstairs in the driveway. In his excitement about seeing her, he'd completely forgotten.

Then he remembered: She's gone to Southampton today, for whatever reason.

He began to circle the huge space, admiring the craftsmanship going into the work. The room was retaining its magical quality, despite the new materials being used to make it a living space.

The light, gray as it was today, poured in through the eight bull's-eye windows and the lantern cupola atop the roof, suffusing the room with a mysterious beauty that was next to impossible to create. Artificially, at least. In this case, Sam mused, Mother Nature and the original architect who had sited the house had worked their magic on Leonie's behalf. He had loved this space since he first saw it with her and could hardly wait to see her in it.

He gave the room a final look, then started back down the stairs again, disappointed that Leonie was not here. He felt a real need to see her today, if only to be in her glowing, vibrant presence. After his last battle with Minette, the peace and ease he felt when he was with Leonie seemed like a kind of salve to the spirit, an anecdote to soothe the world's sharp barbs and stings.

When he got back to the kitchen, he looked for a note from her, hoping to see something that would indicate that she was perhaps thinking of him before she left for Southampton. But there was nothing.

He noticed a coffee mug in the sink, and saw that the coffee maker was still on. The cream and sugar and Sweet 'N Low were still out on the counter. He got a mug out of a cabinet and helped himself to coffee, then stirred in cream and sugar.

'Whoa!' The first sip told him that the coffee was old. Very old. Sludge, in fact. He threw it in the sink and rinsed out the cup.

Jeez, she must have been up at the crack of dawn, he thought. This trip to Southampton must have been pretty important.

Sam watched the workmen through one of the kitchen windows, idly wondering why he was so concerned anyway. After all, he reminded himself, what Leonie Corinth does is none of my business. She's a big girl, and certainly doesn't owe me any explanations for what she's doing. She didn't even have to tell me she was going, for that matter. Or where she's gone.

Besides, he thought, she comes from a world that I know very little about. That I'm not part of at all. A world that she obviously still had a foot firmly planted in. At least from all appearances.

He drew in his gaze, looking at the stacks of magazines, books, and papers on the kitchen table: French and Italian *Vogues*, piled alongside scholarly books on various painters and sculptors, over-size volumes on period furnishings and decorating, catalogues of clothing collections sent to special clients by expensive designers, esoteric-looking novels mixed in with what were some plainly good, old-fashioned 'junk' reads, and several thick engraved vellum invitations to art openings and parties in New York City and Southampton, even London and Paris.

Minette had been rich, but hers was essentially a provincial background with a small, well-to-do circle of 'horsey' friends. Leonie came from New York City and a much more sophisticated, cosmopolitan world and had mixed in rarefied international circles.

Most likely, he told himself, she probably doesn't give me or my world very much thought at all. If she does, she probably doesn't think much of it.

Nevertheless, he could not get her off his mind, could not shake the mental image of her shiny chestnut hair, those black currant eyes, and that long, slender body. The early morning tonic that her cheerful presence always provided left him feeling suddenly lonely . . . as if he were missing something.

Then he realized: I miss her.

And missing her made his problems, serious though they were, seem insignificant in comparison to her absence.

148

N ext stop, Bobby Chandler's: the huge estate where he 'managed to scrape by,' as he laughingly put it, in forty-odd rooms set on seventeen lushly landscaped acres – all by his lonesome, except for the seven full-time staff members to minister to his every need.

As Leonie pulled up to the huge wrought-iron gates, which were swung wide open, as if in welcome – just what she needed after her encounter with the pompous Mr. Henry Reynolds and the scummy Mr. Jeremy Sampson – she couldn't suppress a smile at seeing the name of Bobby's palatial spread spelled out in bronze on the stone piers: Salt Cottage.

Cottage indeed! she thought.

It was one of the magnificent shingle-style mammoths designed by McKim, Mead, and White in the 1880s and 90s for the very rich and very, very social, and Stanford White had done himself particularly proud with this one.

Salt Cottage was a beautifully eccentric showplace, created in a bygone era, but updated by Bobby – with her help – for his very luxurious and contemporary lifestyle. All gabled roofs, huge porches, parades of columns, Palladian windows, it was sheathed in cedar shingles weathered to just the right turn, with pristine white trim, and shutters of the darkest green.

The breathtaking landscaping had been laid out over the last century by some of the world's foremost garden designers. Ancient specimen trees, rose gardens, wisteria arbors, a walled kitchen garden, laburnum pergolas, and lovingly tended perennial beds dotted the grounds.

Set amid the luxuriant foliage were a sculpture court, a croquet lawn, an Olympic-size swimming pool, tennis courts, two small guest houses, staff quarters, a stable with fenced paddocks, and a garage that accommodated twelve cars. Bobby loved speed, whether on the polo grounds or behind the wheel of his Ferrari, Aston Martin, Lamborghini, or any one of the other of his treasured cars. If he was feeling especially adventuresome, he mounted either a Harley-Davidson, a new Ducati, or perfectly preserved old Triumph.

Driving slowly through the short allée created by huge, gnarled old oaks, Leonie felt a mixture of excitement and anxiety. She and Bobby – and Hank – had done a lot of 'living' in this house, and its spirit was closely akin to that of the house she had restored and decorated down the road: the 'love nest' getaway she and Hank had lavished so much attention and money on.

Ha! What a joke that turned out to be, she thought.

She parked in the circular drive up front and eased out of the car, then reached in and grabbed her shoulder bag. Before she could reach the front door, it was opened by Bobby Chandler himself.

'Leonie,' he called out, a big smile on his face.

'Bobby!' she cried, rushing into his outstretched arms.

He drew her into his broad, strong shoulders, and they hugged and kissed cheeks. Any doubts, any minute misgivings, she had harbored about his loyalty and affection were immediately dispelled by the reality of his warm and glowing presence.

'Let me look at you,' she said, standing back, eyeing him up and down. 'More handsome than ever,' she judged with a laugh, noticing that he, too, was in his tennis whites, a once fluffy, now damp white towel draped around his neck.

'And you look beautiful,' Bobby said, offering her his arm.

'Thanks, Bobby,' she said.

Leonie felt gratified because she had made an effort today, for both the lawyer and Bobby – and for myself, she thought – donning an exquisitely soft and lightweight white silk-and-cashmere sweater and crisp white linen trousers, worn with a navy blue linen blazer with big gold buttons. Her feet were shod with navy espadrilles. Her only jewelry was a very thick gold chain at her neck and gold bangle bracelets at her wrists, antique ones studded with small diamonds, rubies, and emeralds set in alternating rounds and diamond shapes.

They sauntered, arm in arm, up the steps and into the house, where the butler appeared.

'Hi, Boyce,' Leonie said.

'Miss Corinth,' Boyce replied, with the hint of a smile on his lips and a nod of his bald café au lait head. 'Shall I take your bag?'

'No, thanks, Boyce,' Leonie answered. 'I'll hang on to it.' How like Boyce to be correct about my name, Leonie thought. He's so correct about everything.

'How's Willie?' she inquired. Willie was his wife, a woman of an ancient, indeterminate age, like Boyce himself, and she was Bobby's first-rate cook.

'She's very well, Miss Corinth,' Boyce replied. 'Thanks for asking.'

'Tell her I'll come visit her in the kitchen today, if that's all right,' Leonie said.

'She surely would appreciate that, Miss Corinth,' Boyce replied.

Then he turned and disappeared on quiet feet through the dining room.

Why is Boyce so . . . restrained today? she wondered. He seemed somehow distant. A tad nervous and . . . hesitant. Or is it just me? she wondered. Probably my paranoia in overdrive, she decided.

'You want to freshen up?' Bobby asked.

'Great,' Leonie said. 'I'll just be in the powder room a minute.'

'I'm going to jump in the shower and rinse off,' Bobby said. 'Sorry. Didn't have time before you got here. Been playing tennis.'

'Don't rush,' Leonie said. 'I'll take a tour of the gardens.'

'Whatever your heart desires. It being such a beautiful day, I thought we'd sit outside,' Bobby said. 'A pitcher of Bloody Marys awaits you out at the pergola, fair maiden. Under the laburnum.'

Leonie laughed. 'Sounds irresistible to me.'

'Then we can do the lunch thing,' Bobby called over his shoulder as he dashed up the stairs. 'Okay?'

'Fine,' Leonie answered.

'Be out in a jiffy,' he assured her.

When she was finished in the powder room, she wandered through the first floor's immense and beautifully furnished rooms.

They had a grand, yet casual, understated air about them. Family treasures, like the magnificently carved and gilded George II Irish console in the entrance hall, were offset by big comfortable chairs and couches covered in striped sailcoth, with touches of flowered chintz here and there. Needlepoint and sisal rugs lay on the parquet floors, and the draperies were all simple, designed to take advantage of the sunlight.

Vases of colorful, fragrant flowers, fresh from the gardens, were everywhere, their beauty repeated in some of the paintings adorning the walls. The overall effect was very light and airy, as befit a summer house on the seaside.

Leonie felt a surge of self-confidence and pride rush through her as she wandered through these rooms. Bobby had helped her, but it

152

had essentially been her ideas and work which had accomplished this peaceful, serene, and beautiful oasis of both luxury and comfort.

It was a look, she knew, that was much copied here in the Hamptons. Probably a lot of other places, too, she thought, since this place had been photographed for a major magazine, as had her own.

Wandering on through the rooms toward the back of the house, Leonie stopped in the terracotta-floored mud room, Bobby's favorite room in the house. She smiled, looking around her, thinking how he had certainly made it his own domain.

The walls sprouted a few hunting trophies – his own, not bought. Stuffed deer heads, antlers, a pheasant or two, and large, glass-eyed fish stared vacantly down at her, and a huge black bear rug growled malevolently from the floor. All very politically incorrect nowadays, but she knew that Bobby couldn't have cared less.

An antique coatrack and wallhooks held coats and jackets, and hats, caps, and helmets for every conceivable type of weather, temperature, and activity. Lined up with military precision on the floor were riding boots, polo boots, hunting boots, wellies, gardening clogs, running shoes, cleated soccer and golf shoes, Roller Blades – practically every sport and activity imaginable represented, Leonie thought.

Huge antique floor stands held umbrellas, riding crops, tennis rackets, polo mallets, lacrosse sticks, fishing tackle, and the like.

Bobby's toys, Leonie mused. Toys he used, too. They weren't for show like in so many of the grand houses New Yorkers owned out here.

Then something caught her eye. There were two pairs of what appeared to be fairly recently splattered riding boots, sitting side by side on the floor. Well, she thought, either Boyce is getting a little negligent in his duties – one pair dirty, okay, but two? – or Bobby had a riding partner she didn't know about.

Odd, she thought. Bobby had always told her about his latest 'loves.' They'd spent many an hour talking about the dates he'd had, the various sexual exploits and conquests. Not the Social Register women he'd squired to parties, but the late-night dates with men he'd seen after all his society obligations were over and done with.

Perhaps, she decided, that's why he hasn't called lately. He'd been too busy with a new partner.

I hope so, Leonie thought. It's just what he needs to give his life a little more focus and . . . maybe a little more meaning.

Then, suddenly feeling like an intrusive voyeur, she quickly dismissed these conjectures from her mind and wandered out the mud room door and on into the garden.

She reached the laburnum pergola, dripping with giant yellow blooms, and headed for the cut-glass pitcher of Bloody Marys and glasses on the white wicker cocktail table. Yummy, she thought. Just what the doctor ordered.

She poured herself a tall drink, sipped, and decided it wasn't too strong. It was just right, in fact. Then she noticed that there were two obviously used glasses on the cocktail table.

My, my, she thought, her eyes full of mischievous glee. Bobby's amour must have left just before I got here. Or could even still be here somewhere.

She settled herself on one of the comfortably cushioned wicker chaise longues – she'd bought the fabric for them herself from the revered Madeleine Castaing in Paris, just before the doyenne of decorators died – and picked up the *New York Times*, but put it back down on the cocktail table again, deciding she didn't really care about the news today.

Her gaze swept the verdancy around her. Bumble bees lurched from flower to flower, and butterflies danced attendance – lots of little solid white ones, some larger brown and orange ones, and a blue and black pair. She was idly watching their frolicking ballet among the flowers when Bobby's voice abruptly jerked her back onto the stone-floored pergola.

'Penny for your thoughts,' he said, coming from behind her. He leaned over the chaise and gave her shoulders a squeeze.

'Nothing, really,' Leonie said. 'I was just watching the butterflies.'

Bobby poured himself a Bloody Mary, then spread out on the lounge next to hers. 'There've been oodles of them this year.'

Leonie looked over at him. Bobby the Bull. His raven black hair was still wet from the shower, and his tanned, muscular body shone with health and vitality. His was a strong, compact body of medium height, packed thickly with rock-hard muscle. His dark-brown eyes more often than not flashed with merriment, but today Leonie detected a slightly tired and apprehensive cast to them.

'Spill the beans, Bobby,' she said. 'What's this nonsense about selling Salt Cottage?'

'I've had an offer I can't refuse,' he said. He sipped his drink, then smiled over at her. 'Twelve million.'

Leonie was stunned. 'Dollars?' she gasped.

Bobby laughed. 'Movie-star dollars,' he said.

'You've got to be kidding,' Leonie said.

'Nope. I'm dead serious.' And he sounded it, she thought. 'In fact there was a bidding war between two big box-office stars. I guess they think that spending beaucoup buckaroos out here will get them into society.' He told her about the bidding war and named the stars – both household names.

'It's incredible what's happening out here,' Leonie said. 'It's like Beverly Hills East. I couldn't afford a shack, if there's one left.'

Bobby looked over at her. 'Do you miss it, Leonie?' he asked seriously.

'Sometimes,' she replied. 'But I'm too busy to think about it most of the time.'

'I don't think you're missing much,' he said. 'It's become a celebrity cesspool, with all that implies. It attracts day-trippers by the busload. Traffic, traffic, and more traffic. There's more silly

155

one-upsmanship than ever, between the old rich, the nouveau riche, West Coast money, and even European money. It's gotten to be so bad, some of the old society matrons are afraid they're going to be seeing tits on the beach. Like St. Tropez.'

Leonie laughed, then turned serious. 'What will you do, Bobby?' she asked. 'I can't imagine you anywhere else.'

'I'm building an ultra-modern place on practically the last piece of beach left. All glass and steel,' he said. 'And small.'

'You!' Leonie laughed. 'Glass and steel! Small!'

'Believe it or not,' he said with dead certainty. 'Something manageable. And everything in this place goes to auction. Everything. To Christie's. They've told me I should see about five million.'

He paused and turned to her with a sudden look of fiery determination in his eyes. 'I'm also quitting the job,' he said. 'I'm sick of Wall Street, investment bankers, the whole bit. I'm retiring, Leonie. I'm going to hunt and fish and play polo and all that.'

Leonie's head spun. This really was news. Bobby had always toed the line, more or less, to please his rich WASP family, and they would not greet the news that he'd decided to retire, still in his thirties, with a great deal of glee. No, indeed. They were firm believers in constantly adding to the already swollen family coffers.

'Have you told your family about this?' she asked.

'Part of it,' he said. 'Not the whole shebang. I'm taking it a step at a time. They'll explode, of course.'

Leonie nodded. 'Knowing them, "explode" is quite an understatement.'

Bobby grinned. 'But you know what?' he said.

'I'm all ears,' she replied.

His grin disappeared, and his voice became a throaty growl. 'I don't give a fuck,' he spat. 'Not anymore. I don't need them or their fucking money.'

Leonie looked at him, seeing a new Bobby. He almost never used coarse language, and never, ever growled.

'I've decided I've got enough,' he continued. 'The stock market's been treating me like a prince, and I've got a new investment advisor who's working miracles. So' – he looked her in the eye – 'screw them.'

Leonie was momentarily nonplussed. She had known that Bobby resented conforming to his family's expectations, but not to this extent. He'd always seemed like a relatively happy and good-natured game player, sometimes even relishing the little subterfuges and schemes that keeping his secrets required.

'Well,' she finally said, 'I hope it all works out for the best, Bobby.'

'It will,' he said.

'How about the rest of your life?' she ventured. 'Are things going smoothly? I mean . . . is there . . .'

'Anybody new?' he finished for her.

'Now that you mention it.' She laughed.

'Ummm,' he said noncommittally. 'I guess you could say that.'

Leonie looked at him. 'Oh, come on, Bobby,' she cajoled. 'Tell me. This is Leonie, remember?'

He looked away, suddenly studying his fingernails intensely. Uncharacteristically, he seemed to shut down and close up, to drift off into another, faraway world all his own, leaving Leonie in a void.

'Bobby?' she softly ventured.

'I'd rather not talk about it, Leonie,' he said slowly, but with conviction in his voice.

'Of course. I'm sorry. I didn't mean to pry,' she said apologetically.

Then he turned to her, and his face brightened. 'Let's talk about you,' he said, with renewed good humor. 'Are you happy up there? Making friends?'

'Yes,' she said, 'and yes. The house is coming along swimmingly. I think you'd really like it. And my friend, Mossy, and I have become very close. Like soul sisters, really. And . . .'

She paused, hesitant to continue, uncertain of how revealing she should be.

'I think I smell a man,' Bobby said.

'Well . . .' Leonie muttered.

'I definitely smell a man,' he said, his voice full of mischievous laughter. 'Right?'

'Yes and no,' Leonie finally said. 'I . . . I have met someone, but . . . oh, God. I'm just not ready for anything, Bobby.'

'That's understandable,' he said.

'I don't know. I just feel so unsure of myself, of my feelings. Even being a good friend is difficult for me at this point. After Hank—'

'A little shell-shocked?' he broke in quickly.

'You might say that,' she said. 'I still wonder what the hell happened. Just seeing him today—'

'Hey.' Bobby interrupted her again. 'I'm starving, aren't you?'

'I'm getting there,' Leonie said. She was both surprised and somewhat irritated that Bobby obviously didn't want to hear what she had to say.

He was getting to his feet. 'I think I'll tell Boyce to start serving,' he said. 'Table's all set, out by the swimming pool. Meet you there?'

'Sure,' Leonie said. 'Meet you there.'

Leonie watched as Bobby turned and sauntered off, toward the house. His macho stride didn't amuse her today.

What's with him? she wondered. Something is not right. No, not right at all. He's not the old caring and listening Bobby Chandler. He's not the Bobby who would ordinarily have leapt at any juicy tidbit of gossip. Not the forthcoming Bobby who was always anxious to share everything with her, secrets included. He was, in fact, unrecognizable.

Perplexed, she got up, set her drink down on the cocktail table, and grabbed her shoulder bag, then decided to head on over to the swimming pool. She could wash her hands and check her makeup in the pool house.

She ambled slowly through the gardens, admiring the profusion of summer blooms. When she reached the pool house, she walked through the neoclassical portico at its façade, engulfed in the heady fragrance of the climbing roses which practically obscured it from view. Old-fashioned pink roses, full to bursting, their fallen petals lavishly embroidering the lawn and stone floor.

She opened one of the French doors and went inside, surprised to see that Bobby had turned the party room into a gym. He used to have a gym in a room up on the third floor of the house.

What a clever choice this is, Leonie thought. It's light and airy out here, and part of the year, at least, you only had to open the doors to take a dip in the pool after working up a sweat.

Making a beeline for one of the bathrooms, something caught her attention. Out of the corner of her eye, she noticed a big black leather gym bag on one of the bench presses. It looked awfully familiar, with its gleaming gilt-embossed initials twinkling up at her from a few paces away.

She stepped closer, and—

—oh, God, no!

Leonie stepped back as if a poisonous snake had slithered out of the bag and raised its head, forked tongue protruding evilly, to strike out at her.

This can't be happening, she thought. This cannot be happening.

Her heart pounded in her chest, and her pulse raced. She thought for a moment she would be sick. Then, taking a few deep breaths, she steadied herself. I must be mistaken, she thought. It's a trick of the eye, that's all. It's got to be.

After a few moments, her breathing returned to normal, and she stepped forward again, and looked closer.

HWR, the gold initials very clearly and definitely spelled out.

Henry Wilson Reynolds.

A hand flew to her mouth, and she uttered a cry. There could be no doubt in Leonie's mind:

This is the very same gym bag I gave Hank for his birthday two years ago.

She reached out and grabbed the bench press for support, knocking over the tennis racket propped against it. The tennis racket clattered to the floor, and Leonie leaned down and picked it up, leaning it back against the bench press where it had been.

Undeniably, the tennis racket Hank gave himself for the same birthday.

Leonie slumped down onto the bench press next to the bag, putting her elbows on her knees, her head in her hands. She sat there for several minutes, her mind a maelstrom of conflicting thoughts and feelings, unable to focus on any one thing, too stunned to cry.

Slowly her racing heart slowed its pace, and she began to feel a sort of numbness come over her, replacing the agitation she felt within.

Suddenly, many of the horrors of the last few months began to make sense, as realization dawned, full blown and malevolent.

Hank and Bobby Chandler are lovers. It's as simple as that, she thought. My husband left me for my best friend. An old story. Only in this case the other woman happens to be a man.

Suddenly, throaty laughter slowly began to rise from deep within her, then it shook her entire body, and finally filled the pool house with its raucous roar. She shocked even herself with her loud and inappropriate outburst of seeming merriment in the face of such betrayal.

That good old cosmic fly swatter! she thought. Yes, that's what it is. Another swat from that good old cosmic fly swatter. You can count on that if nothing else.

When she finally managed to control herself, her mind whirled once again with all the puzzle pieces that, put together, rendered this picture. All the clues that had been there, but she had overlooked, never suspecting a betrayal of this sort.

At last, she slowly stood up and strode purposefully into the bathroom, where she brushed her hair, washed her hands, and checked her makeup. Just a little lipstick, she thought. That'll do it. She took a tube of Beyond Bordeaux out and applied it carefully, then blotted, checked her face in the mirror again, and was ready.

She shouldered her bag, squared her shoulders, and walked out of the pool house and around to the opposite end of the pool, where Bobby was sprawled out at the table, under a big market umbrella.

When he saw her, he started getting to his feet. 'There you are,' he said. 'I was beginning to wonder where—'

He saw the expression on Leonie's face and fell silent.

'Don't get up,' Leonie said mildly.

'What is it, Leonie?' he asked. 'You look like you've seen a ghost.'

'Not a ghost, Bobby,' she replied. 'The truth.'

He stared at her with a baffled expression. 'What . . . what are you talking about?' he finally asked.

'I think you know what I'm talking about,' Leonie said softly. 'You and Hank.'

She watched as his body went rigid and his face drained of color beneath its sunny tan. After a few moments, he visibly relaxed, but remained silent.

'You know I've loved you like a brother, Bobby,' she continued. 'You were my best friend, or so I thought.'

'And I've loved you, too, Leonie,' Bobby replied earnestly.

'Maybe,' she said, with a sigh. 'As long as it suited you and your purposes. But you don't treat those you love so shabbily.' She

161

paused and took a breath. 'I wish you could have found it in your heart to be honest with me. Maybe ... maybe it wouldn't hurt quite so much.'

'I'm sorry, Leonie,' he said.

'I guess in your own way you really are.' She stared at him for a long moment in silence. 'Well,' she finally said, 'I'm going to get on my way. I wish you both great happiness.'

Leonie left him sitting there, turned and walked rapidly away from the pool, through the gardens, around the house, and to her car. She quickly opened the door, threw her shoulder bag in, slid onto the seat after it, and started the engine.

Driving down the short allée to the gates, tears began to well up in her eyes. She brushed at them with her fingertips, and thought: I didn't even get the boxes I came for. Oh, well, fuck it! He's rich. He can send them.

13

The house was in near darkness, only the glow of a small reading lamp in the parlor giving any indication of life. Rain thrashed relentlessly at the windows like hail, and thunder crashed menacingly as the heavens opened up. Lightning, at once spectacular and frightening, flashed in the windows and reflected off the mirror over the fireplace, which magnified its powerful light.

It was a summer storm of such awesomeness that it intensified Leonie's already powerful feelings of vulnerability.

She lay on the daybed in the near dark, propped up on elaborately fringed pillows made from fragments of a lustrous antique Lyonnaise silk. A glass of Pouilly-Fuissé sat on the table beside her. Preoccupied as she had been with her own thoughts, the storm's sheer ferocity and pyrotechnical majesty now distracted her, brought her out of herself. Somewhere a loose shutter flapped a hard tattoo against the house, propelled by the vicious wind which accompanied the storm.

I've got to get up and try to see where it is, she thought. Tomorrow

I can have a workman properly secure it. Then she remembered that all the shutters had been removed for repairs and scraping and painting. What the hell could it be, then? she wondered. I've got to get up and go see.

But she didn't get up. The effort seemed too much for her right now. Her body, like her spirits, felt leaden, dead weight that she couldn't lift. Even raising the sweating glass of cool wine to her lips seemed an exertion she could hardly perform.

A brilliant flash flooded the room in a surreal blue-white light for a moment, and seconds later a tremendous boom of thunder seemed to shake the house to its very foundations, further unnerving her, physically and emotionally spent though she thought she already was.

Leonie shivered involuntarily, then reached down and grasped at a cashmere throw where it lay folded neatly at the foot of the daybed, pulling it up over her all the way to her chin with both hands, as if it would offer her protection from any harm. Then she reached an arm out and picked up her wine. She took a long sip, then set the glass back down and pulled her arm under the cover again.

She had thought about calling Mossy when she got back from Southampton, but decided against it. I would certainly not be good company, she thought. Besides, Mossy has listened to my divorce woes enough as it is, and I don't want to burden her further.

She was exhausted from the drive down to Southampton and back. It was a long trip any day, but today the drive back had been like a roller-coaster ride in some mad carnival in hell.

Her laughter at discovering the truth about her ex-husband and her former best friend had quickly disappeared, to be replaced by an overwhelming sense of betrayal and loss. And it had triggered renewed doubts about her own poor sense of judgment and her own fragile sense of self-worth.

Tears of sorrow and anger had come in fits and starts, forcing her to pull off the road several times until she could get her emotions in check. She had wondered more than once if she would ever get back home to the safety of her own little nest, construction site though it may be.

Now that she was here, Leonie felt immobilized, almost paralyzed from the emotional events of the day. And try as she might, she hadn't been able to snap herself out of it. She hadn't even bothered to bathe or change clothes when she got back – she felt that leaden.

The room was suddenly bathed in an eerie blue-white flash of light again, then another deafening crash of thunder sent tremors through the house. The reading lamp on the table next to her went out.

Oh, God no, Leonie thought. This is just what I need. All alone, an emotional wreck, and Mother Nature decides to bring the house crashing down around me.

Candles. I've got to get candles, she told herself. Somewhere in a kitchen drawer.

Before she could rouse herself from the daybed, she noticed lights – different lights, not lightning – bobbing and waving yellow in the rain-streaked windows. They seemed to be circling around to the back of the house, first flashing in the dining room windows, then the kitchen. She couldn't hear a car because of the storm, but she was certain that was what it was.

She sat up straighter, wondering who on earth could be coming to see her at this time of night. Mossy, perhaps? No, surely not. Not in this storm, and not without calling first. If not, who then?

The lights disappeared, and a moment later there was a pounding on the back door, barely audible above the furious roar of the tempest.

I can't answer it, Leonie thought. Whoever it is will just have to go away. I look too awful to let anybody see me. She lay still, waiting for the knocking to cease, but it didn't.

Then suddenly it occurred to her that it might be someone in trouble. What if there had been an accident on the highway? What if someone needed to use the telephone? What if—

Oh, hell, she decided, I have to answer it.

She got up from the daybed, letting the cashmere throw fall to the floor, then slipped into her thongs and carefully made her way through the parlor, out into the hallway, and down it to the back door in the darkness.

When she got there, she unlocked the door and opened it to see a drenched and worried-looking Sam Nicholson standing there.

'Sam!' she said, pulling the door wide. 'Hurry up, get in here.'

Another flash of lightning rent the sky, followed by an ear-splitting clap of thunder.

Leonie quickly closed the door behind him, and turned around. 'You're soaked!' she said.

'I know.' Sam grinned, and stood there in the dark, dripping water. 'I know it's late,' he said, 'but I was passing by and thought I would stop on the chance that you might be back. You weren't here this morning, and I . . . well, I was just wondering how your trip went. If you got back safely in the storm.'

Leonie's previous state of paralysis instantly dissolved, and her bluest of moods evaporated as if a particularly generous fairy god-mother had waved a magic wand over her, only to be replaced by a quickening pulse and a heartbeat that made her feel almost breath-less. The mere sight of him, she thought, still makes me totally irra-tional. On another level, she was deeply touched by his wanting to see her, for she knew instinctively that that was why he was here.

He wants to see me, she thought. That's all there is to it.

'I've got to get candles,' she said. 'The lights just went out. Come on in.'

'I'll get water everywhere,' he said.

'It's okay,' she assured him. 'You can take off your boots in the kitchen, and I'll get a towel for you.'

He shook out of his lightweight rain jacket and hung it on a wallhook, then followed her into the kitchen where she was rummaging around in a drawer for candles.

166

'Eureka!' she cried. 'Found them. Now for some matches.' Her fingers scrabbled around in the drawer until they struck paydirt. 'Aha! Matches.'

She lit a candle and put it in a holder on the kitchen table, then lit three more off it until both candleholders burned brightly. She turned to Sam and saw that he had sat down and was unlacing his boots.

'Just put them on that old rag rug,' Leonie said. 'Would you like a glass of wine?'

'That'd be great,' Sam said. He put his soaked boots on the rug, and then watched her get out a wineglass and fill it from the opened bottle of Pouilly-Fuissé on the kitchen counter. She seemed to shimmer in the candlelight, her dark hair a lustrous contrast to her pure white sweater and slacks, the gemstones in her bracelets picking up the light and glinting as she moved about.

'Sit back down,' she said. 'I'll just get my glass.' Leonie retrieved her wine from the parlor and returned to the kitchen, where she joined him at the table. She poured a generous measure into her glass and turned to him. 'Cheers,' she said, clinking glasses with Sam.

'Cheers to you,' he replied, smiling. They both sipped at the dry white wine.

She thought he had never looked so handsome or so boyishly virile as he did now, sitting there in the candlelight, drenched as he was from head to toe in rain.

'Oh, I forgot,' she said. 'A towel.' She set her glass down on the table and hurried off in the near-darkness to the bathroom, where she grabbed a big white towel, returned, and handed it to him. 'Now, dry off,' she said. 'Get comfortable.'

She sat down herself and watched him as he vigorously rubbed the towel through his hair and over his face and neck, then his arms, the light dancing over his features.

'How did it go today?' she asked, taking another sip of her wine.

'Fine,' Sam said. 'I don't know whether you saw it or not. But you've got a very big hole out there for the swimming pool.'

'No!' Leonie said. 'I didn't get back until late, and I didn't even look out there, so I missed it.'

'It won't take long to finish if the weather clears up,' he said. 'And that'll be the last of the digging outside.' He looked at her and smiled. 'Which I know will please you.'

'You mean it's not going to look like World War II out there forever? All trenches and mountains of dirt and rock? I don't think I can live without them,' she joked. 'I'd become rather fond of the look.'

They both laughed.

'And,' Sam said, 'I think you'll be pleased to know that maybe . . . just maybe, in the next few days, we'll be able to move you upstairs to the third floor where you'll have more privacy.'

Leonie looked at him with surprise. 'So soon?' she said. 'Do you really think so?'

'There'll be some things to iron out, a lot of finish work to do,' he said, 'but I think it's safe to say that this time next week you'll be ensconced upstairs.'

'That is good news,' Leonie said. 'I'll be out of the way.'

'There's something else,' Sam said. 'You want to bring a candle and have a look?'

'Sure,' she said. 'At least I think so. What is it?'

Sam smiled. 'A little surprise,' he said. 'Just come with me.'

He got to his feet and picked up a candleholder.

'Where're we going?' Leonie asked.

'Just into the library,' Sam said.

She got up and took the other candleholder and followed him out to the hallway and on into the library. They cast giant shadows across the walls and ceilings, padding along in the dark, being cautious with their candles.

In the library, Leonie watched as Sam held his candleholder over an enormous stack of – what? It appeared to her to be a great pile of ruined old windows. What on earth? she wondered.

Sam turned to her, a questioning look on his face. 'Can you guess what these are?' he asked.

'Windows,' Leonie answered. 'Horrible, disgusting, useless, ugly old windows!'

'Exactly,' Sam said. 'But take a closer look. I think maybe the glass will interest you.'

Leonie got closer with her candle and studied the filthy glass. It was only an instant before she jerked up, spilling hot candle tallow onto the floor.

She turned to Sam. 'I don't believe it!' she said excitedly. 'I simply don't believe it!'

'Believe it,' Sam said, grinning.

'Where?' she asked. 'Where on earth did you find them?'

'At an old wreckage warehouse upriver in Troy,' he said. Then he added: 'For next to nothing.'

'My Lord,' Leonie said. 'When did you do this?'

'Today,' Sam replied, 'while you were gone. After the pool people got here and we went over the changes again, I took off up there on the chance that they might have some old windows. They did, and I had them delivered this afternoon late.'

'Oh, this is fabulous, Sam,' Leonie said. 'It's old and wavy glass just like those cracked panes in the cupola. It'll be so perfect.'

'Yes,' he said, 'that's the idea. I can get a glazier to cut it and fit it here. Less risk of damage. I'll get the guys to take it upstairs tomorrow.'

Leonie looked at him in the candlelight and saw the excitement, the enthusiasm, and pleasure on his face. He looks like I feel, she thought.

'Sam, you're amazing,' she said. 'This was really above and beyond the call of duty. Thanks a million. This is just the kind of thing that makes a world of difference.'

'Yes,' he said, 'it does. Well ...' He shrugged. '... How about that wine?'

'Yes,' Leonie said. 'Although if I had it on hand, we should have some celebratory champagne.'

They walked back to the kitchen and sat down at the table. Leonie picked up her wineglass. 'To you,' she said, 'and to the fabulous old—'

She abruptly stopped talking and lowered her wineglass when there was another violent flash of lightning, followed by a deafening peal of thunder which seemed to be directly overhead. Rain hammered against the house with renewed intensity.

'My God,' Leonie said. 'This is downright scary.'

'I'll protect you,' Sam said, after taking a drink of the Pouilly-Fuissé.

Leonie looked across the table, searching his face for humor, but the expression she saw there was earnest and truthful. He's not joking, she thought. She smiled at him, then quickly changed the subject.

'Sorry I didn't leave a telephone number or anything this morning,' she said. 'I know I should in case I'm needed for a decision, but I left in such a rush. I ... I had to go down to Southampton and sign some paperwork.'

'I know,' Sam said. 'You told me.'

'Oh, I'd forgot,' Leonie said.

'Was it a good trip?' he asked matter-of-factly.

Leonie hesitated. She really didn't want to discuss the trip or what had transpired; its emotional sting was still too fresh, too livid, in her mind. She took a sip of her wine, then set the glass down.

'Let's just say that this has definitely not been my day,' she replied.

'I didn't mean to pry,' he said, looking at her curiously. In the candlelight, he suddenly saw that her eyes were puffy and red. She had apparently been crying before he got here, and he hadn't even noticed it before because of the lightning. Sam felt a stitch in his chest, as if his heart actually ached for her, and every protective instinct in his body was aroused and reached out to her. He stretched an arm across the table and placed his hand atop hers.

'I've stopped by at an awkward time, haven't I?' he said softly.

Leonie shook her head. 'It's okay,' she said, but tears welled up unbidden in her eyes. Why am I suddenly weepy? she asked herself. But she knew that after the awful ordeal of her trip, his kindness and gentleness to her were especially moving, and his touch was warm and comforting . . . Oh, God, she thought, it's everything I need right now.

Sam reached his other hand over, now clasping hers in both of his. 'I don't know what's upset you,' he said, 'but if there's anything I can do, I'll be glad to.'

She closed her eyes and shook her head again, biting down on her lower lip in an effort to stem the flow of tears she felt certain was imminent. When they started to spill, she abruptly jerked away and stood up, turning around and placing her hands on the kitchen counter, facing away from him.

Sam got up and walked around the table to her. He could see her body shake convulsively as she silently wept. He slowly and gently encircled her with his arms and hugged her ever so lightly to him. 'Leonie, don't cry,' he whispered. 'I'm here for you.'

Her tremors gradually ceased as he held her, as she heard his tender whispers and felt his warm breath on her neck, but she didn't trust herself to speak.

'I . . . well, I can't stand seeing you sad,' Sam said earnestly.

He sounds entirely serious, Leonie thought. As if he really means it.

He slowly turned her to face him, and delicately traced a hand down her cheek, brushing her hair away from her face with his fingertips. He looked into her eyes. 'Tell me,' he said. 'Please, tell me what hurts.'

171

Leonie looked up into his intense and pleading turquoise eyes. I can trust him, she thought. Yes, I'm certain that I can trust him. After a moment, she emitted a sigh. 'I just ... well, I just had a very saddening experience today,' she said.

'Please,' he persisted, 'tell me about it, Leonie. Maybe it will help you to talk about it.'

Leonie abruptly and uncharacteristically made a quick, on-the-spot decision. He's right, she decided. It would help me to talk about it.

'Let's go into the parlor,' she said. 'We can get comfortable in there on the daybed.'

Sam drew back and smiled at her. 'Good,' he said. He put an arm around her shoulders, and squeezed her reassuringly, then reached over and picked up a candleholder from the kitchen table. They picked up their wineglasses, and Leonie grabbed the bottle of wine. In silence, they walked together into the parlor.

There was the rumble of thunder, now distant, and the rain, though it had slacked off, still beat in a steady rhythm against the windowpanes.

Sam put the candleholder down on the table next to the daybed, then turned to Leonie, as if for direction.

She set the wine bottle down next to the candleholder and perched on the daybed with her glass, patting the spot next to her.

Sam sat down beside her, then looked into her eyes. 'Now,' he said, 'tell me what's making you so sad.'

And Leonie did. She talked and talked, quietly and without tears, pouring her heart out to him. She gave him a quick sketch of her marriage to Hank, their subsequent divorce, told him about her friendship with Bobby Chandler, and finally related the events that had transpired earlier in the day.

Sam listened intently, holding her all the while, with an arm around her shoulder, gently stroking her hair, her arms, giving her reassuring little squeezes. Savoring the feel of her next to him.

When Leonie finished, she looked up at him and said: 'So there you have it, Poor Little Leonie's Sad Little Story.' She laughed self-deprecatingly.

'You're absolutely certain about the two of them?' Sam asked seriously.

'Oh, yes,' she said. 'First, Bobby denied nothing, which was as good as admitting the affair. Believe me, if Bobby wasn't involved, he'd have let me know in no uncertain terms. Like shouting it to the world from the rooftops. That's Bobby. I think . . .' She paused for a moment, and looked at Sam with a curious expression.

'You know,' she finally said, 'I think Bobby actually wanted me to know what was going on, but didn't want to confront me. He was afraid to.'

'Why do you say that?' he asked.

'Oh, because he was careless, which is totally out of character. Allowing Hank to leave his gym bag and tennis stuff in the pool house. An extra pair of riding boots – custom-made boots, dead ringers for Hank's – in the mud room. Strong indications, if not proof positive, that something was going on. Something out of the ordinary. They were never tennis partners, and they never rode together, either.'

She paused thoughtfully for a moment, then looked over at Sam and continued. 'In fact, come to think of it, they'd always kept a certain distance from each other – at least while I was around.'

'So they weren't such good buddies until after the divorce,' Sam said. 'At least as far as you know,' he added.

'Exactly,' Leonie replied. She appeared lost in thought again, then nodded her head and went on.

'It also sheds a lot of light on other things,' she said.

'What do you mean?' Sam asked.

'Well, the divorce makes more sense in terms of why Hank wanted out. I mean, there was no other woman, nothing like that.

173

He simply – and I thought a little mysteriously – popped up one day and wanted out.'

'And you were suspicious about his motives,' Sam said.

'Yes,' Leonie said. 'Because there didn't seem to be any. Of course, now I know better.' She looked at Sam with an expression of certainty on her face.

'But most importantly,' she went on, 'it explains how Hank so easily managed to videotape Bobby and myself, cavorting in the bedroom like sex-crazed idiots. I'd always wondered how he'd done it, but I got so caught up in the divorce proceedings I never really thought about it much. Anyway, now I know. It was all staged by the two of them.'

'That's revolting,' he said.

'Well, it sho' ain't the way to treat a friend, is it?' she replied. 'But you know what the worst thing of all is?'

'What?'

'I gave in to Hank's divorce demands so easily because I didn't want Bobby dragged into it,' she said. 'Hank threatened to use the videotape, which made me look very bad.'

'Yeah, but the whole thing—' Sam began.

'Wait. Let me finish,' Leonie continued. 'My only defense if he did use it against me was to counter that Bobby is gay. You see?'

Sam nodded.

'Well, Bobby certainly didn't want his sexuality exposed in court for the press to get hold of. He's a closet case, and it would have been terrible for him to be exposed like that to his family and friends and business colleagues. So I didn't defend myself at all, thinking that was the only way to protect Bobby.'

Leonie paused again, and looked up at Sam, her eyes suddenly fiery. 'I've got a little bit of the fighter in me, you know? But I just caved in to Hank's wishes without a peep.'

'And Bobby was in cahoots with Hank all the while,' Sam said.

'Exactly,' she said emphatically. 'The one person I thought I could rely on betrayed me.'

'It must feel very strange, knowing that your husband left you for a man,' Sam said.

'No,' Leonie said. 'Not really. I've seen that happen. But what I do feel . . . well, I still feel like I can't trust my judgment. I fell in love with a man and married him. I believed in him, trusted him, and thought he was always honest, at least with me. How could I have been so wrong?'

'Maybe you weren't,' Sam said. 'Maybe he . . . maybe he changed. Maybe he didn't know he was gay. It happens, you know.'

'You're right,' Leonie said. 'But that doesn't account for him treating me so shabbily in the divorce. I still have a hard time believing in myself, much less anybody else. I feel as if all my instincts have gone awry . . . as if they've short-circuited or something.'

Sam grinned and gave her a squeeze. 'I don't think you're guilty of any short-circuited instincts,' he said with amusement in his voice. 'I think they're probably pretty damn good.'

Leonie smiled. 'Maybe,' she said. 'I don't really know anymore.' She paused a moment, then said: 'But I . . . I really appreciate your listening to me, Sam. It's meant a lot to me.'

Sam looked into her black currant eyes and gave her a hug. 'I'm really glad that you felt like you could talk to me. I can't even believe this is happening,' he said in a whisper. 'That a woman like you would give me the time of day, much less confide in me. I feel honored, Leonie. That you've let me into your life.'

She looked at him with genuine surprise on her face. 'Why in the world would you say that, Sam? I mean, look at yourself! You're kind and gentle and thoughtful and understanding. Think about what you did for me today. Who on earth would have done what you did? Going out and finding that glass for me? Huh? Nobody. At least not that I've ever met. Any woman in her right mind would want you!'

'Well,' he mumbled, 'it's just that you come from such a different world. You know. Rich, sophisticated, high society, and all that. There's a big difference between being rich in the local set around here and mixing with the kind of people you have. I'm just a poor farm boy from over in the Berkshires, and I do mean poor. You're a big city woman and all.'

'Phoo-ey!' Leonie cried, laughing gleefully. 'I can see that you don't really know me at all.'

'What?' he said, smiling at her. 'What's so damn funny?'

Her laughter swelled, richly and mellifluously, filling the room.

'Come on,' Sam said, giving her arm a light shake. 'What? What?'

When she finally controlled her merriment, Leonie said, 'It's . . . it's just that . . . well, you've got it so wrong, Sam.'

He looked at her in surprise. 'I do?'

'Yes,' she replied, 'you do.' She looked at him with a serious expression. 'You certainly do. I grew up in New York City, yes. But not the New York City you're thinking of. It was a tenement in the worst part of the East Village – a fifth-floor walkup. Bathtub in the kitchen, shared toilet down the hall. Most of the neighborhood looked like something in Vietnam. All burned-out, boarded-up buildings.'

He looked surprised. 'You're pulling my leg, right?' he said.

'No, Sam,' she said, 'I'm not. My family was very loving, but we were anything but rich. We barely scraped by. My papa was a lawyer, yes, but a civil rights lawyer. He did lots of pro bono work, always defending minorities, the poorest of the poor, bringing them home to eat with us half the time.'

'I don't believe it,' he said.

'Believe it,' Leonie answered. 'My mama was like Mother Courage, always with a pot of soup bubbling away on the kitchen stove. My friends used to laugh about it – the bottomless soup pot, they called it – wondering what year she'd started the soup. They'd never been there when it wasn't on. There was a running joke about never eating Mama's soup.'

Leonie paused, smiling at the memory. 'They were wonderful people, wonderful to everybody and me, but when they died the only thing I inherited was their debts – and the love they'd given me.'

She looked at him levelly. 'And a good sense of values, too, I think.'

'That I can see,' Sam said. 'But the rest? I would never have believed it. You seem so . . .'

'Like an uptown lady?' Leonie supplied, smiling up at him.

'Yes,' he replied. 'Definitely an uptown lady.'

'Well, the crowd I ended up running around with – the high society set – was something I was certainly not born to, as you can see. I met Hank in college and our rise, if you want to call it that, in the social world, came naturally with his work. The richer and more powerful he got, the richer and more powerful our friends became.'

'Yeah, but you fit right in, didn't you,' he said, a wisp of a smile on his lips.

'Well, his friends' wives liked my style, my decorating abilities, and so on,' Leonie said. 'But I never really felt like a part of that set. Oh, sure, I mixed and mingled, and I have a couple of friends – and a lot of acquaintances – among them. I just never really felt like I belonged.'

'You didn't like them?' he asked.

'I'm not knocking them,' Leonie answered. 'Money and power are great, if you know how to use them. But if you're just living for the next party like a lot of the women, even some of the men . . . well, that's definitely not my style. I guess I always marched to a different drummer. Anyway, whatever polish I have is something I've acquired along the way.'

She looked over at him with a sardonic expression. 'So you see, I'm just an East Village girl who made good,' she said. 'Then nearly went bust again with the divorce.'

Sam hugged her to him again, tighter. 'You seem like a survivor to me,' he said.

'That I am,' Leonie said.

'And it seems to me like you're surviving pretty damn well,' he said.

'I would tend to agree with you right now,' Leonie said, loving the feeling of his arm around her. She looked at him thoughtfully. 'I think you're surviving quite well, too. For a poor farm boy.'

The smile on his face faded. 'Yes and no,' he said. 'I married money, as you've no doubt heard since there are no secrets out here in the country. But my marriage is . . . well, it's pretty miserable at best.'

Leonie knew that the stories Mossy had told her must be true, that Sam must be married in name only. 'Do you want to talk about it?' she asked.

He shook his head. 'No,' he said. Then he looked at her. 'I'm having a wonderful time here with you. I hope you are, too.'

'Yes,' Leonie said softly. 'I'm having the best time I've had in . . . I don't even remember when.'

'Do you feel better now?' Sam whispered.

'That, too,' she said. 'Talking to you has really helped, Sam. I wish I knew how to thank you.'

She looked up into his eyes, and she knew without any doubt that she was completely besotted with this man, that she was ready to give herself to him wholeheartedly, that she wanted him to know her as she wanted to know him. It was just as she had suspected the very first time she had seen him.

14

S am pulled her closer to him, gently, with his powerful arm. Soon, she felt his lips delicately brush first her hair, then the side of her creamy neck. She could feel his breath upon her there, and a fire ignited within her.

He gradually turned her to face him, then lifted her face to his and looked into her eyes. She returned his gaze, and felt the fire inside her begin to gather strength and heat.

There was a barely perceptible smile on his face, and he whispered: 'I want to kiss away your sadness, Leonie. I want to kiss away all of your doubts about yourself.' And his lips found her dark, dark eyes, delicately brushing them, caressing them, one at a time.

The fire within her mounted, and an urgency she didn't think she had ever known, ever felt, roared through her now, consuming her in a rapture of impassioned flames. She put her arms around him and drew him closer, relishing the strong, hard, masculine feel of his body against hers.

She moaned aloud as his mouth sought out hers, his tongue

grazing her lips, then parting them, searching, exploring, devouring her. His powerful hands moved up and down her back, pressing her ever closer to him.

She hungrily returned his kisses, his embrace, giving herself up to this carnal pleasure, feeling that it was surely meant to be. That to deny herself would be unnatural, blasphemous even.

He gently lowered her back onto the daybed, and they lay there, side by side.

Now his hands stroked her tight round buttocks and pushed them, firmly pressing her against his manhood.

Leonie gasped at the stirring hardness straining against his jeans, and Sam pulled back, drawing a ragged breath.

She looked into his vibrant turquoise eyes and reached up with a hand to stroke his sun-kissed hair, running a finger across the scar on the bridge of his nose, relishing the stubble on his firm jawline. He took her hand in his, kissing her fingers, licking them slowly, then opening his mouth and taking them in, stroking them with his tongue.

Leonie threw her head back, delighting in the sensations he created in her, when she suddenly felt him remove her hand as his mouth sought out her neck. He kissed and licked her from ear to ear, sucked at her creamy skin, slowly trailing down her long thin neck to her chest. He pulled down on her sweater, revealing the hint of cleavage barely exposed above her bra. His hands moved up now, to her breasts, where he pushed them up, all the while kissing and licking.

'Oh, Sam,' she moaned. 'Oh, that feels so good.'

He kissed and licked furiously, carried away on a carnal tide of pleasure that matched her own. After wondrous long minutes, he brought his head up and once again sought out her mouth, devouring her ravenously, like a man starved. His hands were all over her now, caressing, exploring idling at her breasts and the precious mound between her thighs.

Leonie felt the dampness there, in her most private place, and knew inexorably that she must have him, that she must have him in her – now!

He sat up again, then got to his feet, off the daybed. He reached out a hand to her and pulled her up, then began kissing her again, lightly, on the mouth, drawing back as he pulled her sweater up over her head. He flung it on the daybed, and helped her out of her slacks. They rustled into a heap on the floor, and Leonie stepped out of them, kicking them aside. Then Sam encircled her in his arms and began kissing her again as he took off her bra. He let it fall to the floor and watched as her breasts leapt free, their nipples ripe strawberries against the cream of her skin. He took them in his hands and caressed them gently, then leaned over and began kissing and licking them.

Leonie gasped with pleasure, running her fingers through his hair, as he continued to kiss and lick down her chest to her flat stomach. Slowly he eased down on one knee now, his ravenous lips and tongue never leaving her body, even as he peeled the darkly shimmering pantyhose sensually down to her ankles.

Leonie's legs trembled ever so slightly as she stepped out of her hose, lifting one foot at a time, his fingers so light and nimble that she could feel the barest whisper of his touch. He tossed them away. All the while she could feel the warmth of his breath on her thighs, on her mound.

Totally naked, she stood before him and watched as he stood, his turquoise eyes traveling up and down her body from head to toe, drinking in her naked magnificence, those haunted eyes of his smiling now with anticipation. Her skin was smooth and glowed healthily. Her breasts were high and, though not large, were well-shaped. Her waist was small, her stomach tight. Her hips were narrow, but beautifully curved, and her legs were long and well-shaped. She stood there with a kind of pride in herself, a confidence which was her own, but which was increased by the obvious pleasure he took in her.

He took a step toward her, and wrapped her in his arms again and kissed her deeply and with renewed urgency, then drew back and began to undress himself.

Leonie sat down on the daybed and quickly slipped her jewelry off and put it on the table, then watched him pull off his still-damp polo shirt, which he dropped to the floor. His lean, tanned body gleamed in the candlelight, his muscles etched out as in a classical bas relief. She watched their sensuous, rippling movement as he unbuttoned his snug Levi's and peeled them off, then removed one sock at a time, before finally unselfconsciously taking off his jockey shorts.

Her eyes widened when she saw his manhood, engorged with lust and splendid to behold as he stood before her naked.

Sam reached down and pulled her up to him. His lips closed over hers, and he kissed her deeply again. She moved her arms around his neck, glorying in the feel of his nakedness against her, the taste of him, the smell of his masculinity.

Sam guided her to the bed and lowered her down onto its soft, silk cover. It felt cool and sensuous against her back. He slid on top of her, careful not to hurt her, then feasted on her mouth for long moments.

'I've wanted you since the moment I first laid eyes on you,' he whispered to her.

'Me, too,' Leonie breathed. 'I . . . I've wanted you . . . so much.' And it was true, she thought. She had never wanted anyone so much.

Then his tongue began traveling from her mouth to her neck and slowly down to her breasts, where it darted moistly into the cleft, then encircled each nipple in turn. He took a nipple in his mouth, lightly thrumming it with his tongue, savoring the hardness it became, even as one hand moved inexorably down her stomach to the mound between her legs.

He felt her swollen wetness and heard Leonie's gasps of pleasure.

Suddenly she could sense in him a surging rise of urgency mingled with desire as he stroked her pubis, exploring its secrets, his fingers gently working into her.

Then he was on his knees, massaging her breasts with his hands, fingers flicking at her nipples, while his tongue trailed a fiery path of sensation down her chest to her stomach, deliciously teasing her navel, then moving slowly down to her thighs, where he kissed and licked each one in turn, before finally nesting in her mound, where he feasted on her, as if at some holy shrine, at first slowly, then more and more voraciously, until she was writhing in ecstatic pleasure, shuddering as his tongue brought her to one height of sensation after another.

'Oh, Sam,' she moaned. 'Oh, Sam . . . Sam . . .'

He brought his head up now, and slid atop her again, his mouth on hers, feasting upon her more hungrily than ever. In a fleeting moment he raised his tight, hard buttocks into the air and slid a hand under hers. For a split second he was poised above her, his manhood, rock hard and huge with tumescence, between them, then he lowered himself, down inside her, entering her slowly but definitely. He gradually eased himself in at first, then drove himself in up to the hilt, filling her as she had never been before.

For a moment, Leonie was almost overwhelmed by the indescribable reality of his hot, pulsing, and huge penis within her, then slowly her hips rose to meet his, to welcome him – oh yes! – and her legs parted wide and her feet dug into his calves, as he began thrusting himself into her, gently at first, then faster and harder, until they were both moving in a frenzy of syncopated rhythm.

Suddenly he gasped and slowed, then pulled almost all the way out, pausing for a moment, the head of his manhood pulsing within her. Then he slowly, ever-so-slowly, drove himself back in, up to the hilt, repeating this for almost unendurable minutes, until they were both swept back up into an uncontrollable frenzy, pummeling at each other harder and faster, unable to get enough of each other.

Leonie looked up at him and saw there the straining tendons in his powerful neck and the ecstatic agony etched on his face in the flickering candlelight. Suddenly, she was swept up in an uncontrollable tide of emotion and sensation as she began contracting, the heat within her bursting, a sun flaring its long, delicious tongues of flame outward from the very core of her body, from the very core of her being.

Wave after wave of exquisite pleasure washed over her, and suddenly she couldn't contain the cry of carnal pleasure which escaped her lips, reverberating around the room with its undeniably resonant lust.

Sam's mouth suddenly closed over hers, and his tongue plunged in hungrily, even as he growled in ecstasy. His hips lunged at her in a final powerful thrust to the hilt, and his entire body stiffened and then quivered exquisitely as his juices burst forth into her in a seemingly endless flow, his huge spasms of pleasure inside her continuing for almost unendurable moments before they both collapsed, gasping for breath.

He rested atop her, peppering her face and neck with little kisses, murmuring in a breathy rasp, 'Leonie . . . oh, Leonie . . . that was so . . . so wonderful.'

She returned his kisses, running her hands up and down his back, finally gasping, 'Yes . . . oh, yes, Sam. That was . . . perfect . . . perfect . . . perfect.'

After a few minutes, he rolled off her, lay alongside her, and put an arm around her shoulders, pulling her to him, looking into her eyes as they both still labored for air.

They lay there spent, luxuriating in the afterglow of their intimacy, rejoicing in the pleasure they had given each other, running hands over each other, still touching, feeling, looking, unable as yet to part, the urge to explore and experiment with this newly found indulgence so powerful that it was irresistible.

The storm had diminished in intensity, and the rainfall was

much quieter now, though it still lightly, rhythmically pelleted the windowpanes *sotto voce*. Candlelight flickered around the room and over their sweat-sheened bodies, rendering them as would a master of chiaroscuro.

Finally, Sam kissed her lightly and looked into her eyes. 'I'm not suggesting that what we did is a cure-all,' he said, 'but I hope you feel as good as I do.'

Leonie smiled up at him. 'Yes, Sam. Oh, yes. I think I do,' she replied. 'I know I do. I think this was just the tonic to chase away the blues.'

They lay staring at one another for long moments, still marveling at their newfound bliss. Then Leonie saw the wonder and contentment on his face change to a more ardent expression, and she sought out his lips with hers.

Sam began kissing her more feverishly again, running his hands over her body lightly, her arms, hips, buttocks, and breasts, caressing her tenderly, and Leonie immediately responded, her desires excited by his touch, by his rousing manhood, which she felt already coming to life against her.

'Do you think . . . ?' Sam began, looking into her eyes.

'Yes, I do think,' Leonie answered huskily.

Time seemed to stand still as they began the eternal erotic dance once more, feasting upon one another insatiably and exquisitely, slower this time, exploring one another's bodies, becoming more and more familiar until they both lay finally exhausted, reveling in this new intimacy, this new defense against the darkness outside their candlelit orb.

'I could stay like this all night,' Sam whispered. 'In fact, I could stay here, just like this, forever.'

'Me, too,' Leonie said, snuggling even closer and kissing him. 'It feels so good. I still . . . well, I still can't quite believe this is happening.'

Sam grinned, almost sheepishly, she thought.

'I guess it sounds silly, but I think that somehow or other it was meant to be,' he said seriously, his lips brushing her temple. 'From the very first time I saw you, I've wanted you so much.' Now his lips brushed her breasts. He looked up at her. 'You knew, didn't you?'

'Oh, yes,' Leonie cried. 'I felt the same way.'

'There was some kind of chemistry from day one,' Sam continued. 'I've never felt anything like it before.'

'Neither have I,' Leonie confessed. 'It's . . . it's never been like this before.' She paused and then said, 'It's sort of scary . . . it's . . . it's almost like magic.'

'I know,' Sam replied. 'I think that what we have is very rare and very special, Leonie. And it's very powerful.'

Suddenly the lamp beside the daybed came to life, momentarily startling them both. They laughed.

'I guess that's my cue,' Sam said, planting another kiss on her lips. 'I'd better get back to the house. We both have an early morning.'

'You're right,' Leonie said, giving him a quick peck on the lips.

They slowly began to part, hesitantly at first, kissing as they separated.

Eventually, Sam sighed wistfully, then reluctantly got to his feet. He started getting dressed while Leonie lay supine, watching, enjoying the sight of his rugged, bronzed masculinity, his uninhibited naturalness in her presence.

I feel like one of Manet's odalisques must have felt, she thought, experiencing a satiety – and serenity – she hadn't known could exist.

She leaned over and blew out the candles, her breath casting tallow across the table. Then she reached for the cashmere throw and pulled it around her shoulders, holding it together at her breasts with one hand. She noticed that the rain had become a barely discernible patter against the windowpanes.

When Sam was dressed, she rose from the daybed and stepped into his outstretched arms. They began kissing passionately again, until she drew back. 'You'll never get out of here if we don't stop this,' she said breathlessly. 'If you don't leave now.'

He smiled. 'I know,' he said. 'I'm finding it slightly difficult to tear myself away.'

She patted him on his firm buttocks. 'Go,' she said. 'This place will be swarming with your workmen in a few hours.'

She walked him to the kitchen, where he retrieved his boots, then sat down, pulled them on, and began lacing them up.

'I guess they're still soggy.' Leonie laughed.

He looked up at her and grinned. 'It's okay,' he said. 'It was well worth getting wet.'

When he was done, he got up and put an arm around Leonie's waist. Together, they walked to the back door. Sam pulled his jacket off the coat hook and slid into it. He turned to her in the near dark and began kissing her again.

'Oh, God,' he panted, 'I don't want to go.'

'Go,' she said. 'Now. While I can stand it.'

'I'll see you in the morning,' he promised.

Then he turned and was gone.

Leonie closed the door and padded back into the kitchen on her bare feet. She retrieved her glass of wine from the parlor, and took a big gulp. Then she returned to the kitchen and sat down, staring at the candles, guttering in their holder on the table. She hated to put them out, their glimmering flickers so suited her intoxicated mood.

She heard Sam fire up the Range Rover, circle around, and go out the drive.

Tomorrow, she thought, squeezing herself. I only have to wait the few short hours until tomorrow morning when I'll get to see him again.

15

Morning came.
But Sam didn't.

Summer's brilliant light and air and sky were a tonic for the spirits, perfect as they were. True blue sky, cool air that would gradually warm up, and pleasant breezes that felt cleansing. Oppressive heat and humidity had yet to come to the valley.

Leonie had bounced out of bed with more than her usual abundant resources of energy, looking forward to the day with a new and – the better to relish it – secret excitement.

Her heart still sang from last night's lovemaking – for that is what it was, she told herself. It was not a mere toss in the hay. Far from it. Now, she felt that nothing – nothing! – could take the shine off her day, that nothing could breach her refortified defenses.

She found herself smiling for no obvious reason, whistling, and singing. It was the feeling of indomitability, she supposed.

Yesterday, she decided, had been a day of purest hell, and a night of unadulterated heaven. And there was nothing like it for the spirits.

As the various workmen arrived, she greeted each of them cheerfully, exchanging pleasantries and discussing the progress on the house. As she had done nearly every morning since work on the house first started, she brewed coffee for Sam and herself, popped some bread in the toaster, then got busy out in the garden. Weeding, trimming, mulching. It was hard work, but the garden was already thanking her. Roses had been blooming in abundance in the parterre and on the climbers over the now-repaired gazebo, just in time to replace the colorful display of the peonies and lilacs which had finished their show for the season.

When Sam hadn't arrived by mid-morning, Leonie decided to approach Skip Curtiss, the construction foreman. She didn't want to appear to be too curious, but then decided that was being a trifle silly. She realized her hesitation was only because of last night. After all, Sam was in charge of the project – her project – and he hadn't missed a day yet. He was always there, running the show.

'Skip,' she asked casually, 'have you heard from Sam?'

'Had a message this morning,' Skip replied succinctly. 'Said he'd be in later on. If he could make it.'

'I just wondered,' Leonie said. 'It's not like him to not show up or call.'

'Naw,' Skip agreed. 'Sam's a real Johnny-on-the-Spot.'

'Thanks, Skip,' she said, and went back inside.

Could it be . . . ? Oh, God! Could it be because of last night? she wondered.

Well, I am not going to fret, she decided, knowing, of course, that that was exactly what she was doing.

She heard a car on the gravel drive and looked anxiously out toward it from the garden, hoping to see Sam's Range Rover. But it was Mossy's pristine white Acura.

190

Leonie put down her tools and hurried over to greet her as she got out of the car.

'Bloody hell,' Mossy cried, patting her electric-orange bird's nest of hair. 'You are a sight for these hungover eyes.'

Leonie laughed. 'You don't look the least bit green around the gills, Mossy,' she said.

They air kissed and walked arm in arm to the kitchen.

'You want some coffee?' Leonie asked. 'It's already made.'

'Yum-yum,' Mossy replied, pulling out a chair at the kitchen table and sitting down.

Leonie poured them each a cup of coffee and set them on the table, then sat down herself.

Mossy fished a cigarette out of her shoulder bag and lit it, eyeing the candles as she did so. 'Looks as though you lost power last night, too,' she said.

'Yes,' Leonie said. 'For quite a while.'

'That's one thing you can always count on in these parts,' Mossy said. 'Happens all the time. Rain, snow, sleet. You name it.' She stirred Sweet 'N Low and skim milk into her coffee.

'I'm getting used to it,' Leonie said. 'I've got candles handy, and then when the power's restored I run around resetting all the blinking clocks.'

'Oh, plasma!' Mossy cried. 'This coffee is just what I need. An elixir for these whiskey-soaked old bones.'

Leonie looked at her suspiciously. 'And exactly what have you been up to that's put you in such a state?' she asked with amusement in her voice.

'My dear,' Mossy said, taking a puff on her cigarette. 'You don't want to know. Far too sordid a story for your tender little ears.'

'Oh, come on Moss,' Leonie cajoled, knowing that Mossy was dying to tell her because she was at her most dramatic this morning, all exclamation points and italics. 'Out with it.'

'Well . . .' she began, '. . . if you must know . . .'

191

'Yes!' Leonie said. 'Tell all.'

'Well, there's this new lad in town,' Mossy said. 'Oooooh, divine! Tall! Up to here!' Mossy theatrically waved a hand toward the ceiling. 'And it!' Pausing, she gave Leonie a significant look. 'Down to there!' She swept her hand down to the floor.

Leonie nearly choked on her coffee, sputtering with laughter. 'You're shameless,' she cried.

'Dropped by for a cocktail,' Mossy continued, blowing a plume of smoke toward the dining room, 'and what with the dreadful storm, the poor boy couldn't leave. Has a big Harley-Davidson. Couldn't have him get all wet, could we?'

'Oh, no,' Leonie said. 'Might melt.'

'Indeed,' Mossy said. 'So . . . one thing led to another. And, of course, with the positively Wagnerian storm . . . and a few too many cocktails . . . we ended up thrashing about under the skylights for hours! Hours!' She eyed Leonie mischievously. 'They're soooo much more energetic and appreciative when they're younger, don't you agree?'

'I'm sure,' Leonie said. 'And where did you meet this new . . . amour?'

'Oh, he comes with the best references,' Mossy replied quickly. 'Works in air conditioning repair, or some such trade. Very useful. If your old AC gives out, just ring him up.'

'So your air conditioner broke down, and you called a repairman . . . ?' Leonie said, sipping her coffee.

'Noooo. Nothing of the sort!' Mossy said. 'You know me. Never even use my air conditioning.' She put her cigarette out in the ashtray and lit another one, exhaling smoke through her nostrils. 'Anyway, he happened to be at one of my old watering holes. You know! That dreary place up the road where the lesbians hang about in the afternoons.'

'Oh,' Leonie teased, 'so he's a lesbian!'

'My dear,' Mossy intoned, 'the last thing on earth! They always

192

disappear by nightfall. Anyway, he'd gone in for a nightcap, as had I.' She sat back with a wistful expression on her face. 'Jared, that's his name. So . . . biblical! Don't you think?' She took another long drag on her cigarette. 'The rest, as they say, is history.'

'Will you be seeing him again?' Leonie asked.

'Who knows?' Mossy replied. 'And who cares? I have the memory of that huge—'

'Stop!' Leonie cried. 'You should be locked up!'

Mossy suddenly gazed at her across the table, with a look of utter consternation. 'My God,' she said, 'here I've been prattling on like a madwoman, and yesterday was your trip to Southampton.'

Leonie nodded solemnly.

'I didn't even think you'd be here today. Took a chance. On my way to show a house down the road.' She looked at Leonie quizzically. 'What are you doing here? Thought you'd have spent the night, at least.'

Leonie gave her a matter-of-fact and brief rendition of the previous day's events.

When she was finished, Mossy sat there, eyes wide, aghast. 'I am stunned!' she said. 'I hope you plan to purchase a very large knife and cut their cocks off. That's the ticket! The Lorena Bobbitt solution! The only way to go.'

'I have to admit that revenge of some sort was my very first thought,' Leonie said truthfully. 'But I've decided the best thing for me is to try to forgive and forget.'

'What a saintly and boring decision,' Mossy spat, scowling.

'It may be boring, but saintly has nothing to do with it,' Leonie said. 'I just want to get it all behind me. I'm starting a new life for myself, Mossy. You know that better than anyone. And I don't want a lot of old baggage weighing me down. I think that I'm doing the healthiest thing for me.'

'How wise you are!' Mossy said with a tinge of sarcasm. Then she saw the sober look on Leonie's face and her scowl immediately disappeared and was replaced by an expression of concern mixed with admiration.

'I must hand it to you,' Mossy said, the mockery gone from her voice, which now rang with seriousness. 'You're bloody marvelous. I know that I would be utterly consumed with quite unhealthy revenge fantasies. For years.'

'Well,' Leonie said, 'enough of that.' She took a sip of coffee and set it back down. 'Listen,' she said, 'I have to go into New York for a few days to pick out wallpaper and fabric. Some trimmings, stuff like that.'

'Oooooh, hit those fabulous decorator shops in the D & D building,' Mossy said.

'No,' Leonie said definitely. 'This will be hitting the fabulous bargain basements on Orchard Street, Grand Street. You know, Beckenstein's, all those places on the Lower East Side. Don't forget. I'm on a budget.'

'That's infinitely more interesting,' Mossy said. 'Close to such fabulous neighborhoods. Chinatown! Little Italy! Punks and druggies!'

Leonie smiled. 'Right. Well, anyway, I thought that if you could get away, you might like to come with me. We could split the cost of a hotel room. What do you think?'

'Bloody marvelous!' Mossy said. 'I'll have to force myself away from work, of course.'

The telephone bleeped, and Leonie got up to answer it. 'Excuse me a second, Mossy,' she said.

'Not at all,' Mossy said, sipping her coffee.

Leonie grabbed the receiver. 'Hello.'

'Leonie, it's Sam.'

She felt a frisson of excitement rush through her at the mere sound of his voice and turned her back to Mossy, afraid that she would give away her nervous fluster.

'Good morning,' she said in as calm a tone as she could muster. 'We were wondering where you were.'

'Listen, Leonie,' he said. His voice had a somber timbre to it, a downbeat note that she didn't recognize and that she was certain did not bode well.

'I'm all ears,' she said, trying to put cheer in her voice and a smile on her face, even though a sense of dread was already pervading her senses.

'We've got to talk,' Sam said. 'Right away, if possible.'

'Sure,' Leonie replied, picking up a sponge and absently wiping at the kitchen counter.

'What if I come by and pick you up,' he said. 'Say in about half an hour?'

'That's fine,' she answered.

'See you in a bit,' he said, and hung up.

''Bye,' Leonie said to the dead line.

Oh God, no, she thought. It is last night! I just know it! He's going to tell me he can't see me again. That it's all over before it hardly started. But how can I blame him? He's a married man for God's sake. Married! Suddenly, a wave of guilt washed over her, burning her with its potent sting, wrenching her stomach into a sickly knot of remorse and reddening her face with shame. What the hell was I thinking? she asked herself. How in God's name could I have ever done what I did? She took a deep breath, trying to still her now-trembling hand. How could I have let myself do something so . . . shameful?

Dreading the worst, she hung up the telephone, took a deep breath, and turned to face Mossy, hoping her features did not betray the sense of apprehension she felt, the guilt that she knew must be written on her features.

'Sam,' she said simply, sitting back down.

'I see,' Mossy said, scrutinizing her friend closely and suspiciously. 'And where is the fabulous Mr. Nicholson today?'

'He got held up,' Leonie said lightly.

'Bloody hell, Leonie,' Mossy said. 'Can't fool me. I hope you're

195

not getting yourself involved in something that you'll surely regret.' She paused, taking a puff of her cigarette. 'But my very reliable nose most decidedly senses a carnal plot afoot.'

'Oh, Moss,' Leonie said, 'lay off. Please.'

'Sorry,' Mossy quickly apologized. 'Didn't mean to intrude, dear.' She put out her cigarette and grabbed her shoulder bag. 'I'd better dash. Have to show this sodding dump down the road.'

'I didn't mean to run you off,' Leonie said.

'No, no,' Mossy said. 'I really must run. Ring me about going into the city.' She rose to her feet and shouldered her bag. 'I think it would be great fun.'

'I do, too,' Leonie said. She got up and walked Mossy to the door, where they exchanged air kisses.

''Bye,' Leonie said. 'I'll call you tonight, okay?'

'Perfect,' Mossy replied. 'And while you're at it dear, do put that sponge back where it belongs. It is not a very attractive fashion statement!' And with that, she gave a toss of the orange bird's nest atop her head and was off.

Leonie looked down, surprised to see that she'd been clutching it in her hand. She turned and retraced her steps to the kitchen, where she sat back down, and wondered: Why? Why did it have to be so good? Only to end.

16

The Range Rover bumped down the rocky dirt lane, jolting them in their seats. It was hardly more than a trail through the woods, petering out in a copse of woods, where Sam pulled over. The Hudson River, muddy looking from yesterday's deluge, was barely discernible across the railroad tracks and through the trees.

He had been unusually quiet during the drive, his tanned face set in a grim and determined expression. He seemed so intent, so preoccupied, that Leonie didn't question him, but had waited patiently, biding her time, wondering how he would tell her, what words he would choose to say that he wouldn't be seeing her again.

Despite the cleansed, sunlit beauty of the day after last night's rain, she was nagged all the while by the cloud of conflicting and perplexing emotions within her: trepidation, concern, and – surely the most powerful – lust. A very potent and heady lust it was, too, for this man she had begun to know.

After Sam had killed the engine, he turned to her, looking into her eyes. He abruptly reached across to her, pulling her gently to him, kissing her deeply, passionately. She responded, tentatively at first, puzzled by his behavior, then more hungrily, swept up on a tidal wave of desire.

Almost as suddenly as he had kissed her, Sam drew back, staring into her eyes again, his arms still around her, his breath rapid.

'I'm sorry for being so mysterious,' he finally said. 'It's just that . . . well, it's just that I find it so difficult to talk to you about this.'

Leonie waited for him to continue, not certain what to say.

He pulled away from her now, and they sat, turned slightly in their seats to face each other. 'You've probably heard all kinds of things about me,' he said, heaving a sigh. 'And my marriage,' he added quietly.

Leonie nodded, but remained silent.

'I know a lot of people say I married for money. You know the story. That I waltzed in and took over the family firm and all that stuff,' he continued. 'But it's not so simple, Leonie, and I want you to know the truth.'

'I wouldn't expect anything else from you, Sam,' she replied with confidence.

'God, I don't even know where to begin,' he said, his face tortured, his voice full of pain.

'Why don't you try the beginning, Sam,' Leonie said, her usual practicality not deserting her now.

A hint of a smile appeared on his lips at her simple advice. 'Well, I . . . I guess you're right,' he said. He cleared his throat before beginning, then launched into his story slowly, thoughtfully, measuring his words carefully.

'My family was dirt poor, like I told you last night. Farmers, over in the Berkshires. In Western Massachusetts. They didn't have much of anything, hardly any education,' he said, 'but they were good people. Not religious, but I guess you'd say that they were Christians. We didn't have much of anything material, but they were very loving parents. And they instilled in me a good set of values, I think.'

He paused, looking at her, as if she should acknowledge this similarity in their backgrounds.

Leonie nodded. 'Go on, Sam. I want to hear it all,' she said.

'They pushed me in school, and I pushed myself,' he continued, 'trying to get something better out of life. I guess I was ashamed of what I'd come from.'

He sighed again, momentarily silent, as if coming to terms with this revelation, as if remembering the struggle and the shame. 'Anyway, I ended up with a scholarship to Yale. Studied architecture. One summer I was offered an internship at Van Vechten Architects. It was a great offer, and I took it.'

He turned, looking through the windshield, apparently unable to continue while face-to-face with Leonie, her presence too powerful a distraction.

'I met Minette, Richard Van Vechten's daughter, right away, and – Jesus! Was I ever swept away in their world. They were rich and powerful, very well connected, and had a proud, old lineage. Their lives, it seemed to me, were perfect. And beautiful,' Sam said, a touch of wistful awe in his voice. 'They had everything that I hadn't had, and they represented everything that I hadn't come from. Everything I had aspired to.'

He stopped speaking, deep in thought, before continuing. 'And Minette was beautiful, too,' he finally said. 'And seemed perfect in every way. We were having sex within a week and were engaged in less than a month. At first, it was all . . . magical . . . almost unreal. It seemed to be too good to be true. But as the summer wore on' – he took a deep breath and expelled it – 'I started to see them and their whole world for what they really were.

'They were incredibly spoiled and arrogant,' he said, an unfamiliar harsh tone in his voice. 'They were so used to having their way that they couldn't even conceive of anybody disagreeing with them. The

199

world was their oyster, all right. They were like master puppeteers, and everyone else around here was a puppet – me included – with them pulling all the strings.'

He stopped and turned to her now. 'Do you know what I mean?'

Leonie nodded again. 'Oh, yes. I know exactly what you mean,' she said. 'Only too well.' She stared at him. 'And all this time, I would venture a guess that you felt like an outsider. Like you didn't really belong, and that you weren't as "good" as they were.'

'Exactly,' Sam said emphatically. 'I always felt like I was less than. Less important, less money, less class, less everything. I was an interloper from another world. Maybe even a threat to them. And they made damn sure that I knew that. In little ways. Nasty little ways. So. They had to make certain that I was right under their thumb.'

He took another deep breath before going on. 'Anyway, later on in that summer, I came to the decision that I couldn't marry Minette. I finally realized that I wasn't in love with her. I'd just been dazzled by all that money and status. So, anyway,' he said, 'I decided to end it. We were going to a big party at a cousin's of hers in Old Chatham. She'd been looking forward to it, so I thought I should wait until afterward to tell her. We left there—'

He suddenly stopped talking, the pain of telling the story obviously almost too much for him.

'Go on, Sam,' Leonie said, reaching over and patting his shoulder. 'I'm here. It's okay.'

He sighed and turned to her now, and she could see the anguish in his eyes. 'We'd both been drinking. A lot. I was driving, and Minette was trying to . . . she was trying to get in my pants. I was trying to stop her, and we ran off the road and went crashing down a ravine. We wound up wrapped around a tree.'

'Oh, God,' Leonie said in a whisper.

'When it was all over, Minette was left paralyzed from the waist down. A spinal cord injury.' He looked into Leonie's eyes. 'I couldn't tell her I wouldn't marry her. I didn't have the heart to do it.'

'No,' Leonie said softly. 'Of course not.'

'So . . .' he said, '. . . we ended up married because I was so guilt-ridden. I felt like I'd ruined her life. Rationally, I know that we were both drinking and that if she hadn't been trying to get it on in the car it might not have happened. But it did happen, and I felt responsible.'

'And you still do, don't you,' Leonie said. 'You still feel the guilt and shame.'

'Yes,' Sam said. He reached over and took her hand in his. 'I still do. It's . . . I guess it's diminished some over the years, partly because Minette's used it against me so much. She has . . . well, Minette has a penchant for a selfish kind of self-misery sometimes.'

He looked over at Leonie. 'But who can blame her?'

'I understand, Sam,' Leonie said, 'but people try to move on, to get past these things, to rebuild their lives as best they can. No matter what the circumstances are.'

'I know what you're saying,' he replied, 'but I guess that everything has come to be overshadowed by the fact that our marriage was loveless to begin with.'

'For Minette, too?' Leonie asked.

'Yes.' Sam nodded. 'She's let me know in no uncertain terms that the only reason she wanted to marry me was because I was the best-looking man around, good in bed, and an architect to boot. A Yale graduate, no less. I could carry on the family tradition in business, provide stud service, and be a decoration for her at the same time. So you see?' he said. 'I'm not exactly the gold-digging gigolo some people make me out to be.' He looked at her.

'Oh, God,' Leonie said. 'It must be so miserable for you both.'

'It is,' Sam said simply. 'Loveless and childless. A miserable past, a miserable present – and no future.'

'You wanted children?' Leonie asked.

'More than anything,' Sam said. 'Growing up alone, always wishing I had brothers and sisters, I've always wanted children of my own. But, of course, Minette can't carry a child.'

Leonie looked down, studying their entwined hands intently.

Sam looked at her and gave her hand a squeeze. 'What about you?' he asked. 'Didn't you want kids?'

'Yes,' Leonie murmured, slowly looking up at him. 'Always, like you. But Hank kept saying we had to put it off until we could afford it. Then, when we could afford it, he said we were both too young and too busy to be tied down by kids yet. So why not wait until we could spend more time with them?'

She shrugged her shoulders, a bemused expression on her face. 'I kept playing his game, trying to believe what he said was true.' She laughed self-deprecatingly.

'Now,' she said, 'my biological clock is tick, tick, ticking away, louder and louder. It's like a damn time bomb in my ears.'

'But it's not too late,' Sam said.

'No, of course not. It's not too late,' Leonie answered. 'Just getting closer. And, of course, there are other considerations.' She laughed again. 'Like a father.'

He reached over and put an arm around her shoulders and began kissing her. Leonie responded immediately, urgently.

She wished that she could kiss his guilt and pain away, knowing that that was impossible, but she also realized that the solace they found in each other, however temporary, had healing properties all its own, for them both.

Sam drew back after a few moments and looked at her. 'I hope you understand me a little better now, Leonie,' he said. 'That you know where I'm coming from.'

'Yes,' she said. 'I think I do, Sam.'

'It's just that I . . . oh, my God . . .' he stammered, '. . . I love you so much I want you to know everything there is to know about me.'

Leonie felt a jolt of excitement stir within her, so deep down inside that it was surely visceral. She imagined she could feel her heartbeat quicken and her pulse race, but at the same time her practical mind couldn't help but wonder if part of this was not fear. Fear at becoming involved with a man whose life was so complicated. Fear that her own feelings for him would surely lead her down a path of self-destruction.

She stared into his haunted blue-green eyes and decided that, whatever fears she might have, however ill-advised their relationship might be, her attraction to this man was so powerful, so deep-down chemical, that she must follow her instincts, wrong as they might have sometimes been.

'I think I love you, too, Sam,' she said in a whisper. 'I know that I want you. I want you desperately.'

They embraced again, passionately, giving themselves up to their insatiable hunger for one another, as they had last night in the candlelit parlor. After long, but seemingly timeless, minutes of kissing, running their hands over each other, Leonie drew back, breathless.

'This is unbearable,' she rasped. 'We've got to find a place to make love.'

Sam gently brushed strands of hair from her face with his fingertips and kissed her lips. 'Let's get out of the car,' he said.

They were both out of the Range Rover in seconds. Sam went around to her side and opened the back door. 'Come on,' he said, 'back here.'

Leonie got in and slid across the leather-upholstered seat, and Sam climbed in after her, his hands and mouth all over her, kissing, caressing, exploring.

'What if somebody comes by?' Leonie panted.

'That's highly unlikely,' he replied, sliding a hand under her panties, his fingertips delicately brushing her swollen readiness. 'And if they do, we'll give them a show they'll always remember.'

Leonie shuddered from the feel of him, the intoxication of

what they were doing, the chances they were taking here in this sun-dappled copse of trees near the river, and within moments the leather of the seats was creaking under their ferocious need, its heady perfume a witness to their frantic, inflamed coupling.

Afterward, gasping for breath, they both began laughing. Laughing at the awkwardness of this backseat lovemaking, at its frenzied pitch, and at their carnal delight in each other.

'Oh, God, I'm going to miss this while I'm gone,' Leonie said, ruffling his hair.

'Gone?' Sam sputtered, pulling his Levi's up from around his ankles.

'Yes,' Leonie said. 'Didn't I tell you? I'm going to spend a few days in New York, picking out wallpaper and fabrics for the house, while you guys are doing some of the major interior work.'

She reached down and retrieved her panties from the floor of the car and began sliding them back on. 'That way, I'll be out of your way, and I won't have to live in such a huge mess. The idea of a dust bowl does not appeal.'

'That's smart,' he said. 'But I'm going to go crazy without you.' He put an arm around her shoulders and pulled her to him again, looking into those dark eyes of hers, gleaming now with postcoital bliss.

'Don't you think that in that case,' he said, nibbling at her ear, 'we're going to have to have as much of each other as possible between now and then?' He nibbled, and licked, and kissed his way down her neck toward her breasts.

'Oh, yes,' Leonie said, returning his kiss, aware now of the swollen tumescence against her hand. 'Yes, indeed I do.'

Sunlight flashed off chrome and metal as the Range Rover moved with them once again, rhythmically, matching them thrust for thrust, until it rested at last, as they lay spent, already imagining the next time.

17

Minette replaced the telephone receiver in its cradle and stared stoically out through the verdant glass enclosure of the conservatory to the aqua swimming pool beyond. It sparkled invitingly in the hot summer sun, but its promise of cool respite from the weather's oppressive heat and humidity only served as a reminder of her crippled body's inability to take advantage of its pleasures.

The telephone conversation she'd just finished had left her momentarily numb, as if she had been anesthetized for a painful surgical procedure. Her mind had, at first, but only for an instant, recoiled with horror at the news which she had received. But the utter terror she had felt had very quickly and mercifully been replaced by the stoic, unfeeling, and imperturbable self-possession with which she had always dealt with alarming, even tragic, realities.

Now, however, gazing out at the beautiful pool, her mind very gradually began to process the ominous news, until, after several minutes of idle reflection and deeper thought, it was beginning to be filled with a whirlwind of possibilities, of strategies, of plots, of negatives and positives – all of which amounted to not only ways to cope with the disturbing news, but much more important, various means by which she could use the news to her best advantage.

Oh, yes, indeed, she thought. She had ways to turn its malignant reality into a way she could strike out, to vanquish, to avenge herself very effectively on that – no, who, she told herself – which had caused all of her pain and suffering.

Yes! A smile of hideous vengefulness crossed her lips. I know what I will do. I know how I can get even with that poor little nobody who has ruined my life. That poor little nobody who has made my life a living hell.

For there was no doubt in her mind that one person and one person only was responsible for the predicament in which she now found herself. One person who had set off the chain of events that had caused her to end up here, in this wretched wheelchair, with this useless, near-lifeless body. One person, furthermore, who was responsible for the disturbing piece of news she had just received.

Ha! Minette thought. I know how to take care of this situation. If this interesting bit of news is true, if this is the way I'm going to be dealt with, then I know exactly what I'll do to that single person who is responsible.

Oh, yes!

She looked out at the swimming pool again, framed so beautifully as it was by the foliage here in the conservatory, formulating her plans, coming to decisions, relishing the possibilities for the destruction and pain she would cause. Ah, yes! The revenge she would extract! The idea was more delicious on her palate than even the most delectable and finest small-grained black Sevruga caviar could ever be!

But first she had a lot of work to do, and she must act quickly. Time, after all, was of the essence. There were telephone calls to make, a letter to write, papers to have drawn up and signed. Many tasks to perform, all of which she could easily do right here in the conservatory, from the comfort of her wheelchair.

First, Dr. Nathanson. Yes! She must discuss certain matters with the ever-caring, ever-fawning doctor.

Then, her lawyers. Some changes in certain legal documents. Ah! The mere thought gave her a shiver of excitement, and she laughed aloud.

Next, Andrea Walker, her realtor friend. Oh, yes! she thought. I have some property for sale! At once!

And then, of course, there was the bank. Some changes to make there, for certain. And the sooner the better.

She pressed a button on the intercom which sat mutely beside her on the table.

'Erminda!' she called out.

'Yes, Mrs. Nicholson?' the maid answered.

'Bring me that open bottle of white wine that's in the refrigerator and a glass.'

'Yes, Mrs. Nicholson.'

After Erminda had brought the wine and a glass to her, Minette waved her away. She poured herself a generous portion of the wine, and took a sip. It tasted dry and cool, just the right accompaniment for the task at hand.

She reached over and picked up her small leather-bound address book from the table next to her, then tapped it lightly on the arm of her wheelchair, lost deep in thought.

After a few moments, she quit tapping. I'm ready, she thought. Yes, ready to get down to the business at hand.

But before she did, Minette gazed out at the pool again, smiling at it as if it held her secrets with her, as if it held all the answers to her problems, as if it were a co-conspirator in her vengeance on the one and only cause of all this misery in her life.

And that cause, of course, was Sam Nicholson, who was going to suffer, tenfold, a hundredfold – a thousandfold! – for the news she had received.

18

Sam felt lost.

He was adrift in a world that was an alien, lonely place he had forgotten existed since he had met Leonie. When he'd told her that he would miss her – all those days ago when they'd made love in the Range Rover – he had meant the words, but he'd had no idea of how true they would prove to be. An emptiness, like a dark hollow carved from down within his very being, haunted him.

Had it not been for the work on the octagon house – her house – and the frenzied pace at which he was driving the men, he wouldn't have known what to do with himself.

He wondered now how he had coped, walking such an inhospitable terrain, before he had met her, but thought he knew the answer: I shut down, he thought. Closed up. I didn't allow myself to feel anything. I was going through life, saying the right words, doing the right things, like some kind of automaton with no heart.

At the same time, he realized that by opening himself up to Leonie, he was taking a big risk. He was making himself vulnerable to more pain and sorrow, the possibility of rejection. And, of course, there was Minette to consider. It was a little frightening, he realized, but the alternative was even more so. He did not want to return to that loveless state of nothingness he had existed in for too long.

In the meantime, he was single-mindedly pursuing one goal: making certain that Leonie would return to a much more nearly completed project, and that it would come in within budget.

Now, rolling down the highway toward the house, the summer heat was at its most oppressive. They had been lucky because it was one of only a few such days all summer. The landscape seemed somehow out of focus, a blur amid the atmospheric haze of humidity and heat.

Soon, Sam realized, the heat and humidity would give way to fall's crisp, cool, and invigorating air. All the more reason to drive himself and the men to the limit. Christmas was the deadline for completion, and he was sure that they would make it. But he knew that a lot of the finish work – the details that were so important for the overall look – could eat up time and money.

He pulled into Leonie's drive and drove around to the carriage house. Jumping out of the Range Rover, he decided to quickly inspect the pool and outbuildings before venturing inside.

He had supervised the completion of the stonework around the swimming pool yesterday, satisfying himself that it was exactly like Leonie wanted it.

Looking at it yet again today, he tried to see it through her eyes. He thought that it resembled the long, rectangular reflecting pool she wanted, black inside, although you could see through the water to the bottom. There were built-in steps descending into it at one end, but otherwise it was completely unadorned, except for a single light which lit it from within at night. The effect was breathtakingly beautiful – he had seen it last night – even without the enhancement of the landscaping that was yet to come.

He wondered what she had planned. She had told him she was

going to do the landscaping herself, but he knew that whatever it might be, it would be beautiful.

Checking on the existing stone terraces, he noted that they had all been repointed and repaired where necessary. Then he strode over to the carriage house. It was now an up-to-date two-car garage with a large apartment upstairs for staff or guests. It was completely finished except for its interior painting and decoration. That would begin after Leonie returned from New York with the fabrics and wallpapers. He knew that she had already selected the paint. She'd also ordered the appliances for the apartment's small kitchen, when she'd ordered those for the house. They should be in place in the next couple of weeks.

From there he walked to the barn. It was now completely finished inside except for painting, with two rooms, ideally suited for offices, which had adjoining baths. The rest of its enormous space, with its huge hand-hewn beams, had been finished out to be used as an artist's studio space or workshop. Its northern façade contained huge windows and skylights positioned to give the proper northerly light for painting. Pine floors had been installed and now awaited the shipment of furniture which Leonie had told him she was having sent from storage in New York next week. It was furniture that she would use to decorate the house, and would be sold with it at a nice premium if the future buyers wanted it.

Leonie had been here for the vast majority of the work, of course, but Sam hoped that she was going to be pleased with the finishing touches that had been added in the last week.

She had seen none of the exterior paintwork which had just begun and was truly giving this old dowager a new lease on life. Leonie had chosen an ocher yellow color, one based on archival records, but more often seen on European buildings, particularly old buildings in Mittel Europa. It would be complemented with crisp white trim for the windows and moldings. The shutters and doors were going to be the darkest green. Sam had had his doubts about her choices at first, but now he saw, as the painting had begun, that he needn't have questioned her. The effect was turning out to be even more stunning than she'd described, certainly more so than he'd imagined.

He turned and went into the house, where there were carpenters and plumbers on every floor. The sound of electric saws and hammers created a din that was music to his ears, and the smell of the fresh sawdust was, as always, like a sweet perfume to his nose.

All the gutting that had to be done was finished, and now floors, woodwork, and plasterwork was in the process of being repaired or replaced. The kitchen was now an empty shell, but in another few days it was going to be spectacular. Cabinetry and other woodwork that had to be stripped was well on its way to completion. The original beamed ceiling had been exposed, and the old pine floor was now ready for sanding, staining, and sealing.

Fireplace mantels were being stripped for painting or cleaned and polished. The woodwork was being prepared for painting, and all the old wallpaper was now gone, soon to be replaced by new.

He took enormous satisfaction in seeing the results and thought that, even if he made a little less money than he had anticipated because he had gone the extra mile in using certain materials, he had no regrets.

This was for Leonie. His Leonie.

He was heading up to the third-floor master suite when the cellular phone clipped to his waist bleeped.

'Damn,' he muttered. Very few people had this number, and he had a good idea who it might be.

'Hello,' he said, after stopping to unclip the phone and answer the call.

'Sam! Where are you?' It was Minette.

'I'm at the octagon house, Minette,' he replied equably, though of course she knew very well where he was.

'Please,' she said, 'come home.'

Sam's antennae immediately went on full alert. Her voice, he thought, was suspiciously undemanding, which could only mean one thing: trouble.

'What's going on, Minette?' he asked calmly. 'I'm working, you know.'

'Something very important,' she said mysteriously. 'We must talk right away.' And then she abruptly hung up.

'Shit!' Sam said, punching the end button and reclipping the cell phone to his belt.

He hesitated for a moment, thinking that perhaps he should ignore Minette's order. And that's exactly what it really is, he thought. An order. But he just couldn't bring himself to do that.

'Shit!' he said again, and then dutifully retraced his steps back downstairs, and went back out to the Range Rover. He fired it up, spewing gravel as he tore out of the driveway, and raced up the road, his mood a perfect match to the weather: hot.

Minutes later, he jerked to a stop at the gates to Van Vechten Manor, and moments after that he slammed to a halt at the formidable front door of the great manor itself. Taking a deep breath to steel himself, he leapt out of the car. He made a conscious effort to control his anger, not slamming the car door and stomping up the steps as he would have liked.

The door was swung wide by Erminda before he reached it. 'Mr. Nicholson,' she said, her dark eyes brightening with pleasure at the sight of him.

'Hey, Erminda,' he said. 'Where's Minette?'

'Mrs. Nicholson,' she answered, 'is in the conservatory.'

'Thanks, Erminda.' He strode quickly through the entrance hall and weaved his way back to the library and through it to the conservatory.

Minette was seated, a bulb baster in hand, carefully watering an enormous, carnivorous-looking orchid plant, its dozens of ivory blooms trembling at her every touch.

213

He stood watching her, silently fuming, wondering what emergency might have had her command his presence at this familiar domestic scene. To all appearances, she was quietly, even serenely, contentedly, enjoying this household chore, without any special concerns or worries.

Without turning around to look at him, Minette said: 'So many uses for a bulb baster, aren't there, darling.' She dipped the baster into a watering can, squeezed the rubber bulb, then continued feeding the plant. 'Best way to do it without doing any damage, you know.'

'What did you call me home for, Minette?' Sam asked as mildly as he could.

'Oh . . .' she said, '. . . why don't you sit down, darling. I'll only be a minute.'

'Look, Minette,' Sam said, gritting his teeth, 'I've got a job to do, or have you forgotten? I dropped everything, left a crew of men working, thinking there was some kind of emergency here.'

'Patience, darling,' she said. 'It's a virtue, or didn't you know.'

A few moments later, she put the bulb baster down and clapped her hands together. 'There. All done.' She looked up at Sam. 'See? It only took a moment.'

Sam sighed and sat down in a wicker chair, wishing that she would get to the point, whatever it happened to be. Get this over with.

Minette turned her wheelchair around to face him, then stared across at him levelly, her eyes hard and bright. 'I've put the Van Vechten Building on the market,' she said matter-of-factly.

Sam sat there, both surprised and angry, at the same time wondering why he felt that way, since this was nothing more or less than he would have expected of Minette lately. She certainly hadn't been herself.

'I gave Andrea Walker the listing, and she's very excited,' Minette continued. 'She already has two or three very interested parties.'

'I see,' Sam said simply, nodding his head.

Minette adjusted the pearls at her throat, still staring at him. 'I've sent Dirck and some of the stable boys over to load up all of Dad's things that are still there in his old office,' she said. 'I'm sending it all to auction.'

Sam noticed that the hardness and brightness in her eyes seemed to intensify, turning to icy blue steel. With malevolent joy, he thought.

'So, Sam, darling,' she went on, 'you'll have to clear out all your office toys – fast.'

'They are not toys, Minette,' he said angrily.

'Call them what you will,' she said with a shrug of her silk-clad shoulders. 'Just get your stuff out of there. Van Vechten Architects is history.'

'Why are you suddenly doing this now?' Sam asked curiously.

'Well . . .' she replied, a thoughtful look on her face, '. . . the building is historically important and could be put to good use – and make me a bundle in the bargain. So why not?'

Sam felt his face burn with indignation. God, he thought, she knows how to go for the jugular. Implying that he didn't make good use of the building, that everything he did was useless and unimportant. How like her. But he didn't want to argue with her now. He knew it was futile.

'Okay,' he said, getting to his feet. 'I'll take care of it right away.'

She followed him with her eyes. 'What will you do with your things, darling?' she asked.

'Truthfully, I don't know, Minette,' he answered. 'You know I certainly can't afford an office that's anywhere near comparable, but I'll think of something.'

He started for the door, then turned and smiled ruefully. 'See you later.'

'You do that,' she said.

Leaving the conservatory, Sam puzzled at his reaction to her news. He knew that he should be worried – even panicked – but, surprisingly, he felt instead a new and wondrous freedom. It was as if a burden had been lifted from his shoulders. This is crazy, he thought. Jesus! What am I going to do? I don't even have a damn office, and I feel good about it.

But he knew why: A tie with Minette and their unhappy past had been cut, and she had done the snipping.

As he strode through the library, Sam saw Erminda, furiously dusting at books. Her pace was such that he almost laughed out loud, but he didn't want to offend her.

'Erminda,' he said. 'Slow down. You'll give yourself a coronary at that rate.'

She turned to him, the ostrich feather duster in her hand. It shook with her undisguised fury.

'Erminda,' Sam said, serious now that he saw the state she was in, 'what's wrong?'

'I just don't understand why Mrs. Nicholson is so mean to you,' she said. I would know how to make him happy, she thought.

'Don't you worry about it, Erminda,' he said. 'It's nothing.'

'Okay,' she said mildly. If only she was out of the picture, then I would have him all to myself! she thought. But she said: 'If you say so, Mr. Sam.'

Sam walked on out to the Range Rover and headed back downriver to the octagon house. He wished that he believed what he'd just told Erminda, that as far as Minette was concerned, it really was nothing. But he knew deep down inside that that was not the case.

What the hell is going on with her? he wondered. Minette had always been . . . difficult. Snobbish, selfish, arrogant, and sometimes self-pitying, but she had seldom ever been so outright mean.

Why now? he wondered. And why is she putting the Van Vechten Building up for sale? He realized that she was upset because he

216

was working, but to go to this extent to hinder his work? If this was a game she was playing, she had certainly raised the stakes.

It didn't make any sense to him. No, none at all. This was, in fact, completely out of character. Minette had always been one to hang on to things. Tenaciously. As if a part of her was vested in every object around her, everything she owned. And she fiercely guarded her every possession.

Why then, would she suddenly decide to disperse her father's belongings? She had worshipped her father, and his old office in the Van Vechten Building had been preserved as it was the day he'd last been there, over a decade ago. Sam couldn't quite believe that she would really send her father's treasured belongings – her belongings, he reminded himself – to auction.

She didn't need the cash, of that Sam was certain. He knew that their various bank accounts were very healthy. He also knew what her portfolio of stocks and bonds was worth – a lot – and the income it generated was far more than enough to live comfortably on. And that didn't take into account all of the various properties that she owned, some of which were income producing.

If not for money, what then?

She surely wasn't going to such lengths simply to punish him, to be mean. Or was she?

The closer he got to the octagon house, the more confused he became by the puzzle which was his wife, and she was one he simply couldn't figure out. Furthermore, he knew that trying to talk to her about it, trying to find out what was going on in her mind, would be an exercise in futility. Minette had obviously made up her mind, and once it was made up, there was no changing it. She was possessed of a stubbornness that refused to listen to reason.

Pulling into the drive at Leonie's house, Sam told himself to forget

217

it, that it wasn't worth thinking about. It's probably just another ploy to frustrate my desire to work, to actually be an architect and earn my bread.

Even if I am an architect without an office now.

19

'Bloody hell!' Mossy cried, as she and Leonie stepped out onto the sidewalk, the door to Beckenstein's swinging shut behind them. 'I'd forgotten that the heat here is surely hotter than in any hell imaginable. And the air! One can hardly breathe!'

Leonie laughed. 'Summer in the city. I think you're ready to get back to the country, Moss,' she said.

'No,' Mossy replied. 'I'm masochistic enough to be having the time of my life in this filthy, depraved, uncomfortable, dangerous, fabulous town!' She paused lighting a cigarette. 'And that young man who works in Beckenstein's. What a cutie!'

'He has a boyfriend, Moss,' Leonie said.

'What a waste,' Mossy said. 'I was already imagining the possibilities.'

As they made their way down Orchard Street, Leonie took pleasure in its usual melee: vendors noisily hawking their discounted wares; shoppers, elbow-to-elbow, ogling the windows and the merchandise displayed on the sidewalks; Sabrett wagons sending smoke into the air, the smell of their hot dogs and falafels tempting.

'What about stopping someplace for a drink before we go back to the hotel?' Leonie asked.

'That's the ticket,' Mossy said. 'I've never seen so many fabrics in my life. Chintzes, plaids, damasks, stripes, velvets, brocades, toiles de Jouy, muslins. It's all quite maddening actually.'

'I know,' Leonie said. 'There's so much that everything starts looking alike.'

'I do think you made some fabulous choices,' Mossy said.

'And the prices are right,' Leonie said.

'Not exactly dollar-a-yard specials,' Mossy said, 'but they sure do beat uptown prices. And you knew exactly how much of everything to get. I've never seen such organization. I could never do it.'

'It just takes patience, Moss,' Leonie said. 'And a bit of practice. And of course, measuring, measuring, and remeasuring. I've been living with a tape measure in my pocket.'

They reached the corner of Delancey Street and stepped out to hail a cab. Heavy traffic raced east and west on the wide, bumpy street, and taxi after taxi sailed past them without stopping.

'Sod it,' Mossy said, 'we'll never get a cab.'

Leonie stepped farther out into the street, watching the traffic carefully. She put two fingers to her lips and whistled, loudly and shrilly.

A cruising taxi pulled over and jerked to a stop, right at her feet.

Mossy stood rooted to the spot, her eyes wide with amazement. 'I do not believe what my eyes just witnessed,' she said.

'Hurry,' Leonie said. 'Get in before he leaves us standing here.' She opened the cab's rear door and slid in, giving the taxi driver an East Village address.

Mossy slid in behind her. 'You!' she said. 'A lady of such dignity!'

'You're forgetting I grew up here, Mossy.' Leonie laughed. 'I learned to whistle like hell when I was just a kid. It's all part and parcel of sink or swim in the urban jungle.'

Within minutes, the taxi pulled over on Avenue A, and Leonie paid the fare. The sidewalk café was anything but fancy, but its tables afforded a view of the passing spectacle of the East Village and its collection of the interesting, the fashionable, the bizarre and, lately, the middle classes that had come with gentrification. It was all accompanied by the raucous and ceaseless cacophony of the traffic and the toxic smoke belched out by countless buses, trucks, and cars that sped by.

They took seats and ordered, both asking the young waiter, who sported multiple rings through his ears, nose, and eyebrows, for vodka and tonics.

'I do so like the orange in his Mohawk,' Mossy declared, when the waiter was out of earshot, 'but I think he should dispense with the purple. And all those rings! Isn't it gilding the lily just a mite too much? I mean won't one or two do?'

'Nothing in this neighborhood would surprise me,' Leonie said. 'You know I grew up close by.'

'That's right,' Mossy said. 'I'd forgotten.' She paused, lighting a cigarette. 'What a different world you're living in now!' She expelled a streamer of blue-gray smoke.

'Yes,' Leonie said, 'it certainly is that. But I really do love it.'

'You know,' Mossy said, 'at the rate your place is being done up, it's soon going to be time for you to start looking for another old house to fix up.'

Leonie looked at her. 'Have you seen anything I might be interested in?' she asked.

'Possibly.' Mossy nodded. 'There's no end of old places on the market. Old places that need lots of tender loving care. I'm just keeping my eye peeled for the best deal.'

'When we get back, maybe we should start seriously looking,'

Leonie said. 'I'm thinking that if everything works out all right, autumn would be a good time to put the octagon house on the market. You know, with the fall foliage it will look beautiful. Otherwise, I should maybe wait until spring when everything is flowering.'

'That's clever,' Mossy said, 'but the fall would be awfully fast. Finding a buyer and a new place for yourself. Anyhow, it will look equally beautiful in the snow this winter – if there are any shoppers about. The market is a bit slow.'

'That's why I've been busy calling some of my old clients from the shop in Soho,' Leonie said. 'I think I've actually got a couple of them interested in the octagon house. And you know what else?'

Mossy looked at her questioningly. 'What?'

'Nearly everybody I've talked to has begged, literally begged, me to open another shop. They say they're more than willing to travel up to the country to shop, especially if they know I've been picking out the merchandise. So . . . I have to keep that in mind, too. Do I look for a separate place for a shop? Or do I have it at home? If I renovate several more places, wouldn't it make sense to have a separate space for a shop, so it doesn't have to move, too?'

'You've just complicated the picture considerably,' Mossy said. 'But in any case, I'm sure it will all work out.'

The waiter arrived with their drinks, and they both thanked him and took generous sips.

'I must say,' Mossy said, 'the way you've worked at it so far, it's not impossible.'

'What?' Leonie asked.

'Doing it all this fall, I mean.' Mossy paused, taking a drag on her cigarette. 'In fact,' she added, 'you're nothing short of a bloody miracle worker.'

'The project has worked out exceptionally well, hasn't it?' Leonie said with a hint of pride. 'It's had its ups and downs, but mostly ups. It's been a great team effort.'

Mossy eyed her friend across the little café table. 'I think I know the "team" to which you are referring.'

Leonie looked into the distance with a smile on her face that was both wistful and secretive. 'Yes, Mossy,' she said, 'I guess you do.'

Mossy took a sip of her drink and set it down, staring at Leonie. 'You're in love, aren't you?' she asked quietly.

Leonie nodded. 'Yes, Mossy,' she said, 'I believe I am.'

Mossy cocked her head to one side and smiled, a little sadly, Leonie thought, but tenderly. 'I only hope for your sake that you know what you're getting yourself into,' she said. 'You know that I love you dearly and don't want to see you hurt.'

'I know that, Mossy,' Leonie said, 'and I appreciate it.' She sighed. 'I can't deny that there're all sorts of complications, but ...' She looked at Mossy with a mixture of exasperation and joy on her face. 'I'm head over heels in love,' she said. 'Hopelessly and irretrievably in love.'

'Oh, sod it!' Mossy said. 'I do so envy you. Even if you're up against the most impossible brick wall imaginable! Because let me tell you! Minette Nicholson is like a she-wolf, and Sam is one of her pups.'

'I know all about her, Mossy,' Leonie said. 'And believe me, I've done some soul searching. Don't think for a minute that I don't feel guilt. Sam's told me everything, and I realize it's an impossible situation. But what am I going to do?' She shrugged. 'I'm really in love with the man.'

'I don't know what he's told you,' Mossy said, 'but she is ferocious. She has gone out of her way to cross me at the historical society.' Mossy tossed her head back haughtily. 'I'm not local gentry, you know.'

Leonie laughed and took a sip of her drink.

'But even worse,' Mossy continued, 'I've had potential clients ring me up about listing their houses. Then the same people have mysteriously turned around and rung me back to tell me they've decided to list elsewhere. Nine times out of ten with Andrea Walker, Minette's bitch of an ally. All Minette's doing. I'm sure of it.'

Mossy paused and puffed furiously at her cigarette.

Leonie sipped at her drink, knowing that Mossy had her best interests at heart, but also knowing that none of this mattered, at least not to her. Sam's absence this last week had left her feeling incomplete, as if somehow she weren't whole, and the aching emptiness had convinced her of one thing. She knew now that what she'd told Mossy was true: She truly loved him. This feeling certainly wasn't just the result of a dalliance, and it wasn't just lust, either. No, absolutely not. It was, Leonie had become certain, the real thing. As real as it could ever be, she thought.

'The woman,' Mossy continued, fire dancing in her eyes, 'will stop at nothing. She's the worst sort of snob, and she's vicious and vindictive.'

'I'm sure all that's true,' Leonie said calmly, 'but don't you see, Mossy? I feel the way I feel, despite what I know.'

'Just giving you fair warning, my dear,' Mossy said. Then in a softer voice: 'And, of course, there are the stories about him. The stud marrying for money and all.'

Leonie fixed her friend with a stare, her dark eyes bright with determination. 'You are not telling me anything I don't know, Mossy. I am in love come what may.' Her voice rang with the pitch of finality. 'Case closed.'

Mossy arched a thinly plucked eyebrow. 'Well, my dear. I hope at least he's a damn good screw!'

Leonie laughed in spite of herself. 'You always get down to the nitty-gritty, don't you, Moss.'

'Speaking of which,' Mossy said, 'it's a bit gritty out here in the bus fumes and heat. Shall we go back to the hotel and freshen up before dinner? We can have another cocktail there.'

'Why not,' Leonie said.

*　　*　　*

While Mossy soaked in a bubble-filled bathtub at the Soho Grand, Leonie spread out on one of the beds reading the *New York Times*. It was almost as if a magnet had drawn her eyes to the story's boldface headline:

S.E.C. CHARGES TWO WITH INSIDER TRADING:
HENRY REYNOLDS AND CHANDLER HEIR CHARGED

NEW YORK, August 15 – The Securities and Exchange Commission has charged a former stockbroker and a former investment banking firm employee with insider trading related to the WallBank Corporation's acquisition of SouthBank Inc.

The commission filed a complaint today charging Henry Wilson Reynolds and Robert Winston Chandler, IV . . .

Leonie felt a chill slither up her spine to the back of her neck and continue on up into her skull, and she broke out into a cold sweat. Her pulse began to race, and she could feel its pressure against her eardrum. Her heart seemed to hammer loudly against her chest.

She dropped the paper onto her lap as if it were a poisonous snake, and took a sip of the mineral water at her bedside. But she felt compelled to finish the article. She picked the paper back up and continued to read on, the paper twitching in her trembling hands:

. . . The S.E.C. said the case against Mr. Reynolds and Mr. Chandler will proceed . . . Criminal prosecution . . .

Leonie lay back, a bilious, nauseous feeling in the pit of her stomach. The article had mentioned millions of shares of stock and millions of dollars in profits – from sales that were illegal.

Hank and Bobby in cahoots, she thought. In more ways than one.

She ran her hands through her hair and sat up, letting the paper slide to the floor. Her first thought was to pick up the telephone to call them, to offer a sympathetic ear. She knew that their world had suddenly been turned topsy-turvy, that the embarrassment and shame must be acutely painful for them both.

Haven't I felt much the same way in the not so distant past, if for very different reasons?

She reached a hand over toward the telephone, but quickly drew it back, reconsidering. They've made their bed, she thought, and they'll have to lie in it.

Hank and Bobby had unceremoniously dismissed her from their lives – ousted her, she reminded herself – and this whole affair, she decided, was none of her business. After all, they had certainly turned her world on its head.

She supposed she should take some satisfaction from their public humiliation. Their reputations, no matter the outcome of the case, she knew, would be besmirched for the rest of their lives, both in business circles and the high and mighty social circles in which they moved. Not a pretty picture.

She heaved a sigh and swallowed, tasting the bile which had risen up her throat. Had she been seeking revenge, she couldn't have asked for anything better than this. But she took no pleasure in their spectacularly public downfall. No. On the contrary, she was reminded once again that her own instincts could be grossly amiss. That her love and trust in others could be misplaced.

After everything that had happened in the last few months – the betrayal of that love and trust by her ex-husband and her former friend – after all that, she still found this difficult to believe.

Would human nature, the heart and mind of humankind, always be so elusive? So treacherous?

She didn't have the answer to this or so many other questions. But, she decided, if retribution is indeed the Lord's, then let the Lord take it. She would get on with her life.

226

'My God,' Mossy said, coming out of the bathroom, a large white towel fashioned into a sarong wrapped around her. 'You look as if you've seen a ghost.'

Leonie looked up and smiled weakly, sickly. 'I have,' she said. 'Look at this.' She picked the paper up off the floor and handed it over to Mossy, pointing out the article.

Mossy read it intently, then looked over at Leonie. 'Couldn't happen to nicer people,' she crowed. 'Serves the bastards right.'

She saw the downcast expression on Leonie's face and sat down on the bed next to her. She tossed the paper aside and put a hand on each of Leonie's shoulders and squeezed. 'Don't worry, my dear,' she said. 'If you're worried about those two wankers, I'm sure they'll get out of this just fine.'

'Yes,' Leonie said, 'you're probably right.'

'Fancy lawyers, tons of money,' Mossy said. 'You'll see. They'll buy their way out.' She tapped Leonie lightly on the cheek. 'Now put a smile on that beautiful face of yours, my dear. Just be glad you took back your maiden name!'

227

20

Leonie carefully tied the big chocolatey bow on the matte black-wrapped package and eyed it critically. 'Handsome,' she pronounced, especially gratified because she knew that Sam would appreciate her effort.

On the way back from New York City, she had dropped Mossy off at her house in Chatham, then driven home, anxious to see what had been accomplished while she and Mossy had been in New York. She hadn't known what to expect, but was thrilled when she caught her first glimpse of the octagon house. It did not resemble the house she had left only days before.

Behind the painters' scaffolding which sheathed part of its exterior, she could see that the ocher-yellow paint was at once elegant and suitable, and the crisp white trim and darkest green shutters were perfection with it, as she had known they would be. The effect was truly stunning, for the sad, old, weather-beaten, once-beautiful edifice had been transformed, as if a particularly artful plastic surgeon had been at work on the wrinkles and blemishes of an aging star, restoring her to a once-pristine and unspoiled state.

Atop the house, the lantern cupola gleamed in the sunlight like a refurbished crown, a reminder of Sam and the extra lengths to which he'd gone to see to it that the work had been well done.

As she pulled into the drive, she had drawn a deep breath of relief, pleased to see that not only were her choices paying off, but they were actually exceeding her expectations. She'd discovered in the past that what looked good on paper, or what seemed like the perfect solution in her mind's eye, did not necessarily translate into the reality she had planned for or imagined.

It was late Saturday afternoon, and no one was about, so she had the place to herself. Before unloading the Volvo, she had quickly taken a look at the progress outside. She discovered that more than she'd hoped for had been accomplished while she'd been away in the city. But satisfied as she was, her eagle eye noticed several things – detail work, really – that still needed attention, and she made a mental note to let Sam know.

After making several trips from the Volvo to the still-gutted kitchen with shopping bags, she'd wandered through the house, looking at every room. Here, she could see that there was still a lot to do.

Well, she thought, finally back in the kitchen, hands on her hips, surveying the chaos about her, I'll just have to grin and bear it, won't I?

She could clearly foresee her future. For the next couple of weeks at least, she was going to be doing a lot of eating out of cans and going out for pizza. After the luxury of the Soho Grand Hotel in New York, it was going to seem more like camping out than ever.

However, Sam and his men had moved her daybed and other necessities to the top floor, and she could survive quite nicely with the minibar up there.

She eyed her shopping bags which she'd put atop a carpenter's makeshift work table and decided that she would take them upstairs to the third floor out of harm's way later. Now, she wanted to relax a bit and savor being back in the country after the city's intense heat and noise.

But first she'd dashed up to the master suite and retrieved a glass and a bottle of wine from the refrigerator in the minibar. She poured herself a glass and rummaged through shopping bags until she'd found Sam's present, rummaged some more to find the paper and ribbon, and finally retrieved scissors and tape.

Now, she looked at the wrapped package and debated with herself about whether or not to call him. Late Saturday afternoon, she thought. Cocktail hour for lots of folks. Getting ready to go out for the evening. Should I or shouldn't I? After about ten seconds of deliberation, she picked up the telephone and punched in his number.

'Hello?' He picked up on the second ring, breathless. The sound of his rich baritone was still a fresh thrill, no less so than the first time she'd heard it.

'Sam,' she said, 'it's Leonie.'

'Are you at home?' he asked, excitement evident in his voice.

'Uh-huh,' she said, 'I just got in a little while ago.'

'Can I come over?' He was still catching his breath. What had he been doing? she wondered.

'Yes, of course.' She delighted in his genuine, boyish joy, his unrestrained anxiousness. No game-playing with Sam, she thought. He lets me know what he thinks and how he feels.

'I'm on my way,' he said, and hung up.

My, oh my! she thought. I think he missed me, too.

She dashed to the powder room to check her hair and makeup. Applying a fresh coat of Shanghai Express red to her lips, she studied her face. Great, she decided without hesitation. Even if I say so myself. And she knew it was true, because she felt great.

She picked up the little crystal bottle of Caprifoglia and dabbed it generously at her neck and breasts, inhaling its heady honeysuckle

231

fragrance. It was a scent that transported her back to the hills of Capri, and she'd been using it for years, particularly in the summertime, ever since discovering it in Milan at the ancient and venerable Centro Botanica. Bobby had always called it one of her secret weapons, and she thought that if its delightful fragrance pleased others as it did her, then Bobby was right.

She decided the loose, cream silk midi she was wearing would suffice. Its scoop neckline was a tad revealing, and it felt cool against her skin. She would just have to be careful not to get it filthy in all the sawdust and plaster dust and other debris. She dashed back upstairs again and got another wineglass, then grabbed hers and the bottle of wine and took them outside on the terrace. That done, she fetched her big, bound sketchbook, spreading out on a lounger and leafing through it.

It was filled to bursting with her plans for the interior of the house. She had meticulously drawn each room, then written in its dimensions and the measurements of its windows, walls, even the furnishings. She had even sketched in the tentative furniture placement, and drawn different views of each room. Then she had stapled in the color and fabric samples she was going to use in each. She'd also stapled in Polaroid shots of every room from various angles. It had been a lot of work, but she enjoyed it. She knew that it would save her time in the long run and minimize mistakes. It was this sketchbook with its measurements – so patiently and meticulously made – that she had taken to the city with her. It had made her shopping much easier, and it was also a visual diary of a work-in-progress.

All the fabrics and trimmings she'd purchased in New York City had been sent directly to Mrs. Miller, the wonderful seamstress she'd discovered in nearby Chatham. She would be making all the draperies and slipcovers. She already had all the measurements, and knew exactly what Leonie wanted, after several intensive consultations. The wallpaper and other odds and ends would be sent to her by Fed Ex next week.

Leonie took a sip of wine and looked out over the grounds. The sun was beginning to set, and the view west, over the Hudson River to the Catskill Mountains, was heartstoppingly beautiful. To the east, the giant old willow trees were washed in a silvery gilt by the sun's reflection. Before she could tear her eyes away from the awesome scenery, she heard the sound of Sam's Range Rover on the driveway.

Leonie felt a now-familiar and welcome shiver of excitement, knowing that he was here.

Before she could get to her feet, he pulled in and jumped out of the car, rushing toward her with a broad smile, his teeth gleaming white against his bronzed face.

'Look at you!' she cried. 'You look so ... so great!' And he was resplendent, she thought, in black polo shirt, white jodhpurs, and dusty black riding boots. God, she thought. No wonder I missed him!

'I'd just come in from horseback riding when you called,' he said, 'and didn't take the time to change.'

She rose to her feet, and he took her in his arms. 'Hey,' he said, kissing her gently on the lips.

'Hey,' she said, returning his kiss.

She gloried in the feel of him against her, his hard muscularity and brute strength. And the masculine smell of him! It was an intoxicating co-mingling of the out-of-doors, sun, sweat, and leather. Even a bit of the horse. She nuzzled against him, reveling in his sheer physical presence.

For long moments they embraced, Sam simply holding her pressed closely and firmly against him, his face in her hair, his mouth at her ear, inhaling her intoxicating scent.

'I missed you, Leonie,' he whispered. 'More than you can ever know.'

'I missed you, too, Sam,' she said. 'I ... I would never have believed how much.'

He hugged her tightly. 'I couldn't wait for you to get back,' he said.

She laughed with rash impetuosity, her delight in him impossible to contain.

'What is it?' he asked, drawing back and smiling at her, his startlingly blue-green eyes searching hers.

'Oh,' she said. 'You. Me. Us.'

'Yes,' he said. 'Us.' His hands moved up and down her back, anxiously, hungrily, pressing her to him again.

'Come on,' she said. 'First, you have to sit down and have a glass of wine. I've got something for you.'

'What?' he asked, reluctantly relinquishing his hold on her.

'You'll see,' Leonie said, a mischievous light dancing in her eyes. 'I'll be right back.'

Sam poured himself a glass of wine and sat down. He sipped at the wine, then picked up her sketchbook and flipped through it.

Leonie came back outside, and he looked up. 'This is amazing,' he said, holding up the sketchbook. 'I knew you were organized, but this is phenomenal. A real piece of work. When in the world did you do it? I haven't seen you working on it.'

'Usually at night, after everybody has left for the day,' she said. 'And on the weekends.'

'It's really professional looking,' Sam said.

'It's not my first one,' Leonie said. 'And will not be my last,' she added. She had been holding the package behind her back, and now she had held it out to him.

'Here,' she said, 'this is something I picked up for you in the city. For all your help and . . . and everything else.'

'This is beautiful,' he said, a grin on his face, 'but I'm going to tear it open anyway.'

However, he carefully removed the bow and paper, placing them on the stone terrace beside him, then he studied the present closely, intently, before looking up at her, a wondrous gratitude etched into his features.

'I don't know what to say, Leonie.' His voice was hushed, almost reverent. 'This is beautiful. I don't think anybody's ever given me anything like this before.'

'I was hoping you'd like it,' she said.

'Alexander Friedrich Werner,' he read. 'German, circa 1877.' It was a small pencil and wash on paper, a study of a neoclassical cupola much like the one on the house, which he'd worked so hard at restoring to perfection.

'I thought it would be a fitting remembrance of this project,' Leonie said. 'After all your work on the cupola. Finding the glass and all.'

Sam stood up, embracing her again. 'And it is,' he said. He kissed her. 'Thank you, Leonie,' he added.

'You're welcome,' she replied.

'Have you seen what's been done while you were away?' he asked.

She nodded. 'Yes, and I'm thrilled.' She hesitated.

'But?' he said, smiling knowingly.

She grinned self-consciously. 'Well, there are a few things, little things, that need to be seen to,' she said. 'Why don't we do a quick look-see, so I can point them out while they're fresh in my mind.'

'Always the perfectionist.' He squeezed her.

'Well,' she said. 'I have been accused of it.'

'Let's go,' he said, and took her arm.

Later, after another stroll around the property and a discussion of the work, they stood in the barn, enjoying the theatrical effect of the waning light in its lofty interior.

'It's really beautiful, isn't it?' Sam said.

Leonie agreed. 'You've done a great job,' she said.

He put an arm around her shoulder and hugged her to him. 'We did a great job,' he corrected her.

He leaned down and kissed her cheek, and Leonie responded, suddenly ravenous for him after days of a physical craving she'd never before experienced. Now, his physical proximity made waiting any longer to satisfy this aching need torturous.

Within moments, they were entwined, his lips and hands all over her. She leaned back against a beam for support, and Sam's hands slowly ran under her dress and up her thighs until they found her panties. He pulled them down gently, his hands brushing her buttocks. Then his deft fingers began exploring those buttocks and her mound, simultaneously, rubbing delicately at first, then more firmly, until one hand discovered her moistness.

Leonie gasped in pleasure, her breathing coming in rasps, as Sam moaned and began delving into her most private place, working his fingers in wondrous ways.

Then, he knelt before her, sliding her panties down farther still and pushing her dress up. He began kissing her thighs, his lips working their way up, his tongue licking its way, up, up, up to that soft moist triangle which now awaited him in anxious and distended readiness.

Leonie threw her head back, her hands in his hair, as his mouth found her mound and he buried it there, hungrily devouring her. His hands pressed her firm, rounded buttocks toward him, and his tongue worked its magic, swirling, licking, probing.

'Oh, Sam,' she breathed. 'Oh, my God, that feels so wonderful. Oh . . . oh . . .'

He suddenly stopped, pulling his face away, and stood back up, encircling her in his arms again, his mouth searching out hers. He pulled her against him, and there was no mistaking the tumescence in his jodhpurs, pressing hard and ready against her.

'Oh, I can't wait another second,' Leonie gasped. 'I want you so much. I want you in me.'

Her words were like a jolt of electricity to him. Still holding her, his mouth on hers, he unbuckled his belt and unzipped his jodhpurs. He brought one of her hands down to it, and she rejoiced in its throbbing hardness.

Sam then reached under her thighs with his powerful arms and lifted her up, her back against the beam, her legs spreading out to either side of him. His hands were now under her buttocks, holding her up and open to him. Leonie wrapped her legs around him, and as she did so, he plunged into her wetness, all the way.

She cried out in ecstasy as he pinned her to the beam with his powerful, swollen manhood. Then, unable to wait, he began thrusting right away in a frenzy of desire, hard and long, pulling almost all the way back out, then plunging back in to the hilt, ramming her back against the beam.

Leonie thought she would be split wide open, that she couldn't possibly endure such penetration, but his energetic lustiness only served to increase her own wanton desire.

It was only short moments before she was swept up in wave after wave of sensual release, crying out in ecstasy, unable to control the shudders which rent through her. Her cries spurred Sam to new heights of frenzied thrusts, and in one final plunge he exploded inside her, over and over, spasming in his own stupendous release, and groaning in cathartic joy.

Panting, gasping, so breathless they could not speak, he held her there for long moments, his lips hungrily kissing hers, until he could finally rasp out: 'I love you, Leonie. I love you. Love you. Love you.'

'I . . . love . . . you . . . too,' she managed to gasp.

He slowly eased her legs down to the floor, and they stood facing each other, exhausted for the moment from their efforts. He held her in his arms, kissing her lightly on the face, the neck, the ears, until their breathing finally returned to normal and their racing heartbeats subsided.

'You really mean it, don't you?' he said. 'You're really certain? You really love me?'

Leonie looked up into his eyes. 'I meant it, Sam,' she said. 'I do love you.'

He hugged her to him harder than ever, and held her there, squeezing as if he would never let her go.

At long last, they parted.

Sam picked up her panties and handed them to her, and she slid into them. He zipped up his jodhpurs, buckled his belt.

Leonie shook her head. 'Crazy,' she said, laughing.

'Yeah,' Sam agreed, joining in her laughter. 'Love crazy.'

Arm in arm, they walked back up to the terrace, where they sat down and sipped wine, holding hands, unable to take their eyes off each other. Neither was quite back down to earth after their voyage through the heaven of carnal pleasure.

At last Leonie spoke. 'Why don't we have a snack and go spread out? We can go up to the top floor to my glorious big suite. That is, unless you have to leave?'

'No, no, no,' he said. 'I don't have to leave. There's a big party tonight and Minette's cousin Dirck is taking her. A family thing – all the cousins' – he made a face – 'I always bow out of it.'

He rose to his feet, towering over her, and offered her a hand. 'Let's go in,' he said.

Plates with cheeses, a sweetish mascarpone, a tangy chevre, a ripe brie; and spreads, spicy sun-dried tomato and basil feta, a garlicky hummus; sat half-empty on a tray. Olives – oil cured, wine cured, and Greek – and water wafers, picked over in their bowls, made a semi-circle around them. Sam's riding boots and Leonie's sandals made a pile on the floor next to the table.

The eight bull's-eye windows and those in the cupola were open, letting in a cooling breeze. Flickering candlelight illuminated the remains of the feast and glinted off their wineglasses. On the ornate daybed, Sam ran his fingers up and down Leonie's arm as they lay, face-to-face, while she finished telling him about her trip to New York and what she'd read in *The Times*.

'I don't think you should feel so unsure of yourself,' Sam said.

Leonie sighed. 'I don't seem to be able to help it. To shake the feeling that there must be something wrong with me to have made such wrong choices.'

'Remember what I told you earlier this summer,' Sam said. 'The man you married and the man Hank Reynolds is today – the man he became – are two very different people. He's been through a lot of changes that don't have anything to do with you. None of this is because of you.'

He looked into her eyes. 'And if you ask me' – he kissed her lips – 'I don't think there's any way in the world that your instincts could possibly be improved upon.'

She smiled. 'I think you're just a little prejudiced,' she said. 'But I'll take your word for it. Especially regarding you and me.'

She squeezed his muscular bicep with her hand. 'I don't see how anybody could not believe in you, trust you . . . love you.'

Sam sighed, and that familiar haunted look came into his eyes. 'I wish . . .' he began, but then lay staring off into space, far away, in some sadder world of his own.

'What is it, Sam?' Leonie asked. 'You can talk to me. You know that.'

His eyes roamed the dark corners of the lofty room before finally settling on hers. 'I wish I could always be here for you,' he said. 'I want that more than anything.'

He heaved a sigh. 'But I know that, even though she doesn't love me, Minette would fight like hell to keep me around. And of course you know why I stay there with her.'

'I understand,' Leonie said.

'Now she's put the Van Vechten Building on the market,' Sam went on. He hadn't told Leonie about it before. He'd felt uncomfortable discussing Minette's increasingly hostile behavior, perhaps because he was afraid that Leonie might feel in some way responsible. He looked at her, a wry smile suddenly brightening his features. 'So you have an architect without an office,' he said.

'What?' Leonie said. 'Out of the blue?'

'I'm not really surprised,' Sam said. 'She's been trying to get me to quit working for a long time. I guess this is just another one of her retaliatory tactics to make it that much more difficult. I'm really not sure.'

'Sounds like she wants to punish you,' Leonie said.

'I think you're right on the mark,' Sam said. 'But enough of that. I just wish things were different. That I could always be here for you.'

He paused and pulled her closer, kissing her deeply for long moments. 'I love you so much.'

Leonie looked into his eyes. 'And I love you, Sam,' she whispered. 'And remember. No matter what happens, I'll be here for you.'

She ran a hand down his strong back to his hard, tight, rounded buttocks, stroking, caressing, and he eased himself up against her, one hand sliding under her dress and up the backs of her legs to her buttocks, pulling her even closer to him, kissing her now more urgently.

Leonie felt his hardness pressing against her again, and the flickers of desire once again began flaming up within her.

Sam drew his head back. 'Let's get undressed, okay?'

Leonie nodded, smiling.

They got up off the daybed and undressed each other, slowly, reverently, reveling in their nakedness together.

Not knowing or caring what tomorrow would bring.

PART THREE

AUTUMN

21

Ominous storm clouds gathered on the horizon. There was the hint of a nip in the air, and pale gray light seeped through the windows of the breakfast room just off Van Vechten Manor's large country kitchen. The smells of freshly brewed coffee, orange juice, and Erminda's apple pancakes did little to dispel the air of gloom that pervaded the otherwise cheerfully decorated room.

Minette sat buttering a slice of crispy whole-wheat toast, gazing across the table at Sam, who was munching, vigorously and hungrily, on a slice of pancake and looking at the *New York Times*, which was spread out beside him.

She took a bite of toast, chewed, and washed it down with black coffee, then cleared her throat. 'What did you do with your stuff?'

Sam looked up. 'My stuff?' he asked, so preoccupied that for a moment he was uncertain what she was referring to.

'Oh,' he said evenly, realization quickly dawning, 'I got one of those storage rooms at a place near Hudson.'

'Seems like a waste of money to me,' Minette said. 'Why don't you just get rid of it?'

'I plan on finding another office,' Sam said, taking a sip of coffee. 'I'm going to go on working, you know.'

'As you please,' she said, smiling sweetly, 'but you'd better watch your pennies, darling.'

'I always do,' Sam said. 'You know that, Minette. In fact, there was a time when you joked about my penny-pinching.'

'Well, it's no joke anymore, darling,' Minette said. 'I've closed our joint checking account.'

'You what?' he said, truly surprised. Sam put his fork down and knocked the newspaper onto the floor.

'The money's in a new account. In my name only,' she went on. 'It's my money after all. My trust fund.'

'I'm well aware of that, Minette,' Sam said heatedly. 'But if you'll recall, the only use I ever made of that money was to do things like pay your help and feed your horses.'

'Dirck will be doing all that in the future,' Minette said. 'If you insist on working, then you're going to have to live off what you make.'

'Is that why you're suddenly doing this?' he asked. 'Because of my working?'

Minette shrugged. 'Think what you will,' she said inconclusively, obviously unwilling to discuss the matter any further.

'Fine, Minette,' Sam said. He took the napkin from his lap and threw it down on the table next to his plate, his patience finally worn too thin to accept her abuse with equanimity. 'Does that mean I'm supposed to move, too? This is your house, after all.'

She looked at him with a smile. 'Oh, darling. I wouldn't be too hasty. I wouldn't give you a divorce, no matter what,' she said. She took a sip of coffee.

'Who asked for one?' Sam asked, his voice taut with exasperation and anger. He shoved his chair back and got to his feet.

'Running off to work, are you?' Minette said. 'Well, I hope you've got gas money, because you're not getting it from me.'

Sam stared at her without speaking. He didn't trust himself to respond to her taunts, so he turned and left the breakfast room, trying to control his rage, his fists and teeth clenched, his head spinning with this, her latest and most castrating news thus far.

Jesus, it can't get worse, can it? he wondered, slamming the front door behind him.

Rolling down the highway toward the octagon house, he wondered again what on earth had gotten into his wife. Was it truly a simple matter of his working that was enraging her so, pushing her to such mean extremes? She had never lashed out like this before.

First, putting the Van Vechten Building – a part of her family's precious heritage – on the market. Now this. He didn't care about the money. After all, he was working, making good money off Leonie's project. Plus, he had savings from projects he'd worked on over the years. No, it wasn't the money. It was the principle of the matter.

Why was she suddenly doing it? What the hell was the matter? When he tried to discuss it with her, she simply refused or offered some lame excuse. Sam felt that there was bound to be more to it than met the eye, something he was missing, something she was keeping from him. But what?

Was it possible that she'd heard something about him and Leonie? This was not the first time he'd wondered about this, especially in light of Minette's behavior. But, if so, from whom? And how? They'd been extremely discreet, their truly intimate moments so few and so private that he couldn't imagine that there was any talk about them.

What, then? he asked himself.

He drove on toward the octagon house, more perplexed than ever. At the same time, he'd about decided that he couldn't take much more of Minette's outrageously humiliating behavior toward him. He had just about reached his limit with it.

245

But what am I going to do?

He wished he knew.

Erminda approached the breakfast table, and silently began removing the remains of Sam's unfinished breakfast. She looked over at Minette, who sipped at her coffee, thumbing through *Horse and Rider*, seemingly oblivious to her servant.

Erminda cleared her throat before speaking, but Minette still ignored her. 'I know it's none of my business, Mrs. Nicholson,' Erminda finally ventured, struggling to keep her voice calm even though she was a cauldron of heated emotions, threatening to boil over at any moment. 'But why do you make an argument with Mr. Sam? He tries to please you, to make you happy, all the time.'

Minette looked up from her magazine now, her blue eyes wide and glinting, first with surprise, then with amused contempt. 'You're right, Erminda. It's none of your business,' she said. 'You just work here, remember?'

'I don't mean to interfere,' Erminda said. 'I just know that he is a very good man. A nice man—'

Minette made a moue of distaste and peered at Erminda down the full length of her aristocratic nose. 'I was going to give you the weekend off, Erminda,' she said, cutting off her maid, any hint of amusement gone out of her voice.

Erminda looked at her, her eyebrows raised quizzically. 'Oh?'

'But I'm firing you instead,' Minette spat. 'Now pack your things and get out.'

'The bloody bitch!' Mossy snapped. 'Of course she's listed the building with her dear, dear friend, that sodding Andrea Walker. No surprise there.'

She paced the living room's gray carpeting, telephone in one hand, ubiquitous cigarette in the other.

'Then why are you so upset?' Leonie asked.

'Why am I upset!' Mossy cried. 'It is a multiple listing. I've tried to show it three times to a very interested gentleman from New York. And do you know what they do?'

She didn't wait for a response, her words coming in a torrent of outrage. 'Every single time, they've made lame excuses about having lost the keys, or some such shit! They will not let me show the place! It is infuriating.'

'Listen, Moss,' Leonie said, 'why don't you let me take you out to dinner tonight, and we can talk about it then? Is that okay?'

Leonie wanted to hear her friend out and try to cheer her up, but she had her hands full right now, busy mixing paints, trying to achieve the precise shade of yellow which she wanted in the parlor – a butter yellow not easy to come by, she'd discovered. Her T-shirt and old khaki shorts were paint-splotched testimony to her efforts thus far, as were her hands, arms, and legs.

'Heaven!' Mossy replied. 'Let's go to some low bar and get shit-faced!'

'That isn't exactly what I had in mind,' Leonie said, laughing, 'but whatever your heart desires. Okay?'

'Bloody marvelous,' Mossy enthused.

'Why don't you come on by here when you're done with work,' Leonie said, 'and we can decide where to go.'

'I'll ring you before I head over that way,' Mossy said.

'Great,' Leonie said. 'See you.'

'See you.'

Mossy hung up the receiver and stubbed her cigarette out in an ashtray. Tonight would be a much-needed break from work. She'd had a lot of catching up to do after being in New York City. Still did, for that matter. And now, thanks to Minette Nicholson, Andrea Walker had thrown a wrench into what might have been a very nice sales commission. A veery nice sales commission, indeed.

That bitch has interfered with me and my business for the last

247

time, Mossy thought. I may not be a bloody nabob around here, but I've got my own means for revenge.

And revenge, she decided, it would be. Somehow or other, sometime or other.

Erminda carefully folded the last of her clothing – a white cotton blouse – and placed it neatly in the suitcase which lay open on top of her bed. Then she carefully checked to make certain she had left nothing of her own behind.

First, the closet. Bare.

Next, the drawers. All empty.

Finally, the bathroom. Like the day she moved in.

Satisfied, she hung her uniforms in the closet and shut the door. Good! The detestable, ugly things belonged to Mrs. Nicholson, and she certainly wouldn't miss them. She went to the bed to close her suitcase, but had a sudden inspiration.

She rushed from her room to the library, making certain that Mrs. Nicholson didn't see or hear her. There, she grabbed a very valuable keepsake, and tore back upstairs to her room with it.

She went over to her suitcase and picked up the top two or three articles of clothing and reverently laid down the photograph of Sam Nicholson in its sterling silver frame. She stared lovingly at it for long moments, then placed the clothing on top of it, and, her eyes now brimming with tears, closed the suitcase.

She stood and looked around the room. The life we could have here, she thought. Just me and Mr. Sam without that witch.

She picked up the suitcase and started out of the room. If it's the last thing I ever do, she thought, I'll get even with Minette Nicholson for ruining my life.

Now, one more little job to do, and my work here is finished.

Mossy had spent hours showing houses, even mobile homes, but her efforts had all proved fruitless today. Not a single one of her potential buyers was interested in a single one of her listings. To top off a day of one disappointment after another, she was once again given the runaround when she telephoned Andrea Walker for the keys to the Van Vechten Building.

'Oh, I'm soooo sorry, Mossy,' Andrea had drawled, 'but a man is looking at the building aaaall afternoon. You knooooow how it is. With partners and inspectors and so on. Probably be there quite late.'

'Tomorrow then,' Mossy had said.

She heard Andrea shuffle around some papers. 'Oh, dear,' she'd said, 'looks like it's all booked up for tomorrow, too. Hmmm. Tell you what, Mossy. I'll call you when it's okay to pick up the keys. All right?' Then she'd abruptly hung up.

Mossy slammed down the receiver. 'Bloody little shit!' she spat. She grabbed her cigarettes and lit one, smoking thoughtfully for a moment. Then she reached over and picked the receiver back up and punched in Leonie's number.

'Hello?' Leonie was out of breath.

'It's Mossy, dear,' she said quietly. 'Have to take a raincheck on the dinner. I've . . . I've had a change of plans.'

'Who is he?' Leonie asked with amusement in her voice.

'No, no,' Mossy said, 'nothing like that. Just . . .'

Leonie waited.

'Just some business to take care of,' Mossy said, being uncharacteristically reticent.

'Okay,' Leonie said, wondering why Mossy was being so mysterious. 'Give me a ring when you get a chance.'

'Will do, dear,' Mossy said, and replaced the receiver.

She grabbed her cigarettes and lighter and shoved them in her shoulder bag, snatched up her car keys, and sailed out the door, headed for her Acura. She got in and fired up the engine, spewing gravel as she tore out of her driveway.

The workmen had left for the day, and the house was quiet.
Leonie scrubbed off the last of the paint that she could see
and toweled herself off. I looked like a Jackson Pollock, she thought,
checking herself in the bathroom mirror again. She had been covered
with various colored splotches from head to toe, and was certain that
there was still a veritable palette of colors dotting her body.

Oh, well, she decided, if that's the worst the day brings, I'm a
pretty lucky lady. She left the master suite on the third floor and
walked downstairs to the kitchen. The terrible stench from the
polyurethane sealer had almost completely dissipated now – thank
God! – and the floor looked magnificent. Its old wide-board pine
floors shone to perfection in the light. The big old beams overhead
had been cleaned and oiled, and she thanked her lucky stars that
they had been there, only to be exposed.

The cabinetry and appliances had now been installed, and she
thought they worked very well. She had decided on a green for the
cabinets; it was a hue with a bit of olive in it, based on the early

American paints made from milk and often used in these houses of this age, and it looked great with the sunny yellow walls. The cabinet knobs were a contrasting pine, with a natural finish which was sealed to protect them. The real stunner was the countertops – real butcher block. It was thick, substantial, expensive, and, she decided, worth every penny it cost.

As were the appliances. She had known that she would have to spend big bucks for appliances, especially if she wanted to market the house to well-heeled New Yorkers. Fancy, pricey, professional kitchen equipment was all the rage, even for those weekenders who rarely, if ever, cooked. She knew that many of them hardly ever stepped into the kitchen, but the equipment had better be there for show, if nothing else. So there was a huge, stainless-steel Garland gas range with double ovens and hood, a Subzero stainless-steel refrigerator, and two Asko super-quiet dishwashers.

She heard a knock at the back door, and left the kitchen to answer it. It was Sam.

'You're still here,' she said, smiling. 'I didn't see your car and thought you'd already left.'

'No,' he replied, 'thought I'd stick around and see if there was anything I could do to help you around the house.'

'You didn't have to do that,' Leonie said. 'But I'm glad you stuck around. I want to show you the top floor. Jimmy and I got a lot done today.' Jimmy was the young man Mossy had found for her to help her out around the house.

'Good,' Sam said. 'I wondered what you two were up to. I've hardly seen you.'

'Let's go upstairs,' she said. She took one of his hands and led the way up to the third floor, to the master bedroom suite.

'My Lord!' Sam said, as they stepped into the huge room. 'It's going to be beautiful, Leonie. It already is beautiful.'

'Yes,' she said, 'it is, isn't it.'

'The fabric on the walls is great,' Sam said. 'It looks like something in a French country house with the old beams.'

The toile de Jouy was a creamy off-white with pastoral scenes printed on it in blacks and grays.

'I wanted more color,' Leonie said, 'but it was too expensive. Anyway, this works well. So the color will come in the accessories.' She and Jimmy had spent all day cutting fabric, sewing strips together where necessary, and stapling it up over the batting she'd already stapled to the walls.

'I've still got to glue the trim up,' she said, holding up a length of cream braid. 'Mrs. Miller is making the hangings for the bed, and a spread and bed skirt and shams. All out of the same fabric.' The bed was an old iron one she'd gotten out of storage, with a canopy soaring above it. To either side of the bed, country French fruitwood tables held black tole lamps and stacks of books, magazines, and small vases of full-blown roses from the garden. Her trusty daybed was now used as a couch, set against another wall, piled with beautiful silk cushions.

'I haven't brought up most of the furniture yet,' Leonie said. 'It can stay out of the way in the barn for now.'

Sam looked at her. 'Where did you learn to do all this?' he asked.

Leonie laughed. 'Mostly by watching the people do it in the apartment in New York City and the house in Southampton. I figured I could do it myself. Plus, Jimmy has been a real help. He's a fast learner.'

'Did the men get the mirror in today?' Sam asked.

'Oh, yes,' Leonie said. 'Come and look.'

They walked into the bathrooms, two capacious rooms adjoining one another, all white marble and mirror now. Their only difference was that one held a Jacuzzi, while the other had a glassed-in shower.

'The men did a good job,' Sam said, examining the seams where mirror met marble.

253

'That they did,' she said. She looked up at him. 'Come on, let's go see the rest,' she said. 'Okay?'

'I'd better,' Sam said. 'It's getting to the point of no return as far as changes go. So if you want any, now's the time to let me know.'

'I don't think so,' Leonie said. 'I just want you to see what Jimmy and I did today.'

On the second floor, she led him through all four bedrooms and the two bathrooms to show him where she and Jimmy had tested paint samples on the walls and woodwork and stapled up pieces of the fabrics to be used for curtains.

'There's a red room, a blue room, a green room, and a sort of gold room,' Leonie said. 'Although none of them are really all one color. Those are just the predominant colors.'

Sam looked at her and grinned. 'I see where your sketchbook really comes in handy,' he said.

'You bet it does,' Leonie said. 'Let's go on downstairs.'

In the library, she showed him where she had stapled up a length of green felt. 'This is like the color of a billiard table,' she said. 'And I got it for nearly nothing. The walls will be covered with it, and the curtains will be this fabric that looks like a kilim rug. See?'

'What about the bookcases?' Sam asked.

'My friend Pierre is coming up from New York to paint them to look like mahogany,' Leonie said. 'He's great and so is his work. You'll see.'

'It's really impressive,' Sam said. 'And it looks so much more expensive than it really is.'

'That's the idea,' Leonie said.

In the parlor she showed him the yellow she had finally arrived at by trying several different mixes. 'It goes really well with the yellow silk for the curtains, don't you think?'

'Yeah,' Sam said. 'It looks perfect to me.'

'It'll be pale and airy in here,' she said. 'The library, of course, is much darker. More . . . masculine, I guess.'

They walked from the parlor into the dining room, where Leonie stopped and frowned. 'This room has been a real challenge,' she said. 'It begs to have murals above the wainscoting. But.'

Sam smiled. 'One of your famous "buts"? What's it all about in here?'

'Well,' she said, 'having them hand-done would be far too expensive. Buying enough of the really beautiful wallpaper murals, like Zuber, is also too expensive. Like an arm and a leg. And if you buy the cheap ones, well, they look . . . cheap! So I had to compromise. I finally found this chinoiserie wallpaper that will work well. It wasn't cheap, but it looks great.' She pointed to a strip stapled to the wall.

Sam looked at the paper with its Chinese motif. 'I approve,' he said with a grin.

'Now,' Leonie said, 'it's just a matter of your men finishing up the parquet down here. None of the painting and papering can be done until the floors are finished. No more fabric can be put up either. I don't want anything to get ruined.'

'It won't be long,' Sam said. 'But I'm not going to rush them any more than I already have. I want them to do a first-rate job.'

'I'm not being pushy,' Leonie said, hoping she hadn't sounded that way. 'That's just where things stand right now.'

'I didn't think you were being pushy,' Sam said, turning to her. He took her in his arms and looked into her eyes, then kissed her brow.

Leonie hugged him closer and kissed his lips, then drew back. 'How about a glass of wine?' she said.

'Good idea,' Sam said.

They sat in the kitchen, sipping wine. The storm clouds of early morning still hovered, promising rain, but it had not yet come. The gray clouds and the slight nip in the air made for a gloomy combination, but Sam and Leonie were impervious to the weather's unpleasantness.

'I've started calling old clients in New York,' Leonie said. 'And I've got two or three very interested in this place.'

'Already?' Sam said. 'Jeez. That's fast, isn't it?'

'Well, you know how it is,' Leonie said. 'For most people time is money, especially these filthy rich types. Luckily, they trust me enough to do a place up that they will really love. I know what they want, their tastes and so on. And they know that if I do it, they can move in A.M. and entertain P.M. No hassles, you know. Practically everything done for them.'

'Unbelievable,' Sam said.

'Believe it,' she said. 'So, anyway. I've got Mossy seriously on the trail of another house to renovate. And guess who I'd like to work on it with me?' She looked at him, a mischievous smile on her face.

'Who?' he joked. 'Not me, surely?'

'You bet,' Leonie said. 'And maybe soon. We'll see.'

Sam studied her face intently, gratified by the mixture of pure and simple excitement, joy, and – yes, he thought – hope which graced her features.

'I can't even pretend that it wouldn't be the best thing I can imagine happening,' Sam said. 'Can you picture it? The two of us getting to work on another project. Together.'

'I was hoping you would cotton to the idea,' Leonie said. 'I think we make a great team.'

Sam reached a hand across the table to one of hers and squeezed it affectionately. 'I think so, too,' he said.

She looked into his eyes. 'I've also been thinking,' she said, a more serious note in her voice, 'that we could maybe even . . . well – and I hope I'm not being too forward or presumptuous here – maybe even go into business together.'

She took a sip of her wine before continuing. 'I could purchase properties, and you could use your inestimable abilities to renovate them.' She gave his hand a squeeze.

'I could also do up the interiors, just like here, then let Mossy handle the selling. I feel pretty confident that we'd be able to attract well-heeled New Yorkers, especially after we've snagged a couple. Birds of a feather and all that.' She paused again, searching his face for a clue to his thoughts. 'It's just an idea, Sam, but what do you think?'

For a moment, he simply looked at her, digesting this piece of news in silence. 'Sometimes I'm certain that some kind of fate threw us together, Leonie,' he finally said. 'That our meeting was destined. Now, I guess I'm more convinced than ever that it's true. It's just so . . . so perfect.'

Relief and exhilaration washed over Leonie in equal measures. She had not been absolutely certain that he would like the idea. He might think that whatever independence he had was being threatened, or that she was trying to get too close, too fast.

God knows, she thought, our physical relationship is sublime. I've never had better sex in my life. And mentally, they were on the same wavelength, most of the time at least. Emotionally, deep down inside that mysterious place called the soul, could it be better? No. She didn't think so.

But working together? A lot of men would probably draw the line there, she thought. Some sort of male pride might be at work that she was unsure of.

She looked at him now, nodding her head in agreement. 'I've felt exactly the same way. That this is our destiny. Our fate.'

And it was true. She thought that together, they were a force united, a force that could push back the dark shadows in each other's lives. That together, they could do anything.

Sam couldn't remember ever having been so happy, so full of love, so full of hope for the future. His fears of commitment, of his own emotions, of trusting himself – let alone another person – seemed to be dissolving, becoming mere phantoms, and he knew that it was because of his love for this woman who sat so serenely before him.

It was a love that had grown from that first powerful physical attraction in the spring, through the summer, and now had become a full-blown force to be reckoned with.

There was only one blight on the landscape, he thought. One malignant and very powerful force which threatened the perfection he and Leonie had found together: Minette.

When they finished their wine and he got up to leave, Sam felt empowered by a new determination, a new resolve: He knew what he had to do, and he was going back to the manor and do it.

23

The body floated facedown in the swimming pool.

Pale blond hair fanned out to the sides from its head, shifting ever so slightly as the water, shimmering in the wind, moved almost imperceptibly. A wheelchair, oddly incongruous, sat empty by the narrow stone coping at the edge of the pool.

Except for the swishing of the wind in the trees, an eerie quietness enveloped the setting in a shroud of tranquility. Even the early fall cicadas appeared to have hushed their chorus out of respect for the dead.

He stared at the body in silence, still as a statue, for what seemed like eternity, but might have been mere seconds. He didn't know. Time had stopped at this place, focused on this appalling tableau.

He felt as if he were floating above the scene, looking down at it, seeing the body in the pool, the wheelchair at pool's edge, and his own lone figure, standing there mute and immobile, staring at the body, transfixed by its inert lifelessness.

Finally, in an unearthly trancelike state, he turned and retraced his steps to the conservatory and picked up the telephone. He punched in 911 and waited, his eyes glancing about the room, seeing it in a different light, as if for the first time.

The luxuriant, flowering plants and vines, once so beautiful in their verdant profusion, were suddenly mocking, their tendrils seeming to reach out to him, threatening to choke, to suffocate, pointing fingers of guilt and shame.

'This is Sam Nicholson,' he told the operator when she finally answered. He gave her the address.

'It's my wife,' he said, calmly and quietly, in complete control of himself. 'She's dead. In the swimming pool.'

When the call was over, he walked over to the drinks table and poured himself a splash of Scotch. He drank it down neat, then poured another one, mixing this one with ice and a little water. He stood staring into space for a few moments, then sat down to wait, controlling his desperate impulse to call Leonie, to tell her what had happened.

Suddenly, he jumped to his feet and strode to the entrance hall. He couldn't sit in the conservatory any longer, not with its view of the pool. He had to distance himself from the scene. From the body – her body.

He sat down heavily on the graceful steps leading upstairs, elbows on his knees, head in his hands, his eyes riveted to the front door, as if it was there that he would find the answers to the questions swirling through his mind like so many poisonous eels.

Long, distended minutes later – a lifetime of waiting – the intercom from the front gates buzzed. Sam got up and pressed the button that opened the gates, not bothering to ask who was there.

'What time did you get home, Mr. Nicholson?' the policeman asked, his eyes sweeping around the library, taking in its darkly rich grandeur, then coming to rest like lasers on Sam.

'About seven or seven-thirty,' Sam said. 'Somewhere around there. I'm not really sure.'

'Where were you?'

'I was working at a construction project, a house downriver. Then I went by my office . . . my former office,' he amended, 'to pick up some paperwork I'd left there.'

The questions dragged on and on, relentlessly and often repetitiously, while the medical examiner and a photographer worked in the pool area, and other police officers swarmed over the house and grounds.

After a time, the detective excused himself to confer with the medical examiner, and Sam went out to the conservatory to pour himself another drink. Through the glass the pool area was brightly floodlit, and in this harsh brilliance, he watched these men – perfect strangers – as they zipped up a body bag, Minette's aristocratic elegance rendered featureless, inhuman, by its ugliness, its blackness. Its finality, he thought.

He was repulsed by the sight, but couldn't tear his eyes away from it until the men, body in hand, disappeared around the side of the house.

Finally turning away to go back to the library, he saw the homicide detective, Biegner his name was, watching him. From his hand a clear plastic Baggie dangled.

'We may have ourselves a real problem here, Mr. Nicholson,' he said.

Sam stared at him. 'What is it?' he asked, not really moved to curiosity, just going through the motions. He'd immediately given them permission to search the house and grounds, just as he'd agreed to answer their questions.

'It's a note, Mr. Nicholson. I would guess in your wife's handwriting,' he said. 'It was on the desk in that office off the kitchen.'

Sam heard his words, but they didn't register.

'Says here, somebody hated her. "He" hated her, wanted to see

261

her out of the way.' He looked at Sam through tired, puffy eyes. 'You wouldn't know anything about that, would you?'

'No,' Sam said. 'I don't know anything about it.'

'You said the maid should have been here, right?' Biegner went on.

'Yes,' Sam said, 'Erminda. She lives here. I don't know where she is.'

'Well,' Biegner said, scratching his head, 'why don't you take me to her room. Let's have a look.'

Sam took him upstairs to the now-deserted maid's room. He stood looking around, then turned to the detective with a puzzled expression.

'Huh.' Biegner grunted, scratching his head. 'Looks like she cleared out.'

'I don't know what the hell's going on,' Sam said. 'Erminda was here this morning when I left, and as far as I know, she wasn't planning on leaving.'

'Any idea where she could be?' Biegner asked.

'No,' Sam said. 'I know she has relatives in New York City. I don't know who or where exactly.' He suddenly realized how little he actually knew about Erminda; how, in fact, this woman who had been living in the same house with him and his wife for some time was an almost complete stranger.

But one thing he did know: She hated Minette.

'Do you want to come over here?' Leonie asked. Her voice was concerned, but even. She was struggling to keep her composure. She didn't want to upset Sam any more than she knew he already must be.

Her initial shock had worn off to some extent, but she had not yet fully digested the news, its reality being so horrifying that it simply hadn't sunk in. It still seemed too unbelievable to be true.

This happens in movies, she thought. Not in real life. Certainly not in my life.

She knew that Sam needed her now more than ever, and she desperately wanted to be with him, to comfort him as much as was possible under the circumstances. 'Maybe you should get out of there,' she added.

Sam hesitated. 'I don't know if I should leave here.' He sounded perplexed and unsure of himself. 'I mean, of course I want to come over. I just don't know if it's the best thing to do under the circumstances.'

'Oh, Sam!' Leonie said indignantly. 'My God! They can't think for a minute that you had anything to do with it.'

'I don't know,' he said worriedly. 'But they told me to stick around. And in no uncertain terms. This fellow Biegner, a homicide detective, I think, said there would probably be more questions for me tomorrow. They're doing an autopsy.'

'How long will that take?' Leonie asked.

'Probably only a couple of days,' Sam said. 'Biegner said that the medical examiner wasn't too busy, and that being who Minette is – was—' Sam corrected himself, 'they would probably do a rush job.'

'Well,' Leonie said, 'you've already told them everything you know. Don't worry. Christ, you were here when it happened!'

'Probably,' Sam said.

'What do you mean "probably"?' Leonie said. 'You went home from here.'

'I stopped at the Van Vechten Building to pick up a box of files I'd left there,' Sam said. 'I'd cleared out everything else, but needed this stuff for my accountant. So I didn't want to store it. I left it there to pick up later.'

'Well, that couldn't have taken long,' Leonie said. Despite her staunch belief in him, she couldn't help but feel a sense of dread creeping over her, little needles of worry pricking somewhere at the back of her consciousness.

'No,' Sam said. 'I wasn't there for more than fifteen or twenty minutes. You know, I looked around the old building. Sort of said goodbye to the place. It's the only office I've ever had.'

'I know what you mean,' Leonie said. Her head was spinning now, the news beginning to sink in, reality's ugly head asserting itself in no uncertain terms. It was perhaps not as simple as she had first thought.

'What about the maid?' she asked. 'Do you have any idea what could have happened to her?'

'No,' Sam said. 'She'd completely cleared out.' He sighed. 'The police are looking into that. I got telephone bills for the last few months out of the files and found some number out in Queens or Brooklyn that she'd called. At least I assumed she called it. Neither one of us even knows anybody with a seven-one-eight area code.'

'That was good thinking,' Leonie said.

'I guess so. The whole damn thing's so crazy, I don't know what to think,' Sam said. 'No sign of forced entry. Nothing! And this place is like a fucking fortress.'

He paused for a moment, then said, 'I don't think it looks very good for me, Leonie. Not good at all. Particularly with that note.' His voice was world-weary.

'Don't jump to conclusions, Sam,' Leonie said. 'You don't even know exactly what the note said. And it doesn't sound like it could prove anything.'

'I guess you're right,' he said. 'I'm just not thinking straight. I don't know what's wrong with me.'

'Sam!' Leonie cried. 'My God! Is it any wonder. You've just found your wife's body in the swimming pool. You're probably in shock. Why don't you come over here, or I'll come over there. You really shouldn't be alone now.'

'I appreciate it, Leonie,' he said. 'You know I do. But I think I should stay here where the police can reach me in case they find out anything. I'll be all right. Besides, that cop said I'd better stick around.'

'Maybe you should call a doctor,' she said. 'Do you have any tranquilizers?' she asked. 'Or sleeping pills?'

'There's some stuff here,' he said. 'I'll take something if I have to, but I don't think there's any need to call a doctor. I just feel so . . . strange. So . . . numb. It's like everything's unreal . . . like none of this really happened.'

'Oh, Sam,' Leonie said. 'I wish I could be with you. Is there anybody you can call?'

'There's nobody I want to,' he answered. 'You're the only person I want to talk to.' He sighed. 'I hate burdening you with this, but I – I—'

'Stop right there!' Leonie said forcefully. 'You are not burdening me with anything. Understand? I love you, Sam. And that means that whatever happens to you concerns me, too. I'm part of this, and it's perfectly right and natural that you called me.'

'Oh, God, I love you,' he said. 'You make me feel so much better. Just hearing your voice.'

'Well, you can hear it anytime,' she said. 'We can talk all night if you want to.'

'I'll call you in the morning,' he said. 'I guess I'd better get going. I have a feeling that I'm going to have visitors from the police bright and early.'

'Do you think you can get some sleep?' Leonie asked, knowing that it would surely be impossible.

'I don't know,' Sam said. 'But I'm going to try. It's probably going to be a long, long day.'

'Sam,' she said, 'don't hesitate to call me at any hour of the night. Promise?'

'I promise,' he said. Then: 'I love you, Leonie. More than anything in the world. I hope you know that.'

'Yes, Sam,' she said. 'I do.'

They hung up, and Sam aimlessly wandered about the house, from room to room, not knowing what he was looking for, not really seeing anything. He finally spread out on a big leather Chesterfield couch in the library with a drink, and tried to shut his eyes to the day's events.

But sleep wouldn't come. In its stead, he saw the body – Minette's body, he reminded himself – floating grotesquely on the surface of the pool.

The instant Leonie hung up the telephone, its shrill chirrup rang out, startling her. She picked up the receiver. Sam, she thought. Calling me back.

'Hello?'

'Leonie, dear.' It was Mossy, whose voice was devoid of its characteristically cheerful irony.

'Hi, Moss,' Leonie said, her tone now weary. Physical and emotional exhaustion were quickly taking their toll.

'I wouldn't have rung you so late,' Mossy said, 'but I heard the news.'

'Already,' Leonie said. 'It is a small world, isn't it?'

'Nothing like the local grapevine,' Mossy replied. 'Anyway, I rang to see if you want company.'

'I'm all right, Mossy,' she replied. But she thought: I'm not all right. No. In fact, I'm far from all right.

'Are you certain, dear?' Mossy persisted. 'I would gladly come over straightaway.'

'No, Mossy,' Leonie said. 'I really just want to be alone and try to get some rest. I'm exhausted. It was a very long day, and Sam and I hung up right before you called.'

'How is he?' Mossy asked, her curiosity piqued. Although she'd promised herself that she wouldn't pry, the temptation was irresistible.

'I think he's in shock,' Leonie said. 'This hasn't really hit him yet.

He's also a little nervous, maybe even scared. He thinks the police are suspicious of him.'

'Little wonder,' Mossy said. 'The general consensus is that he did it.'

Leonie's hackles instantly went up, every protective instinct in her body on full alert. 'Where did you hear that . . . that garbage?' she sputtered defiantly.

'I just had a quick nightcap in Kinderhook,' Mossy replied. 'Some of the local lads had already heard every gory little detail from some of the cops at the scene. You know how it is in these small towns.'

'Yes,' Leonie said, 'I do. Or at least I'm certainly finding out. And I know what shit it is, too.'

'Oh, sod it, dear. I am only reporting what I heard,' Mossy said defensively. 'I'm not accusing him of anything.'

'But you think he's guilty, too, don't you, Mossy?' Leonie said in a quaver, making no effort to conceal her hostility.

'I do not think any such thing,' Mossy said, trying to placate her. 'Jesus!'

'Good! Because he's incapable of doing something so . . . so reprehensible. Christ, Mossy,' she went on, 'he was here with me until dinnertime! Then he stopped by his old office to pick up some stuff.'

'Wait a minute,' Mossy said. 'You do not have to prove his case to me, dear. It's those bloody good old boys in the police that think he did it.' She paused a moment, taking a puff on her cigarette. 'And, of course, some of that lot who know him, or think they do.'

'What do you mean?' Leonie asked, still angry.

'Oh, you know,' Mossy said. 'The same old idle gossip – of mostly idle people. He married her for her bloody money. She was a cripple. He wanted to get rid of her. The usual rot.'

Leonie took several deep breaths. She wanted to scream in frustration and rage, even though she knew that Mossy was only repeating malicious gossip. But, she thought, malicious gossip like this can be dangerous. Very dangerous.

'I think we'd better change the subject, Mossy,' she said. 'This kind of talk makes me completely crazy. I feel like tearing my hair out.'

'I'm sorry, dear,' Mossy said. 'I can see that I've upset you, and I certainly didn't intend to. That is the very last thing I wanted to do. I guess I'm so knackered that I'm not thinking straight.'

'What's wrong?' Leonie asked. 'What have you been up to, anyway?'

'This and that,' Mossy said. 'Nothing important, really.' Her voice suddenly rang false in Leonie's ears, with a light and airy quality that she immediately recognized as evasive.

Deciding that Mossy was not going to be forthcoming, that she was perhaps hiding something, Leonie decided not to pursue the subject. 'Listen,' she finally said, 'I'd better get going, Mossy. I'm really tired, and I should try to get some sleep. And I want to leave the phone line open in case Sam tries to call again.'

'Of course. Just remember, dear,' Mossy said, 'if you need me, I'm only a phone call away.'

'Thanks, Mossy,' Leonie said. 'I appreciate it.'

After they hung up, Leonie thought: God love you, Moss, but I don't think I need a friend like you tonight, well-meaning though you may be. No. I need someone who'll comfort me in my misery.

It was the middle of the night, and Leonie had finally dozed off on the canopied bed upstairs, a silk robe draped around her otherwise naked body. Suddenly, she was startled from her light sleep by a sound in the house.

It was a sound, wasn't it?

She jerked up, wide awake now, all her senses on full alert. Fumbling for the light switch on the lamp at her bedside, she thought she saw a movement in the darkness, through the doorway that led to the stairs and down to the floor below.

Oh, my God! It isn't my imagination!

Her heart began pounding, and her pulse raced, beating noisily against her eardrum. But before she could think what to do, before her mouth could even form a scream, she heard her name softly called out.

'Leonie?'

It was Sam. Wasn't it? Whispering from the shadows?

'Sam?' she cried out. 'Sam!'

He rushed into the room and encircled her in his arms, peppering her with kisses.

'Oh, my God,' she said. 'You frightened me half to death.'

'I'm sorry,' he said. 'I'm so sorry. I didn't mean to.'

'It's okay,' she said, patting him on the back as if he were a child.

'I had to be with you,' Sam rasped. 'I just had to be with you.'

Later, in the darkened room, as they lay spent, Sam slumbering on her shoulder, Leonie reflected on the irony of their lovemaking. In the face of the sorrow and death in their lives, she thought, their making love was at once joyous and life-affirming.

But it was a joy that for once didn't bring a smile to her lips.

And she wondered, not for the first time, Oh, God, is this the beginning or the end?

24

The weekend seemed to last forever, dragging on and on, a tortured wait for – what? Sam and Leonie had no idea what to expect.

Saturday and Sunday, Leonie had worked around the house in a frenzy, trying to keep her mind off the nagging worries which continually nibbled away somewhere just beneath the surface of her consciousness. She stapled up fabric, glued on trim, mixed more paint, and weeded in the garden. But hard as she tried, those worries asserted themselves time and again, refusing to leave her in peace, threatening to undermine her newly regained self-confidence and sense of worth.

Was her world – their world – a world so abundant with happiness and hope only a short time ago, going to come crashing down around them? On and on she drove herself, slavishly, madly, doing anything to keep the painful flickers of worry and doubt at bay. It was at night, when he came to her, that the doubts and fears dissipated, only to resurrect themselves when he left in the mornings.

Sam spent the days at Van Vechten Manor, difficult as it was to be alone in the huge house – a house of death, he thought of it now – dutifully fielding telephone calls from Minette's friends and relatives and waiting for further word from the police. But word didn't come. Only the agony of reality, which was slowing sinking in, almost overwhelming him with sorrow and guilt and an increasingly paralyzing fear, filled the void left by Minette's death and Leonie's absence.

Gone was the numbness which had dulled his senses after discovering Minette's body. Now, in its stead, was a constant gnawing anxiety that he couldn't shake, that dominated his every waking hour and made sleep difficult and fitful.

He was at the octagon house early every morning to get his men started, reviewing the work that had to be done, then he'd return to the manor.

It was days later before the police finally arrived, around noontime. When the buzzer for the front gates sounded, it was a shrill and foreboding din in Sam's ears. Biegner, the homicide detective, ambled in unaccompanied, wearing the same weary expression on his face that had been there Friday night.

'Preliminary autopsy results are in,' he said in a matter-of-fact voice.

They were sitting in the library again. Sam still couldn't bring himself to venture out to the conservatory that he had so lovingly built and had once been so proud of. Because of its view of the pool, its atmosphere was now tainted with a potent malignancy that he couldn't ignore.

'What did you find out?' he asked. He studied Biegner's face, but couldn't read his expression.

The homicide detective answered him with a question. 'Did your wife drink a lot?' he asked.

Sam looked at him in surprise. 'No. Well . . . I mean . . . she had a drink now and then,' he replied. 'You know, socially. Sometimes a drink or two before dinner, but that's about it. Why do you ask?'

Biegner ignored him and answered with another question. 'Pop pills? Take tranquilizers, anything like that?'

'No!' Sam said definitely, his voice strained with irritation. He was beginning to lose patience with the man's questions. They seemed pointless and irrelevant. 'Hey, look,' he said. 'What the hell's this all about?'

Biegner looked at him with hangdog eyes. 'Blood tests show she had a potentially lethal combination of alcohol and secobarbital, a prescription sedative, in her bloodstream. That, and a load of oxycodone. It's in Percodan, a painkiller.'

Sam was stunned, and for a moment only stared at the detective. 'I . . . I don't believe it,' he finally sputtered. 'That's impossible. I've never seen Minette drink too much.' Sam grimaced. 'Well, not in years. Not since . . . not since we were dating. You can ask anybody who knew her.'

'What about pills?' Biegner asked.

'No way,' Sam said. 'She almost never took anything. Not since we had a car accident years ago. Minette hated any kind of drugs. She wouldn't even take an aspirin unless she had to.'

He paused and looked at the detective intently. 'There's got to be some kind of mistake,' he said.

'There's no mistake, Mr. Nicholson,' Biegner replied. 'The medical examiner said she'd have died from an overdose. If she hadn't drowned.'

Drowned.

The word made Sam's skin crawl. Hearing her cause of death reduced to this single offensive word, put so bluntly, made it all the more real and horrendous. In his mind's eye, he could see her lungs filling with water, could see her arms thrashing about in the water, could see her crying for help.

Suddenly, bile rose in his throat, and he thought for a moment he was going to be sick. He jumped to his feet and started toward the bathroom, but at that moment the telephone at his side bleeped. He stopped in his tracks, swallowed, then retraced his steps and picked up the receiver.

'Hello?' He listened, then got up and handed the cordless phone to the detective. 'It's for you,' he said.

Biegner nodded thanks. 'Yeah,' he growled into the telephone. Then he listened, Sam watching.

'Bring her over here,' Biegner said.

He punched the off button and handed the phone to Sam. 'That woman who worked for you . . .' he said.

'Erminda Gomez,' Sam said.

'Yeah.' Biegner heaved a sigh. 'They're bringing her over here.'

Leonie gingerly took the newspaper from a closet shelf where she'd put it out of sight. It was the big Sunday paper, but she and Sam had decided not to look at it. While they were together, they didn't want any unnecessary reminders of what had happened, and they certainly didn't want to read any speculation from a scandal-hungry press.

Alone now – the workmen had knocked off for lunch, some of them leaving, others sitting out in the shade eating – Leonie felt compelled to look for the article she knew would be there.

She placed the newspaper on the kitchen table and looked at it in trepidation and fascination. She didn't have to search for the article. The headlines screamed:

VAN VECHTEN HEIRESS DROWNED

AT LUXURIOUS ESTATE

Accompanying the story was a large photograph of Minette Nicholson.

Leonie took a deep, steadying breath and studied the picture closely. Minette was dressed in a beautiful ball gown and she was wearing what appeared to be a king's ransom in jewelry. Not gaudy.

274

No. Discreet, tasteful. But glinting very expensively for the camera, nevertheless.

My God! she thought. She's absolutely breathtaking. Sam had not exaggerated. She was strikingly beautiful, the newspaper photograph confirming what he had told her. Minette's pale blond hair and elegant features were shown off to perfection in the picture. She was seated, but unless you knew she was in a wheelchair, it wasn't obvious.

Leonie expelled a sigh and ran a hand nervously through her hair. There was no mistaking what Sam had seen in this lovely creature. And even though she knew appearances could be deceiving, Leonie found it hard to believe that a woman who looked so beautiful and so refined – angelic even – could have an ounce of meanness, of cruelty, in her.

Suddenly, Leonie couldn't bear looking at the photograph any longer, nor could she bring herself to read the story. She quickly snatched up the newspaper and put it in the recycle bin. Then she covered it up with old papers already there. She wanted it completely out of her sight again – and out of her mind. As if that were possible!

She paced the kitchen floor nervously, taking deep breaths of air. She looked at her watch. Shit! It was after noon. Sam usually called her around this time of day, checking in, keeping her posted on whatever was going on at the manor.

Why hadn't he called yet? What was going on?

She began to fret, imagining a dozen different scenarios, the tapes running through her head like evil cartoons. The most powerful and frightening, of course, being that the police had found evidence to prove that Sam had killed Minette. That Sam was being charged with murder.

She shook her head. No. That's impossible. I can't have been wrong about Sam, she thought.

She stopped pacing for a moment. There's no way he could have had anything to do with this, she told herself. I have complete faith in him. Complete and utter faith!

She resumed her anxious pace, remembering their conversation last night. They had discussed Minette's death at length, but had come up with absolutely nothing, deciding that none of the possibilities they considered were viable.

'I left here Friday with my mind made up,' Sam told her. 'I decided that, when I got back to the house, I'd tell Minette I was going to file for a divorce.'

He looked at Leonie, anguish dimming the gleam of his blue-green eyes. 'I made up my mind that, no matter what she said or did, I would go through with it.'

'Oh, my God, Sam,' Leonie said, realization dawning. 'You feel guilty about it now, don't you?'

He nodded solemnly. 'I came to the decision that the love we have for each other is so strong that we can't deny it, Leonie,' he continued. 'I thought – and I still think – that we deserve a chance. That no matter what, we have to be together.'

She hugged him to her, knowing that he was in pain, and desperately wishing that she could make it go away.

'When I left here, I knew what I had to do,' he said. 'And you know the rest. When I got there, I . . . I found her. I found her . . . floating in the pool.'

He looked at Leonie. 'I felt as if I had murdered her,' he'd said. 'I know it doesn't make any sense. It's . . . it's crazy. I hadn't even told her yet.'

His eyes welled up with tears. 'Now, I can only wonder, Who did this? And why?'

Leonie had believed his words last night, and she still believed him . . . didn't she?

She turned and strode through the dining room and into the parlor, wringing her hands.

I've got to stop this right now, she told herself. It's absurd to even consider the possibility. How could I betray Sam, even in my mind?

But what if he somehow . . . ?

No. He couldn't. He wouldn't.

She dashed upstairs to her bedroom. She wanted to make certain that she was away from the prying eyes of any workmen. There, she looked at the disheveled bed where she and Sam had so recently made love, and the tears began to well up in her eyes, threatening to spill.

Please God, she prayed. Don't let me be wrong again.

Erminda smiled at Sam nervously when he met her at the front door, her eyes flicking sideways with barely concealed fear and contempt at the two policemen who had brought her here.

'Erminda,' Sam said, placing a hand on each of her shoulders. 'Thank God, you're all right. I was worried about you.'

She shrugged. 'I'm okay, Mr. Sam,' she said. 'These policemen, they brought me all the way here just to answer questions.'

'Where've you been?' Sam asked.

'In Queens, at my brother's,' Erminda said. 'After Mrs. Nicholson fired me—'

'Fired you!' Sam exclaimed.

'Let's go back in there, and talk about this,' Biegner broke in. He indicated the library with his head, then turned to the policemen who had brought Erminda. 'You boys wait out here.'

In the library, Sam saw Biegner looking at Erminda curiously. The detective clearly didn't know what to make of this Latin beauty who had been the Nicholsons' maid, and the expression on his tired face was a mixture of suspicion and befuddlement.

Little wonder, Sam thought with amusement. Erminda was barely recognizable today, out of her usual dowdy uniform. She was dressed all in black – tight knit top, body-hugging jeans, and platform heels; thin gold chains glinted at her neck and on both wrists, and big gold hoops pierced her ears. Her shiny jet-black hair swung loose at her shoulders, and she wore a lot of makeup which, though artfully applied, was somewhat startling here in the country.

'You say Mrs. Nicholson fired you?' Biegner began, when they were seated.

'Yes.' Erminda nodded. 'She fired me.' She looked at Sam. 'You didn't know this?'

'No.' Sam shook his head. 'I didn't.'

'Friday morning,' Erminda said. 'After you left for work.'

'Why did she fire you . . . ah, Miss Gomez?' Biegner asked.

'Mr. Sam and her, they had an argument at breakfast,' Erminda said. Sam shot a look at Biegner, but he couldn't read the expression on the detective's face. Oh, Jesus, he thought. The hole for my grave is getting deeper and deeper.

'After Mr. Sam left,' Erminda continued, 'I told her that she shouldn't be so nasty to Mr. Sam. I told her he was a good man and tried to please her. She got mad and fired me.'

'What did they argue about?' the detective asked.

'She told him she closed their checking account,' Erminda said. 'She said she wouldn't give him any more money.'

Biegner shot Sam a look with laserlike eyes, as if he now had a certain knowledge.

Sam returned the look, a doleful expression on his face. I think it's time I quit cooperating and call an attorney, he thought.

'What happened then, Miss Gomez?' the detective asked, refocusing his attention on the maid.

'I just packed my clothes and things,' Erminda responded. 'Then I called a cab to take me to the train station in Hudson. I had to wait over an hour for the next train.' She glanced contemptuously at the detective, as if her inconvenience had been his fault.

'Which train did you take?' Biegner asked.

'The two twenty-nine,' Erminda answered.

'Was Mrs. Nicholson okay when you left here?' he asked.

'Yes,' she said. 'She was fine, I guess.'

'She didn't act odd or anything?' he asked.

Erminda shook her head. 'No.'

'Nothing out of the ordinary?' Biegner persisted.

She twisted a gold chain around her wrist, considering his question, her heavily painted lips puckered in thought.

'Noooo,' she finally replied. 'Nothing different. I just packed and called a taxi, like I said. Then I reset the videocameras and alarms right before I left.'

Sam suddenly jerked upright in his chair and slammed a fist down on its arm. 'Je-sus!' he cried. 'Why didn't I think of it!'

Biegner looked at him, a puzzled expression on his face. 'What— ?'

'The videocameras,' Sam said, jumping to his feet. 'They're motion sensitive.' He looked at the detective. 'They're hidden all over the place. Including the pool. They'll show us who killed Minette.'

'Ready?' Sam asked.

Biegner nodded. He had started to confiscate the tape as evidence and view it at the station, but decided that since Sam was willing, and anxious, to see it, he would go ahead and look at it here and now. Get it over with.

In the darkened library, Sam fed the videotape into the VCR, then, remote in hand, sat down in a chair next to Biegner. He and the detective had gone down to the basement room where all the security controls were housed and retrieved the videotape generated by camera sixteen, the one which covered the pool area.

Biegner had told Erminda to wait out in the entrance hall while they viewed the tape, but she had defiantly gone to the kitchen, where, judging from the racket she was making, it was apparent that she was making a meal.

Sam took a deep breath, his sense of dreadful foreboding fueled as much by the known as the unknown. He hesitated a moment, then punched the play button on the remote.

The big television screen sprang to life, gray and grainy. Then, in an instant, the camera's motion sensors were triggered by a significant movement in their area.

Minette suddenly flashed up on the screen, vividly alive, the camera automatically zooming in and focusing on her movements. Her wheelchair rolled to an abrupt stop at the pool's coping, the diving board at her side. Her movements were jerky, marionettelike, because the camera automatically cut out intermediate frames, consolidating movements. The resultant picture was like a series of freeze-frames strung together.

Sam suddenly felt a chill run all the way up his spine, then up the back of his neck, and on up, to the top of his head. He broke out into a cold sweat, for only the second time in his life. The first had been when he learned of Minette's paralysis. Its recurrence was like a flashback to something unforgettably evil.

He grasped the arms of his chair to keep his hands from trembling and stared intently at the screen, mesmerized by the sight of his wife there, very much alive and—

What the hell?

Minette was alone.

It was not easy to see, but he would swear that the expression on her face appeared to be blank, devoid of any emotion whatsoever, registering – nothing.

She leaned slightly forward and to the side, grasping the edge of the diving board with both hands, pulling herself out of the wheelchair. Her arms and shoulders, strengthened by years of using the wheelchair and compensating for her useless legs, made it look easy, especially with the jerky movements on the videotape. But Sam knew that, despite her strength, that couldn't be so. He thought he recognized the steely determination that came into her eyes, replacing the stony, dull look that had been there.

She pulled herself out of the wheelchair, dragging her feet over the coping, all in a seemingly single, concerted effort, then let go of the diving board.

There was a splash as she went down.

Like a broken puppet, Sam thought.

The camera focused momentarily on her body underwater, then the picture flickered and went gray. The movement that had triggered it – Minette's movement – had stopped. But only an instant passed before the motion sensors kicked back in again.

Now seemingly lifeless, Minette's body surfaced, floating on the wind-ripped water, facedown. The camera focused on it momentarily – it was only a flash – then went dead again.

Sam sat with his head in his hands, the shock of the macabre marionettelike images almost unbearable.

Biegner looked over at him after a minute and shook his head slowly. 'Jesus! I would never've believed it.' He heaved a weary sigh. 'Not in a million years.'

Sam sat mute, unable to speak.

The detective stood up, walked over to Sam, and took the remote from his hand. He pushed the rewind button, waited a moment – the tape had lasted only a minute or so – then hit the eject button. He retrieved the videotape from the VCR and stood looking at it in his hand.

'I'll have to take this with me,' he said. 'The boys aren't going to believe it. Suicide.'

Sam looked up at him. 'I don't understand,' he said.

'Well, Nicholson, I've seen it before,' the detective said. 'When a person wants to kill himself, he can show the strength of five people. It's like arresting a nutcase. I've seen a hundred-pound woman take on five or six cops. Hold them off, too. Like some kind of Sumo wrestler.' He paused, looking at the videotape in his hand. 'Your wife was determined to do it.'

'That's not what I meant,' Sam said. 'I meant why? Why? Jesus! She had almost everything in the world to live for.'

'Maybe she got tired of being a cripple,' the detective said bluntly. 'Who knows? What I don't understand is why she tried to pin it on you.'

'You mean the note,' Sam said.

'Yeah,' Biegner said. 'It was in her handwriting, so it sure didn't look too good for you.'

'I don't know,' Sam said. He sat lost in thought. 'I guess she assumed the security system was off, too,' he finally said. 'So what she did wouldn't be recorded. She didn't take into account Erminda resetting the system before she left. I just wasn't thinking straight. I assumed it was off because Erminda had been here earlier. Jesus, if Erminda hadn't . . .'

Suddenly Sam felt completely drained, as if there weren't an ounce of life left in him. He didn't want to discuss any of this right now. Not what had happened, or why. Not Minette or their history together, and certainly not with this stranger. Their relationship was none of his business.

The detective tapped the videotape against his hand. 'I better get going,' he said. 'You want to take care of Ms. Gomez there, or want my men to take her back?'

'Don't worry about it,' Sam said. 'I'll take care of her.'

He showed the police out, then hurried to the office off the kitchen. He wanted to call Leonie at once.

He punched in her number on the telephone there, still so shaky it took three tries to get it right. Waiting for her to answer, he leafed through the mail on the desk. He'd been stacking it here for days without looking at it. Bills, flyers, catalogues, magazines, more catalogues, a couple of letters.

'Hello?' Leonie picked up.

'It's me,' Sam said.

'Oh, my God,' she said. 'I was getting half-crazy with worry. Are you all right?'

'Yes and no,' he said. 'The police have been here. Finally.'

'And?' Leonie said worriedly.

'You're not going to believe this,' he said.

'What?' she asked, more agitated than ever.

'Minette committed suicide,' he said.

'What?' Leonie cried. 'How do you know, Sam?'

He told her about the videotape. 'I can't believe I didn't check,' he said. 'But you know how I hated the whole paranoid security system here. I just never paid any attention to it.'

'You must be crushed,' Leonie said. 'To know that she was so miserable and she would do this.'

'Yes,' he said. 'I just can't figure it out.'

'At least now, despite everything, I hope you feel some relief,' Leonie said. 'Being in the clear.'

'Yes,' Sam said. 'I mean, I'm in the clear. Thank God. But that still leaves the mystery of why Minette would have killed herself. I don't understand it at all. I would never have believed that Minette, of all people, would kill herself. She just wasn't the type.'

'From what you've told me,' Leonie said, 'and from what Mossy has said, I wouldn't have believed it either. I wouldn't even have thought of it. Like you said, she just didn't seem like the type.'

'No,' Sam said definitely. 'She was a very strong lady. A fighter.' He paused, rifling through the mail again. 'I just don't know what to think, Leonie,' he said. 'Anyway, I've got to see about Erminda, God bless her. Angry as she was, and as much as she disliked Minette, she turned the security system on before she left.'

'Is she going back to New York or stay up here?' Leonie asked.

'I don't know,' Sam said. 'I've got to talk to her. I thought I would do that, then head over your way.'

'Good,' Leonie said.

'How's it going?' Sam asked. 'Are the men behaving themselves?'

'It's unbelievable,' Leonie said. 'It's only going to be another week or so. Maybe a little longer. The paintwork's almost finished and some of the wallpaper is up now. They started this morning. Miss

Miller is here now, fitting slipcovers, and I'm helping her. I've sort of been cleaning up after everybody as fast as I can. Trying to keep all the windows and doors open to get the polyurethane stink out. It's really awful.'

Sam laughed. 'It won't last too long. Just make sure everything's well ventilated so nobody gets sick.'

'Will do,' Leonie said. 'So I'll see you in a bit?'

'Yes,' Sam said. 'I'll be there in a little while. And Leonie?'

'Hmmm?'

'I love you,' he said.

'I love you, too, Sam,' she said.

Sam hung up the telephone and started dumping catalogues and fliers in the wastebasket next to the desk. Then he put the bills in a stack, looking at them again. Suddenly, a letter caught his eye. It was addressed to him and marked personal, in an old-fashioned-looking black script.

What the hell? he wondered. He tore it open and saw it was on Dr. Nathanson's stationery, Minette's physician in Manhattan. Why me? Sam wondered. His bills were always sent to Minette.

But then he saw that it wasn't a bill at all.

Dear Mr. Nicholson,

It is with grave concern and perhaps questionable medical ethics that I write to you regarding the medical condition of your wife, Minette Van Vechten Nicholson, as she has expressly told me that under no circumstances are you to be informed of her recent diagnosis.

After a great deal of deliberation, I have decided that I must give you the unhappy news that Minette has been diagnosed with a cancerous tumor of the spine, and has no more than six months to live, although it could be a matter of a few weeks.

Technically—

Sam read on, the letter trembling in his hands as he did so. When he finished it, he sat in stunned disbelief for the second time that day, a thousand questions running through his mind, and at the same time, the mystery of Minette's death – her suicide, he reminded himself – finally answered.

His heart felt heavy with sorrow. As miserable as their relationship had become, Sam couldn't help but think that Minette Van Vechten, beautiful heiress that she had been, was dealt a bad hand in life. The crippling car accident, an unhappy marriage, and finally a gruesome cancer that was literally crushing her spine. Worse cards couldn't have been dealt her.

It isn't fair, he thought. Not fair at all.

And he wondered: Am I going to be able to have a life after all this? Will I always be haunted by the darkness of the past few years?

His eyes now became wet with tears. Will I only be like some terrible talisman of bad luck for Leonie?

26

Red, gold, pink, orange, purple, yellow.

Like a peacock with fully unfurled tail feathers, the valley was ablaze with a fireworks show of color such as it hadn't displayed in over a decade. Day after intoxicating day it went on, revealing its rich hues, delighting the eye with its magnificent plumage. Now, its rainbow was at its peak, and the nip in the air had turned to a distinct chill. Winter was around the corner.

The light – that same light that had drawn artists to this valley for generations – was extraordinarily crisp and clarified, rendering the landscape as an unspoiled and revived canvas after summer's heat and humidity.

It was apple-picking time, and the trees were heavy with fruit, the air scented with a sweet, heady fragrance. Pumpkins, round and fat from summer's growth, mutely awaited their fate upon dinner tables and front porches.

Leonie was spreading out the picnic feast she had prepared for Sam and herself in the octagon house's leaf-strewn gazebo. She stood up and, hands on hips, surveyed her domain. The house rose freshly scintillating and majestic, like a pristine jewel in nature's perfect setting.

Heaven, she thought. It's truly heaven, dressed in its autumn finery. So beautiful now that it was finished, in fact, that not for the first time she thought that perhaps she should put down roots on this very spot. Open a shop in the barn and stay put.

She stepped out of the gazebo and crunched through the fallen leaves as she made her way back to the kitchen. On the terrace, she stood and gazed out at the Hudson River, shining bright and silvery in the sun, and over to the mighty humps of the Catskill Mountains beyond.

I never imagined I would feel so proprietary, she thought. So attached to this place emotionally and – dare my practical mind even think it? – spiritually. For that was the word which sprang to mind, although she hadn't a clue where it came from. It was an alien word to her, so strange, in fact, that she could hardly roll it off her tongue.

She took a deep breath, inhaling the invigorating autumn air. She'd had no idea so much would happen here, on this blessed ground, for that was how she thought of it now. It had been such a short time, but so much life had been lived here, so many changes wrought. Leonie smiled to herself.

When she'd first seen this ragtag grand dame of a house, she had identified with it instantly and powerfully. It had needed help. Salvation, really. And in retrospect, Leonie surmised that part of her strong bond with it had been her own need for a kind of salvation, of a healing. She had needed to heal the wounds left by a marriage gone wrong, of friendship turned to betrayal. She had been in need of a cleansing of her spirit, she supposed, after years of benign neglect.

Working on the house, she now realized, had been a kind of therapy for the mind and the body, and her very soul. As it was returned to its former glory, so had she gotten back in touch with herself, with the values and beliefs that she had virtually forgotten she'd once had, with an inner life that had gone almost completely by the wayside.

She wondered now whether or not she would feel the same way about it had she not met Sam Nicholson here. Maybe, she thought, but she didn't really know, and it was impossible to guess. Because overshadowing everything else, of course, was finding Sam.

Never in her wildest imaginings would she have dreamed that, here in this magical land that time had nearly forgotten, she would meet and fall in love with a man she truly felt was her soulmate, her destiny. It was as if fate had conspired to bring them together at her hour of greatest need. And Leonie knew without any doubts that the same was true for Sam, too.

Once again, she was struck by the wonder of it all. Whatever powers there are, she thought, they really do work in mysterious ways.

She went on into the kitchen, stopping to admire its now exposed and beautifully finished wide-board pine floors, its mighty old beams and beautifully painted cabinetry. Even its top-of-the-line, state-of-the-art equipment. She still felt a gratifying sense of accomplishment when she looked around and realized that, with a lot of help, she was responsible for the transformation of this dilapidated ugly duckling into an elegant swan that was also warm and welcoming. It had been no mean feat.

She wandered through to the dining room, with its chinoiserie-covered walls in reds and greens and yellows and the plain but elegant mahogany George II table, chairs, sideboard, and china cabinet. Over the table a Russian neoclassical 'waterfall' chandelier sparkled in the autumn light.

She strode through the dining room into the butter-yellow parlor, thrilling at the sight of the refurbished parquet floors and the newly polished marble fireplace mantel with its huge gilt mirror. Pale golden silk draperies shifted slightly in the breeze from an open window. The chairs and sofas in here were English – large and comfortable, slipcovered in a pale but sturdy and durable linen. There were antique tables, lamps, and chairs of various vintages and origins – English, French, Italian, Austrian – but the whole was cohesive and inviting. The ivory-painted woodwork here, and in the hallway, dining room, and nearly all the bedrooms, was clean and crisp, yet it didn't glare. It seemed to have a patina that was appropriate to the house and furnishings.

She walked on into the library, now a hushed retreat, darkly handsome with its faux mahogany bookshelves and woodwork, its magnificent Directoire billiard light, and green felt walls. On the floor was a multi-hued Tabriz rug, and on it sat comfortable old Edwardian leather-upholstered chairs and sofa and a huge antique partners desk in mahogany.

Yes, she thought, I've achieved what I set out to do, making the house elegant yet comfortable. Somewhat formal, but not stiff or fussy.

On upstairs she wandered, strolling through the second-floor bedrooms. The Red Room – inexpensive red damask walls, curtains, and bed hangings. It looked rich and regal. She smiled, recalling that Sam had dubbed it the Pope's bedroom. The Blue Room – pale, ethereal, perhaps ladylike, she thought, with ivory and palest pink and gold accents. The Gold Room – with its brocade walls, curtains, and bed hangings and lots of ivory woodwork, also regal, but eminently comfortable.

Suddenly, she heard Sam's Range Rover on the pea-gravel driveway, and turned and dashed back downstairs to the kitchen. She grabbed a tray, which was loaded down with food, off the butcher-block counter, then started back outside.

Sam leapt out of the Range Rover, his eyes brighter than ever and his teeth gleaming Beverly Hills white against his tanned face.

'Hey,' he called to her. 'Wait right there.'

Leonie laughed, thrilled at the sight of him, as she always was. 'What is it?' she asked.

He bounded up to the terrace. 'Here, let me,' he said, giving her a kiss on the lips and taking the tray from her in one swift movement.

They crunched through the leaves down to the gazebo where Leonie had set the table and begun putting out the food. Sam set the heavily loaded tray down on the table, then turned to her.

He took her into his arms and kissed her deeply, staring into her dark, dark eyes. She gloried in the feel of him against her, hoping it would never end, but she finally ruffled her hands through his sun-kissed hair and drew back.

'I want to hear all about your morning before anything else,' she said, sitting down and getting comfortable. 'There's some white wine or apple cider.'

'Cider, please,' Sam said, sitting down on the chair next to her.

Leonie filled two glasses with the fresh cider and handed Sam one.

He clinked her glass with his. 'To us,' he said, looking into her eyes, smiling.

'To us,' Leonie repeated, returning his look. As she sipped the cider, she thought that he had never looked better. Despite the horrors of the last few weeks, his features were finally relaxing, radiant with happiness and fulfillment.

Like me, she thought. I could be looking into a mirror.

'How did it go?' she asked, heaping a plate with fried chicken, a spicy apple chutney, and other testaments to her culinary skills.

'It was . . . interesting,' Sam said. Then he looked at the plate she was serving. 'Wow! This food looks fantastic. What's that?'

'Bourbon sweet potatoes,' Leonie said, spooning some onto his plate. 'Guaranteed to cure what ails you. And they taste as good as they smell.'

He laughed. 'When you said picnic, I thought you meant some cheese and wine.'

Leonie served herself, then looked over at him. 'You want to tell me about it?' she asked.

Sam chewed and swallowed. 'This chicken is great,' he said.

'Thanks,' Leonie said. 'Bobby Chandler's cook, Willie, taught me how to do it.'

Sam wiped his hands on a napkin. 'To make a long story short,' he said, 'Minette left me two dollars in her will.'

Leonie looked over at him in disbelief. 'Two dollars?' she said.

His face broke out into a grin. 'Said it was all I had in my pocket when we met.' He laughed, a genuine laugh from deep down inside.

Leonie laughed with him, thinking that they must both be a little crazy to be finding this funny.

'It's so like her,' Sam said with amusement. 'Ah, well. You know what?'

'What?' she asked.

'I'm actually relieved,' he said.

'You are?' Leonie said, forking up some wild rice with portobella mushrooms. 'You really are?'

'Yes. Definitely. I would have felt like I was still tied to her and her family if I hadn't been cut out of the will,' Sam reasoned. 'This way, it's like a nice, clean break. I'm not beholden to anybody.'

He reached over and brushed stray hair out of Leonie's face, appreciating the way the sun picked up the red and magenta. She gave his hand a kiss.

'The lawyers seemed to think I might contest the will,' he said, 'and I could if I wanted to. My lawyer says I've got a very good case. But' – he looked into her eyes – 'I assured them I won't. I just want to get the whole thing behind me.'

'I couldn't agree with you more,' Leonie said sincerely. How alike we are, she thought. Letting go. Letting bygones be bygones.

'So who ends up with all that Van Vechten loot?' she asked.

'Dirck, her cousin,' Sam said. 'I'm not crazy about him personally, but I think he'll take care of everything just like Minette would have wanted him to. Anyway,' he went on, 'I told him I would have all my stuff out of the house within the next week. Put it in storage.'

'You don't have to do that, Sam,' Leonie said. 'You can bring it over here.'

'We'll see,' Sam said noncommittally, taking a sip of cider. 'Dirck and I went by the house together, after the meeting at the lawyer's office. He's asked Erminda to stay on.'

Leonie nearly choked on her cider. 'What?'

Sam grinned. 'I think there're a few sparks flying between the two of them. In fact, I think it's safe to say there's a real bonfire about to be lit.'

'I don't believe it!' Leonie said. 'And she's been pining after you like a lovesick schoolgirl!'

'Well, you know I had that talk with her after Minette's death,' Sam said. 'I made it clear that I was in love with you.'

'And you really think there's something between her and Dirck?' Leonie asked.

'You can bet on it. I know Dirck,' he said, 'and believe me, he's on the make. And' – Sam laughed – 'the attention is not lost on Erminda. She's really appreciating it.' He looked at Leonie with a smile. 'Wouldn't it be wonderful if Erminda became the next chatelaine of Van Vechten Manor?'

'Poetic justice,' Leonie said, laughing.

'Anyway,' Sam said, 'I left there and grabbed a pot of chrysan-themums at the nursery and took them by Minette's grave.'

Leonie stopped eating and looked at him. 'That was sweet of you, Sam,' she said. 'I just hope you didn't do it because you still feel responsible. Like it's your fault that all this has happened?'

'No,' he said, 'I don't. I feel like I've done my duty the best that I can. I may not have been perfect, but I tried. I think her death was something beyond my control.' He paused thoughtfully. 'I guess I went by the cemetery to . . . to say good-bye. For . . . for a kind of closure.'

'I'm so glad to hear you say that,' Leonie said. She reached over and gave him a kiss.

There was the sound of a car on the driveway, and they both turned to see who was coming. Mossy's shiny white Acura pulled in, and she parked next to Sam's Range Rover.

When she got out of the car and started for the back door, Leonie called out to her. 'Mossy, we're back here.'

Mossy turned, her electric orange bird's nest of a hairdo shining brilliantly, and quite unnaturally, in the sun. 'Oooooh, how divinely romantic you two look,' she said, kicking leaves as she made her way to them through the garden.

Sam and Leonie got to their feet and each kissed her in turn. 'Come on,' Leonie said, 'dig in. There's enough for an army.'

'My dear,' Mossy said, 'I'll just have some of that delicious looking wine. It's time for some serious slimming. I'm not eating until the new year.' She perched herself on a chair and immediately rummaged in her bag for a cigarette, which Sam then lit for her.

'Thanks, Sam,' Mossy said.

'You're welcome.' He poured her a glass of wine and handed it to her.

'Thanks even more, Sam,' Mossy said. 'And to your health. Both of you.'

'What brings you to this neck of the woods?' Leonie asked.

'Ummm.' Mossy seemed determined to be mysterious. 'Need to have a word with you.'

'Me?' Leonie said.

'Indeed,' Mossy said, exhaling a plume of smoke. 'Both of you, I should think.'

'What is it?' asked Leonie, who found mystery maddening.

'Well,' Mossy said, 'this divine place has come on the market.

Granted, it needs a lot of work, but it could be absolutely to die for. An old mill house. On Kinderhook Creek. Secluded. Cheap. And . . . I think I can get it for you even . . . cheaper.'

Sam and Leonie exchanged quick looks. They had discussed the possibility of working together in the future, but hadn't reached any definite decisions. Plus, Leonie had already made it clear to Sam how strong her attraction to the octagon house was, and her feelings about possibly putting down roots here. What's more, she had also told him that she wasn't certain she wanted to live through another renovation project anytime soon.

God, no.

Now, Mossy's sharp gaze, which rarely missed anything, studied first Leonie, then Sam. 'Bloody hell!' she exclaimed. 'Is this what I get for my efforts? Silence?'

Leonie and Sam laughed. 'Oh, Moss,' Leonie said. 'I'm sorry. It's just that we don't know what we're going to do. At least not yet.'

'Tired of camping out, are we?' Mossy said, arching a thinly plucked brow.

'A little, to be honest,' Leonie said. 'It's been months now, and this place is finished . . . and so . . . beautiful.'

'But what will you do?' Mossy asked. 'And what about your plans to make the proverbial bundle on this place?'

'Well, there hasn't been an offer on this place yet,' Leonie said. 'So . . . I could always start dealing architectural elements and antiques out of the barn. You know. Invest in a few pieces, then notify my old clients in New York that I'm back in business.'

'What if there should be an offer?' Mossy asked.

'Moss,' Leonie said. 'What are you getting at? Huh?'

'Well, my dears, there are these obscenely rich New York City folks who gave me a call a few weeks ago,' Mossy said. 'Former clients of yours, Leonie.'

'Who?' she asked.

'The Carsons. Claudia and Richard Carson,' Mossy said.

297

Oh, ho,' Leonie said. 'They're rich all right.'

'I've been showing them place after place. This all started about the time Minette died.'

'So that's why you were always disappearing!' Leonie said.

'Yes,' Mossy said. 'I wanted to see what happened before I told you about it. Anyway, these absolutely maddening people have seen nearly everything in the county. I even showed them that fabulous place on the Kinderhook. They positively hated it. They want something ready to move into. Absolutely perfect. You know the type. As you always say, they want to move in A.M., entertain P.M. Soooo . . .' She took a drag off her cigarette.

'So what?' Leonie asked.

'Soooo . . . I brought them over here,' she said. 'The evening you two went over to the inn for dinner.'

'You did?' Leonie said. 'You didn't even mention it to me!'

'I am now, my dear,' Mossy said with irrefutable logic.

'Oh, Moss, really,' Leonie said. 'Why are you being so cagey?'

'I wanted to surprise you,' Mossy said. 'Anyway, I brought them back just the other day. You'd gone to that art show at the Clark Institute.'

'What happened?' Sam asked.

Mossy took a sip of wine, savoring the suspense she knew she was creating.

'Moss!' Leonie cried. 'Out with it!'

'Well, my dear, you would not believe!' Mossy finally said. 'They wanted to buy it on the spot. On the spot. A cash deal! All furnishings included!'

'You're kidding!' Sam said.

'What kind of money are you talking about?' Leonie asked, her practical mind already at work.

Mossy looked at them, a triumphant expression on her face. 'Nearly four times what you paid for it,' she announced.

'What!' Leonie cried.

'Over double what you've got invested in it with the renovation work,' Mossy said.

'Jesus,' Sam said. 'I don't believe it.'

'It's true,' Mossy said. 'I decided to take a real chance with these bozos and test their limits. They'd certainly tested mine. So I began by asking for the sun, the moon, and the stars. They were ready to sign a binder, but I wouldn't allow it until I'd discussed it with you two.'

Leonie looked at Sam, a quizzical expression on her face.

Mossy took another sip of her wine. 'They loved the house,' she went on, 'were mad for the renovation work, and were in a frenzy over the decor.'

Leonie hugged Sam to her, and he pecked her on the cheek.

'I told them you might be willing to part with some of the furnishings,' Mossy continued, 'but that a price hadn't been set as of yet.'

'Well, Mossy,' Sam said, grinning. 'I think you've given Leonie some food for thought.' He squeezed her next to him, and Leonie looked up into his eyes.

'What do you think, Sam?' she asked. 'Think we ought to have a peek at the place on the creek?'

'Might be a good idea,' he said. 'If it's as good a deal as Mossy says, then . . . well, it could be worth looking into.'

'And buyers like the Carsons don't come along every day, either,' Leonie said.

Mossy set her wineglass down and got to her feet. 'I must dash off, dears,' she said. 'I've got a new personal trainer coming by the house this afternoon, and I mustn't be late.'

'New trainer?' Leonie asked.

'Oooooh, indeed,' Mossy said. 'You should see him. Young! Tall! Built! And—'

'Moss! Stop right there!' Leonie said, laughing.

'Sod it,' Mossy complained, fumbling in her shoulder bag. She finally extracted a set of keys and dropped them on the table. 'There,' she said. 'The keys to the old mill house.' Then she fumbled some more and came up with a piece of paper which she handed to Sam. 'And that,' she said, 'is the directions to the place.'

'Thanks, Mossy,' Sam said.

'Now, I really must dash,' she said, turning toward her car. 'I mustn't keep him waiting. This young man is do-able!' And with a toss of her very autumn-appropriate orange head she was off.

Sam turned to Leonie, and they both laughed. 'She is some piece of work,' he said.

'That she is,' Leonie replied.

Sam took her hand in his. 'You really want to have a look at the mill house?' he asked.

'Sure,' she said, 'I can hardly wait.'

'But I guess we'd better finish up the fine-tuning here first,' Sam said. 'Don't you think?'

'Yes,' Leonie said, giving his hand a squeeze. 'You're right. But I do wonder what we may have facing us.'

'We'll see,' he said, brushing her lips with a kiss. He looked into her eyes. 'Who knows what the future holds?'

PART FOUR

WINTER

The snow fell in huge flakes, as if, Leonie thought, Mother Goose and all her friends and family were shedding their soft white down from the heavens above. It had started the night before, and now the valley was truly a winter wonderland, blanketed in a pristine white beauty that begged for crackling fires in toasty, comfortably snug rooms with warming drinks and stick-to-your-ribs food. And someone you loved very much to hold very close to you.

She looked about her in awe, the beauty and drama of Mother Nature impressing her anew, as it never could in the city. Up ahead on the road, she spied three deer, two grown ones and a large fawn, stopping to stare at the Range Rover before loping on across and charging into a thicket of trees on the opposite side, where they finally disappeared from sight.

'Aren't they beautiful?' she said to Sam.

'They sure are,' Sam said. He smiled. 'But I sure do wish they'd learn to avoid the roads.'

'Yes,' Leonie said. 'They aren't very sensible, are they?'

They were finally on their way to see the property that Mossy had given them the keys to. An old mill, she'd said, in need of lots of tender loving care. They'd had the keys nearly a month, while Mossy had shown the place – with no one interested in buying – using another set. With the inevitable fine-tuning on the octagon house renovation and the settling of Minette's estate, they had simply not taken the time to look at it yet.

'This is it,' Sam said. 'The road where we take a right. The property is just on down this way according to Mossy's directions.' He slowed the Range Rover and turned off onto a road leading into the woods.

'Good thing we've got four-wheel drive,' Leonie said. All the main roads were already well plowed and salted, but the back roads, like the one they were turning onto, were virtually nonexistent, buried as they were under a foot of snow.

Sam eased the big car on down the road. It was lined with huge old trees bending down nearly onto the road, heavily laden with snow.

'It's like an ice tunnel,' Leonie said. 'My God, it's so beautiful.'

On they went, slowly and carefully, until they reached a dead end. Off to the left and straight ahead were thickly wooded acres of land, and off to the right was a clearing, opening onto acres of parklike grounds. Sam turned in here, to their right, and drove a short way into the clearing and then stopped the car.

Leonie jumped out of the Range Rover the instant Sam hit the brakes, enthralled with the sight that greeted her eyes. Sam joined her, sliding an arm around her waist. He kissed her neck tenderly, taking in the spectacle of the old mill himself.

It was set directly on Kinderhook Creek and surrounded by several acres of fields and woods on both sides of the stream. The creek itself was broad here, probably fifty feet across, and strewn with boulders and large rocks. Its constant rushing burble was hypnotic as it wound its way through the property.

The mill rose three stories high and was a behemoth of unpainted timbers with several small-paned windows and a tin roof. Off to their right, about a hundred yards from the mill, was the house.

Leonie squeezed Sam and pointed. 'Look,' she said. 'A perfect Greek Revival.' And it was. A two-story white frame Greek Revival house of classical proportions, in dire need of help, as was the mill. It was all peeling paint, loose shutters, broken windows, and sagging porches. The lawn, what you could make out of it in the snow, was studded with giant old oak and maple trees, pines, hemlocks, and spruce, all swagging heavily to the ground with snow. Birches, Leonie's favorite, rose skyward in clumps of three or more, their silvery bark reflecting the almost hallucinatory light reflected by the snow.

They trudged arm in arm in their snow boots around the property, quietly taking in the exterior, then Sam produced the keys. 'Ready to go inside?' he asked.

'Yes,' Leonie said anxiously, looking up at him. 'I can hardly wait.'

'Me, either,' he said.

He opened the door to the house, and they stepped through.

Leonie's mouth fell open. 'Oh, my God,' she said, surveying the spacious entrance hall with its beautifully curved staircase, wainscotting, and fading murals. 'Look at the murals! The stairs! This is fantastic!'

Sam stood next to her, silent, every bit as excited as she was by what he saw.

'Look, Sam!' Leonie cried. 'The woodwork's all intact. At least in here.'

. 'I'll be damned,' he said. 'It looks like nobody's "improved" it. Ever. Just given it about a hundred coats of paint.'

They walked through the house together, finding delight in

its wide-board floors, fireplaces, neoclassical woodwork, and the generous and elegant proportions of its rooms.

'You're right,' Leonie said, after they'd finished their inspection. 'It looks like it's hardly ever been touched.'

'Which would save us an extraordinary amount of time and money,' Sam said. 'We wouldn't have to try to put it back like it should be.'

Then he turned and looked at Leonie, a wry smile on his face. 'Except for the kitchen and bathrooms,' he said. 'They'll be an arm and a leg.'

'Yes.' Leonie laughed. 'I don't think they've had anything done to them either. At least not in this century. In fact, it doesn't look like anything's been cleaned in several decades.'

'You want to take a look at the mill?' Sam asked.

'I'm ready, if you are,' Leonie said.

They walked over to the old mill, and Sam opened the door.

'Whew-eee!' he breathed, stepping in after Leonie.

It was an enormous space, all hand-hewn beams and wide-board heart pine floors.

Leonie turned to him, looking at the expression of genuine wonderment on his face. 'It's magnificent, isn't it?' she said. 'At least I'm pretty sure it is, under all the layers of grime. It reminds me of the first time I saw the third floor at the octagon house. Except this is at least twenty times the size.'

'This would make the most sensational offices anybody around here's ever seen,' Sam said. 'And there's tons of space. Enough for . . .' He looked at Leonie. '. . . for both of us,' he finished.

She squeezed his arm. 'I'm glad you put it that way,' she said.

'I wouldn't have it any other way, Leonie,' he said.

They walked through the old mill, then went back outside and wandered over to the banks of the Kinderhook, entranced by its movement and its continuous burbling over and around the rocks. Today, it was running high, powerful, and loud. Sam put an arm around her shoulders, and Leonie slid an arm around his waist.

'What do you think?' Leonie finally asked him.

'I think the place is fantastic,' he said. 'And besides that, it's practical. It would be a great place to both work and live, you know?' He leaned over and brushed her hair with his lips. 'What do you think?' he asked.

'Exactly the same thing,' Leonie said. 'Use the mill for offices. Architectural preservation and renovation in part of it . . . and my shop and interior decoration services in another. And the house would be a great place to fix up and live.'

'We'd have to talk to Mossy about the deal,' he said.

'I can call her when we get back,' Leonie said. 'We'd have to act awfully fast. The Carsons want to move into the octagon house for Christmas.'

'Well,' he said, rubbing his chin, 'how do you think a Christmas tree would look in an empty, dusty, old Greek Revival house begging for some of our own special brand of TLC?'

'Do you mean it?' Leonie asked, almost breathlessly.

'You bet I do. But if we do this,' Sam said, 'we're doing it together. Even-Steven. Okay?' He looked at her.

Leonie returned his look, seeing the seriousness in those depthless turquoise pools. She nodded, suddenly overcome with emotion.

He means it, she thought. A real partnership. The two of us, taking on the world together. She wondered if they were ready for this, if two souls, wounded as they were, could really make a go of it together. If they could overcome their pasts, and live in the present – and build for the future.

Sam put a hand under her chin and turned her face gently to him. He kissed her lips chastely. 'Are things moving too fast for you?' he asked.

Leonie shook her head. 'No . . .' she began. 'At least I don't think so.'

He hugged her to him. 'I can understand it if you've got cold feet,' he said. 'But I think we make a great team, Leonie – in business and in life.'

'I do, too, Sam,' she replied, flushing with the warmth of his words. 'I want that more than anything.' She looked into his eyes.

'We don't have to commit to each other if you're afraid,' he said. 'We can wait. I won't push you. But I want you to know that I'm . . . well, I'm ready when you are.'

Leonie nodded, almost afraid to speak, so choked with emotion was she. He was offering her everything she had ever wanted, ever dreamed of, and the reality of it was almost overwhelming and unbelievable.

'You know, I don't believe that life's a rehearsal, Leonie,' Sam continued. 'This is a chance – maybe our only chance – for happiness, and I think we should grab it.'

Leonie looked out over the far banks of the creek at the beautiful snow-laden trees, so magnificent in this Currier and Ives setting. Even as the snow fell, she knew that springtime's buds were already there, storing up energy and strength for their showy rebirth after winter's dormant sleep.

We're part of it, she thought. The endless cycle of death and rebirth. And suddenly her heart swelled with gratitude. She felt grateful to be a part of all this splendor, and she felt unafraid.

She turned to Sam slowly. 'You're willing to take that chance, aren't you?' she said.

'Yes,' he said, 'with you. I've wanted that ever since I first met you, but now more than ever.' He hugged her again. 'This place,' he said, gesturing around him with a hand, 'would be a great place to start a home together . . . and a family. It's a great place to build a life, Leonie, and when I build something I expect it to last till the end of time.'

Leonie felt another flood of emotion surge powerfully through her. She had thought that her last marriage was for always and forever, that it would withstand the tests of time. But she had been proven wrong, hadn't she? Why trust herself – and Sam – now? she wondered. Why would it be any different this time?

Because, she told herself, we share not only goals and ambition, but values and beliefs. We each have an inner life that we nourish in one another, a life of the soul.

We've both had awakenings, she decided. Yes, awakenings. And she didn't really know how to articulate it any further, because these feelings were so new, so alien to her. But what she did know was that she would let these feelings carry her where they would. And that included taking a chance with Sam.

Finally, she looked up at him. 'Do you mean that, Sam?' she asked. 'That when you build something you expect it to last till the end of time?'

'Oh, yes,' he said. 'You know I do. And I hope that's what you still want, too.'

'Oh, yes,' Leonie said. 'Yes and yes and yes! I want us! I want your children . . . our children! . . . So much. So damned much!'

Leonie's lips sought out his, and they kissed deeply, passionately. She thought that this afternoon on the banks of the creek in winter's silvery white light would surely never lose its radiant holiness in her mind. Each moment, she was certain, would stand out clearly and beautifully, and somehow eternally significant.

Her time with this man, no matter how profound or trivial their moments together had been, no matter how happy or sad, impressed her with a peculiar vividness and intensity, and she was reminded of what she had thought so often before: that the two of them together were a force that could push back the darkness in each other's lives.

She looked into his eyes – those eyes which no longer haunted, no longer sad. 'I love you,' she said.

'I love you, too, and I always will,' he said. He smiled broadly. 'You know, if you don't want to wait, we can get started on that family right now.'

309

'I like that idea,' Leonie said. 'I like that idea a lot. And here I thought you'd never ask!'